Freya North

Freya gave up a Ph.D. to write her first novel, *Sally*, in 1991.
For four years she turned deaf ears to parents and friends
who pleaded with her to 'get a proper job'. She went on
the dole and did a succession of freelance and temping
jobs to support her writing days.

In 1995 throwing caution to the wind, Freya sent three
chapters and a page of completely fabricated reviews to a top
literary agent, and met with success: five publishers entered a
bidding war for her book. In 1996, *Sally* was published to
great acclaim and Freya was heralded as a fresh voice in fiction.
Her next books, *Chloë, Polly, Cat, Fen, Pip, Love Rules, Home
Truths* and *Pillow Talk* have all been bestsellers. Freya won the
Romantic Novel of the Year Award 2008 for *Pillow Talk*.
She lives in London with her family.

To find out more about Freya and her books,
log onto www.freyanorth.com

love rules:

home truths:

Also by Freya North:

Sally

Chloë

Polly

Cat

Fen

Pip

Love Rules

Home Truths

Pillow Talk

Freya North
secrets

HARPER

Harper
An imprint of HarperCollins*Publishers*
77–85 Fulham Palace Road,
Hammersmith, London W6 8JB

www.harpercollins.co.uk

A Paperback Original 2009
1

A catalogue record for this book
is available from the British Library

ISBN: 978 0 00 724593 2

Set in Sabon by Palimpsest Book Production Limited,
Grangemouth, Stirlingshire

Printed and bound in Australia by
Griffin Press

For Jessica Adams, Sarah Henderson, Kirsty Johnson
– and Jo Smith –

for your unconditional and bountiful support,
love and laughter.

thank you xxx

RESOLUTION

1 resolve, determination, purpose, dedication,
2 promise, commitment, pledge, undertaking
3 answer, solution, disentanglement, sorting out,
4 Captain Cook's ship for his second (1772–5) and third (1776–9) voyages of discovery. James Cook, born Marton, Middlesbrough, 27 October 1728. Died Kealakekua Bay, Hawaii, 14 February 1779.

I could not get tae my love if Aa wad dee
The waters of Tyne cem betwixt her and me
Sae thor Aa wad stand wiv a tear in my ee
Till the Smoggies[1] cem and built a bridge
Ower them for me

(regional version,
'Waters of the Tyne', trad.)

[1] Geordie moniker for Middlesbrough folk

Prologue

House-sitter wanted.
Sea views.
Immediate start.

As Tess and Em crept soundlessly to a corner of the kitchen and crouched down to make themselves as small as possible, Tess chanted the words to herself. It helped to block out partially the banging at the front door and, like a mantra, it gave her some composure.

The banging, though, continued, almost in time to her quickened heart rate, but louder. Stronger.

Go away.

But she had known they'd be back. They were hardly likely to have had a change of heart since their last visit, never to return. She knew that. Of course she did. However, she had not anticipated them coming back quite so soon, certainly not on a Thursday afternoon, the day she didn't work. She put a smile on for Em and they continued to crouch in silence.

House-sitter wanted.

House-sitting sounded so much better than crouching.

After one final aggressive barrage, the banging ceased at last, though Tess and Em remained in situ for a cautious minute or two longer until they were quite sure that the people at the front door had gone. Em didn't object, she was used to it by now, content to follow Tess's lead – going along with

1

the silence when Tess put her finger to her lips at the sound of banging; appearing not to notice if Tess answered the phone in a cod American accent. Being silent and feigning absence were two things that Tess and Em did well. Quite the double act. After all, Tess has managed to make it all a form of entertainment, both to lighten the load and fill the loaded silences between banging or ringing. Sometimes, she'd even run through her repertoire of daft faces.

Let them bang all they bloody want – I stick out my tongue and pull my fish face at the lot of them.

Today, though, those six words had provided the diversion. *House-sitter wanted. Sea views. Immediate start.*

No more banging for today. They'd gone, for now. Tess and Em hugged as they always did when they were sure the coast was clear – in a congratulatory manner. It reminded Tess of the stories her late grandmother had told her of blackouts during the Blitz. The feeling of triumph, of personal success to have come through bombardment unscathed.

'If ever two people deserved cake, it's you and me, Em.'

She passed Em a slice of chocolate roll with a chipper wink.

She kept her anxiety hidden from view.

It is only when she's by herself later that evening that Tess relents and lets her pent-up fear creep around her like an odourless, toxic gas, chilling her to the core like a soundless scream. It has her sweating and short of breath; alternately pacing the confines of the small sitting room or paralysed to the spot. It's a detestable feeling but like severe turbulence during a flight, she has to believe she can weather it and that it will pass. She tries desperately to stifle sobs because if she starts she won't be able to stop. She blinks hard and breathes deeply and eventually she feels calmer. She closes her eyes for a short while, concentrating hard on the colour of nothing behind her eyelids. When she opens them, they alight on the newspaper. She'd found it on the tube home from work yesterday. Right now she is happy to be seduced by the serendipity that, amongst the scatter of all the free London papers in that carriage, the one on her seat was the *Cleveland Gazette*. She thumbs through it with a sense of urgency, as if the offer she'd chanced upon the day before, which has lingered with her all day today, was so good it would have been snapped up by now and disappeared from the listings.

But it is there. The house with the sea views in need of a house-sitter.

She knows the words by heart, but it is the phone number underneath them which now looms large, turning the abstract mini-poem into a real proposition. Tess knows well enough how today's newspaper can wrap tomorrow's fish and chips. But what if yesterday's newspaper had escaped such a fate? If she'd saved the paper from a brief and greasy end at the chippie – in return, might yesterday's *Cleveland Gazette* become her map for tomorrow? Did it matter that she didn't know exactly where Cleveland was? It sounded far-flung from North London – and any distance from here and all that had happened, had to be a journey worth making.

I'm crazy, she thinks, as she dials the number. I've been driven completely mad.

Joe considers not taking the call. But once the ringing stops it starts up again.

'Hullo, my name is Tess and I'm phoning about the ad,' someone is saying. 'Could you tell me more?'

He pauses. Isn't he on the verge of offering the position to Mrs Dunn? 'Well, I just need someone to oversee the old place when I'm not here. I work away from home mostly.'

'It's old?'

'It was more a term of affection. Detached. Victorian. Six bedrooms.'

'Oh.' Tess wonders if affection can ever be detached. 'Where is it, exactly?'

'Saltburn.'

'Saltburn?'

'On the outskirts of town, the Loftus Road. The pay isn't much, I'm afraid, but I'm offering a long-term position. Hullo?'

Tess is computing the information. *Sea views. Immediate start. House-sitter wanted. Wage provided.* 'Is there a garden?'

'Of course there's a garden.'

'You didn't put it in the ad.'

'No – I thought "sea views" would clinch it.'

'Is it a big garden?'

'Not compared to some round here. But sizeable compared to others. A good half an acre. Hullo? Are you there?'

'Currently, I have a patch of paving stones, mostly cracked. And they're not mine anyway.'

Joe pauses. Suddenly he likes the idea of someone tending his garden who's only had a patch of paving stones that don't belong to them anyway. Perhaps he won't phone Mrs Dunn just yet. 'Do you want to come and see it?'

'I'll leave first thing and be with you whenever.'

'From?'

'London.'

'*London!* You do know you're talking a five, even six-hour drive on a Friday? And the weather's meant to be vile tomorrow even for March?'

'That won't matter to me. Thank you so much. You won't regret your decision.'

Joe frantically replays the conversation to see just when he'd even implied he'd given her the job. But he can't very well ask her now, nor can he object – she's already hung up.

*

4

Tess's grandmother used to say, think before you speak; she also used to say, look before you leap. Tess can imagine how her grandmother would be tutting at her now. She hadn't actually thought about what she was going to say or what she was hoping to hear when she had phoned the number under the ad. What she does know now is that, at a time when she's desperate to run away from the banging and the fear that peppers her life in London, six words in the classified section of a paper from somewhere far away have offered her a way out.

She still isn't quite sure exactly where Cleveland is. She's never heard of Saltburn-by-the-Sea. But there's a six-bedroom house there, in which she is going to be paid to stay. It might just be the answer to her most impassioned prayers, it might be the solution to her problems. It might assist her need to right wrongs. It could well be a safe-house for her secrets, somewhere to lie low until she is back on an even keel and able to start over. It is a long way from London and that's a start. She has to believe that she can do something about the people who come banging at her door. Had Tess known running away could be such a good idea, she'd have considered it much sooner.

Chapter One

There was something about the way the small red hatchback slunk onto the gravel of the drive, coming to a shuddering standstill as if it was giving up, as if it was about to conk out, that reminded Joe of an animal in need of a rest; some poorly-kept packhorse exhausted from an arduous day's work. He watched through the window of his study, on the ground floor, through the tangle of honeysuckle branches which clambered around that side of the house and provided useful camouflage at moments like this. Nothing happened for quite some time; whoever was in the car was staying put. Eventually, the car door opened and Joe watched as a woman climbed out. She stared and stared at the house while still clinging to the open door as if it was a shield. She ducked back in and Joe was prepared for her to drive away, for this woman not to be the Tess of the bizarre phone call last night. She looked nothing like the people who had house-sat for him in the past. But now she was out of the car again, walking around to the other side of it, opening the door, leaning in, apparently rummaging around.

And then, when she reappeared, Joe thought, oh, for fuck's sake.

But by now, she was walking slowly towards the front door.

He considered disappearing elsewhere in the house, feigning not to be at home. But even from this distance and through the network of honeysuckle, her look of awe placated him. Suddenly he wasn't staring at his worst nightmare, but at a scene straight from Thomas Hardy. From his vantage point, he watched as she stood timidly on the weathered slab of doorstep like a peasant girl braving the estate of the wealthy squire. Joe hastened to open the door before she rang the bell, fearing the old mellow clang would all but finish her off.

'Hullo,' he said. 'Are you Tess?'

Still he couldn't be absolutely sure. Over the phone she'd sounded older, somehow bigger and physically rather more nondescript. If this was Tess, he hadn't accounted for strikingly amber eyes darting from behind a privacy screen of an overgrown fringe. Despite the droop of mousy brown hair, he could see that her features were fine, her skin porcelain pale. Her lips were pursed, as if to imply something on the verge of being either said or swallowed. She was not tall and her slimness diminished her further, yet she stood square and defensive. Joe wondered why she would drench her frame with a drab hooded sweatshirt which fell to mid-thigh length, emblazoned with a college crest that made good design whether or not the establishment existed. He saw that her jeans were old but too scruffy to be acceptably vintage and her trainers were scuffed, with laces that were inexcusably dirty. He thought about first impressions, and why she would choose to turn up looking like this. Previous house-sitters arrived very spruce and professional. But then he glanced at himself and thought he'd better change the subject.

'Well, Tess, I'm Joe.'

From his brusque manner on the phone, she had him down

as a suit-and-tie dour businessman. At any rate, she'd envisaged him much older, sterner. She hadn't considered his wardrobe to contain jeans and a well-worn grey woollen turtleneck. Nor that he'd answer the door shoeless, in socks of the same yarn as his jumper and similarly bobbled. Least of all did she expect quite a handsome face, even if it did need a shave. Good hair, she noted, for someone in his – say, late forties? Thick, short, salt-and-pepper. Dark eyes. Dark brows. Arms folded nonchalantly.

But her arms were obviously too full to shake his hand so he hadn't offered it. Instead, they nodded at each other. She looked up at him through her fringe and he tried not to look down on her with an expression that was too patronizing. But then he regarded the reality staring him in the face – and once again his dominant thought was, oh, for fuck's sake.

'You never said anything about a child,' he said.

He watched her freeze, shift the infant higher on her hip, suck in her bottom lip and knit her brow. Oh Christ, she's not going to cry, is she? But her eyes darkened as a scorch of indignation crossed her cheeks.

'And *you* never said anything about a dog,' she retorted.

Wolf had been standing casually at Joe's side. Tess glanced at him with distaste, noting that his coat appeared to be fashioned from the same material as Joe's jumper and socks. Or was it vice versa.

'I could be allergic.'

'And are you?'

'No. But that's not the point.'

'Maybe I'm allergic to children.'

'No one's allergic to children.'

'Do you not like dogs?'

'That's not the point either.'

'Wolf is a soppy old thing.'

8

'Does he come with the job, then?'

'Yes. Sometimes I take him with me. Not if I'm abroad, obviously.'

'Does he like children, though?'

'He prefers Pedigree Chum.'

Tess looked at Joe. It was a bad joke but the timing was perfect. She clamped down on a smile, wanting to cling onto the upper hand and invent a moral high ground despite knowing that actually, she was in the wrong. Because she hadn't, on purpose, told him about her eighteen-month old daughter, had she? Whereas he simply hadn't thought to mention his enormous dog.

'Shall I come in?' she asked more jauntily, because she was suddenly aware of the threshold still between them and feared the job offer might be rescinded.

Joe looked at her; wondered again how old she was. Thirty? Or possibly late twenties and just tired?

'Sure,' he said, 'come on in.' He turned and walked into his house.

Nice doggy, he could hear her saying in a voice that was for the baby's benefit and not Wolf's, *nice doggy.* He heard the infant attempt to emulate her mother's words. It was a very odd sound to hear in the house. Joe had been the last baby here. And that was forty-five years ago.

He thought of the bustling Mrs Dunn from the agency, and her doughy forearms. In comparison, this Tess was a slip of a thing. The flagstones would surely defeat her. The flagstones were not baby friendly. The flagstones alone could be a deal breaker, to say nothing of the draughts. The rickety banister. The occasional whiff of gas that no one had been able to find or fix. The water that sometimes ran brown. The pipes that bickered loudly. The mutant spiders. Wolf. The wasps that returned to the eaves each summer and fell about the house drunk, drowsy and aggressive each autumn. And then

Joe thought how Mrs Dunn would not have tolerated any of this and he looked over his shoulder at Tess standing there in his entrance hall, all wide-eyed in inappropriate teenage clothing. Her baby: wild curls, rosebud mouth and beautifully, perfectly, appropriately dressed. And Joe thought that there was something about Tess's poise and the fact that she'd taken the job without it being offered and had made the long journey in that old red jalopy at a moment's notice, that suggested to him she was here to stay. That it would take more than wasps and a Wolf and water that runs brown to see her off.

'Tea? Coffee?'

'Tea, please,' said Tess.

'And the – what's your daughter's name?'

'Em.'

'Full stop? Or, as *in* –?'

'As in Emmeline.' She saw Joe raise an eyebrow. 'You were thinking Emma or Emily like most people. She's named after my grandmother.'

'And was Granny known as Em?' It came out wrong, Joe could hear it. It implied no lady of that generation would tolerate such a diminutive of the name. 'I just meant – it's unusual. It's pretty. Shame to shorten it.'

'Well, you can call her Emmeline,' Tess said a little tartly. 'I like to call her Em Full Stop.'

'OK, I will,' he said. 'Emmeline, what would you like to drink?'

'She's eighteen months old.'

'Don't they drink at that age?'

Tess paused. It was like the Pedigree Chum remark and she was unsettled to feel simultaneously annoyed yet amused.

'Emmeline,' he said very slowly, 'what would you—'

'It's OK, I have –' and Tess contorted herself to keep the child on her hip while she delved around the large holdall

10

dragging on her shoulder. 'Somewhere in here –' Finally, she retrieved a colourful beaker with a spout. 'She's fine.'

Joe looked from mother to daughter. Silently, he agreed with Tess. Emmeline was fine. The house might be fine too, with the two of them. Certainly, the set-up wasn't what he'd had in mind, what he'd had before, but if Tess agreed to Wolf, then he'd agree to Emmeline.

'Doggy.'

The adults swung their attention to the child.

Clever Em, he heard Tess whisper and there was pure joy in her voice.

The tea was good.

'Builder's tea,' Joe said. 'We don't do gnat's pee in this house.'

They sat opposite each other, with more than just the expanse of a particularly large farmhouse table between them. On it was a veritable mountain range too, complete with landslides and crevasses fashioned from books and mail and newspapers and documents and something scrunched up that appeared to have foodstuff on it. Tess eyed it all.

'What exactly does a house-sitter *do*?' she asked. 'Am I to tidy and clean then?'

Joe tapped the side of his mug thoughtfully and Tess sensed he wasn't thinking of an answer, he was thinking of the best way to make it known. 'Well, it's not really a defined role like house*keeping*. For me, I need someone here for times when I'm gone – and I'm away for work a lot for varying periods of time. In the past, I've had people stay for a few weeks – and that hasn't really worked. That's why I want someone who can stay long-term. I don't want you buggering off after a month. You need to really learn the ways of this house. If lights aren't switched on, they soon enough don't come on at all when you need them to. If rooms are left untended, a staleness hangs in the air that is troublesome to clear. The water, especially, needs to run. The freezer tends to frost up. The sofas go hard and lumpy if they're not sat on. At this time of year, some of the doors can warp and can't shut or others can't be opened. So, unlike some house-sitting jobs you may have done, I don't designate quarters for you. And so – yes, a little light cleaning is part of the deal. And you're OK about the pay?'

It struck her that he presumed she'd house-sat before – whereas she'd always assumed house-sitting was more a brief opportunity than a profession. A stopgap. But he said that this position was potentially long-term. She hadn't thought of that. Perhaps she should have packed more. And then she thought she might make quite a good house-sitter. She thought how there might be muck and mess in her life but she'd always kept her surroundings tidy and clean. She thought back to the flat at Bounds Green that she'd left just that morning and as she did, she felt a plug of lead plummet straight through her, buckling her a little and causing a blear to glaze her eyes. Landlord, nasty man, breaking and entering. Finding her gone. Chucking her stuff out with the rubbish in disgust, even though she'd left her TV set behind in the vague hope it might go some way towards the outstanding rent. Perhaps he'd called the police.

'Excuse me, are you OK?'

Tess looked up from having been miles away, 250 miles south, and she was momentarily surprised to see Joe and not Landlord, nasty man, sitting there. She nodded and kissed Em, over and over. She gave Wolf an energetic rub, discovering that his coat was far softer on the hand that it was on the eye.

'I'm just tired – it was a long haul to make my way here.'

'Well, here you are – and I have work to crack on with so how about the guided tour?' And, as Joe led the way out of the

12

kitchen, into the utility room, through to the boot store before retracing the route back to the expansive entrance hall, he thought to himself that there was something gently peculiar about all of this, something oddly compelling. However, his prevailing feeling was that it was OK for Tess and the child to be here, for the knackered red hatchback to take up a little patch of the sweeping driveway alongside his Land Rover. For a baby's voice to enliven the stillness of the old house, adding variety to Wolf's low woofs and whines. For a woman's touch to dissuade the dust. For Wolf to have company. And, on the occasions he himself was to be home, for Joe to have company too.

'Am I allowed to watch your TV? I had to leave mine in London. Do you have a record player and am I allowed to play it?'

Joe stopped and turned. 'Most house-sitters I've known bring their own stuff – but if you want to watch my TV or play my music, or play your music on my equipment, you are welcome.'

Though he was friendly and obviously at ease, Tess found him slightly detached; he met her questions with a quizzical expression, a rather aloof response. Tess's mind scurried over possible rules that a more experienced house-sitter might want to establish.

'Should I keep my food separate from yours? Is there a shelf for me in the fridge? Are there times when the heating or hot water isn't to be used?'

'Start running a bath early,' Joe advised, 'the hot water takes a while. And I'd much rather you availed yourself of whatever's in the fridge or cupboards – as long as you restock when I'm due back.'

It occurred to Joe that this woman had never done this before. Some previous house-sitters had even brought their own compact fridges. Most brought their own televisions. They didn't enquire about his hi-fi. They all but stipulated private cupboard space in the kitchen. They usually marked up their food with stickers. And then he thought to himself that, if she didn't really know what was expected of her, then he could change the rules and alter the conventional set-up. He quite fancied doing things a little differently. He was rather amused by the idea of coming across her watching something on the box that he'd planned on viewing himself anyway.

*　　*　　*

There were times – they were infrequent and it had taken some time for her to feel comfortable in acknowledging that they existed – when Tess really would rather not have Em around. Not permanently, of course, but just for those moments she'd prefer to be on her own. Meeting this marvellous, vast old house was one of them. Room after room where she craved time by herself to drink it all in, see the view from that window, look back into the room and regard it from this aspect or that corner. Run her hands over the wood panelling. Feel how cold, or warm, the marble mantelpiece was. Let her fingers bounce along book covers – the way she used to bounce a stick along the wooden fence which ended at the wall heralding her grandmother's house. Instead, she found herself having to assess rooms in a glance, attempting to absorb what Joe was saying while trying to be low-key and even-toned when repeating, don't touch, Em, don't *touch*. Come back here. No, no – put that back. Careful!

It wasn't that Tess actually minded Em touching or exploring; rather, she didn't want anything to jeopardize this job being hers. This job now seemed more than the answer to her present predicament; it seemed to be the embodiment of long-held dreams. This house was a haven, if a slightly unkempt one.

*

14

And if I look after it, it'll care for me.

'Sorry?' Joe was looking at her.

Tess, appalled that she might have spoken out loud, quickly turned to her child. 'Em! Mummy said be *careful.*'

'This is the other sitting room,' Joe was saying as he led them into a room whose walls were dark red, with two sofas of well-worn brown leather, curtains half drawn. Tess wondered, if you sat still enough, whether no one need know you were there at all.

'When do you use this room?' she asked.

'TV,' Joe said. 'I know it's naff – but look.' He opened a cabinet door to reveal a sizeable flat-screen set.

'Do you have *CBeebies*?'

'What's that?'

'It's a kids' channel,' Tess said, brushing the air as if her question was unimportant and an affirmative answer was no big deal.

'Probably,' said Joe and he zapped at the remote control. 'Is this it?'

'No.'

'This?'

'No.'

'How about this?'

'No. It doesn't matter. It's not a problem. I brought DVDs that Em likes. If that's OK, I mean. If you have a DVD player? Oh – and if it's OK for me to use it?'

'Sure. Why not. See here – and you need this remote control. Now, come through. This is another loo. And this is a room that – well – I just keep stuff like this in. Quite a useful room, really – though it's become a bit of a dumping ground. Now – upstairs. This is my floor – I'm down there. But I keep the hoover in this room here. Slightly extravagant – and actually, there's another hoover downstairs. But I'd say life's too short to lug a lone vacuum cleaner up and down all these stairs.'

'Or to use either of them much at all, really,' Tess remarked, eyeing fluff and stuff on the floors. She caught Joe looking a little taken aback. 'That's what I'm for,' she said brightly, 'that's why I'm here, it's part of the job, isn't it – and I quite like hoovering.'

Joe's expression was odd but he walked on ahead and up a flight of stairs before she could read too much into it.

On the second floor were three further bedrooms and a large bathroom, floored in shiny black-and-white chequered lino. There was a smaller bathroom on the landing going up to the top floor where another two bedrooms, without beds, were in the eaves. There was more attic space too, he told her.

'Take which you like,' Joe said, walking back down to the second floor, 'I don't mind. Mostly the house-sitters squirrel themselves away right at the top.'

'Is that where I should be?'

'I said – take which you like.'

'Sorry.' She paused. 'Really?'

He shrugged. 'Of course.'

'Could I take the front room on this floor?'

'Sure.'

Tess returned to it. A bay window. A window seat. A double bed, stripped to the mattress, with a dark wood bedstead. Nearly but not quite matching chest of drawers and wardrobe, both almost fitting into the alcoves either side of the fireplace. Cherrywood perhaps. A similar colour to the design decorating the tiles of the fireplace.

'Which one for Emmeline?'

And Joe had to repeat the question because Tess was looking into the wardrobe as if she could see right through to Narnia.

16

'Which one for Emmeline?'

'Em?'

'A bedroom – for Emmeline,' Joe said. 'Which would be suitable for her?'

'She can have her *own* bedroom?' Tess said, flabbergasted. Joe looked flabbergasted to the contrary. 'She can bunk up with me,' Tess said, as if availing herself of anything more than Joe had already offered her would be obscene. 'She has done so far. I have a travel cot. Well – it's her only cot.'

Joe shurgged. 'Whatever suits you. But you're welcome to the other rooms. To house-sit successfully, you need to feel at home.'

At home, thought Tess when Joe had gone downstairs leaving her to gawp at her leisure.

This house is a home.

And she sat down and looked around her and thought, how did I come to be here?

How on earth did *I* come to be *here*?

Chapter Two

Joe could hear her, clattering around. He listened to his furniture being moved and he wondered if he minded. When all went quiet he reckoned she was making the beds – he'd heard the yawn of the linen cupboard door being opened repeatedly, as if she was searching for the best thread-counts. The other house-sitters had always come so prepared. Some had come positively armoured, especially those from agencies. They never seemed much interested in his offer of a home from home – instead, they turned up bringing portable habitats with them – boxes and suitcases of pillows, towels, lamps, TVs. One young man brought his own cutlery and a bespoke wooden container for it, the Scottish lady brought her own armchair and Joe doubted that she ever sat in one of his. It was as if they pitied Joe or disapproved of the contents on offer and so constructed their self-contained pods within the fabric of his home. Which was probably why they were happy to move on – however long they stayed, the charms of the old house never seduced them and Joe ended up thanking them far more than they thanked him.

He had helped Tess in with her bulging suitcase and numerous bags that appeared to contain solely the accoutrements required

18

by a toddler. There was an iron on the passenger seat of her car and a box on the back seat billowing wafts of the *Cleveland Gazette*. She told him it contained two bone-china cups and saucers and would he mind if she put them in the kitchen. They were her Grandma's, apparently, and made tea taste its best. The footwell in the back was taken up with carrier bags full of vinyl LPs, which Joe said she was welcome to unpack in his sitting room. There were also three taped-up cardboard boxes in her boot. He'd offered to bring these in – but she'd said, *they'll stay there, thank you very much*, as if they were in disgrace.

That was a couple of hours ago. He hadn't seen her since, but she'd been calling down to him at various intervals. Checking it was OK for her to swap the lampshade in 'her' room for the one in the top bedroom. And did he mind if she brought in the bedside drawers from the other bedroom. And could she move the single bed in Em's room through to the furthest bedroom because the iron bedstead concerned her and the paint was probably lead-based. And if she moved the Persian rug from that furthest bedroom into Em's room, would that be all right? Because then the iron bed wouldn't put unsightly dints into it and anyway what a shame for such a lovely rug to be stashed away in an unused bedroom. Joe really didn't need the details, or the rationale, and in the end he shouted from the bottom of the staircase, *mi casa su casa* – sorry, but I really need to crack on with my work. And she called down, oh! sorry! And he called up, don't worry. And she called down, OK! sorry again! And he didn't call back up. But he found that he did wait until he heard the floorboards creaking again before he closed the study door.

He saw to his emails, organized his diary, looked through his file and then went to sit at his drawings. It was always the same when he next looked at his watch. He tapped it, held it to his ear as if it had malfunctioned and could not possibly be telling the correct time. It was gone nine o'clock and it was very quiet upstairs. Even in the silence, another's presence in the house was palpable and a few minutes later it became apparent that it was so quiet upstairs because actually she was downstairs, in the kitchen. Help yourself, he'd said earlier and he assumed she was now doing just that. He was tempted to wander in on the pretext of a cup of tea and was about to do so when a glance at his drawings and their glaringly overdue incompleteness drew him to his desk.

But then she started singing.

He wished she wouldn't.

Not that she couldn't hold a tune.

Just that it was a distraction.

He switched the radio on and tuned it to the World Service and turned the volume down so the voices sounded hushed, reverential, as if in a library. He concentrated on the plans in front of him, his initial freehand drawings on torn scraps Blu-tacked around the large sweep of graph paper; notes and measurements and calibrations pinned around his desk.

It was odd having young female energy in the house. It was unexpectedly compelling, really. New and different. But of what concern was it to him? He'd be away, mostly. France at the beginning of next week. London. Possibly the Far East later in the year. A trip to California in the late autumn. Various interludes in Belgium in between.

Concentrate.

It's only the house sitter finding her way.

Tess was making an omelette when she caught sight of a photo of Joe propped against a milk jug on the Welsh dresser. She had wondered whether she should offer to cook for him too, or if that was more a housekeeper's job than a house-sitter's. She decided not to. Anyway, there were only two eggs left and he looked like a three-to-four-in-an-omelette type of bloke. She'd make him a cup of tea instead, builder's tea not gnat's pee, and leave it outside his study door, knock once and then disappear. Perhaps she'd make it in one of her own teacups. Or would that be rude? Would that suggest she thought his crockery not good enough? Or was she being slightly ridiculous? First she needed to have her food and a sit-down. Her back was nagging – she'd never driven such a distance and then manoeuvred so much furniture before unpacking her life to make things just right for Em, now sound asleep in her new room. She took her plate to the table, picking up the photo of Joe on her way. He was younger then; his hair not so flecked. Bare-chested and tanned, wearing baggy khaki shorts, work boots and a hard hat. There was a bridge in the background. San Francisco, perhaps. He was smiling, looked ecstatic, actually. Probably grinning at a girlfriend, Tess thought. They probably swapped positions and somewhere there's a picture of her in front of this bridge too. Is it San Francisco? Perhaps not – isn't the Golden Gate Bridge a reddish colour? She put the photo back. Glanced at a postcard in pidgin English from a Giselle Someone, postmarked *Brasil* a couple of years ago. Tess liked to browse recipes while she ate but there appeared to be no cookery books, only an old *National Geographic* on top of the pile of unopened letters and discarded post on the kitchen table. She tapped Joe's chest in the photo. Bet you're one for the ladies, she thought.

She sat down and gazed at the food on her plate. She marvelled at how Em had been so compliant, eaten well, welcomed sleep so amiably for once. Tess smiled at the thought of her daughter snuggled down for a really good night's sleep. In a *house*. Fingers crossed she'd sleep through tonight – Tess knew she was in desperate need of a few hours' total rest herself and she wasn't sure how Joe would react to Em's midnight or dawn chorus. Or Wolf for that matter. She felt she'd done a good job making Em's room homey and suitable; finding a low bookshelf in one of the attic rooms on which she'd arranged Em's toys invitingly. She'd vacuumed the Persian rug and placed it centrally so that Em had somewhere warm on top of the bare floorboards on which to play. She'd tacked up the paper border she'd bought ages ago but had never fixed to the rented walls in London. Funny how she'd thought to bring it with them. She'd used sellotape, lightly because she planned to ask Joe if she could do it properly, with paste. She'd ask him tomorrow because by tomorrow she suspected there'd be a lot more to ask him. She'd make a list in bed.

The omelette tasted so good. She hadn't eaten all day because her car had needed fuel more than she had and there had only been money for the one of them. She thought she was possibly romanticizing the omelette – she'd been so hungry even stale bread would have tasted ambrosial. She looked around her and realized she liked this kitchen so much because all the stuff was owned, it all belonged to someone, it belonged here; it hadn't been bought on the cheap for tenants past, present and future. *Mi casa su casa*, he'd said. Don't mind if I do, Tess said under her breath as she took her plate to the sink. Conversely, she also sensed that she could relax because if the phone went in this place, it wouldn't be for her. And no one could come thumping on this front door for her because they couldn't know that she was here. She was a lifetime away from London and it was a relief. As she boiled the kettle, she thought how she was making tea for Joe and a new life for herself.

She hovered outside his door. She could hear a radio. She didn't even know what he did for work, what it was that took him away for periods long enough to require a house-sitter. She didn't even know his surname. She put the mug down and knocked gently, twice. Heard huffing and panting and was taken aback for a moment before she remembered Wolf.

22

It was not yet ten o'clock; too early to turn in though she was fantastically tired. However, recalling how the bath had taken an age to run for Em, Tess decided to start it now. While it was filling, she would make a final check of the car. It looked a little lonely, very small, out there on the gravel drive.

'Thank you for bringing us here in one piece and on a single tank,' she whispered. In the boot, the three cardboard boxes. She poked one accusatorily, as if it was animate. There was probably little call for the contents up here in Saltburn but Tess could not have left them behind. She might hate them and level blame against them, but there was a little bit of her inside them too. She dug around in the two smaller boxes, retrieved a pot from one and a tube from the other. '*Made With Love*,' she muttered, as if reading the label for the first time. She was about to twist the lid off one, a moisturizer, but resisted when she remembered the twelve-month shelf life once opened. Anyway, she'd packed a tub of Nivea which was still almost full. The thought of it brought her grand-mother to mind. She'd have given Tess short shrift. Put Tunisian *what* on my face? she'd have said. *How* much do you charge for one of those tubes, did you say? Good God, girl, she'd have chided, *what's wrong with Nivea?*

What's wrong with Nivea indeed? If only I'd asked myself that question in the first place. Suddenly Tess was tearful. One of her earliest memories was deep in that iconic navy-blue pot. Her grandmother's face slathered with the thick, white, gently-scented cream, used in such quantity and applied in such a way that it coated her face in little peaks like a miniature mountain range, like Christmas cake icing. Her skin had been very good, Tess reminisced and, looking back into the boxes in the boot of her car, she liked to think that her grandmother might have liked her hand-cream at least. Made with love. Too bad she didn't live long enough to see

23

any of it. But there again, thank God she hadn't lived to witness the current mess of it all.

I miss her still.

Tess shut the boot gently and walked back to the house, quickening her pace as she wondered if she'd been lost in thought long enough for the bath to have overflowed.

Inside, however, the pipes were still clanging and protesting at having to deliver another bath and the water was retching in fits and starts out of the tap so Tess went for a walk through the house again. At last, she could take time to run her fingers over things, see what books were on the shelves, find out which channels were available on the TV, feel the heaviness of the curtains, sniff at the fireplace to tell whether it was real or gas, test out all the chairs and sofas and find the one most comfortable to her. She pressed her face against windowpanes to look outside from every window even though it was dark.

The house really was immense – not just because she was conditioned to thin stud-walls subdividing the meagre space characterizing the London rental market. Here, the doors were definitely wider, the furniture larger, ceilings higher, floorboards broader, stairs longer. She could imagine turning cartwheels in the expansive hallway when she had the place to herself. She wouldn't need to talk in a whisper when Em went to bed, she could sing at the top of her voice and not wake her.

Sitting curled in a cavernous armchair in the grander sitting room, Tess invited the notion of a dog sprawled at her feet – even if it was to be a giant, mangy old thing. She knew little about dog breeds, but she very much doubted that Wolf was anything other than a mutt. Surely no one would actively breed dogs to look like that? There was something of the greyhound about him, but with none of the requisite grace in either conformation or movement. His colouring suggested

German Shepherd but his coat was fashioned along his back and the top of his head with the wiry curls of a terrier, while limp-long stringy sections, which alluded more to an old mop than any breed, hung down from everywhere else. He had one blue eye and one brown, which gave his face a lopsided look enhanced further by him being apparently unable to keep his tongue in his mouth. It was like a flap of chewed leather always lolling out on one side or the other. His owner said he was harmless. Perhaps it would be a good experience for Em too.

Tess thought, why have a dog if he has to leave him here so frequently? And then she thought, why choose a dog who looks sewn together in big clumsy blanket-stitch from a melange of various elements animate and inanimate? Do owners grow to look like their dogs – or aren't they meant to be attracted to breeds that look like them? Well, there was little physical correlation between Wolf and Joe – the dog really was as eye-poppingly ugly as his owner was easy on the eye. Opposites attract, beauty is in the eye of the beholder, don't judge a book – Tess ran through her grandmother's sayings as she left the sitting room to check on her bath. Then she hovered at the top of the stairs, wondering whether to call out goodnight, two flights down.

What's he doing in there? Why is he working at this time on a Friday night? Why does he need a house-sitter anyway – what is it that takes him away? Shall I call down – is that the correct etiquette?

She ran the palm of her hand over the newel post as though it were a priceless orb. There was no female presence in this house, that was for sure – the dust and drabness attested to that. Hence the need for me, Tess thought, grateful.

As she soaked in the bath, alternating one big toe and then the other up inside the tap which was a long-held habit she found meditative, she wondered if running away hadn't just been easy, but actually a very good thing to have done. It was going to be a better life for Em, with all this space and fresh air. Tess told herself she was hurting no one and no one would miss her, really. She'd texted a couple of her friends and told them she'd be in touch, that she was going away for a bit, added the mandatory Txx so that they wouldn't worry. Tamsin would worry but she'd known Tess long enough to trust her and root for her. They'd probably assume she was going to Spain on a long overdue visit to her father. Or up to Edinburgh to see her older sister. She sank down in the bath, up to her chin. It was hot and her tired limbs needed it. She'd used a squirt of her shampoo for bubbles because she hadn't wanted to help herself to Em's all-natural, camomile-scented hypo-allergenic bath-soak with added baby-sensitive moisturizer. Tess's supermarket own-brand shampoo suited her needs just fine. Appley and fresh and satisfyingly foamy. What a day. All that driving. Here now – a new place. Unlike anywhere she'd ever been. Unlike anything she'd ever done. Sometimes – especially when she'd been low or trapped awake by her worries – she'd wondered about such houses but hadn't really expected them to exist.

When she finally climbed into bed half an hour later, she started to worry about the enormity of what she'd done, that she was in a huge house in the middle of nowhere and no one knew she was here apart from the man downstairs tucked away in his study. How stupid to have thought she could drive away from London and leave her secrets in the flat in Bounds Green. Then she told herself she was too tired to think but tired enough for her thoughts to run wild. Be sensible.

She turned on the bedside light, planning to formulate a list of queries for Joe, but caught sight of her mobile phone. The signal was scant. No messages or missed calls. She gave but a moment's thought before removing the SIM card and cutting it in half with blunt nail scissors. Then she turned off the light and lay in the darkness, soothed by the stillness. Eventually her eyes made their acquaintance with the shadows. Wardrobe. Drawers. Standard lamp from Em's room. Mirror from the back bedroom. Painting of a seaside pier. Lloyd Loom chair brought down from one of the attic rooms. Today's clothes heaped by the door to wash tomorrow. Across her body, under the bedclothes, the soft throw she'd brought with her which Tamsin had given her on her birthday. Just before she fell asleep Tess remembered the utility room. A whole room devoted to a washing machine and tumble dryer and ceiling-mounted airer with its pulley system. Off that was the boot room – just for footwear and coats. Imagine that. The lap of luxury. A house that had everything. Buckingham Palace had nothing on this. Bounds Green was far far away. This wasn't running away! This was a new start – a sensible thing to do. An excellent idea! Brave, too. Tess felt utterly liberated.

Joe went to bed stiff and tired. He'd worked until two in the morning. He climbed halfway up to the second floor, observed how the doors were closed on the rooms that were empty, but were ajar on the rooms now occupied. He liked that. Usually house-sitters barricaded themselves in at night. This woman was open. Then he told himself to stop being soft – the baby hadn't slept on her own before and the mother would need to hear her in an instant. And as he tucked down on the floor below, he thought, where there's a baby and a mother – then there's most usually a father, isn't there? And he wondered, for a moment, who he was. And where. And why wasn't he here with them? Was he on the scene? Or was he the reason Tess had suddenly turned up on his doorstep, babe in arms?

A girl and her tot in his house was one thing, a whole

bloody family unit would be quite another. Boyfriends lounging around and playing man of the house were not on the job description. And then he touched upon the fact that little over twenty-four hours ago, he had not known this woman at all. And he still didn't. Yet here she was, without references, without even giving him her surname. Here she was in his house having brought her life into his home.

She can make changes to a couple of the rooms, he thought, but that's it.

Chapter Three

Joe came into the kitchen, still fugged from a heavy sleep. He was wearing pastel-striped pyjama bottoms, the same woollen socks from yesterday, and a T-shirt. Tess glanced at his arms and thought, he has a tan – in March.

'Morning,' he said. 'Been up long?'

'Since the crack of dawn,' Tess answered curtly. 'I'm not used to everything being so quiet everywhere. The dog's been sick – does it happen often?'

He looked at her, standing there with her hands on her hips and a tea towel he knew wasn't his slung over her shoulder, her sleeves rolled up as if she was ready to fight.

'Where?'

'I've cleaned it up,' she said. 'I wasn't going to leave it there.' She folded her arms. She looked peculiarly defiant and Joe found he didn't know what he was meant to say but felt she was waiting for an apology and fast.

He glanced at the clock and then regarded Wolf who didn't look like a dog that'd just been sick. The dog was engrossed in a hearty lick of his nether region, his tail spread across the kitchen floor like a length of old frayed rope. 'Sorry – I overslept. I don't usually. And no, Wolf isn't sick often. You should have left it for me to deal with.'

'What – with Em around?'

Now he felt guilty – as if he'd brought a lack of hygiene into the home of a child. Ridiculous – this was his house, wasn't it! And only her first day. He looked over at her sternly but she shrugged and popped her hair into a pony-tail. He'd quite liked her spirit yesterday – but not this morning when he'd just woken up.

'It's not a problem,' she said as if she sensed his reservation. 'I just thought you needed to know.' Now her equanimity made Joe feel a different sort of guilt, which was just as unnerving. All the more so when Tess then handed him a cup of tea in the china cup and saucer she'd left outside his study last night and he'd left, unwashed, in the sink. He sipped, giving himself time to think, but he was distracted as much by the unblinking attention of the infant as by the very good cup of tea.

'So, you haven't done this job before?'

'No – it's a brand new adventure.'

He thought she must mean *venture*. 'What did you do in London?'

'Nails.'

'Sorry?'

'Manicures, pedicures.'

He glanced at her nails. They were unspectacular, un-varnished and there was a Mister Man plaster around one. If these were the tools of her trade, they were not a particularly good advertisement. Manicures and pedicures? He didn't feel such a career could have suited her. He reckoned she looked more like a potter, or a photographer's assistant, or a landscape gardener at a push. He couldn't see her in a salon. She was pretty behind her slightly unkempt exterior – but her hair didn't have a particular style, her clothes were nondescript, asexual, and well worn. The lace of her left trainer was shorter than that of the right – the bow being tied on the penultimate eyelets. He thought, OK – fashion is not her thing. He thought, she hides behind her hair. He thought, you wouldn't notice her if you passed her on the street. He thought, perhaps that's a look she's honed.

There's more, Joe thought, noticing a twitch of discomfort cloud her face. A nail-person, whatever they're called, doesn't stand there fidgeting with her own – it's bad for business.

'Well, actually, I'm trained as a beautician,' Tess pre-empted, 'a beauty therapist. Highly qualified, in fact.'

'I'm not sure there's much call in Saltburn,' Joe told her. 'There are a couple of salons already. You might have luck further afield.'

'But now I'm looking for a change and that's why I'm here,' she said, as if she'd been mid-sentence.

'A change?'

'That's why I'm here,' Tess said and she folded the tea towel briskly to signify the matter was closed.

'Well – welcome to your first day. I need to go through my diary with you.'

'Of course,' Tess said, 'but perhaps when Em has her nap after lunch.'

'Well, actually I would rather—'

'I ought to figure out where I am,' Tess interrupted and Joe, to his bafflement, found himself saying, OK, get your coat and I'll show you around town.

Joe had overslept, for the first time in his adult life. Strangely, the sound of someone else was less intrusive than the usual silence. It was as if, with the clatter and attendance of someone else in the house, Joe could sleep longer. He hadn't yet checked a single email. Nor had he shaved because the hot water had sputtered lukewarm in his shower. And when he walked into the kitchen, he was met with a reprimand for his vomiting dog and a change to the order of his day.

'Joe?' She was calling him. 'Five minutes? Ten?'

Twenty would have suited him but he agreed to ten.

Tess had driven in daylight but her urgency to arrive at the destination had precluded any appreciation, or awareness even, of the new landscape. The drive had been arduous, it had all felt interminably uphill from London; even through the monotonous flatlands of the Fens and the plains around York, she'd still sensed she was climbing north. She had never driven such a distance and her eyes had continually darted to the fuel gauge. She needed the journey to be done on what she had in the tank. But having never been further north than Milton Keynes, she didn't know how to judge it. It had added stress to the journey, but not enough to warrant thoughts of retreat. 'Space, Em,' Tess had said, over and again. 'Proper space.'

And this is the sentiment she is repeating today as she walks down the drive with Joe. Em in her buggy. Wolf loping circuitously alongside.

'It wasn't the pollution or the second-hand aspect of London air and water,' Tess tells him, 'I just felt hemmed in. There are places – in the city – where the buildings are so tall and packed they appear to converge and steal a part of the sky.'

'Living place plotted and pieced by subdividing space into a size that is simply sufficient,' Joe says and it is so perfectly phrased that Tess stops to consider it. 'Paving stones butting right up against tree-trunks.' He's walking on. She catches up so she can listen. 'People living on top of you, underneath you, crowding into you on buses, pushed up against you on tubes, encroaching on your personal space but avoiding eye contact at all costs.'

'But how do you know this?'

'I lived there too. When I was studying. A century ago,' he laughs. 'I lived in Peckham.'

'From here to Peckham? What is there to study in Peckham?'

'Peckham – because it was a cheap place to live,' he says. 'I studied Design. And then I studied Engineering. Not because I wanted to be an eternal student. But because I knew what I wanted to do.'

'Are you doing it still?'

'Yes.'

'What is it that you do?'

'I build bridges,' he says.

'As a metaphor? Are you a counsellor? Marriage guidance – that kind of thing?'

Joe laughs and she looks cross that he should. 'No – real bridges, the type that go from A to B. Bridges that span valleys and rivers and cross divides. Bridges that enable one to traverse air and water; bridges that take you closer to the sky or allow you to skim the sea. Bridges that join and unify places otherwise kept apart, that pacify areas previously hostile.'

Tess is struck, again, by his turn of phrase. She recalls that photo on the Welsh dresser. Perhaps it *was* San Francisco, the Golden Gate Bridge? She's embarrassed to ask. She knows nothing about bridges. In fact, she's probably always taken bridges for granted, having grown up in the shadow of Brunel's mighty Clifton Suspension Bridge. She decides she likes Joe's passion for his job, how it obviously enhances his life. She feels gently envious. She had similar passion once that she'd ploughed into a Small Business Loan, but that verve and the funds are long gone. Nothing remains. Nothing of anything apart from those bloody boxes in the back of the car and the weight of it all on her shoulders. She glances at her nails now and alters her grip on the buggy so she

33

doesn't have to see them. The whites of her knuckles will
have to do instead.

'It's nice here,' she says, priming her gaze outwards to blank
out thoughts of London that have suddenly slid around her
like a coarse scarf pulled too tight. They are walking downhill steeply; the street is residential but quiet, with grand
Victorian buildings to their left, while lush and wooded land
delves down sharply into a valley to the right, the land climbing
up to the cliffs beyond. A little way ahead lies the North Sea,
a motionless grey slab from this distance; on the horizon a
tanker looking like a toy. Tess slows her pace, giving little
tugs at the buggy. On the right, just before the woods roll
downwards, a war memorial, a bandstand, a playground with
a view. And an intriguing sign for Italian Gardens.

'There's a miniature railway,' Joe is saying. 'It runs from
the gardens to the sea.' And then he tells her, just wait until
the summer.

'Hear that, Em,' Tess leans forward awkwardly over the
buggy, 'a train to the sea.' And to herself she says, hear that
– he'd like me to house-sit until the summer.

She really likes his accent and she really likes what he's
said.

'You can also take a lift down to the pier.'

'A lift?'

'A water-balanced cliff lift. Eccentric Victorian ingenuity.
You'll see.'

'Did you grow up here, then?'

'I did.'

'And apart from your student days in London, you've lived
here, you'll never leave.' It is not a question. She says it as
a statement, as if she wants it to be true.

'Yup. I'm tied to the place all right,' Joe says.

'You make it sound a burden. I'd love to own a house half

34

as beautiful and half the size as yours. Do you have family here too?'

But Joe has already bristled inwardly. Why is he doing this? Why is he walking with her? Why didn't he just give her the map and the info pack he'd prepared for house-sitters? In fact, why didn't he give it to her last night? Or leave it on the stairs when he realized she'd gone to bed. Why does she want to know about his family? Enough! A more informal set-up than he's used to in his house is one thing – but personal history is another. It has nothing to do with what's in the fridge or the hot-water system or the fact that the boot-room door to the garden needs a shove to open and a tug to shut.

Anyway, missy, what about you? he's tempted to say. You and your child up here on a day's notice? He lobs a stick into the copse and Wolf streaks off to fetch it. House-sitters shouldn't ask so many questions, Joe wants to say though he can't deny he has some of his own. It's not part of the job, he wants to point out. He ought to have stayed home this morning, he ought to have made it plain that the only time his life should be of any concern to her will be clearly written on the calendar. She can consult it to know when he is due back and when he is off again so she can organize milk and bread and other basics. But he doesn't say any of this – he knows it sounds too harsh. However, that just makes him wonder if he's soft to think so.

What had possessed him not to ask for references? Most people wanting the job had presented them to him before even looking around. Pages of testimonials praising their hygiene and trustworthiness and responsibility and experience. He glances over his shoulder; she's lagging behind again, pointing things out to the baby though the baby appears to be asleep. It's difficult to tell, under the swaddling of hat, scarf, blanket, mittens and foot-cosy all made from spongy cerise fleece.

'Look! Plane!'

She says it out loud, automatically, as if she is conditioned to conversing only with her child. As if she has been unused to adult company and conversation, down there, wherever it was that she'd come from in such a hurry. Joe looks up at the plane and his antagonism wanes a little. She does seem genuinely enamoured of the house and the remit of the job. She has mopped up dog sick and she does make a good cup of tea. How is she to know about which of his raw nerves not to touch?

Joe decides the best option, for both their sakes, is to keep the conversation anodyne. He sees he has the very opportunity, spread out in all its faded Victorian splendour in front of them. This woman doesn't know Saltburn-by-the-Sea but he does. In a few days he'll be out of the country. He does need to go through his dates with Tess but OK, it can wait until Emmeline's nap. He also needs to go the bank and Wolf is straining for a good blast on the beach. En route however, there is plenty to politely point out – landmarks for Tess, an opportunity for Joe to de-personalize the conversation.

Tess has now caught up with him. 'These buildings are stunning,' she says, 'they'd cost a fortune in London.'

'Good old Henry Pease,' Joe says. 'He was the Victorian gentleman who came for a walk, sat on the hillside over there overlooking Old Saltburn's single row of cottages and the Ship Inn and had a vision for the town and formal gardens you now see.'

'Why isn't it called Pea-on-Sea then!'

'*Pease*,' Joe repeats but he has to smile. 'Actually, Saltburn comes from the Anglo-Saxon *Sealt Burna*, or salty stream, on account of all the alum in the area. But moving on a few centuries – Henry Pease built the place with George Dickenson of Darlington in the 1860s. They constructed a model of homogeneity – uniform roof lines in slate, white

36

firebricks exclusively from Pease's own brickworks, and no fences.'

'You have a fence,' Tess says. '*You* have a tall wall with a fence on top all the way around.'

'The house is from a later period,' Joe says, thinking she is an argumentative thing. 'Anyway, twenty years later the town was done – the station complex, the Valley Gardens you've just passed, the chapel, the pier and the cliff lift which back then was a glorified hoist. Best of all the Zetland Hotel – see, over there? Isn't it magnificent? It's flats now – but it was the world's first railway hotel and very grand it was too, with its own private platform. Pease's father built the Stockton and Darlington Railway – the first passenger railway in the world.'

'It's a very good-looking town,' Tess says, thinking how her own family had so little to be proud of.

'That's partly because when Pease died in 1881, the Saltburn Improvement Company was disbanded and the town's driving force was gone – so no new features were added and the resort has remained a sort of time capsule, a perfectly preserved Early Victorian seaside town.'

'Like a living museum.'

'You should see it in August during the festival – everyone dresses in period costume. Well, not everyone.'

'Not you.'

'No, Tess – not me.'

'I'd like to.'

'Don fancy dress?'

'No – see it in the summer!'

'You should be here over Christmas – there's a tradition of running into the sea.'

'Oh. Do you do that?'

'I have been known to.' He looks at her. She seems concerned. 'It's not obligatory.'

'It's just I don't really like beaches all that much.'

Joe continues to look at her; again she is irritating yet intriguing in equal doses. What an odd thing to say – not least on account of her impromptu beeline for Saltburn. 'Why ever not? And why come here, then?'

'You said *sea views*.' And once again, she's implying that Joe is guilty of misrepresentation.

'Who doesn't like beaches?' Joe says because the beach is clearly in view now. The tide is out and the view is stunning: the sand is long, wide and glossy and the North Sea is now licked with silver and scattered with diamonds while the pier marches on its cast-iron trestles almost 700 feet out.

'Me,' Tess says. '*I* don't like beaches.'

Two surfers ride the waves, weaving in around each other like shuttles on a loom. Wolf is at the shoreline already, barking at them but apparently loath to get his paws wet. Joe passes a tennis ball from hand to hand. 'Coming?'

Tess looks at the beach cursorily. 'I think I'll stick to dry land. I think I'll explore the town.'

Joe shrugs. 'I'm going to the bank after I've tired out Wolf. I'll see you back at the house. Can you find your way? It's straight up there. Shit – you don't have keys. Here, take mine.'

'Say you're back before me?'

'I won't be. You'll know town inside out in the time it'll take me to walk half the beach. Pick up some milk, would you?'

There's a plunge to her gut as she realizes she has brought no money. Rice cakes, a beaker, baby wipes, nappies, a spare hat, two cardboard books and a squeaky toy. But no money.

'I left my purse at home,' she calls after Joe who is already tormenting Wolf by feigning to throw the ball. The wind, though, snatches her words away. 'Joe!' He turns and cups a hand to his ear. She pulls the empty pockets of her jacket inside out and gives a mortified shrug. He jogs across the

38

beach back to her, Wolf bounding and lurching and leaping at his arm in desperation for the ball which Joe holds aloft like the Olympic flame.

'I left my purse at home,' Tess says when he's close. 'Sorry.'

She looks acutely embarrassed. Joe throws the ball for Wolf and passes Tess a pound coin and says, don't spend it all on sweets. As he heads back for the shore, he recalls how she said she'd left her money *at home*. He liked that. Hers are undeniably a rather odd pair of hands – this manicurist with the chipped nails from London – but Joe senses they are a safe pair and that in them, his house and all that is in it will be fine. He can go to France on Wednesday without a backward glance. In fact, he might even head off early. Perhaps tomorrow. See if Nathalie is around.

Chapter Four

Tess kept the pound coin tightly in her hand though it made pushing the buggy awkward. Though Joe had mentioned the pay, he hadn't told her when she'd be paid, but she expected it would be in arrears. Which meant no income for a month. Which meant she really was going to have to phone her sister at some point soon. But at that moment, she let the practicalities drift out to sea and she turned her undivided attention inland, to the new town before her. Tess had been in London for a decade, gradually becoming inured to the challenges of the big city; learning not to be intimidated by its scale or bothered by her anonymity. However, on her first full day away from London, Tess found the smallness of Saltburn quite startling. The pavements felt narrower. The cars appeared to move slower. It all felt quiet and empty. There was a total absence of the familiar coffee chains and though she had often cursed their proliferation in London, it made Saltburn seem half asleep. Wake up and smell the coffee, she felt like calling out. But actually she felt a little shy and too conspicuous to cast her gaze too far afield, so all she spied in her first glances was a newsagent, a grocers, an off-licence, butcher, baker, gift shop and chemist. There also appeared to be a startling lack of the gaudy homogeneity to which she'd become accustomed in London. As a child, Tess had visited Bekonscot Model Village and now she felt she was walking around a life-size version. On that first morning, Saltburn seemed quaint and odd in equal doses. However, people were undoubtedly friendly as she passed by, giving her a nod or offering her a quick word, counter-acting her private misgivings of blimey, is this it? She wouldn't phone her sister, not today. Let today be full of promise.

She'd seen Joe and Wolf still bounding about the beach so she made haste to be the first one home. There, she paused at the gate and drank in the sight of the house which after the arduous slog uphill from town, had a similar effect to downing a long cool drink. Despite the general sharp chill in the air, she'd needed to take off her coat and bundle it into the hood of the buggy. At a standstill, she could feel the race of her heart and she was surprised at her lack of fitness.

Odd how, apart from its size, she'd noted very little about the building on arriving the previous day. Now, she had the time to. Compared to the creamy white bricks of Pease's buildings in town, the house, a large Victorian villa, was constructed with bricks which had a rose tint to them. Even on a cold March day, they appeared to soak in the sun and radiate its warmth. Decorative arches, some in bas-relief, some indented, broke up the expanse of brickwork between the tops of the windows and the roof. The roof was a mauve slate, its uniformity given interest by the tall chimney stacks of different design and the terracotta pointed crenelations along the ridges which might be to deter birds but could be purely ornamental. The white-framed sash windows were edged in cream stone. There were windows everywhere at all angles – no vista would go unseen from this house. When she had the time and the privacy, Tess would certainly look out from inside from every one of them.

Em was on the cusp of dozing off so Tess pushed the buggy on a tour around the garden – or gardens, for the half acre had been compartmentalized. There were polite lawns at the front, flanking the drive, another large expanse at the back demarcated by a blousy shrubbery and rolling herbaceous borders in something of a straggle. A little path mown through longer meadow grass at the back led to two sheds, one sizeable, one ramshackle. There were specific areas for a compost heap and bonfire site, an overgrown raised vegetable patch where only weeds shot out along the heaped rows. Behind a group of conifers was a plot apparently designated as Wolf's toilet. Well, she'd be asking Joe about fencing that bit off; she couldn't risk Em toddling in that direction. If that wasn't too much for a house-sitter to demand. What a place, though, what a space.

Suddenly, she was clinging onto a tree as if she was teetering on the edge of that great Huntcliff Nab, the majestic cliff which towered above the beach and plunged into the North Sea. The ground felt as if it were moving away from her feet like a conveyor belt in overdrive. Her breath was shorter, her heart racing harder than when she'd just slogged up the hill.

Em, Em, what have I done? Setting out to secure the best life for you? Or have I just run away? Where the hell are we? Where on earth have I brought us? What was I thinking? I didn't stop to think. I never stop to think. Am I running away? Will I be caught? Is this just hide-and-seek – have I gone to ground while kidding myself this is My New Life? These stupid ideas of mine.

When she finally felt able to open her eyes and prise her grip from the tree, she stood still awhile, blinking in the reality of her surroundings in a series of snapshots. The beauty and breadth of the grounds. The majestic poise of the house. The warmth of the bricks. A date stone carved with 1874. She repeated the date out loud quietly, over and over, the sound of the words regulating her breathing. She honed in on another stone plaque over the front door just visible from this angle. She wheeled the buggy over to take a closer look. The lettering was in relief. *RESOLUTION*, it read. Strange name for a house, she thought. And then she thought, it's time for resolutions of my own. It was a bright moment of calm after a storm of turbulent emotions. She placed both palms flat against the bricks. This house, by name alone, had instilled a new sense of purpose in Tess and she didn't feel merely soothed now, she felt bolstered. She returned to the main swathe of garden and parked the buggy in a quiet spot under a tree within sight and earshot of the kitchen windows and went inside to boil the kettle.

She made a cup of tea, more to hold than to drink. And there was Joe again, grinning from the photo on the dresser, yellow hard hat and the bridge in the background. Thank you, she said, thanks for this chance. She turned her gaze outside. She could see that Em was asleep in the buggy, Em was just fine.

'Here.'

Joe's back.

Tess hadn't heard him come in and her vantage point from the kitchen window precluded seeing the approach to the house.

'Keys – though as you've probably found out, the doors are rarely locked.' He reached up for an old toby jug on the top shelf of the dresser, full of keys, and jangled a set. He looked at her quizzically. 'Or you could keep mine,' he said, 'and I'll take this pair.'

It was then Tess realized the keys were still firmly in the clench of her fist as if she had no intention of letting them go. She looked at them. A Chubb and a Yale on a key ring from Brazil spelled with an 's'. Like the postmark on the card on the dresser from Giselle.

'Have you been to Brazil, then?'

'Yes. Many times.'

'Have you a bridge there?'

'Yes.'

Tess wondered why she wanted to say, and have you a Giselle there too? 'Tea?' she said instead.

'Ta.'

'Resolution.'

'Pardon?'

'Your home – it's a good name. Different.'

'Next door is Endeavour.'

'That's different too. But I prefer Resolution. I like the meaning.'

'Not that up on British history, then?'

'What?'

'*Resolution? Endeavour?* They were the ships James Cook sailed on his voyages of discovery. This is Cook Country – he was born not far from here, just outside Middlesbrough. He sailed from Whitby – just down from here.'

Tess grasped the information. 'Where did he go to on the *Resolution*? Where did he discover? When was that?'

'1772. Cook sailed the *Resolution* for three years, disproved the southern continent by sailing round Antarctica and discovered Tonga and the New Hebrides. 1776 was his third and final voyage – off to the North Pacific on the *Resolution* to find the end of the North-West Passage which of course he didn't. But he did sail through the Bering Strait and he did discover Hawaii where, on a return visit, the natives killed him.'

Tess felt shy for her ignorance but she thanked Joe and said that Resolution was a beautiful name for a house.

'Better than Dun Roamin',' said Joe who appeared to Tess to be oddly immune to the romance of it all.

44

She thought about the house, inside and out. 'All the windows,' she said. 'It's like a compass – views from every point.'

'Well, your maritime analogy is strengthened by the fact that there are mice in the cellar and in a raging storm, the rain finds its way in through the lower windows.' With that, he let Wolf out into the garden from the boot store off the utility room. Tess realized this must have been the way he'd come in just now. She followed him.

'Does Wolf always go in that patch – over there? You know, "go"?'

'Yes, he's very particular.'

'Could you fence that part off, then?'

Joe looked at her. 'How about I put a sign up instead. Like in municipal parks – you know, like *Keep off the Grass*.'

'What – *No Dogs* instead?'

'I thought more along the lines of *No Children*.'

There was a loaded pause between them.

'Em can't read,' Tess said, and her tone harked back to when she first saw Joe's dog. 'She's only eighteen months.'

'Wolf can't read,' Joe said bluntly. '*He's* only a dog.'

'*You* didn't say anything about a dog,' Tess muttered.

'Ditto child,' said Joe. He felt curiously irritated. Not because of the child or the dog or the shit, just because this girl was doing it again. Unnerving him. Maybe it was sharing his space that caused it. Maybe those house-sitters who did the job unseen and not heard, suited him better. 'I'm going to go to France early – tomorrow,' he said.

'Very good,' she said because then she could have the place to herself.

The chill between them lasted a few moments longer but then Joe watched a whisper of vulnerability cross Tess's face.

'Tea?' she said though he hadn't finished his first cup.

'No thanks,' he said. 'I need to crack on. We'll go through my diary in a while.'

Alone again, Tess looked out to the garden. Wolf was mooching around like a hairy metal-detector, never far from the buggy. Em's little fists were agitating the air around her.

They'll be OK, those two, Tess thought, they'll get along fine. It's not that relevant if Joe and I don't. He won't be here that often.

But she was appalled that her mind's eye had returned to the smatter of dark hair running from his stomach down to his jeans that she'd seen when he had reached up for the jug of keys.

Get your mind off that, she scolded, and fix your eye on your child outside.

And, though she had no reason to glance again at the photo on the dresser, she was helpless not to. It wasn't the hard hat or the bridge or the bare chest, it was the smile. A blend of euphoria and tenderness and utter focus. There had never been a time when someone had smiled at her like that.

Who were you smiling at, Joe? Where is she now?

*   *   *

'It's a peace offering.'

Tess turns around, mortified. She is stooped over the bath with her bottom in the air and she knows her jeans are not the most flattering at the best of times. From this angle, there's no escaping builder's bum.

How long has he been standing there, holding the bottle of red wine?

'A peace offering?'

'I was arsey,' Joe says, 'before – about Wolf and the garden and Emmeline.' He takes his eyes off Tess and focuses on the slippery pinkness and the foam Afro demarcating her daughter.

Tess scoops Em out of the bath and cocoons her in a towel.

She sits down on the side of the bath not knowing what to say. 'Well, that's OK, Joe. I was a bit – demanding. I'm just the house-sitter anyway. Not a house mate.'

Joe considers this. 'Well, whoever you are, would you like to share a glass of wine? Save me from drinking the whole bottle?'

She felt herself ricochet between desire and reticence like a ball caught on a bagatelle. Yes, Tess wanted to say, yes please. Adult company. Someone to share an evening with. Someone with a nice stomach. Who can smile so well. Someone currently standing casually against the doorway of the bathroom just a foot or so away. But it is easier to be harsh on herself, lecturing herself as she lowers her head and rubs Em dry that she is here for a very different purpose than sewing seeds of friendship or being charmed by a member of the opposite sex. She's been rubbish at so much else over recent years, but this house might provide the fabric for her at least to be an excellent mummy and a fine house-sitter. And that'll do. That'll really do. She is not going to ask for more than that.

'Thanks,' she says, 'but I'd better not. I'm a bit headachy. I'm going to have an early night.'

Chapter Five

When Joe shut the front door and Tess watched, unseen, as he drove away at eleven o'clock the next morning, she mourned the glass of red wine that had never been. But then Wolf sauntered by and headbutted her and Em was squawking and Tess told herself to get a grip and get on with it.

'What'll we do, gang? Fresh air?'

Wolf, it soon transpired, would be taking Tess and Em for a walk. She didn't dare let him off the lead so he plunged and strained, dragging her and the buggy in his wake. The steep downward gradient of the hill on tarmac was onerous enough but when Wolf led them into the woods and the path became an uneven assault course of hairpin bends, it was quite terrifying. How safe she'd been in London – nothing more than the occasional raised paving stone to negotiate.

'Wait!' she said. 'Halt!' she said. 'Sit!' she said. 'Stop, you great oaf, just *stop*.' They stood in the dappled lilac-green light of woodland. Em and Wolf looking expectantly at Tess. With her composure and breath back, and Wolf having to walk with a peculiar high-stepping slo-mo gait, Tess became leader of the pack. The steep woodland suddenly opened out and levelled off in a little dell of meticulously organized

Italianate design. Raised flower beds in intricate quatrefoils and curlicues currently nurtured embryonic planting that would no doubt proliferate as the weather grew warmer. Running in straight lines around the beds, a pathway plotted with regularly placed benches and punctuated by stone columns currently skeletal but which, by the summer, would be cloaked in extravagant floral displays. It was eerily quiet and though Tess tried sitting, she soon moved away.

They walked on until again the woods gave way to open meadows and a river over which catkins trickled off branches and there was a Poohsticks bridge. She found a bench for herself, plied Em with rice cakes and threw sticks for the dog. He seemed unable to track any of them but was eager to belt off in the approximate direction, bounding back to Tess as if to say, again! again! again! It made Em laugh. And it made Tess consider how pleased she was that Joe hadn't said anything about a dog because if he had, she wouldn't have taken the job. But the dog's character had won her over; his doleful mismatched eyes and soppy head-cocking were so appealing that she was now immune to his bizarre appearance. It was a novelty, having a pet part-time. And it was going to be a good thing for Em, Tess justified.

'Fetch,' she said, though she sat on her hands. Wolf looked at her in confusion. 'Fetch,' she said, hurling something imaginary which Wolf bolted off for. Daft bugger. She stroked him affectionately when he came galloping back. His ears felt like the rags she had in the back of her car. They were of a similar colour, and just as frayed. 'Dog-eared,' Tess laughed. 'Come on, let's go home and get you two some lunch.'

Pushing the buggy uphill as it dinked and lurched over the pathways, while having to haul an exhausted Wolf lagging behind her was a slog and Tess decided she wouldn't be pitching quite so many imaginary sticks for the dog tomorrow. Maybe tomorrow she'd venture a little further – not afield, but into town again. Today it felt enough to have walked and walked in the woods, to have found the Italian Gardens and the river.

Back at the house, rooting around in cupboards for a tin of baked beans, she came across a jar of preserved apricots over two years out of date. And a dead moth. And then sugar that had congealed into a solid block. Next to it, a lidless jar of Marmite with a layer of fluff furring the surface. Further inspection revealed plenty more in there – crumbled packets, tins with unfurling labels, sticky bottles. But the baked beans at least were in date and there was still half the loaf of the good bread Joe had bought yesterday. She glanced at the clock. Lunch-time. Where would Joe be right now? When exactly would he be back?

The afternoon was washed away by rain which came down like old-fashioned beaded curtains so, while the child and dog were napping, Tess made a start. The only apron she could find, in a scrunch with a collection of old batteries in one of the kitchen drawers, had a cartoon illustration of a naked female body on it, complete with foam breasts that, with time and storage, had puckered like a bad boob-job. Never mind, it would have to do. After all, there was no one here to see her. The kitchen table now had a usable surface large enough (since Tess had liberated it from the piles of Joe's stuff) for her to place items to be kept. Anything out of date, or just plain dodgy (some yellowish powder that was neither sugar nor flour, some worrying dried brown pellets, the apricots, Marmite and moths) she dumped in a bin bag. The cupboards she would disinfect before reorganizing. She looked everywhere for cleaning fluid and though it appeared Joe bought Fairy liquid in bulk and had plenty of pristine cloths that looked nothing like his dog's ears, that was about it.

She thought of the dog. And the baby. And the hill. And the enclave of shops. And the hill back. And the ache in her arms and the nag in her shins. The woods were one thing – she'd liked the company of only oak, ash, hazel and alder; the solitude had made her feel so together. Human contact, she anticipated, was quite another. Too much, too soon. On her own, she could be busy and in control – but how would she answer if someone said, hullo, love, are you new to these parts? Anyway, she wanted Em to have another half-hour's sleep and by the look of Wolf, sprawled halfway across the kitchen floor, he needed the same. She rooted around in the utility room. More Fairy liquid. And cheap washing powder. Even at her most impecunious, Tess had never scrimped on buying leading brand, dermatology-tested hypo-allergenic tablets.

Better make a list – prioritize what's essential. Where's a pen when you need one? Probably up in her bag, hanging on the back of the chair in her bedroom. But two flights of creaking stairs risked waking the baby so she looked around the entrance hall, searched through the drawers of the console. Found a biro. A glove. Some loose playing cards a fair few short of a full deck. A necklace of paperclips. But no scrap paper. Well, there was a Chinese takeaway menu and an address book but all the pages were densely written in the copperplate hand of a much older generation. She cursed herself for having so ruthlessly chucked out the heap of scrap on the kitchen table. Joe had laughed and had said, OK, I get the hint. He had taken some of the papers away while authorizing her to bin the sizeable mound still on the table.

Joe's study. Tess hovered by the door. What were the rules and would this be breaking any? An invasion of privacy? Out of bounds? It hadn't been discussed. He hadn't given her the house-sitter's pack he'd mentioned. She turned the handle, half expecting the door to be locked but it wasn't.

51

A floor-to-ceiling bookcase ran across two entire walls, the proliferation of spines serving the eye like detailed wallpaper. On the third wall, a collection of frames. Diplomas it looked like, some authenticated by red sealing wax. Certificates. Awards. An old print of a run of classical bridges that Tess knew had to be Venice. Against this wall, a large old writing desk with an inlay of moulting green leather and a stack of drawers with brass hinge handles to either side. A specialist would wince, no doubt, that it was in desperate need of French polishing and the leather, frayed and papery, should be replaced entirely, but Tess felt that would be missing the point. The swivel chair appeared to be a little skew but she imagined that it was perfectly aligned for Joe. The fourth wall wasn't really a wall at all, dominated as it was by full-length French windows looking out to yet another aspect of the garden. From the main approach, the house appeared as an imposing solid block. But Tess now felt how it was far from this. Windows at angles, rooms at tangents to the main walls; it felt fortified, there were no blind spots, the house had been configured so that every inch of its grounds could be viewed.

To either side of the French windows, a column of thick maroon velvet hung, faded along the folds to suggest the curtains were rarely drawn. In front of them, at odds with the entire room yet dominating the space and proclaiming Joe's authority, was a vast, stark white draughtsman's table; its top angled up, a high-tech stool in position.

I'm here for a scrap of paper.

But that did not preclude finding it being a lengthy process. She glanced at the clock. Em would be waking soon – Joe, perhaps landing. Tess imagined him fastening his seatbelt thinking, Christ, who the hell is this woman I've left in charge of my house – she's probably rummaging around my study this very moment.

52

One of the brass handles on the desk drawers was sticking out, as if suspended in time waiting for someone to pull it. She folded it gently down. She brushed her hand over the surface of the leather inlay and took her face to it to inhale. Ink and dust and history. She smiled, recognizing some of the documents and papers that had been in a scatter on the kitchen table now in a neater pile here, on top of a less ordered pile that was itself balanced on a jumble of others. She didn't give the laptop more than a glance; it was closed, and jarringly sleek and silvery for the desk. She thought of her Hotmail account and then thought better of it. She looked at all the framed certificates and found out Joe's middle name was Randal and his surname was Saunders. She imagined he was teased about this when he was younger. There couldn't have been many Randals in Saltburn in his school days. Nor now, probably. It seemed he was top at everything he'd done. Cross-country running included. There was a beautifully calligraphed, extravagantly embossed certificate in French. Tess's knowledge of the language was limited. Some fancy accolade for M. Joseph R. Saunders. Perhaps it was the freedom of a city for which he'd built a bridge.

Building bridges is what he did and the meticulous sketches on the draughtsman's desk attested to this. Tess perched herself on the stool and peered at them. A myriad of details, they resembled completed studies of architectural fragments, replete with angles and figures and arrows and symbols. Unable to interpret the details, Tess felt a little small, intimidated by the apparent complexity and Joe's obvious expertise. How ever do these two-dimensional clippings materialize into vast structures which carry, cover and join? She swivelled the stool and thought about this. As the stool stilled, she caught sight of a wastepaper basket under the old desk. Bingo. She retrieved a handful of scrap paper and sat at the desk to write her shopping list.

Washing powder (E)
Disinfectant
Nice cheese (me)
Marmite
Organic pasta (E)
Ditto rusks (E)
Biscuits (me)
Fruit & Veg

That would do for now. She did wonder whether to replace any of the out-of-date items she'd thrown away. But then she decided if a man hadn't had the desire for preserved apricots or brown pellet things during the last two years, he probably wouldn't crave them anytime soon. She glanced at the back of the paper – or what would have been the front when it had served Joe. A column of names. Her own included. It was a list of those applying for the job. The first name had a question mark and *O.C.D?!* written alongside. Mrs Mackey had been rewritten as *Mrs Mucky* and had a large X by her name. John Forder had *mass murderer* and a doodle of a dagger dripping blood by his. Mr and Mrs Potts had *ANCIENT!!* in capital letters by theirs. Mrs Dunn, however, had a tick and an arrow to a telephone number. Then another arrow to a sizeable cross with the word *busybody!* Then Tess saw her name. Next to it was no tick, no cross, no arrows, just a single word. *Barking*. No exclamation mark to lighten it. She thought back to the phone call, where she'd used her phoney American accent before exchanging it for a whisper. She remembered accepting the job before it had been offered. Barking, she had to concede, was an acceptable definition. But she would have liked a doodle by her name all the same. She wondered how Joe would rethink this categorization having had a couple of days of her. She slumped a little as if she could physically feel how she'd let herself down. *Stroppy Cow*, she wrote alongside *Barking*.

Then she wondered, would Joe declare her a busybody

for fumigating his kitchen? Would he think she had OCD for planning to enforce structure in his store cupboards? Perhaps such enterprise would earn her a great big tick, maybe even a doodle. It had been a long, long time since anyone had bestowed a seal of approval on her. Even the paltry tips at the salon had fallen short of being anything but a formality. She looked at her nails and added *Emery board (me)* to the list. She'd left her manicure set on the sofa in London. A feeble gesture, but a gesture all the same. It was a professional kit and had been expensive. She hoped her landlord, nasty man, might know so. Would he have called by now? Three days, she reminded herself, that's all it's been.

Wolf seemed unable to stand upright, let alone go for another walk, so Tess gave him the benefit of the doubt and let him out into the garden where she chided him for doing his business and then felt bad because he looked so confused. It made her think she should leave him be and instead train Em not to venture to that particular area. After all, wasn't the garden large enough to accommodate all of them? She'd poop-scoop, that's what she'd do. She'd timetable it in, every day.

'Come on, Em. Wolf – you can stay here.'

She took the buggy though Em toddled alongside for part of the way. This time, they stuck to the pavement on the opposite side to the valley gardens, passing by the magnificent Victorian buildings, trying to sneak a look through the beautifully proportioned windows.

'See sigh!' the baby's pudgy hand waved excitedly.

'Not today, baby,' Tess said, skimming wary eyes along the beach. There was a pebbly area where the river-mouth met the beach, everywhere else the sand was a perfect blond. Today the wind whipped the surface sending sand whispering over the beach like smoke.

'See sigh,' Em repeated as if indignant that enunciating

the words hadn't led to the reward of the real thing. They were standing at the railings again, from where they'd watched Joe and Wolf cavorting the day before yesterday.

'Sorry,' said Tess, 'Mummy doesn't like the beach.' Then she looked around her and said, but Mummy *does* like the pier.

Tess pushed the buggy along the lower promenade, passing the old beach chalets in red and white all battened down against the spring squalls; on past a closed café, an open surf shop. She walked around the small amusement centre at the entrance to the pier, went through the ornamental gateway and walked out onto the boardwalk. The tide was out leaving the sand with a mirrored surface on which a string of horses was being ridden. They were passing right under the trestles and Tess and Em looked down on them from one side of the pier to the other, like large living Poohsticks. For all its impressive length, the pier was plain, austere almost, with none of the lurid jollity of Brighton or the tasteful and innovative renovation of Southwold. But when Tess looked around her, up and down the coast, inland, out to sea, to the sky, she thought how the point of this pier was perfectly realized – to serve the views.

Along the length were occasional benches, sat upon by elderly couples in a huddle to watch time pass while allowing the bracing sea air to do them the power of good. They cooed over Em who smiled on cue. Tess looked down to the shore line as she continued to walk along the pier; the spray from the wave crests was being blasted back to sea – nature breaking the rules. At the end of the pier, a snuggle of men fishing. Tess ventured up to them, gingerly – it was windy and the pier was high. Their buckets were empty but that didn't seem to be the point, rather eating sandwiches and sharing their flasks of tea did. Plenty more fish in the sea, one man called after Tess. She laughed though she said to herself, yeah right. Been there. Done that. Got the baby.

56

Tess shivered. She wanted to scrub out the kitchen before having to prepare supper. She picked up her pace which allowed for only a cursory glance at the cliff lift Joe had pointed out, now rising steeply right in front of her. Gaily painted in similar shades to the chalets and the promenade buildings, it appeared to be a near-vertical funicular. Another day. No rush. She wasn't going anywhere, after all. Hadn't Joe said he wanted her to stay long-term? Leaning the top of her head into the wind, she retraced her steps briskly.

'Easy!'

She looked up, just in time to avoid a slippery mound of neoprene, which appeared to have been just stripped off and flung in the middle of the walkway outside the surf store; like some felled mutant creature from the deep. The voice belonged to a young wet man saronging himself in a towel. His hair, in long shaggy blond ringlets, held drips of water at each tip and they flew off in a sprinkle as his head moved. He was pale-skinned but brawny. Briny too by the look of his slightly bloodshot eyes and soggy hands and feet. With his chiselled features, he looked rather exotic for his surroundings.

'In the water I don't feel the cold,' he said, in a light Australian accent, 'but as I walk back across the beach I start fantasizing about my towel.'

By the look of his nipples, the shiver of his torso and the blue tinge to his lips, Tess reckoned he could do with another towel around his top half. She didn't say so, she just nodded and walked on.

'Do you surf?'

'No fear,' she said as she walked.

'Well – if you've no fear, as you say, then come by one day and I'll teach you.'

'Not likely,' Tess laughed.

'Can't swim?'

57

She stopped and turned. 'I can. I just don't do sand,' she said.

'I'm Seb. I work here.'

She called over her shoulder as she walked away again. 'I'm Tess. I work up there.'

Not rude, Seb reckoned. Just shy.

Chapter Six

And work up there she did.

The kitchen was to take her two days, during which time fresh air for herself, her child and the dog was restricted to the garden and one excursion down to the small everything shop for milk, bread and fish fingers. She'd been through Joe's chest freezer which occupied an entire room off the utility room, with only a couple of mops for company. She'd chucked out much of what was in it, having to defrost it enough to release the hunk of meat and packet of peas and something that looked like a bag of soil that were entombed in ice at the bottom. The work was hard on her back and tough on her hands, but it was energizing and satisfying and pre-occupying because it gave her no time to dwell. But when the hard labour was done and she could immerse herself in the smaller details, she freed up thinking time and in doing so, gave anxiety an opening to vex her. She'd had no contact with those close to her since her absconding. Because she'd cut up her SIM card, she'd made herself uncontactable but had inadvertently severed many links too. Initially, it had all felt liberating. Now it felt hasty and stupid. There had been no need, over recent years, to commit phone numbers to her own memory when the wonder of the SIM card could take its place and store more. She reckoned she might just be able to recall Tamsin and her sister's numbers – but she couldn't face phoning either just yet.

Stop thinking about it.

It doesn't matter at the moment.

Concentrate on Joe's spice jars. They're filled with little wriggling things burrowing amongst the flakes of herbs.

She chucked out the contents then disinfected the glass containers with boiling water. They looked pretty; dazzling clean with their scruffy labels washed off.

Stickers. She wrote the word on a new shopping list.

Parsley.

Sage.

Rosemary.

Thyme.

Scarborough is around here somewhere, she thought, singing Simon and Garfunkle during which Wolf left the room and Em woke up. With the baby and the dog snaffling rusks, Tess put the empty jars away in their new position in the slim wall cupboard nearest the cooker. Seven of them. She racked her brains but was pretty sure Paul Simon had specified only four. She returned to her list.

Basil.

Coriander.

Etc.

From the hallway, Wolf suddenly started barking. I'm only humming, Tess protested but the dog skittered over the stone floors from kitchen to front door and back again, turning circles while yowling at the top of his voice.

'Hush.'

But he wouldn't so Tess went over to him and looked through the spyhole. 'No one there, Wolf,' she said and she went out into the drive to prove it. She looked down the street too but apart from an elderly lady walking downhill, the road was empty of cars and pedestrians.

'Some guard dog you are,' Tess laughed at the sight of Wolf simultaneously barking but cowering on the front doorstep. 'There's no one there, Wolf. In you go, you daft dog. There's only us here.'

But two days later, Wolf started again. And a split second beforehand, Tess did think she caught a glimpse of someone passing by the living-room window (she was busy alphabetizing the books). But when she ventured outside, there was no one and she felt an idiot. She scolded Wolf for – well, for crying wolf.

'When the real baddies come – I won't believe you.'

But she did quietly wonder to herself whether she was imagining things; perhaps conjuring people to populate her world that currently had in it only a dog and a child for company. One week in, she thought again of Tamsin, of her sister; she needed both for very different reasons. But she didn't know what she needed to say to the former and she didn't want to have to say what she needed to the latter.

She'd been here just short of two weeks. Joe was expected back, briefly, in a couple of days. She'd quite like to finish the larger living room in that time – to beat the hell out of the rug and pummel life back into the cushions, to complete her work on the books, to dust them down and put them back up from A to Z. The kitchen was now spotless but forlornly bereft of supplies. For all she knew, Joe liked to cook up a storm on his short returns. She decided she ought to put the living-room books on hold and complete the herb section in the kitchen instead. Stock up on a few basics, too. Ensure there was fresh produce in the fridge for him, as requested. She looked in her wallet as if she expected it to

61

have spontaneously filled since she last opened it, but discovered less than she remembered. Might Joe pay her when he was back? She knew she'd be too shy to ask. She really should phone her sister, swallow her pride and just dial. She folded her sole banknote and slipped it into her back pocket. She told herself she should have cut up her bank card, rather than her SIM card, because it was the former that was really of no use any more. But she wanted to hang on to it, as if it was a talisman – like a pair of jeans that used to fit and that might fit once again if a few pounds could be lost. But Tess knew her bank account needed to gain a lot of pounds before she could use that card again. She would have to phone Claire. But perhaps it could wait until Joe had been and gone again.

For the first time since her arrival, Tess took her time around town. She'd been in to buy essentials, of course, but had made her visits quick. However, her days during this first fortnight had designed themselves into a series of concentric rings whose diameter had increased with time. Initially, Tess had needed to constrict her surroundings to feel she could cope – just a few feet in front of her, or a few minutes in any direction. As time passed and she unwound and slept better and enjoyed her days more, so she found her energy and her confidence and discovered a new urge to increase her field of vision – what she saw, how far she'd go and how long she'd be gone from the house. Almost daily, she'd increased these elements, stepping onto a larger ring each time, keener to discover what lay along its length.

Venturing up and down the shopping streets on recent days, she'd been surprised at the diversity. From the iron awnings and dusty glass along Milton Street and Dundas Street harking back a little forlornly to their Victorian heyday, to the price-promos plastering the windows of the small supermarket near the station; from old-fashioned boutiques promoting a proliferation of drip-dry beigeness modelled by oddly posed mannequins in slipped wigs, to a hippy-chic kids' clothing store; from the chippy, to the small but sumptuously stocked deli; from a shop selling a knot of fishing tackle to a high-class chocolatiers. It appeared there was even the demand for gluten-free pizza, right here in Saltburn – but that didn't mean that the Chinese takeaway would be going out of business any time soon. She learned as much from the small cartographic gallery as she did from Tourist Information, buying two postcards of local paintings from the former and taking all the leaflets or papers that were free from the latter. She passed by the library and jotted down details of a playgroup at the church two mornings a week and saw that the one-act drama festival had completely passed her by. She read the signs and flyers in shop windows. She took a calendar of events and saw that in May there'd be a film festival, in June a food festival, in July a comedy festival, in August a folk festival as well as Victorian Week.

A friendly woman much her own age, with a child Em's age, struck up a conversation with Tess in the queue inside the bakery. She was Lisa, she said. Born and bred here, she said. You're coming to Musical Minis, she told Tess – your daughter will love it and we mums need someone new amongst us. We go for lunch afterwards, Lisa said, then on to the playground. She even waited for Tess to be served and then said, goodbye, see you soon – great to meet you, pet. To Tess it all sounded as intriguing as it sounded exhausting and she told herself she ought to do it. It would be good for her, and Em.

She walked on, meandering down towards the pier and half wondering if there'd be a flung pile of wetsuits and a semi-naked Seb today. The surf shop was open; there was a rail of sale clothes outside but there was no one tending the shop and no one browsing the wares. No Seb today, at least not on shore. She walked along the pier and watched the surfers but they were indistinguishable in their wetsuits from that distance. The tide was in, lapping greedily around the trestles of the pier, the swirling sea visible through the gaps in the boardwalk. The fishermen at the end of the pier had yet to catch anything.

Tess turned and faced inland and looked at the peculiar little cliff lift waiting for the tourist season to start; the vertical line of the track up the cliff looking like a zip. With the two tiny tramcars stationary midway up, it appeared the cliff's flies were half down. To her right, far along the beach, she noted the industrial chimneys of Redcar, the sunlight today investing the scene with the hazy romanticism of Monet as much as the prosaic charm of Lowry. Some distance to her left, the great lumbering mass of Huntcliff Nab commanded the beach to end in a perfect cove. So much to explore, she thought. How long before all this newness becomes my stamping ground?

Her visit to what she now thought of as the Everything Shop brought increased conversation with the proprietor today. Tess asked for rosemary and a shoebox full of packets of dried herbs was produced.

'Sorry, love. No rosemary, but how about this – *fines herbes*. Sounds exotic, doesn't it.'

Tess agreed.

The lady continued. 'Mind you, the way I pronounce it, sounds like a Scandinavian lurgy. Finiz herpiz.'

Tess laughed and had to agree again. 'Well, I'll risk a packet anyway,' she said. 'Oh, and I need two more types as well.'

Between them, Tess and the lady went through the packets of herbs before Tess decided on tarragon and sage.

'You cooking up a treat then, pet?'

'I'm restocking. The old ones had creepy crawlies in them.'

'You vegetarian, then?'

It was said so deadpan that it took a long wink from the proprietor to release Tess's laughter.

'Would you have a nice vinegar? Try where? Real Meals – is that the deli on the corner of Station Square? Thanks for the recommendation. I'll have some of that jam, please. And do you sell wire wool? Of course you do – you're the Everything Shop.'

There wasn't much change. Tess calculated that balsamic vinegar might have to wait.

'Stopping here a while, love?'

'Stopping here, full stop,' Tess told her. 'I'm still finding my way around, still finding my feet. I met someone today who told me about a mums and toddlers group.'

'Where are you from?'

'London.'

The woman nodded her head gravely. 'Why?'

Tess was stuck. 'Why what?'

'Why London – and why here?'

'My sister lives in Edinburgh.' But that was just the pat reason Tess had decided to use when the time was right to finally inform her friends where she was. She smiled at the lady as she prepared to leave. 'Actually, why *not* here – it's good.'

The lady nodded.

'I'm a house-sitter,' Tess said. 'Up the top. Anyway, I'd better go. I'm dying for a cup of coffee and it's a steep hike home with this old buggy.'

'You want to take yourself to Camfields, pet. It's near the car park by Cat Nab, the funny little hilly mound near the beach – bottom of the Gardens. It's your kind of place, I would think, coming from London and all. You'll get your

65

cup of chino there, or a latty or whatever. It's a café – you know – not a caff.'

'I might just try it,' Tess thanked her. And the next day she did just that. And the coffee really was excellent.

Chapter Seven

Nathalie stretched. She didn't really need to, there were no sore muscles or nagging joints to necessitate it. She did so because she was well aware how it presented her figure to its best advantage. So she stood in the front room of her apartment, on a Thursday evening, her hands clasped above her head, a slight hitch to one hip, knowing that her top, skimpy enough, was now stretched over jutting breasts as well as having ridden up to expose her toned stomach. She'd kept her high heels on because they elongated her legs and she'd locked her knees to increase further the sleekness of her limbs. Holding the pose a moment longer, while casting a nonchalant gaze out of the window, she then sighed as if she'd just had a satisfying yawn and she let her body go soft, her hands coming down to rest on her hips, one knee now cocked, breasts still up and out there.

'So,' she said, letting it hang, her lips maintaining a perfect 'o' of the word. 'You will miss me, Joe?' She did the same thing with her lips to the sound of his name. As pouts go, hers was textbook, but she made it look involuntary, as if it had slipped her mind to return her lips to neutral because sex was always on her mind and never far from her mouth.

Joe was sitting on the sofa, watching Nathalie as if she was a performance, a one-woman show, a private viewing exclusively for him. She didn't need an answer – it hadn't really been an enquiry. He went over to her and placed the tip of his finger against the hole her lips still made. Her tongue flicked at his fingertip before her mouth sucked it all in, down to his knuckle. He moved his other hand deftly up under her short skirt, rubbing his thumb along the gusset of her knickers while he closed his eyes. That mouth of hers, from which came her dirty, husky French accent. That mouth of hers, pretending to be a pussy, pretending his finger was his cock. Yes, he'll bloody miss her.

'You come back to me soon, *non?*'

And she was pouting again, coyly, as she fingered the mound straining behind his jeans. He plugged her mouth with his tongue and ran his hands over her body; a grab at a breast, a squeeze at a buttock, a grasp for the back of her neck, a pull at her hair to release it from the chignon so that it fell and bounced around her face and caught across her lips. She started to pull her top over her head, stretching her torso into its best aspect again. Joe took charge of her top and worked it up into a blindfold while he stroked her, at first tantalizingly through the transparent lace of her bra before ripping it down to reveal her skin and those eager, nut-brown nipples. With her eyes still masked, he returned his mouth to hers while unbuttoning his jeans, released his cock from his pants and took her hand down to it. Like petals closing around a stamen, her fingers lightly encircled his cock before tightening their grip. He gasped. She flung the blindfold away.

'You want my mouth or you want my cunt?' Such a question. And the preview she'd provided of both options rendered Joe speechless. She knelt down, and looked up at him while she sucked him into her mouth. She stood up and grabbed his hand, easing his finger up inside her panties, up inside her. He buckled down to the floor, pushed her prostrate, pulled her knickers to one side and penetrated her for a few forceful thrusts before he came.

She smiled at her chandelier. It was always the same with Joe; he could not contain himself. He loved to fuck her fast and selfishly, to fuck her hard, and she loved it. They'd do it again later, at her instigation and it would be less urgent, lasting longer with him concentrating on her orgasm. For the duration of this trip – as on all his trips here – they'd had sex every day. It was never boring with Joe. Kinky sex, fun shagging, horny sex, oral, aural – but it was the near-aggressive fucks which she enjoyed the most despite being over quickly with no time for her own climax. Just to feel a man so utterly abandoned in his desire for her was turn-on enough. Now he was exhausted and hot, heavy on top of her, spent. She could gyrate against his weight, she could stimulate herself against his semi-stiffness and the ooze of his come to bring herself to orgasm. But she knew he'd take her later that night, tomorrow morning too, no doubt, before he left for England. She traced her nails over his back, right down to the dip at the top of his buttocks.

'You miss me, Joe?' she asked, still consciously lascivious. 'I think you'll miss me big, *non?*'

Chapter Eight

'Look, Wolf, I've told you – there's no one there. I thought I saw someone too – but it must have been shadows cast by the trees.' Wolf turned a few more circles by the boot-room door, baying while he did so. 'You've missed him, haven't you,' Tess said, watching Wolf settle with a sigh. 'I can't say I have because I don't know him at all, really. But that isn't to say I'm not looking forward to his return.'

Because she was standing in the kitchen holding a knife, the dog assumed she was talking about food so he drooled and mooched over to his tin bowl, looking back at her imploringly. Tess shook her head. Daft dog. 'Your master, you dumb hound. Joe? Daddy?' He pushed the bowl with his snout and cocked his head to one side. Tess gave him the crust of the toast she'd been eating. She looked around the kitchen and felt quietly house-proud. She hadn't done it for Joe alone, but that did not preclude her keenly anticipating his response. Or looking forward to adult conversation and human company in the evenings.

When Wolf started barking and charging around as if his paws were on fire, Tess wondered whether it was the phantom presence at the window again until, a moment later, she heard the car crunch onto the gravel. A zip of adrenalin momentarily immobilized her. Shit – the main living room was still a battleground of organized chaos, with books in piles waiting to be re-shelved, the cushions from the sofas airing outside in the garden, the rug hanging on the washing line after a thorough bashing. The room looked dreadful to the untrained eye. And so, for that matter, did Tess. She caught sight of her reflection in the window and winced at her hair hanging in limp tangles. She looked down at herself – baggy sweatshirt, shapeless leggings, bare feet with toenails in need of attention. As she made to dart upstairs, she suddenly remembered Em in the highchair in the kitchen. She raced back in there and out again.

And so it was barefoot Tess looking slightly manic, and Emmeline with porridge or cement or something smeared around her face, and Wolf turning in a tizzy of barks and leaps, who Joe came across when he came through the front door. Fortunately for Tess, the dog hurled himself to the fore-front, craving Joe's attention as much as she slunk from it so she was able to just call, hi there! just going to change a nappy! while springing up the stairs with Em.

Keep away from the front room, keep away from the front room, she chanted to herself while changing Em. Go to the kitchen, go straight to the kitchen.

Quick, quick, quick.

Socks. The good jeans. A clean black top. Hair tamed into a pony-tail. Baby fragrant, pink, cute, clean face.

Slow down. Slow down. Silly to be so excited. Really silly.

He was in the kitchen, with a cup of tea.

'The French are very, very good at most things,' he said, 'but making tea is not one of them.'

'Welcome back,' Tess said and she glanced around the room. Has he noticed anything?

71

'Everything OK? Did Wolf behave himself? He looks well.'

'All's fine,' she said. 'How was your trip?'

'Good. Productive. The project is progressing. I ate a lot of garlic. I ate horse. I argued with the concrete company, I assured the planners that there's been no change to the height, I persuaded the client it may be a little more expensive than we agreed. Oh, and I drank too early in the day – France is France.'

Tess was nodding as if she'd been there. 'Well, welcome back.'

'*Merci, mademoiselle.*'

'Must be nice to be home after hotels.'

'Oh, I was in an apartment,' Joe said and he wondered why he made the place sound corporate rather than Nathalie's.

'Did you have a balcony? And cast-iron twirly railings, long thin French doors and wafting organza drapes?'

He regarded Tess – by the look of her, she dearly wanted the answer to be yes. He recalled briefly Nathalie's ultra-modern pad. 'Of course. And I drink my morning coffee out of a big white bowl.'

He started to glance around his own kitchen, as if it was taking him minute by minute to reacclimatize to his surroundings. 'It's all looking very –'

Tess didn't want him to finish his sentence before he'd seen it all.

'Let me show you!' She rushed through the room, cupboard after cupboard, flinging open the doors and presenting the interiors like a showroom sales manager.

'You've been busy,' he said, flicking through his post. She realized she had hoped he'd jump to his feet, to inspect and marvel.

'Just making myself useful. You don't mind, do you? It's the sort of job that's a shag to do yourself – but I thought it could be part of why I'm here.' She was a fast fidget of words. 'I'm making a start on the drawing room—'

'– the *where*?'

She reddened. 'The grander sitting room – the one without the telly.'

'Making *a start*?'

'Just cleaning and organizing. Doing your books – you know, in alphabetical order. I could do your CDs in the other room too, if you like. You can decide the system – you know, whether Bruce Springsteen comes under B or S. If you have Bruce Springsteen.'

His expression was illegible.

'Your herbs were alive,' she continued, 'and you had stuff two *years* out of date. And *no* disinfectant. So I took the liberty – you know, out with the old, in with the new. But I did replace most stuff, at least store-cupboard essentials. And fresh food in the fridge, like you asked. Have you seen the fridge? A lemon cut in half put in the egg tray keeps whiffs at bay – my grandmother told me so.'

She was tying herself in knots of trivial information and it amused Joe. He'd put his post to one side.

'I can't pay you more,' he said and he really didn't mean it to sound curt but it did – harsh even. And if she'd given him the chance to retract it and apologize for it, he'd have thanked her and praised her too. But she'd already leapt to the defensive.

'I'm not doing it for the money,' she said, intentionally spiky.

And they stared at each other and thought to themselves, oh, it's *you*. I remember now, you have the ability to wind me up.

Tess took Em out for a walk straight away. Wolf took it upon himself to follow them out. Joe called the dog from the house,

73

when he thought he was straying, but the dog ignored him, much to Joe's annoyance and to gentle satisfaction on Tess's part. Once she'd gone, Joe looked in at the disarray in the large living room or drawing room, said, Jesus Christ, shut the door and made for his study. At least his study was as he'd left it. He swivelled on his stool. He'd intended only to tease; he'd meant no offence. But that Tess should bristle so excessively had served to shut down his apology. However, he regretted the situation now. And he was sorry that the house should have emptied so soon after his arrival. He went to the kitchen and glanced in a cupboard. He'd never seen it like that. He looked in the others and had to admit to himself that he was impressed and not irritated. She really had been busy. What had she done in her rooms? He made another cup of tea and took it upstairs, to have a nose.

The child's room looked just that: a room for a child – toys in mutiny all over the place, miniscule clothes on scaled-down hangers, a floral border mounted not very precisely at dado height, pastel-patterned bedding folded neatly over the sides of the travel cot. It had been Joe's bedroom this, once upon a time, but he had no memories of it being so – he pondered – being so *what* exactly? What was it that it seemed now, that it had never seemed then? It took a while to pinpoint. Friendly, he decided. Friendly. He was tempted to sit cross-legged on the floor. It alarmed him a little. He left the room without looking back into it.

Tess's room appeared peculiarly feminine. She'd changed the configuration of the bed but apart from that, and adding furniture from elsewhere in the house, the room remained much the same. She'd found tiebacks for the curtains from somewhere and had taken cushions from elsewhere to put on the window seat. A throw Joe knew wasn't his made the bed seem, well, *made*. Against the fireplace, the LPs he'd lugged in from her car. The little table in the corner, which he hadn't seen for years and she'd found God only knows where, had on it a notebook and pen, a pot of Nivea, and a jaunty little pouch containing make-up. He casually flipped through the notebook. It was blank. Over the chair, her handbag – a beat-up brown leather thing. Maybe not genuine leather. On the Lloyd Loom seat, the scrunch of clothes he now remembered she'd been wearing when he first arrived this morning. Under the chair, a cardboard box. In it, he saw an iron, a kettle, a strange little wire basket and three rather dated fitness videos. Rather strange equipment to have brought with her, he thought. On the windowsill outside, three small handmade terracotta plant pots. Crocus and narcissus in flower. She must have planted those in London last autumn. Overall, the room smelt nice. Of clean things. Of fresh air having been let in on a daily basis. It didn't seem anything like the room his father used, that he escaped into for hours on end when his mother was being unbearable. The uninvited memory made Joe leave quickly.

The bathroom was gleaming. He sniffed at the baby shampoo and bubble bath and discovered it was this gentle scent which permeated the two bedrooms. Nicer than his Head & Shoulders. He noted that Tess had been through his entire towel supply to carefully choose only those that matched. Flannel, hand-towel, bath sheet. The baby, it appeared, had brought her own personalized set; soft, thick and fluffy with an embroidered duck and a curlicue 'E'.

There was a spare loo roll. A bottle of bleach. A book called *Splishy Splashy* made out of plastic. Rubber ducks in pink, mint and yellow. A new, higher wattage light bulb. Toothpaste for sensitive teeth. Another tube for one-to-three-year-olds. A little toothbrush that looked like it was for a doll. A sponge in the shape of a frog. A lovely room. Magazine worthy. Yet was this not the room he'd been locked in as a child, when he'd been bad or had been perceived as such?

His parents' version of today's Naughty Step. It was also the place he'd been sent to when his parents needed him out of sight and sound so they could fight uninterrupted. Today, the transformation of the bathroom was so extreme it was as if an exorcism had taken place. He was sitting in there, feeling no need to shudder. If she could do this to these three rooms, she could do what she liked with the rest of the house, he decided. He'd be sure to tell her so when he next saw her. He'd give her carte blanche to alphabetize his CDs; she could choose whether Bruce Springsteen was filed under B or S. He'd let her know all this once she was back from her walk. Maybe they could have a late lunch, a chat.

He was hungry now, though, and he went back down to the kitchen and made himself a sandwich, admiring the gleaming interior of the fridge, the fresh contents that were in it. Then he took a longer look in all the cupboards and he checked out the freezer and he wondered to himself, was I really that much of a slovenly old dog? And he thought perhaps he had been. And he wondered, why did she do it? Doesn't she have anything better to do? And he thought perhaps she doesn't which, for his ends, was no bad thing. He thought back to Mrs Dunn. He'd made the right decision – for the old place. He wondered if Tess felt the same – it continued to strike him as odd that a young woman should move from the liveliness and opportunities of the capital city to keep house for a sometimes snide bloke in a sleepy seaside town in the North.

'I could throw a pasta dish together,' he told Tess when she arrived back soon after. 'The cupboard fairy appears to have updated my herb rack.'

Tess smiled a little shyly; aware of the peace offering. 'Thanks,' she said. 'I bought olive oil and balsamic vinegar – they're only small bottles but it was a twin pack, on special offer in Real Foods. I reorganized your wines in that cupboard. White on the upper shelf, red beneath. I hope that's OK.'

'Thank you,' he said. 'It *is* OK,' he said. 'Say, eight-ish?'

So she repeated eight-ish and they nodded at each other, appeased.

Joe went to his study, shutting his door, leaving Tess to fill the rest of the afternoon doing whatever it was she finds to do in this old house of his.

Do I dress for dinner? Tess wonders while popping the snap-fastenings on Em's night-time babygro. 'Shall I?' She pauses. 'Stop it.' She pauses again. 'Not you, Em – me. We'd probably be in the kitchen preparing our supper at the same time anyway. It's just convenience.' She snuffles Em's tummy much to the baby's delight, scoops the child up and watches their reflection in the window. She often gazes at the sight of herself holding her child in this particular embrace; it is an image that cannot be bettered.

I love you, little girl. I love you. You and me, my baby, you and me.

She puts Em down in the cot, switches on the night-light, winds up the music box, watches her a while longer, then tiptoes from the room.

She hasn't many clothes but she does want to change. There's her denim skirt, a skinny black polo – a total makeover from the bagginess of her daytime garb. There's an unopened pair of black tights too. No suitable footwear really, only trainers. She'll go shoeless – she's noted that Joe never wears shoes inside, just chunky socks with or without his well-worn moccasin slippers. The latter are usually at the say-so of Wolf, who likes to take them tenderly to bed with him.

She puts on a little mascara for the first time since London and sits at the mirror having a look. You are a bit mad, she says to herself. Dressing for dinner with a man you don't know in a house you're treating as your own, you deluded thing.

It has just gone eight. She waits until ten past – indulging in a woman's prerogative to be late-ish when the plan was eight-ish.

But he isn't in the kitchen and there's nothing on the stove and the herbs are still in the cupboard and there are no sounds of life coming from the study. She stands there a while, furious that she should feel dejected, for feeling suddenly self-conscious in a stupid skirt. And brand bloody new, black bloody tights. Don't even mention the mascara. The stone floor is cold; through the soles of her feet she can feel the chill snaking an insidious path up her body. She is just wondering whether to add socks to her ensemble or change outfits completely when the back door opens and Joe appears, followed by Wolf who bounds to her in a skitter of muddy affection.

'Bloody hell, Wolf,' Joe says, 'it's only been a couple of hours.' He looks at Tess. 'It must be love.' He looks at the kitchen clock. 'Shit. Sorry.' He looks at Tess again. She looks different. She's in a skirt. Good legs. Something about her eyes. Nice though. Shame Wolf has left his mark. 'Are you hungry?'

She nods.

'Thirsty?'

She smiles as she nods.

'Wine? Water?'

She looks a little embarrassed.

'Wine?' Joe helps.

'Please – I mean, if you're having.'

'Red or white?'

Again, she looks self-conscious.

'This is a nice red,' Joe says and they chink glasses and sip quietly.

'Many hands make light work?' Joe says as he plucks up an onion and throws it underarm to Tess. She catches it, much to Wolf's chagrin, who has been sitting quietly focused at her side.

'Slice?' she asks. 'Dice?'

'Finely chop, please.'

'Is this for a secret recipe?'

'It's my "if-you've-got-it, chuck-it-in" speciality,' he says and once she's done the onion, he sets her to work on the tomatoes. Bolstered by the wine, it is a genial and industrious atmosphere and, when they aren't working their knives or humming to themselves, they talk lightly about their time apart. Joe finds out what she's been up to whilst he's been gone and Tess discovers he's off again, to London, then possibly straight on to France.

'This smells good, don't you think?'

'It smells lovely. A welcome change from toast and Marmite.'

'Is that what you live on?' Joe gives her a stern but theatrical frown. He stirs the sauce and proffers the wooden spoon towards her lips. She would have preferred to take it off him but, a little self-consciously, she comes closer and sips straight from his spoon. She licks her lips and hums approval. He is looking at her intently and for a suspended moment they lock eyes before Tess turns away; calls herself crazy, tells herself she's been too long without male company, that it's ridiculous to melt just a little just because he's spooned sauce into her mouth. Joe notes the reddening to her cheeks and, when she turns away, he is left looking at the nape of her neck and he can't deny that it is all rather Thomas Hardy again. He's doing an Alec D'Urberville – albeit feeding this Tess sauce off a spoon instead of a strawberry by hand. He can see that she feels awkward and actually this quite stirs him. Also, he can see that she is unaware how this emotion affects her looks

79

and actually, he likes the look of her. And he liked the look of her lips parting for his spoon, the feel of her mouth against it, the closeness of her body. The nape of her neck.

'I'd better check on Em,' she's saying and while she is upstairs, she takes off her mascara, looks at herself in the mirror and thinks she looks worse which, bizarrely, makes her feel better.

The pasta is in bowls on the table when she returns.

'Seasoned with tarragon and sage,' Joe announces, not actually noting any difference in barefaced Tess. 'I like the labels you drew – very artistic.'

Tess has no complaints about toast and Marmite but Joe's pasta really does taste good. As it warms her, it thaws her awkwardness. 'That Everything Shop is a treasure trove.'

Joe laughs, he knows exactly which shop she's referring to. 'That's why I have a tab there.'

Tess stops chewing.

'If you need anything for the house, just stick it on my tab,' he clarifies.

She swallows thoughtfully.

'Have you spent much?' Joe asks and she should say, well, yes actually. Relatively speaking, she's spent quite a lot. Her purse is all but empty now. She should be recompensed, she's the house-sitter after all. Instead, Tess brushes away the suggestion as if it's grains of salt on the table. She twists her fork gamely into the pasta.

'I'll add it to what I owe you. I need to pay you anyway,' Joe says. 'I'll write a cheque tomorrow.'

Tess stops eating again. She takes contemplative sips at her wine before finally saying that, actually, if it wasn't a problem, cash would be better, if that was OK.

'Cash?'

'If that's OK?' Tess thinks, please say it is.

'No problem. We'll walk to the bank tomorrow morning,

if you like – assuming you'll be taking Emmeline out. Been to the beach yet?'

'I told you – I don't like beaches.'

Joe is about to ask why ever not, but there's something about the way she has lowered her face, how her look has gone all inward, that stops him. It appears sand is dangerous territory so he moves their conversation to neutral ground and they chat easily about bridges and fingernails, dogs and babies, late into the night.

Chapter Nine

'Cash, then?' Joe confirmed, standing outside the bank the next morning.

'If that's OK.' She fought to sound casual and nonchalant though the notion of money soon fleshing out her purse filled her with near manic relief. She hoped Joe might just think it was the whip of the mid-March wind making her quiver a little.

'You guard the Wolfster,' he said, handing Tess the retractable lead, which Wolf took advantage of just as soon as he was in her hands and his master was out of sight.

An unbelievable length of cord spewed out of the casing and though she said, shit, and pressed anything she thought could be pressed, Wolf was around the corner in no time and she was having to set her feet against his almighty lug.

'So, I'm taking it that you don't water-ski either, let alone surf?'

Seb. She'd met him only the once and he'd been semi-naked. Today he was fully dressed and appeared taller than she remembered, but his accent was as distinctive as the shaggy fair hair spiralling out from his black fleece beany. He put his thumb and index finger in his mouth, blasted out a long whistle and within an instant, Wolf was back. 'Universal Language of Dog,' he shrugged and he placed his thumb over Tess's. 'Push it forward – don't press it in.'

'Does my dog know you?'

'Nope – but that whistle always works. Well, it does for the larger, stupider dogs – no offence, big guy. Whereas the little 'uns – they'll just give you the canine equivalent of the finger.' He didn't have to pause long for Tess to smile. 'I have another whistle I use on the ladies.' He gave a lusty wolf whistle through his teeth and finished with a wry, cocky grin at Tess. 'Never fails,' he shrugged and he laughed when Tess raised her eyebrows at her gullibility. He fanned a paying-in book. 'I ought to go.'

Tess found herself hoping Joe wouldn't come out just yet and Seb wouldn't go in just yet. And would bloody Wolf stop his frisk and frolic.

'Pop by,' Seb said. 'You know where to find me. And if I'm not in – just whistle. You know how to whistle, don't you?'

'Of course I can whistle.'

Funny girl, this one. With her blonde baby and oversized dog.

'Do you know him?' Tess asked Joe who'd come out of the bank at much the same time as Seb went in.

'Who?'

'The guy from the surfing place?'

Joe looked back briefly, not sure to whom in the queue Tess referred. 'Er, no. Do you?'

She shook her head. 'Not really – he said hi the first time I went to the pier. He's friendly.'

'We are, mostly,' Joe said.

'He's Australian.'

'They're friendly too, mostly.' He gave Tess a fold of

banknotes which she put in her jacket pocket. He could see that her hand remained curled around them, clinging on tight. But he did note that her eyes were watery and her cheeks red. But there again, the wind was particularly brisk this morning. 'Beach?' He said it very, very casually.

'Not today,' Tess replied briskly, as if she already had plans. 'Em and I will see you at home.'

See you back at the house, Joe said to himself, watching Tess walk away.

What is it about the beach, Tess? And what is it about home?

She says she's eaten, when he offers to cook again later that day. He doubts it, though. She looks pale and tired. It seems her daily tea quota is down too – her two china cups and saucers have not been moved from the dresser.

The baby has been fractious; Tess working hard not to appear harried. But he's heard her cuss the dog and the sing-song voice she usually employs to feed the baby has a strained edge to it. Her smile is there, but her eyes, which appear dark and dull, do not confirm it. Bath-time jollities have been less audible too.

She disappeared into Em's room long ago.

All is quiet. So quiet that Joe hovers on the first-floor landing, then again halfway up the second flight of stairs.

He looks up and there she is. He can see her, she's all in a crumple outside the baby's room. She's slumped on the floor, her back against the wall, her knees up, her head in her hands. Her shoulders are heaving. She's crying soundlessly – she appears to be consumed by utter sadness. He detects the effort it's taking her to counteract the need to let go with a stronger need for silence and invisibility. Mustn't wake the baby. Mustn't let anyone know. But her desolation descends the staircase heavily and every now and then, he can hear how her voice breaks through involuntarily; hollow and desperate.

Joe backs away.

What does she have to cry about?

Why so sad?

He wishes he could ask. He oughtn't to. He senses it is unequivocally private.

He'd like to make her a cup of tea.

Or offer her a glass of wine.

A chat.

But she doesn't appear again until the next morning.

She looks so fragile she's practically transparent.

It's so windy today, Joe thinks to himself. If she goes out in this, she might be blown away.

'I'd stay in if I were you, Tess. I'm not venturing out myself in this weather. Thank God April's round the corner. Cup of tea? Kettle's just boiled. No? Later then – lunch too, perhaps.'

Chapter Ten

'My father was a doctor,' Joe told her, 'and his father before him. And so on. Right from the beginning. When Victorian Saltburn was thriving, they required the finest doctor around – so they perused the revered physicians from York to Durham and offered the position to my great-great-grandfather.'

They were standing at the foot of the valley, near the Cat Nab car park where the clear water of Skelton Beck is joined by the rust-coloured water of Saltburn Beck and they tumble out to sea. Tess and Joe were looking back up inland, both telling themselves that it was perfectly normal for the house-sitter to be out and about with the employer.

'My dad lives in Spain,' she said. 'With his second wife. He's dodgy.'

'Pardon?'

'My dad. I don't really know what he does – career-wise. My grandmother used to tell me he "flew by the seat of his pants". When I was little, I took this to mean that he had magical powers and the months he was AWOL I comforted myself imagining him flying to exotic lands – really flying, with no need for a magic carpet, his trousers sufficing.'

Joe smiled but curbed a chuckle – it was amusing but

rather sad. He had to curb a stronger urge to tuck away the strand of hair caught across Tess's cheek. 'Your mum?'

'She remarried too. She lives in Florida. In a condo with a man called Merl.'

'Do you visit?'

'No. She comes back, once a year, to see my sister.'

'And you,' said Joe because he didn't like the way Tess had cut herself out of the equation.

'Well, she stays with my sister who has a nice place in Edinburgh. And two children. I can't offer my mother anything close.'

'But what about your Emmeline!'

Tess shrugged and looked downcast before visibly pulling herself together.

'And your sister? Are you close?'

'Claire's fifteen years older than me so no, we're not that close. Our lifestyles are very different. We don't really know each other.'

Joe was about to comment.

'For example,' Tess continued, 'Christmas just gone, they went skiing. I mean, I don't ski, I couldn't have afforded the trip and I couldn't have gone with Em being so little. But I wasn't invited anyway. So it did mean I didn't have plans for Christmas.'

Joe thought about this. 'Well, if it's any consolation, I was on my own too.'

'Are your parents not around?'

'Not around,' he confirmed without further detail but also without the burning reticence he'd experienced when Tess had enquired about his family soon after she'd arrived.

Despite revealing the shortcomings of her family set-up, Joe thought she seemed particularly bright today. Or maybe it was because she was facing inland, with her back to the beach. Certainly there was no trace of her desolation last night.

87

'See up there,' Joe said, gesturing towards the valley, 'that's the reason I'm not a doctor.'

The view was certainly picturesque, the perpetual sea breeze had caused the trees to point their branches inland. Tess looked, not quite sure on what she was meant to be focusing, so she nodded.

Her confused politeness touched Joe. 'There used to be a bridge here – spanning the valley,' he said. 'The Halfpenny Bridge – or the Ha'penny Bridge. It was built in 1869 to link the other towns of Skelton and Loftus with Saltburn, to enable travellers to avoid the steep drop down to the sea and the arduous trek up the other side of the valley. The bridge rose 120 feet above the Valley Gardens and it was a fantastic piece of Victoriana. Seven cast-iron supports, ostentatious in height and length. Spectacular views of coast and country.'

'Why Halfpenny?' Tess asked. She might be looking at nothing but she could clearly envisage Joe's bridge now.

'Pedestrians paid half a penny. Carriages sixpence.'

'But where's it gone? Why isn't it still here?'

Joe wasn't going to answer that just yet. 'You'll find so much about Saltburn has a darker side. It always has – throughout its history. From smuggling to suicide. It's not all creamy dreamy buildings, a jolly pier and a quirky funicular. The Ha'penny Bridge became a hotspot – or should that be black spot – for suicides. As a bridge builder, that's often what gets me most about suicides from bridges. Jumping from tall buildings is one thing; similarly Beachey Head – those structures, whether natural or man-made, are static – they go up and then they stop. There's a top, if you like, and a bottom – the emphasis is vertical and finite. But bridges, by default, are there to *carry* you. They dominate a different axis altogether. And it – well – it breaks my heart, actually, that some people can't see the other side. They are too lost to see there is a way across. That A flows over to B. That

88

there's another side, another way. They walk along a little distance – and then they let go. In that moment, the bridge somehow fails its function and it fails *them*.'

'The Clifton Suspension Bridge has the Samaritans' number on each approach. I grew up in Bristol. Is that why it's gone, the Halfpenny Bridge?'

Joe shook his head and gave her a smile because she grew up in the shadow of one of the most seminal bridges of the world. She was currently all ears, all eyes and she hadn't noticed that Emmeline was testing the taste of coastal soil. He retrieved the child and hitched her onto his hip, not minding the grubby fingers exploring the bristles on his jaw.

'No. Actually, that had little to do with it. From the 1960s the bridge started to need repairs, and then total refurbishment. It was going to be too costly to fix, but too dangerous to leave standing. So they demolished it.'

The way he said it made it seem so violent. Senseless, almost. Tess frowned. 'What a tragedy.'

'Sort of. It was 1974. The seventeenth of December – my tenth birthday. That was my party, that year, I suppose. My parents brought me down with my little gang to watch. It took four seconds, exactly, to reduce a hundred and five years of cast-iron beauty and engineering into a twist of tangled metal.'

Tess let it hang for a moment. 'And that's when you decided not to be a doctor?'

'That's when I decided I wanted to build bridges.'

She let Joe have his memory in private while she enjoyed imagining him as a boy, clothing him in her mind's eye in a ridiculous cliché of cloth cap and hobnail boots, shorts and a knitted tank-top. It made her giggle, which brought Joe back to the present and that returned Tess's focus to the here and now between them.

'The view must have been so different – when the bridge was here.'

'Spot on, Tess, spot on. The vista isn't the same. I mean, for purists, it's more natural today than it was for those hundred and five years. But I don't know – for me, that bridge enhanced this landscape aesthetically, never mind practically.'

They looked up the valley quietly. Seagulls bickered in a noisy scatter overhead. The sea breeze, south-easterly and quite strong, pestered one side of their faces, the sun the other. They had to squint but they stood there a while longer, still and thoughtful. Joe didn't tell Tess that, on his tenth birthday, building bridges became not just his chosen career but also a metaphor to serve as a life lesson. He didn't tell her this, just then, because he'd have to explain that the drive for it came from his parents' disintegrating marriage. The one chasm, the only hostile space, the single seemingly untraversable rift that he'd been unable to bridge. The distance between them was never to be spanned.

And just then, Tess didn't tell Joe that she detected both strength and sadness in his story. That his silent thoughts had a heaviness that confronted her. But she did tell herself that she wanted to slip her hand into his. But then she told herself off for thinking such thoughts. And pushed her hands deep into her pockets.

*   *   *

Joe is going to London tomorrow. The day at the Ha'penny Bridge was two days ago. In the intervening time, he and Tess have walked and talked, eaten together, laughed a lot and spent yesterday evening reading quietly in the drawing room before watching *News at Ten* in the sitting room. She does still sometimes wonder whether she should ask permission. And he does recall the structure he'd imposed on previous house-sitters. He still hasn't given her the pack. But he has to concede, the house seems to have shown that it works well for the two of them.

It is now mid-morning and Joe has finally emerged from his study and is pottering in the kitchen, taking a break from work. He sees Tess is outside, pegging out washing. Emmeline and Wolf are lolling about in the garden. It is surprisingly balmy today, as if a switch has turned off the chill of earlier in the week until next winter. April is two days away; spring is within easy reach now.

He studies the scene in the garden. It is less a Thomas Hardy novel and more an Edward Hopper painting. Tess, with her back towards him, wearing a faded tea-dress and woollen cardigan with the sleeves pushed up, a pair of old cream trainers. The breeze furling the washing around her forearms and causing the skirt to cling to her bare legs, licking at the fronds and curls of her hair which have escaped her scratchy pony-tail. Every now and then she turns her face a little as she stoops to pick up the next item or to check on Emmeline. And it is then that the sun glances off her skin and spins silken skeins from her hair. Joe wants to watch but he doesn't want to be seen and it confuses him that the scene is so compelling. He goes upstairs to his bedroom to pack for London but finds himself drawn to the window, peering down onto the garden, again transfixed by the sight of her sorting socks.

And look, my boxers. I didn't know she'd done my washing.

He is concerned, bemused, how a picture of such dull domesticity can be arousing, but this is the undeniable effect on him. Perhaps it is the feminine presence. Perhaps it is because at this angle, the sunlight has made her dress see-through. Maybe it is just because he likes her, he has enjoyed her company these last few days; it has been simple and uncomplicated yet entertaining and energizing too. And there's that frisson – how she can be stroppy and how he winds her up, that she can make him snappish and curt. It doesn't make him dislike her, far from it, but it unnerves him that he should feel eager to seek peace soon after. He tells himself, London, you prat, London. So he goes back to his packing.

But before he returns downstairs, he hovers on the landing and then goes up a flight to Tess's room. He's not really sure why. She's outside – he has only to go to a window to watch her, unseen. But he doesn't want to see her, he wants to sense her. That's why he's standing at her doorway.

There's not much to see: a pair of jeans on the floor. Socks in a scrunch. And a pair of plain black knickers kicked off nearby. Nathalie accosts his mind's eye; resplendent in her carefully selected and unfathomably expensive lingerie. Gold mesh and miniscule. Joe steps further into the room and picks up her knickers from the floor. Black cotton. He holds them to his nose, inhaling deeply while calling himself a crazy, dirty bastard. But still he goes to his bathroom to masturbate urgently. It isn't thoughts of Nathalie that have excited this state in the middle of a nondescript morning. He didn't think back to all that sex he'd had the week before. Rather, it was the sight of Tess this morning, in a shabby dress and old cardi. It's the proximity of her right now, just out there in the garden. The girl with the plain cotton knickers. And so, it isn't images of Nathalie that he now wanks to, but the still prevalent sense and scents of Tess. He comes and it's exquisite.

He opens his eyes after a moment and stares at the tessellation of tiles. Alone in a bathroom. He feels a little hollow. Tess's voice drifts up from the garden. She's rabbiting on at Wolf and laughing. She's sewn herself into the fabric of his life in Saltburn and yet for years now, he's felt no emotional anchor here – just the practicality of the house. He cleans himself up and goes back downstairs. He feels perplexed and shuts himself in his study where the complexity of calibrations for a forthcoming pitch offers him a welcome distraction.

'May I use the phone?'

Tess knocked on the study door later that afternoon and called her request through. Joe's been in there all day, she hasn't seen him at all.

'Sure.'

'Oh – and would you like me to rustle up some supper later?'

After a pause. 'Don't worry about me.'

Tess's turn to pause, laying her forehead gently against the door. 'I'm not worried about you,' she said quietly. 'I'll be cooking for myself anyway. It's no trouble.'

A sigh from inside. 'OK.'

'Don't let me twist your arm!' she muttered and stomped off.

'Look – sorry. Fine – I'd love some food.'

'OK. And it's OK to use the phone?'

'Yes. I told you – it's fine.'

That he should sound irritated irked Tess but her desire to spend time with him is stronger. He's just hard at work, she told herself, building bridges.

'Hullo, Claire? It's your long-lost sister . . . I'm fine – how are you? How are the kids? Good. Good . . . I'm in Saltburn – in the North-East . . . Me – on *holiday*? Don't be daft! . . . I've left London – for good, hopefully . . . A few weeks ago . . . Heard from Mum? Dad? My mobile doesn't work – shall I give you this number, you know, just for emergencies? No . . . No . . . Yes . . . Pretty shit, really . . . No – that's not why I've phoned . . . Pardon? No, I haven't heard from him – not for months, not since Em's birthday . . . Don't say that. You know

what he's like. Anyway, I think he's still in the States. No –
no, he hasn't. I didn't ask again, not after the last time ...
He hasn't got any money, you know that, Claire. Can we
change the subject, please? I'm working here in Saltburn ...
No, not *that* – not any more. I'm doing Property
Management ... Well, I'm house-sitting ... No, it's more than
that – actually I'm looking after a bridge builder and his home.'

She was relieved to have made the call, which wasn't to
say that she'd enjoyed it in the slightest. It would take her
an hour or so to recover and feel better about herself. But
she was used to that. She simply couldn't afford not to touch
base with her sister every now and then.

The only phone in the entire house is the one in the main
entrance hall. And Joe found himself helpless not to hover
at his study door and eavesdrop. And afterwards, he found
it impossible to work but he stayed in his study and thought
about things until Tess called him for supper.

He looked at his plate heaped high with locally caught fish,
home-made chips, peas and carrots. On the table a new bottle
of ketchup, flakes of sea salt in one of the little dishes from
Hong Kong he'd forgotten he had. White wine in one glass and
water in another. He glanced across at Tess. She'd been quite
right to tell her sister how she was looking after him and his
home. Quietly, he considered it a shame he had to go tomorrow,
to be away quite so often. But then he remembered this morning,
when she was hanging out washing. He didn't want to think
about it but he knew he didn't want to forget it either. It was
confusing. Perhaps it was good that he was leaving tomorrow.

'So, Tess,' he said between mouthfuls, 'what'll you get up
to when I'm gone again?'

She thought about it. 'With your say-so, I'd like to start on
the sitting room – the TV room. And we really could make
better use of the boot store. It is a *room*, you know.'

'*We?*'

Tess reddened a little. 'There's good paint you can buy now – it's scrubbable,' she hurried. 'It would be perfect. Will the Everything Shop sell it, do you think? Could I put it on your tab?'

Joe nodded. 'No doubt they have a pot or two at the back somewhere, under the jigsaw puzzles, next to the ericaceous plant food, behind the home-brewery kit.'

Tess laughed. 'Opposite the cotton reels and just across from the mousetraps?'

'Or I can bring you some back,' Joe said. 'I may not stay in London that long – I may come back before heading off to France.'

He'd only just thought of this.

They caught each other's glance and looked away.

'Or I may go and visit friends in Kent,' he said with a nonchalant tap at the base of the ketchup bottle. 'Chislehurst.'

'Cool,' Tess said breezily, as if it was no concern of hers where he went, when.

'More wine?'

'Please.'

Joe held the wine bottle aloft, appearing to scrutinize the label as if he harboured some concern over the vintage or the vineyard. He wasn't. But he needed a moment.

'Pass your glass, Tess, and call me a nosy old sod and you don't have to answer, but Emmeline's dad? I mean, I was wondering – you know – about him. Whether he'll be coming – here – to visit, perhaps?'

He said it all so quickly, so conversationally whilst he poured wine, that however intrusive the question might have been, it didn't come across as such and Tess found herself answering. She hadn't noticed the two small lines that remained between Joe's brows; punctuation marks of discomfort that belied the light tone of his voice.

'He won't be coming up to Saltburn. You see – well, you'll have guessed we're not together. Actually, he doesn't really visit much.'

'Were you together for long?'

Tess traced her finger around the rim of the glass as if to elicit sound. Her voice, when it came, had the volume on low. 'For about six weeks,' she said. Then she cleared her throat, smiled a little meekly and spoke up. 'We were together for about six weeks. And then he went travelling. Which was when I found out I was pregnant. It's all a bit of a cliché.'

The food was finished but Joe dabbed at the smear of ketchup on his plate and then sucked his finger thoughtfully.

'He's a musician,' Tess continued though Joe hadn't asked. In fact, all he was going to ask was whether she wanted a cup of tea. He thought she might want a change of subject; he was surprised that she didn't.

'Or at least he likes to say he's a musician, though he never seems to play much more than themes and variations on "House of the Rising Sun". The problem is, he's very handsome. Well, it's a problem for everyone else, you see. He's stunningly good-looking, really – luckily Em's inherited his looks. But he's one of those free spirits. Born in the wrong generation, you could say. The Woodstock era would have been so much more his thing.'

'Where is he based?' Joe asked though he'd eavesdropped about the States earlier from Tess's phone call. He'd prefer facts over these superlatives of the bloke's beauty.

'He's a "wherever he lays his hat is his home" type.'

Joe was surprised that she smiled so wistfully and spoke with generosity when he felt that this fake rock-star sounded like a vain, irresponsible loser.

'He's Canadian. I met him in London. He was en route to Europe. Now he's in the States. He wants to *do* Australia. And then he'll probably start all over again.'

'Is he a good father?'

Tess wished she could reply quicker and in the affirmative so she employed vagueness instead. 'He means well. He's not what you'd call "hands-on". But he's simply one of those people it's just really difficult to get cross with. He has another child. Another daughter – she's five, apparently. So Em has a half-sister, somewhere in Toronto. Which'll be great when she's older. He's full of love and wonder at the world – he's just a bit crap with the practicalities.'

Her response baffled Joe – such equanimity from the woman who could be belligerent with him in an instant.

'And his name is?'

'Dick.' Pre-emptively, she flicked a stray pea on the table at Joe. 'Don't laugh.'

'I'm not,' said Joe. 'The name fits. Does he support you?'

'Dick?' She was incredulous. 'He's the archetypal penniless musician – he's like a latter-day strolling troubadour! He's only a step away from having worldly possessions small enough to fit in a hanky on the end of a stick, à la Dick Whittington.'

'Dick Whittington went on to become incredibly famous and wealthy.'

Tess shrugged. 'Dick's no Dick Whittington, Joe. He's gorgeous and charismatic and I fell for him, but I knew. I knew from when I first saw him, strumming away in Finsbury Park. I knew after the first kiss. After our first night together. During those madcap six weeks. I knew he wouldn't stay. And when I found out I was pregnant. I knew he wouldn't come back.'

Joe rolled the pea gently under his fingertip as he considered this. 'Brave of you, Tess. To – you know – proceed.'

Tess shook her head. 'Not brave, Joe, not really. My sister said I was stupid. Tamsin, my best friend, warned me how difficult it would be. But it was easy to make the decision.

Being pregnant was the first thing in my life that seemed to slot into place seamlessly with my future. So many other uncertainties. But carrying Em was not one of them. My child would be my constant.'

'You and her together, hey?'

'She and me.'

He topped up their glasses. She gave him a half-smile combined with a small shrug.

'Do you find it hard, Tess?' The wine had made the question flow and there was an audible trickle of tenderness with it.

She looked at him with her head tilted, as if assessing the intent behind his enquiry. 'Dick?' She gave the same smile–shrug. 'My love for Em soon made me realize that what I'd felt for Dick was just – well, it wasn't love at all. It was a crush. And hormones.'

But Joe wasn't smiling; he was still looking at her intently. 'I didn't mean not having this Dick in your life – if you'll pardon the expression. I meant – *your* life. As a single mum. Do you find that hard, Tess? All *this*, on your own?'

Though Tess was quiet for only a moment, her silence was pronounced.

She wore the same carefully composed smile but her eyes now belied it, filmed by a sudden smart of tears which he could see she was fighting to control. Eventually, she looked up and nodded. 'It is hard, Joe,' she said. 'Sometimes. I feel quite alone. Sometimes.'

He thought of her on the landing, enslaved by loneliness. 'Yet you've come all the way up here – did you not leave a support network behind in London?'

'Em *is* my family. And I might be stupid – but I'm strong and I *will* cope. Actually, it's a breath of fresh air up here – even if I have filled it with paint fumes.'

She was trying to lighten the conversation but Joe wanted

98

to say, you're bullshitting, Tess. And he wanted to say, the thing is I saw you crying by yourself. And though he wanted to ask her what was making her cry, he really couldn't do that, could he. And therefore he couldn't very well say, Tess, don't cry on your own. And there were two reasons he couldn't voice any of these thoughts.

What could he do about any of it – not least because he'd be gone again tomorrow?

And who was she anyway? He had to keep reminding himself. Just his employee – that's how she saw herself, wasn't it?

Joe had to concede that any dynamic which had developed over the last few days, was tonight both heightened and limited by wine and time. He was off again tomorrow. Whatever he asked tonight and whatever she told him could have only temporary resonance. He told himself, you're pissed you idiot, so shut up.

Then he told himself he ought to draw on the ability he'd honed over the years to fade a woman into the background of his mind's eye whenever he left a location. Just as she really ought to fade into the background on the occasions he returned to this location. As his previous house-sitters had done without him even asking. The ones who'd asked him for a contract or the pack he'd prepared at the very least. This strange girl might be just another house-sitter, but she was currently doing the sitting at his table at his behest, drinking wine and giving compelling answers to questions he was kicking himself for asking in the first place.

She was a house-sitter who called his place home. Who'd filled it with a baby and constantly clean, line-dried washing. Who'd scrubbed out his cupboards and alphabetized his books. What was he *thinking*? He simply didn't know. But what he did know was that he was *feeling* more than he was thinking.

Think London, think London. He thought tomorrow couldn't come soon enough. He thought, I'll phone Rachel – she's always game when I'm in the city. He thought how tomorrow he'd be safely en route back to the way of life he'd cultivated over twenty years; feeling no greater link to London than he felt to France or anywhere else where he had a bridge and a girl.

'Joe?' He'd been lost in thought. 'Tea?'

He cleared his throat but he still sounded hoarse from his long conversation with himself. 'Please.'

The sound of the kettle busily boiling echoed the fast rattle of his thoughts. Ping. I'll take myself right out of her equation.

'Maybe Dick'll make his millions, come back, swoop you up and take you to live with him on his ranch.' (Joe decided that, just as he chose to call Em Emmeline, he'd be referring to her father as Dickle from now on.)

'Dick? On a *ranch*?' Tess baulked. 'Dick's just a gorgeous, useless, beautiful, crazy dreamer. Even I can see that he's an utter waste of space.'

And, though Joe wasn't too keen on the swoon to Tess's voice, her conviction – heaped as it was with affection and generosity – made Joe quite certain that this Dickle was one area of her life that she really had worked out.

Chapter Eleven

Tess awoke feeling she'd been deprived proper rest. Her sleep had been so busy, so detailed, so involving, that she woke assuming she'd overslept because it felt that her dreams had ensnared her for so long. But the clock said six o'clock and the light, filtering through a gap in the curtains but not making it far into the room, verified this. She knew she had around twenty minutes before Em would wake and these she spent bemused that after over two years during which sex hadn't really crossed her mind, let alone featured on her agenda, three men had infiltrated her sleep in explicit dreams.

She thought back over the details. Dick was in all of them wearing the same beatific smile he famously employed, along with touch, to override the need for much cogent dialogue. In reality, it had irritated her; in last night's dreams it had her fooled. She recalled Dick and Seb together in one scene; that she was running along the pier, coming across the two of them at the end, fishing. Buddies, it appeared. They turned to her and closed in on her and she wasn't entirely sure who kissed her first and who it was kissing her then, and whose were those hands on her breasts, in her hair, grabbing her bum.

Switching on the bedside lamp, Tess dipped into the John Irving paperback that she'd taken from Joe's collection. But drifts of the other dream soon distracted her. Dick again, but this time, Joe too. They weren't in Saltburn. They were crowded with her in the kitchen of the Bounds Green flat. The three of them, pushed against the units. An overriding sense of furtive urgency. Someone, Dick, Joe – she couldn't tell – lifting her onto the work surface. A mouth against hers. A hand between her legs. The feeling of a man's hardness rubbing up against her thigh. One of them taking her hand down to the bulge in his trousers. The feeling of flesh. Her softness. Their firmness. The wetness and the heat. Being about to come.

Tess frowned. She shook her head because she really didn't want to do any more remembering. She didn't want to think about it, because thinking about it was undeniably arousing. That her hand was absent-mindedly between her legs proved the point. The buzz, the release, the sexual attention bestowed on her in the dreams – but she could only chastise herself for being turned on. You should be appalled, she told herself. Because the conclusion to both dreams had been horrible, unimaginable.

Em fending for herself.

Em neglected.

A small distressed baby toddling off down the pier while her mother made out with a surfer and a musician. A tiny tot, alone in the sitting room of a rented flat in Bounds Green, crying while Mummy was having a threesome in the galley kitchen with a musician and a bridge builder.

Tess stared hard at the Loom chair with yesterday's clothes that would have to do for today. What a load of crap. She decided that analysing dreams was as ridiculous as heeding horoscopes.

Mystic Bloody Meg and Sigmund Effing Freud.

This made her smile though still she felt discomfited. If there was meaning to these dreams, what was it exactly? That her desires as a woman, a grown-up, were not compatible with her responsibilities as a mother? That she could be one or the other but not both? In reality she'd all but dispensed with the sexual side of her nature. In the dreams, she'd actively chosen to forsake being a mother. She had heard the baby, seen the baby, been aware of the baby in both – but her lust had ridden roughshod over all sense of maternal duty.

Only stupid dreams.

I am wide awake.

So why am I feeling so wretched?

Because it felt good. I forgot how good it feels to come.

Because it's been a long, long time.

She couldn't afford to consider that these long-dormant cogs, now starting to turn, had come not from dreams, but from events preceding them. Talking about Dick. The realness of Seb. And whatever it was about Joe.

She left the bed to sit cross-legged on the floor, having opened the wardrobe door to see herself in the mirror and give her reflection a stern talking-to.

It doesn't mean anything. Once I had a kinky dream featuring that ugly old bloke who does the weather on TV. It does not mean that I fancy him in reality.

So Seb is cute but that's it. He's about a decade younger than me and lives a life of surf and beaches. And Dick left me high and dry and he's just a stupid boy who thinks he's Jim Morrison but he doesn't even come close.

Tess left the room in a hurry and went to her child's room, chanting to herself 'Come on Baby Light My Fire', which was totally inappropriate but it was the only Doors song she could recall just then.

Em was sitting quietly in her cot, bashing the toy lion against a cardboard book, its bead-eye making a satisfying tap. Tess scooped her up and whispered, Emmy Emmy Emmy into her neck.

And I don't fancy Joe. I absolutely cannot fancy Joe. Not just because he can be arrogant and sharp and he takes his beautiful house for granted. But because I'm only his house-sitter. It's like having a stupid crush on the boss. Ridiculous.

'Aren't you staying around to give me a send-off, then?' Joe asked an hour or so later, seeing Tess preparing the dog and the child for a walk.

'Things to do,' Tess said, busying herself with the zip on Em's cardigan, squatting down on her heels, inadvertently giving Joe an enticing view of the small of her back and beyond. '*Carpe diem*, and all that.'

She was preoccupied but Joe sensed this wasn't caused by a child's zip or a dog in a tangle. Just then, he wanted to crouch beside her, still her hands, say, hey – you OK? But he felt he couldn't very well do that, not least because his departure was imminent.

'I'll call – if you like,' he said instead, 'to let you know when I'll be back.' He paused. 'Or just to say hi.'

Tess stopped fiddling, though the dog and child continued with their fidgeting regardless. She looked across and her gaze came to rest at Joe's lower legs. He was standing relaxed, leaning against the wall, his arms folded, looking down at her. He could see the top of her knickers from here. From this advantage point, he thought to himself.

'OK,' she said, glancing up at him, wondering why he was smiling like that.

'OK,' he said, 'I'll keep in touch, then.'

She stood. 'Bye then,' she said but she loitered. She tickled Em under the chin. 'Say bye bye to Joe, Em. Bye bye Joe. Say – bye bye.'

But the baby just stared at Joe.

'Goodbye, Emmeline. Look after Wolf.' And Joe gave her a little wave that she mimicked.

Ultimately, it was Joe giving them the send-off. He'd be gone by the time they were back.

'Hey, Tess!' he called down the driveway. She was just beyond the gate, just about to disappear from view. 'I'll leave you my mobile number.' She gave him the thumbs-up.

'Hey, Tess!' She turned again. 'Shall I take yours?'

'Don't have one,' she called, 'not any more.' She paused. 'Just call the home phone if you need me.'

Returning to the house, Joe thought he must be losing the plot for thinking how the house seemed deserted without that little lot. Then he scolded himself as a soft sod for again liking the way Tess said 'home'. She never referred to the Resolution as the house, or your house – nor to the phone as the landline or house phone. Home was the word she always employed, whenever she could. Conversely, he chose not to use it much – the word or the place. He didn't want to hang around; he wanted to be on his way, with his London head on. But still he looked in at Tess's room and Emmeline's before he went. The doors had been closed but he left them ajar; as if inviting the new spirit those rooms now exuded to emanate through the house.

He'd miss them.

For fuck's sake, what was he thinking.

*　　*　　*

It took the rest of the day for the residual feelings from her dreams to dissipate and by the following morning, Tess felt restored. She also felt more than ready to tackle the tasks she'd set herself. One of which was to keep the doors to Joe's study and bedroom firmly shut.

It was fine and dry and Tess decided to make a start on the boot and utility rooms, taking all the old boots and coats into the garden. She pegged the jackets on the washing line, chucked onto the bonfire heap a waxed jacket so old and neglected that the fabric had cracked, shook out a dusty jumper and decided it still had life in it and just needed a wash. She thought about adding the gumboots to the bonfire pile, so ancient that the rubber had blanched and disintegrated, but she decided to dump them directly in the bin. The same fate awaited the single flip-flop. As it did the golf umbrella that, when opened, rattled and spewed its broken spokes like a science-lab skeleton that had come unscrewed. Anyway, Tess didn't think Joe was the umbrella type. He probably just turned his collar up against inclement weather. Or donned one of those yellow hard hats. She'd come across two already, had tried one on but resisted the urge to fit the straps and take a look.

With all the footwear out on the lawn either airing or awaiting their fate by fire or bin, she came across a bootjack. It was in the shape of a beetle, its antennae forming the heel grip, and she liked it so she gave it a reprieve. It would only need a clean and a lick of black gloss paint. However, the boot scraper resembling a hedgehog with a thatch of old coir as the spines was dumped without a second thought. It had turned mostly green, was covered with cobwebs, with evidence of large spiders lurking beneath. Sizeable ones had already made their displeasure known when Tess first started to clear out the utility room, putting themselves and Tess into a scuttle of panic.

On the shelves above the washing machine and tumble drier, crates were stacked; some plastic, some wood, some full, some empty. So *that's* where the spare light bulbs are. And batteries. Now Em's little singing tortoise could finally make music again! Jesus, how many packets of fuses does a man need? Rat poison? Meths? And what the hell is *this* stuff, with the skull and crossbones emblazoned all over it? Tess bagged it before she binned it.

She sorted through myriad items. Many were destined for the bin. A few would be better off living in one of the kitchen drawers. Some would stay in the utility room. Others needed to go into one of the garden sheds – but she'd have to sort those out too and they were currently padlocked. It amused her trying to correlate this Joe-of-the-Utility-Room with the Joe-of-the-Study. She wondered what Joe-in-London was doing. Then she told herself to change the subject.

As if reading her mind, Wolf scrambled up from his snooze in a barrage of barking and belted past Tess out into the garden. That mangy cat, no doubt. She was too engrossed in her sifting, and knew Wolf well enough by now, to think much of it. Into an old wooden wine crate (which she thought would scrub up nicely itself and could be re-employed else-where), she piled the items that were to live in the kitchen and took them through.

And there, she froze.

There *was* someone outside.

This time, there really was. It wasn't a shadow. It wasn't her imagination. It wasn't her reflection.

There was definitely someone out there looking in at her, and this time they weren't darting away.

So why wasn't Wolf continuing to bark?

And what could an elderly lady want? All the way up here? Was she lost?

And if she was smiling benignly, why did Tess feel rooted to the spot?

It was because something she couldn't yet decipher was oddly familiar.

The woman knocked on the window, as if unsure whether Tess had seen her though they were observing each other directly. She waved; the kind of gesture that suggested she was popping by for a prearranged cuppa. Then she disappeared from view. This was like a starter's gun for Tess and she hurried out through the utility room taking Wolf's route.

And there he was, the great oaf. Some guard dog. There he was, sitting beside the intruder looking very relaxed by the state of his lolling tongue. She was wearing sturdy lace-up shoes and dark tan tights and she had no ankles to speak of. Her hair was styled in a vague approximation of the Queen's and, though she was quite upright in figure, her coat was buttoned up wrong and her eyes were pale and searching. Though Tess realized she certainly was not ancient, she did appear infirm. One arm lolled by her side. The other hand was busy in her pocket. She was sneaking out treats for Wolf while she looked at Tess, as if she was waiting for her to make the first move. She certainly didn't have the air of a trespasser about her.

'Hullo?' said Tess.

'Hullo, dear.'

'Can I help you?'

The lady laughed. 'I was about to ask you the same thing. I live here, dear – what were you doing in my kitchen?'

* * *

In the short time it took for Tess to wonder how on earth to respond to this, she watched the lady become visibly puzzled. Her thin lips worked over her teeth as if she was in deep conversation with herself. Suddenly, she'd aged. She touched her hand to her hair, pressing firmly through to her head as if to check it was still there. Doing so left an indentation in her hairstyle.

'I just popped out to the shops. To get something. Didn't

I?' She looked at Tess. 'Can you remember what?' Wolf was trying to put his nose right into her pocket. 'Stop it, Wolf,' she said.

She knew the dog's name. And then Tess knew why. She walked over to her and held out her hand – not for the lady to shake, but for her to take as support.

'I'm Tess,' she said kindly.

'I'm Mrs Saunders,' the lady said, holding onto Tess as a child holds onto their mother. 'But you can call me Mary.'

Tess felt tears prick but had no idea why they were there. 'Would you like a cup of tea?' she asked.

'Lovely, dear,' Mary said. 'I think I probably baked a cake yesterday too. If Wolf hasn't scoffed it.'

They sat at the kitchen table, the contemplative, measured tock from the grandfather clock in the hallway adding a soothing structure.

'Sugar?'

'Two, please. Though I used to be sweet enough.'

Mary enjoyed the way Tess laughed at this.

'Biscuit?'

'Well!' She took one daintily, as if she was taking tea at the palace.

'Joe isn't here,' Tess said.

'I should hope not! Unless he's playing hooky from school. He'll be home soon enough.'

'Soon enough.' And Tess thought, won't you come home, Joe – won't you come home and see who's here?

Every now and then Mary looked at Tess with momentary confusion but didn't seem to mind being unable to quite place her. It was as if Tess's benign presence rendered insignificant the finer details of who she was and why she was here. Crumbs spittled from Mary's mouth and she dabbed them away. Tess noted her hands were elegant but the nails were uneven and the skin was not only blemished with age; it was also dry and thin from lack of attention. She spread her own fingers out across the edge of the table, like a pianist about to play. Mary took note.

'Not married yet?'

Tess shrugged and shook her head.

'Joe'll be down on bended knee – when he's back from university. Though what sort of life he can offer you, I don't know. Now – if he'd followed the family path to the doctor's door, well, that would be a different situation altogether.'

'I don't mind that he's not a doctor,' Tess found herself replying before pulling herself up sharp and wondering if facilitating a confused lady's imaginings was tantamount to fraud – or cruelty.

'What's that?' Mary looked through to the hallway at much the same time that Wolf took himself off to sit at the bottom of the stairs with his ear cocked.

'It's the baby,' Tess said.

'The *baby*?'

Tess thought about it. 'Little baby Emmeline,' she said. 'She'll be waking from her nap.'

'Little baby Emmeline,' Mary murmured, as if convincing herself that she'd only momentarily forgotten about little baby Emmeline.

If Em hadn't quite woken from her nap then the sharp rapping at the door-knocker and the clangorous din of the doorbell certainly ensured she had.

'Someone at the door,' Mary said. 'Whoever can it be at this time of day?'

'I'll go and see,' Tess said, patting Mary's hand. 'You relax.' She called upstairs to Em to hang on, Mummy's coming. Then she climbed over Wolf and opened the door.

A plump young woman stood there, in a uniform that was

so generic Tess wasn't sure which profession it served – dinner lady or paramedic, cleaner or nurse.

'Sorry to bother you,' she said and her accent was local and strong. 'Is Joe Saunders around?'

'No,' Tess said, 'sorry, he's in London for the time being.'

'And you are?'

'Tess. Housekeeper.'

'Laura Gibbings.' She was frowning at Tess. 'From Swallows.' Tess looked none the wiser. 'Swallow House Residential Care Home. We've lost—'

'Mary?'

Laura looked both shocked and relieved. 'She's *here*? Already?'

'Having a cuppa and a biccie,' Tess said in what she hoped would be a collusionary sort of way. She didn't want Mary taken from her, from here, just yet.

Laura nodded. 'I thought I'd pop up here myself – before they send out the search party.'

Tess nodded.

'The others – they can be a bit – you know – impatient.'

Tess nodded again.

'She can't half move, that one, when she wants to,' Laura laughed.

Though Tess continued to nod she thought of Mary's thick ankles and the level of dogged conviction the steep drag up to the house must have required. 'Laura, why don't you come in for a cuppa too – then I could drop you both back off. Use the phone if you like – tell them the runaway hasn't, well, run away.'

Laura was smiling her gratitude when suddenly she froze. 'What's that?'

'That's my baby.'

'A *baby*? Here? At *Joe's*? Whatever does he think?'

Tess thought about it. 'Actually, I don't think he has a problem with it.'

'Well, I suppose he's not here that much.'

'Exactly,' said Tess.

So Tess went upstairs to see to Em, and Laura went into the kitchen to see to Mary. They drank more tea and Em and Mary made a similar mess with the biscuits. The baby seemed entranced by all this female energy, whatever the age. Wolf made himself scarce.

'We'd better go,' Laura said a little reluctantly. 'It'll not long be high tea.'

How different the view from the car than from on foot. How odd it felt to be back behind the wheel for the first time since her arrival. How strange to be travelling at a faster pace than a walk. It almost seemed steeper than on foot. Laura directed Tess down to the front then up along Marine Parade and into the Swallow House driveway some yards later.

Tess looked at the grand building.

'Worse places to work, I can tell you,' Laura said. 'I was three years at one in Redcar. Dear God, the smell of piss.'

Tess looked at her sharply and glanced in the rear-view mirror but Mary was as engrossed in Em as Em was in her, and they were busy examining each other's buttons.

'I mean, it was a shitehole compared with Swallows. Just couldn't get the place clean, I couldn't. The smell – seemed to have got into the bricks, you know? It closed down. Too right too. So here I am. Coming up three years.'

'But how old are you?' Tess said, thinking she looked way too young to have six years of elderly care to her credit.

'Twenty-one next month.'

'That's amazing,' said Tess. 'I salute you.'

Laura thought it was odd, a little over the top, but she could see Tess meant it.

'How old are you, then?'

'Thirty,' Tess said.

'Thirty,' Laura marvelled as if it was a distant goal. 'You're not from round here, though?'

'Down south,' said Tess, wanting to leave it at that.

'London?' Laura said expectantly.

'For a while,' Tess said as she parked and turned off the engine. Everyone seemed content to remain in the sudden stillness. 'Nice to meet you, Laura Gibbings.'

'And you.'

'Listen – if Mary, you know, goes missing again, I'll let you know, shall I, if she comes home? And you'll phone me, will you, to let me know if she might be on her way?'

'Early-onset dementia,' Laura said quietly. Then she brightened, turned round and clucked at Mary sweetly. 'She gets confused. Don't you, love?'

'But she always heads home?'

'That's my instinct,' said Laura, 'and hers too, apparently. I know her best, see. She's a bit of a bag with the others – but we rub along just fine. Don't we, love! The others worry she'll go off the pier or peg off down the beach. It's all about Health and Safety and not getting sued, nowadays. Anyway, she doesn't much like the beach, our Mary.'

'Nor do I,' Tess said darkly before visibly brightening. 'But shall we do that – you and me – keep in touch?'

'Sounds like a plan, Stan,' Laura said which made Tess laugh. Followed by Em.

'Stan?' said Mary.

And Laura said, bugger me – Stan was only her old boy, wasn't he.

'You're all right, Mary,' she said, twisting around again and offering Mary her hand. 'You're all right. We're home now, love.'

Tess helped everyone out and up the front stairs, thinking Laura was an old head on young, capable shoulders.

'Do you want to come in?' Laura asked.

'Another time,' Tess said though she was loitering.

'Any time,' said Laura, 'inside visiting hours, of course. Come on, Mrs Saunders, let's get you in.'

'Bye bye, Mary,' Tess said and Mary turned and stared at her vacantly.

'Goodbye, dear.'

And as Laura led her into the house, Tess heard Mary say, do I know her? and she heard Laura say, 'Course you do, Mary – that's Joe's girl, that is.'

She drove off and kept driving, right out of town out along the Loftus road. All the way past the Boulby potash mine, which looked like a *Dr Who* backdrop, before driving inland, into the countryside. She parked the car and took Em from her seat, perching the child on a five-bar gate looking out across fields.

'It is nice here, isn't it, Em. I think we'll stay. I really do.'

It wasn't until Tess had driven home, fed the dog, fed and bathed Em and sat down by herself with a bowl of soup that she allowed herself a little surge to be thought of as Joe's girl.

Chapter Twelve

Joe did ring. The day after his departure, the evening of the day when Tess met Mary. Tess heard the phone and hovered, wanting it to be Joe but not wanting to take it for granted. When the answering machine clicked in and she heard his voice, for all the button-pushing configurations she tried, she could not interrupt it. She considered dialling 1471 in case he was phoning from a hotel or apartment, or she could call him back on his mobile – he'd left the number on the kitchen calendar. But she did neither because all his message actually said was that he was phoning, 'like I said I would'. In the silence of the house after the answering machine clicked off, his message continued to reverberate in her mind. No 'how are you'. No 'hope all's well'. Joe's girl, indeed! Still, she found it impossible not to dither the evening away with whether to pick up the phone or not. She justified that she was too tired to speak anyway, what with all the cleaning and hills and Mary business.

While the TV flickered away in her peripheral vision, Mary accosted her mind's eyes. Tess realized she'd simply assumed Joe's parents were long dead because he spoke of both with an air of neutral finality. The more she thought about it, the more unnerving she found it that his mother lived in the same small town. Why hadn't he mentioned her before, let alone warned Tess of the probability that she'd come knocking? Ah, but was it any of her business – did it have anything to do with house-sitting? Well, yes, actually, it did – if someone was going to give her an almighty shock by lurking around the property and peering in through the windows, whatever their age or frailty. Didn't Joe usually warn his house-sitters about this? Or was it a more recent thing? Early-onset dementia. Mary was probably only in her mid-seventies. Was it still Mary's house – was Joe just house-sitting too?

Tess would be mentioning it to him when he next rang or returned. Your mum popped round for a cup of tea and a digestive. Nice place, that Swallows Residential Care Home, great view.

It was the view which Tess used as an excuse to push Em's buggy into the drive at Swallows at the end of the week. There'd been no further contact from Joe. No contact from anyone, actually, apart from the friendly but limited hellos, good mornings, and good afternoons of passers-by and the Everything Shop lady.

'Would you look at that view,' Tess marvelled to Em as they stood at the top of the driveway looking out over the downy clifftop and straight out to sea.

'Can I help you? Visiting isn't for another ten minutes.'

'Oh – I – we.'

The woman was in the same uniform that Laura had worn. Hers, it appeared, came without the smile. 'That'll be quiet, will it? Some of them in there can get a little – *excitable* – if there's noise. Not that they're a quiet bunch themselves at the best of times.'

Tess looked at the woman and wondered where Laura was. She didn't like her daughter referred to as 'that' or 'it'. Nor did she like the woman's implied exasperation when referring to the residents.

'*That* is Emmeline,' Tess said, 'and Mrs Saunders is *our* friend.'

The woman folded her arms. 'You're welcome to wait. But visiting's not for another ten minutes.'

'Seven,' Tess said as she pushed the buggy away.

The view was so lovely, the weather was good – but why were the benches in the garden empty? Why were the residents cooped up inside on a day like today? Was it staffing issues or strict scheduling? Then she asked herself what she was doing here anyway, taking it upon herself to visit this secret mother of Joe's. But she answered that it was a nice thing to do – for everyone concerned. And what else was she going to do with her day? She was tired of the scrubbing and the spiders and the hoicking; her body was stiff from stretching and ached from bending. And this was a change from walking to the pier, having only the fishermen and their empty nets to exchange nods with and sometimes a smile or a wave with Seb.

Returning to the front door a defiant seven minutes later, Tess was greeted by Laura.

'I thought it sounded like you,' she welcomed her warmly. 'Don't mind Di – she's a crabby old slink. But she does have a heart. Somewhere.'

'How's Mary?'

'In one place today,' Laura said, helping Tess up the steps with the buggy. 'A little quiet, I'd say. How's this little 'un?'

Tess liked the way Laura squatted down regardless of the way it made her uniform stretch and strain.

'How are you, Em?'

Em brandished her beaker in reply.

The place didn't smell of wee. It smelt more like a library, less like a hospital though it shared the linoleum floors and

117

particular signage of the latter, and really only the hushed ambience of the former.

'She's in the day room,' Laura said over her shoulder as she led the way. She stopped at a door and peered through the safety glass. 'As I said, you might find her a bit, well, *distracted*. Well, she was this morning.' Laura looked at Tess. 'But you can never tell, really, how long it's going to last. It goes as quickly as it comes – one minute they're away with the fairies, the next they're back in the land of the living. Sad when you think they'd rather not be.'

Tess looked into the room through the glass in the door and felt suddenly a little apprehensive. Was all this fair on Em? Or Mary? And even Joe too?

Laura sensed her reticence. 'Come on, love, she'll be delighted with the company – whether or not she knows you from Adam today.'

The door opened into a world Tess knew existed but had never been party to. Her grandmother had died in hospital a day after being admitted from her own home. Here, though, were the infirm elderly en masse; all of them displaced because, for whatever reason, home was no longer an option. Yet there was a sense of calm about the place, perhaps because of the lack of movement: everyone was simply sitting, sitting as if waiting. Waiting for what? Three o'clock? But it was now five past. Visitors? There seemed to be only Tess and one other. The next meal? That wouldn't be for a while. Some looked as though they were barely breathing, jaws slack, eyes glassy and unfocused. As if they were simply waiting to – Tess didn't want to finish the thought so she smiled at everyone hoping to mask her pervasive feelings of sadness and, she had to admit, discomfort.

The light from the sun, from the expanse of North Sea and

the huge sky, flooded the room spinning silver into grey hair and an opalescence to otherwise thin old skin. Even the minute lady whose wig had slipped had an air of composure about her – sitting serene, the light playing off the folds and creases of her baggy stockings like a Da Vinci drawing. Sitting beside her, a resident whose sandals revealed toes so overlapped Tess thought it made her look as if she'd been telling lies all her life. The lips of the lady with a startling blue rinse moved constantly, though whether she was talking to herself or just had an involuntary twitch Tess couldn't tell. But her eyes were fixed very darkly on the clock and Tess hoped it was for someone only five minutes late. Em toddled right ahead, looking intently at everyone as she went. Pair after pair of eyes that had been gazing listlessly at nothing in particular now had a welcome focus. One or two of the residents made a noise similar to beckoning a cat. A couple said a cheery hello. One gentleman, with no teeth, still broke into an expansive smile.

Someone said, little Daphne?

Mary, sitting in the corner, looking out to sea, said, Emmeline!

Em went to her outstretched hands. Tess following, nodding and saying hullo to all whom she passed. Mary was delighted, the crows' feet around her eyes were like rays of sunshine suddenly radiating out from the interminable cloud of old age.

'Little Emmeline! Where's Wolf?'

The child barked, to a round of applause. She and Mary knitted fingers for a while and communicated with nods and coos. As Tess sat beside them, it slowly dawned on her that she hadn't been noticed by Mary. And then it took for her to say, hullo, Mary! – Mary? Mrs Saunders? – to realize that actually Mary didn't recognize her at all. So Tess became a silent observer, proud to witness the pleasure Em was bringing to the room. Wherever Em went and whatever she picked up (and Tess noticed many similarities between an old-age-friendly room and a baby-friendly one) she received a chorus of approval. This community spoke in a language Em readily understood. They said, 'apple' when she picked one up. And when she pointed, they confirmed 'book' and 'shoe' and 'blanky' and 'tick-tock'. And they nodded knowingly when she talked in gurgles and they clapped when she showed them something or pointed something out. But Mary just gave Tess a distracted, yes, dear when she tried to talk to her.

'I could bring Wolf one day?' she suggested to Laura. 'I've heard of people doing that – taking dogs to care homes, hospices, prisons even. Petting lowers the blood pressure, it's been proven.'

'It'll raise the blood pressure of Health and Safety,' Laura declared. 'A nice idea, love. Just you come back with Em. She's a little actress that one, isn't she. They've liked it – more successful than the flaming bingo I tried to organize last week.'

Tess looked at the lady with the blue rinse, with the ever-moving lips and the eyes fixed on the clock. She was the only resident on whom Em had had little impact. 'That lady,' she whispered to Laura. And then she didn't know what it was she wanted to know, it was none of her business after all.

'Can't stop her doing it and believe me I've tried,' Laura said anyway. 'Whatever room she's in, if there's a clock, that's her – gone.'

'Is she waiting for a visitor?'

'Possibly,' said Laura, 'though she hasn't had one in all the time I've been here.'

An exhausted Em was asleep by the time her mother had strapped her into the buggy. Tess felt low. She'd suddenly felt desperate to leave Swallows, couldn't get out of there quick enough; she'd felt claustrophobic, unwell, but now in the fresh air she felt wretched. For the first time in weeks, she longed for someone to talk to. She wanted to say, Christ, let's go and have a coffee and a cake. She wanted someone with whom she could share the unexpected emotion of the visit. Will we too grow so old? Will you choose your hair to be blue? Will my toes knit like that? Will our chins get whiskery? Will we not mind if our teeth are in or out? Might that be us – waiting and waiting for no one to visit us? Will we sit and wait to die?

She pushed the buggy along the clifftop and stood awhile looking down the path leading to the cliff lift. There was no one around.

'I'm lonely,' she said quietly. 'I'm really really lonely.' She was immediately ashamed of the emotion.

She took Em home, cursing herself for destroying her SIM card, cursing SIM cards for damaging her memory for numbers in the way that a computer spell-check had compromised her ability to spell. She didn't even know Tamsin's number by rote. Then she wondered about her mobile handset itself. Did it have a memory of its own? She switched it on. And found that it did.

Tamsin didn't recognize Joe's landline number so she didn't take the call. Tess, though, rang again and again until she answered curtly out of frustration.

'Tamz?'

'Tess? Jesus freaking Christ, where the fuck are you?'

'Hullo.'

'You can't send me a text out of the blue saying you're fine and going away for a bit without telling me the whys and wheres, and then go completely off the radar for – what is it now – a *month*!'

'Sorry.'

121

'Where *are* you? I even went round to your flat and tried to break in. I thought – I don't want to tell you what I thought but it was grisly. Don't laugh. It wasn't bloody funny at the time.'

'Tamsin – sorry. I didn't think.'

'Where. The fuck. Are you?'

'Saltburn.'

There was a pause. 'Where. The fuck. Is Saltburn?'

'In Yorkshire.'

'In *Yorkshire*.'

'Yes, in Yorkshire. On the north-east coast. It's gorgeous.'

Another pause. 'I'm so glad you're enjoying your extended holiday.'

'Tamsin, don't sound like that.'

'Look, lady, people have been worried *sick*.'

Tess paused, racked her brains. 'Who?'

'Don't pull the "I don't have any friends" stuff on me. *I've* been worried. Geoff too. And I bumped into that girl you worked with – she said it was the gossip at the salon.'

'But I told them.'

'You didn't tell them why or where.'

'I couldn't.'

They both paused. 'When are you coming back? And where are you going to live when you do? I'm moving in with Geoff next month – otherwise, if I'd only known – And I saw your landlord, bizarrely, when I went round to find your corpse – he had a face like thunder saying you'd done a runner.'

'I have.'

'So I said he should calm down and there was probably an explanation and maybe there'd been a family crisis – *what* did you just say?'

'A runner. I *have* done a runner, Tamsin. I've run away. I'm not coming back.'

122

Tamsin didn't dare pause. 'I sort of want to hang up on you, but if I do I'll risk you never calling me again.'

'Don't hang up, Tamz. Please don't. You have this number now.'

'Don't hang up on me either – I just need to know if you're OK?'

'I think so. I will be.'

'Tess, were things really that bad? Why didn't you turn to me? I know Clapham is the other side of the world to Bounds Green – but Yorkshire's even further.'

Tess paused. 'I had to go.' Memories came back and she shuddered. 'People made it seem that things were very bad for me.'

'So you're hiding? How the hell can that help? You can't hurl your secrets out to sea and hope they'll disappear into the deep depths.'

'Actually, I'm house-sitting, not hiding, and it can help. It already has. It's the most beautiful, beautiful place. And the man is called Joe – he builds bridges. And there's an old lady – Mary. I've just found out she's his mother. And there's a surfer called Seb. And a dog called Wolf. And a garden, the size of which you just can't imagine.'

'It all sounds charmingly Mary Wesley, Tess.'

'I had to leave, Tamsin. I know it's cowardly. But it was the only option. I was really starting to panic.'

'I kept telling you to go to the Citizens Advice Bureau.'

'I don't want advice. I know what they'll say. All I want is to bury the bad stuff. I just want a new start.'

'Tess Tess Tess.'

'I know,' Tess said, 'I know, I know.'

'Don't you think you might be burying your head in the sand?'

'I don't do beaches, Tamsin.'

'You know what I mean.'

'I don't think so. I'm not actually *hurting* anyone.'

'But you – are *you* OK? And my goddaughter – is she OK too?'

'We're both very OK. Em's really blossoming. It's just that today I felt a little – I don't know. Lonely. I don't want to cry –. Shit.'

'Oh, Tess, come back – I'll help you work things out.'

'You can't.'

'Well, what *can* I do? Who knows you're there?'

'Just you. And my sister.'

'And I bet she's really interested.'

Tess considered this. And she realized that her sister hadn't even sounded surprised to hear from Tess, let alone to discover she had packed up her life and left London for a seaside town in the North. Tamsin's initial fury at Tess was different. It came from genuine concern. It came from love. And that helped. Tess didn't feel quite so lonely. She might not have Tamsin to hand, she might not see her for quite some time. But the fact that she was there for her, in spirit and now, at the end of the phone, was a comfort.

'Please keep in touch, Tess? *Regularly*. Let me know you're OK.'

'I will but I binned my mobile phone – it's snail-mail or landline only.'

'How frightfully quaint,' Tamsin murmured in a BBC accent.

'Quaint is quite a good word for Saltburn, actually,' Tess told her, 'though it's gritty too, but that's what I like about it – it's *real*. I saw the most incredible sunset the other day. Then the next afternoon, I came across some young scamp glue-sniffing.'

'You can see that down here,' Tamsin said.

'I know what you're saying. And I know why you're saying it. But there is something about this place – at this time – for me.'

'OK, I hear you. Just stay in touch – please.'

'I will. But I'd better go – the dog and child need feeding. Bye.'

'You're loved!' Tamsin interjected and with such urgency that Tess couldn't reply.

She stood looking at the replaced handset for a while, then wondered what to do about paying for the call. So she went and found one of the clean, empty jam jars she'd stored away and put a fifty-pence piece in it. Then she fed Em and Wolf, after which she bathed the former and turfed the latter out into the garden for his ablutions. She spent her evening designing a label for the jar, complete with a narrative of doodles and fancy lettering.

Telephone Tab.

Every now and then she'd say, oh shh! when the house creaked or the pipes groaned or a door squeaked open all by itself. But it didn't unnerve her. She quite liked it, now she'd grown used to it. The house – its sounds and smells and quirks – was now familiar. The place had such personality. It was as if the house had been a welcoming stranger at first, but Tess now felt she was living with a friend.

* * *

If she picks up the phone, I'll be phoning to say I'm coming back tomorrow. If she doesn't, bugger leaving another message – perhaps I'll squeeze in another weekend in London, see Rachel, head to Belgium on Monday. Or maybe I'll stay put, here in France. I don't know yet, until Tess answers.

Odd, though, that out of all the scenarios I'd probably forego rampant no-strings sex to spend time instead with her

125

– to return to the North, to that faded old town, to that hulking old house and to that slightly odd single mum who is rearranging my home.

*   *   *

Tess could hear the phone ringing but she was not going to disrupt her luxuriating in such a decadently full bath. Whoever it was could leave a message. And if they didn't leave a message, then it wasn't her they wanted anyway.

Chapter Thirteen

The house was filled, during daylight, with the gibberish chatter of the toddler and the huffing and occasional yowls of the oversize dog. In the evenings, the pipes took over with their cacophony of gurgles and groans while elsewhere the house creaked and rattled sporadically. Recently, such sounds had faded benignly into the background and Tess began to notice instead the quiet that seeped its way through her once her baby was asleep and the dog was dead to the world. Initially, she wasn't sure if she liked it; it felt intrusive and confrontational because the only thing she could listen to was herself. She tried to trivialize it by thinking, well, it's a damn sight better than London where by now Upstairs Bloke would be crashing around, Over the Hallway would be having their flaming row and Ocado, Tesco and Sainsbury vans would be leaving their engines running, making their deliveries. How she used to exclaim, shut up, everyone, you'll wake the baby! Shut up everyone, I can't hear myself think! Thinking back, Tess realized how those warring sounds of London were easy to listen to because they had nothing to do with her. Hearing nothing, here in this old house, was far more confrontational.

Now, she could think. A bit too much, some days. Some evenings the quiet would wrap itself around her like a soft blanket and lull her into gentle fantasies of the life she intended to make for herself and Em. At other times, however, it could goad her relentlessly. See! No one here but you! You're on your own, hiding out here, slave to your secrets, stupid idiot girl!

On such occasions, the silence was like a clock that had stopped, trapping Tess in the present – a situation caused by her past and which tarnished the future. Those evenings, she felt frightened and though she rarely reached for the phone or turned to the TV, nor did she face her fears. Instead, on that initial surge of adrenalin and at the first prick of tears, she'd lunge for a book and immerse herself in the lives of others instead. She had to start off by reading out loud, until she felt settled enough to have the silence surround her again.

For the first time in her life, she read voraciously. Anything that was on Joe's bookshelves she considered to have a worthy seal of approval. She tried authors she'd never heard of and authors she'd always meant to read. Every now and then she read passages twice, three times even, enjoying the wordcraft, the drama – but imagining that Joe had liked that book and wondering when he might be back and if there would be dinners they could share to discuss books they'd both read. His collection was vast and varied, from sumptuous coffee-table tomes to dense books about engineering, from the classics to modern masters and cutting-edge contemporary fiction. Tess was well aware it was escapism but what a way to pass another evening on her own. And anyway, wasn't that a function of fiction – a magical place that could transport you a world away? It wasn't as if she could solve anything just sitting there letting thoughts and memories and doom descend like a dark, damp veil. She'd done enough of that on evenings in London. Anyway, didn't Joe do just this when he was here, home alone – settle down with a good book until bedtime?

Sometimes, on a nondescript evening when her thoughts left her alone, Tess would tinker instead. This was different to the committed spring clean and reorganization she continued to devote much of her days to. Tinkering meant moving vases or clocks or the odd photo frame from here to there or from room to room; swapping the cushions in the TV room for those in the den, setting out the chessboard on the occasional table in the drawing room because, occasionally, it was good for such a table to have a purpose. Tinkering was finding a place for the phone books away from the lovely maps and atlases whose shelf they had shared. And it was when Tess was tinkering in the drawers of the hall console – let's put the pens here and the pads there, have the address book here, the takeaway leaflets in that folder there – that the phone rang. The suddenness of it was shrill and intrusive, having not been heard since that night in the bath that evening last week. Her hands were full of pens that she'd been systematically testing out on a scrap of paper rejecting any which were faint or which smudged. It had been a satisfying job that allowed for inventive doodling, which she was enjoying, but she ought to answer the phone. Putting the pens to one side, she picked up the receiver.

'The Resolution – good evening?'

She makes the place sound like a hotel.

He waited a moment.

'I'd like to book a room for tomorrow night, please,' he said, 'for a week.'

Tess thought, he sounds a bit like Joe. But then she thought, why would he phone to book a room?

'I'm sorry, you must have the wrong number,' she said. 'This is a private residence.'

She sounded so affronted that Joe had to laugh. 'Tess – it's me, Joe.'

She cringed but hid it behind a defensive tone. 'I know that. I knew all along.'

'You have a very – particular – telephone manner. Made the old place – the *residence* – sound like a posh guest house.'

'Would you rather I didn't answer the phone then, Joe?'

The barb to her voice snagged against him and he thought, dear God, here we go again. But tonight it amused him more than it irritated him because it was – well, it was so Tess, really. And he could clearly envisage her in his hallway, her cheeks reddening with her silly indignation. It was tempting to wind her up a little more.

She listened hard to Joe's silence and wondered if she'd irked him and whether he might say, yes, Tess, don't answer my bloody phone.

'I didn't mean it that way,' she said.

'I just thought I'd let you know I'll be back tomorrow.'

'We were half expecting you last weekend.'

'Things ran on.'

'Good things?'

A flashback to Rachel's blow-job shot to mind. 'Not bad.'

'What time tomorrow?' asked Tess. 'Ish.'

'Mid-afternoon, I would think,' said Joe. 'Ish.'

There was a pause.

Joe's coming back.

It was a concept privately welcomed by both. Tess thought of the beans on toast she'd had for supper – today, yesterday, probably the day before that too. Perhaps supper tomorrow would be different now. Proper. With wine. With conversation. And laughter. Joe just thought it would be nice to see her again.

'Shall I – you know – have stuff in?'

'Stuffing?' But he knew what she meant.

She tried to sound casual. 'Stuff – you know, fish, meat – for supper?'

She couldn't see him smiling; she could only hear the silence, which unnerved her. She wasn't to know that she hadn't over-stepped a mark, that over in Antwerp Joe was thinking to himself that he liked it that she'd asked. And that had she not, he liked to think he might have suggested the very same thing to her.

'Sounds good,' he said. He wasn't to know that suddenly she was in a knot as to whether there was enough in her purse – which she'd been keeping out of sight under her bed – to cover much stuff at all. 'See you tomorrow, Tess.'

She wanted to keep him longer on the phone, to run away from her nagging thoughts to yak instead about the minutiae of her day. She could tell him how she'd enjoyed the Joseph Heller but not the Doris Lessing, that the downstairs loo was now a sunny yellow, that she'd worked out how to record from the television and had saved him a programme called *Megastructures* about a huge bridge somewhere, oh, where! oh, what *was* the bloody thing called! It's in Japan! She didn't want him to go just yet because then it would just be her in the house and another evening stretched ahead and made tomorrow seem a very long way off.

'Bye then.'

'Bye.'

She placed the handset back in the cradle thoughtfully and looked at the pens, all in a scatter, and couldn't remember which were for keeping. So she had to test them all out again. She saw that she'd doodled the word 'Joe' a number of times. She told herself it had been absent-minded scribbling, that if it had been Tamsin she'd just spoken to, she'd'd've written *her* name a number of times in a variety of colours and squiggles instead. But she certainly didn't want Joe seeing this. She'd be screwing it up and chucking it away.

Don't screw it up.

Don't chuck it away.

Well, the paper, yes. But not the thoughts released by his name.

She told herself to stop it at once. But then she reasoned that it was so quiet tonight – Wolf hadn't even piped up when the phone went and the pipes hadn't made a sound all evening. There was nothing on the box. Her eyes were too tired to start a new book. There was nothing to do but think about tomorrow. She was all on her own and that meant she didn't need to tell a soul what she was thinking. Deluded? So what! The little buzz was – nice.

Later, as she lay in bed still thinking about tomorrow, it crossed her mind whether to invite Mary to tea over the next few days. But she wouldn't – not just because Joe had never mentioned her so Tess oughtn't to interfere. She'd be doing nothing of the sort because actually she was looking forward to having Joe all to herself.

* * *

All morning, Em had been saying 'wol' over and over and Wolf had been careening around in circles, taking sudden bites at the base of his tail. Tess couldn't work out what Em was saying or why Wolf was doing this. She looked through his coat but could see only healthy skin, pink in places, grey in places. He continued to turn on his imaginary sixpence while Em implored wol at regular intervals.

'Do you mean Wol-f?' Tess pointed to the dog but Em continued to say wol.

'Good God – Wolf, would you *quit*? You two need fresh air. Come on.'

For a girl born and bred in a city, Tess was not quite sure from where her belief in fresh air being the answer to all ills had stemmed. She'd never been particularly sporty, nor had long walks or the great outdoors shaped her childhood. Her memories of that time were of her parents' emotional and physical inertia: her mother motionless, staring out of windows as if she could see no way out. Her father seemingly absorbed into the fabric of the armchair, *Racing Post* on his lap, racing on the television, telephone at his side. 'It's a flutter – some men spend all Saturday at the bookies,' he'd snap, implying they should be grateful for his company. How Tess had craved the house to herself back then. And now she has one.

She'd grown to enjoy living at the top of a hill and the physical exertion it demanded. She'd looked at herself in the bath the previous evening and had noticed how her legs were shapelier than she remembered. And she'd stood naked in front of the mirror and had liked what she'd seen. She'd felt the firmness of her limbs as she lay in bed, giving her thighs a squeeze, tensing and releasing her calf muscles, running her hands along her upper arms to feel the pleasing dip and rise of muscle definition. Sea air and steep hills were doing wonders for her health and physique, she decided. Negotiating West End crowds and having to share the recycled air on the underground never had.

'Wolf, come. *Now*, you silly dog. Stop spinning. Let's get some fresh air.'

'Wol!'

Down the drive, across the road, steeply down the divvety path to the Gardens. Daffodils that should be dead by now, a cheeky bluebell out way too early, a profusion of crocuses, bright primroses flirting at all who passed by. Occasionally, the fertile soil beneath certain trees encouraging ancient plants like wood anemone, dog mercury and toothwort. The buggy dinked and lurched over the uneven ground sending tremors up Tess's arms, but Em was too busy saying 'wol' to be bothered. Wolf was off foraging; Tess loved how convinced he seemed of his treasure trail despite always bounding back to her empty-mouthed save his huge lolling tongue.

Through the natural tangle of the woods, they came to a vantage point where they could look down onto the sudden and fantastically incongruous splendour of the fastidiously planted Italianate beds, all swirls and ogees and complex symmetry. The planting was rapidly covering the soil now and Tess thought how it would not be long until the flower buds, currently a scatter of multi-coloured beads, would be pulled by summer into full bloom. What are you? Tess wondered, what colours will you be? She'd like to know more about plants, she thought. Maybe Joe has a book about local flora. Did he really, really mean it when he said the position at the house was long-term? With so much that had never been definite in her life, it was stranger still how comforting was the notion of her stay here being potentially indefinite.

She looked at all the empty benches, imagining them occupied in warmer times ahead. Not by the kids from the jewel streets – Amber, Pearl, Diamond, Emerald, Ruby, Garnet, Coral – who loitered and larked around the station but, Tess imagined, by visitors or the retired folk of town like Mary. People with the time to sit, who liked to look at flowers and feel the day on their faces. And for me, she thought. All year round, there'd be room enough in the gardens and the woods for her little entourage too.

They continued to walk down the steep bank; rather Tess walked, Em was transported and Wolf galloped a circuitous route. Em's arm suddenly shot out, a fat little index finger pointing with great conviction as she gave a triumphant 'wol!'. Tess looked. And then she grinned as she crouched by the buggy kissing Em's hands and burying her nose in her tiny palms.

'Clever, clever Em,' she said. 'Mummy's clever, clever girl.' She gazed through the gates at the Woodland Centre. Closed it may have been, but on the side of the wall a large colourful cartoon owl with binoculars around his neck solicited them with his friendly wave. She'd never noticed him before, which was not to say that her daughter hadn't.

'Wol,' said Tess and Em agreed. 'Can you say Owl?' Tess asked. Em nodded earnestly and said 'wol' again. 'Wol it is,' Tess said softly, 'wol it is.' They stood, looking through the gates, waving at the wall and the wol.

When they finally continued their walk through the gardens, crossing the Poohsticks bridge and following the miniature railway and Skelton Beck down to the coast and the coffee shop looking out to sea, Tess felt a surge of immense contentment and wellbeing. Fresh air was only partly the reason. Another was having just bumped into Lisa and her toddler again, and a further open invitation to the singalong, or the mums' coffee morning or the playground. Lisa marvelled at Tess's news of Wol. And actually, what struck Tess was that for Em too this place now had its own significance; its own unique gifts, albeit in the shape of a cartoon owl. There might be times when she kidded herself but Tess couldn't kid Em. Over and above her mother saying, this is a jolly nice place, Em! let's live here! Em had somehow found something in it all for herself that she liked too.

When Joe pulled into the drive, the first thing he saw was the increased size of the bonfire pile and he thought to himself, Christ, what has she thrown out now? And then he thought, Christ, what's she done inside the house this time? And then he realized, bugger, I forgot the mould-resistant paint I promised her. He sat, drumming his fingers against the steering wheel and, though the journey had been tiring and he wanted nothing more than to unpack, do a few emails and then unwind with a large glass of wine decadently early, he couldn't bring himself to switch off the engine. Instead, he put the car into reverse, turned fast and drove away.

They didn't see him but he saw them. An unassuming girl in jeans, trainers, a sludge-coloured shapeless top, her hair haphazardly tied away from her face; a rangy mangy dog lagging behind her, a buggy which she pushed ahead. Every few footsteps, the girl slowed down, looked over her shoulder and implored the dog to catch up. All the while, her lips moving, chatting to the dog, to the child, about goodness knows what. It struck Joe how Tess looked so much younger and plainer than he knew her to be. He'd seen her prettiness and wondered why she would downplay it. She could make a bit more of herself easily enough. Have a haircut. Choose a nice sweater. Ditch the trainers. Buy a new pair of jeans. Yet there was something that was just right because of its unwavering naturalness. Another glimpse in the rear-view mirror revealed Tess standing in the middle of the road urging Wolf over, like a lollipop lady ushering a recalcitrant schoolboy. What you see is what you get with Tess, Joe thought. Unlike Rachel who, without make-up, looked totally different. Or Nathalie, who in plain underwear just might not hold the same allure. He thought it was probably a better thing to hide under nondescript clothes, than to brandish a fraudulent appearance with a palette of make-up or drawers of dazzling lingerie. And then he thought, for Christ's sake, just get the bloody paint.

At the bottom of the drive, Tess told herself not to be disappointed if Joe's car wasn't there. But it wasn't and she was.

An hour later, she heard the car before Wolf because he was still preoccupied with the gremlins in his tail. And Em wasn't aware that she should be listening out for anything, so she continued an intricate game with the tube from the toilet roll and a ping-pong ball. Tess, though, didn't have anything she ought to be doing so she'd been loitering at the edges of windows.

The car door opened and shut. Front door or back door – she wavered. She thought she should be seen to be doing *something*, not just standing there waiting. She took a step towards the back door. Stopped. Walked towards the hallway. Stopped. Picked up Em then put her down again. Wouldn't he be in by now?

She looked through the window in the hall, standing well back and swaying to increase her field of vision but remain unseen. Joe was not in the driveway. She went into the kitchen and sneaked a look out to the side of the garden. And there he was, circumnavigating the bonfire heap. He picked something up. Oh God, not that dreadful old stringless tennis racquet. Tess laughed abruptly and found herself rapping on the windowpane. He looked up and located her, saw her wagging her finger at him. He gave an imaginary backhand and forehand with the racquet before shrugging and returning it to the heap.

Tess thought, I really ought to wipe this grin off my face.

* * *

'Paint.'

'I'll start immediately, Mr Saunders.'

But she knows he doesn't mean it as a command; he's holding out two tins so she says thank you and takes them off him and through to the boot room.

'No problem,' he says, following her and he doesn't say, actually, it *was* a bloody problem finding the sodding stuff.

She feels a little hyper, nervy; she wants to show him what she's done – the utility room, the downstairs loo, the start she's made on the den as he calls it though she's taken to calling it the snug. She wants to ask him about Wolf's tail. She wants to tell him all about 'wol'. She wants to say, shall we have a cup of tea? and then make it good and strong,

137

served in her own cups and saucers. She wants to say, it's nice to see you, Joe. She wants to say, I'm going to cook us up a treat this evening.

'I'm putting a wash on – do you have any darks?'

And though Joe would rather have been asked if he wanted a cuppa, in a peculiarly domestic way the emotion behind her offer feels much the same.

'Thanks,' he says. 'I'll just unpack, then.'

And as he goes upstairs to his room to sort out his darks for the wash, Tess calls after him.

'Cup of tea?'

And he smiles, which she can't see. She can only hear his pause. But then he says, lovely. And she exhales a sigh of relief that she hopes he hasn't heard.

She knows she feels disproportionately happy. But so what, she says to herself. So what.

She'd overcooked the fish and was furious with herself. If she hadn't apologized over and over and if she'd taken her eyes off his every mouthful, he would have enjoyed the dish more.

'Anything's better than room-service,' he said lightly. 'That came out wrong,' he added, not wanting to incite her stroppy side. Not tonight.

Tess acquiesced. 'Was your trip good, then?'

'Busy,' Joe said. 'France, Belgium, London since I last saw you.'

'Do you like London?'

'Love it.'

'Friends there?'

'A few – clients and colleagues, mostly, but they're a good bunch.'

'Are you wined and dined, then, in the evenings?' and she knew she wanted to hear him say, no, I just chill out on my own in the hotel room and order room service.

'Mostly,' he said.

An emotion swooped down on her so suddenly it was like a fishbone caught in her throat. She wondered about its provenance as she tried to sip away its sharpness but the wine tasted a little sour. Was it envy? Did she envy him his trip – the wining and the dining and the throb of London or Belgium or France? But what did this say about her newfound affection for *here*? Hadn't this place nourished her, provided her with a very literal breath of fresh air? Hadn't it nailed the coffin closed on city living? Lonely she might feel up here, some evenings, some afternoons, whole days too, all on her own, but she hadn't felt stir-crazy. Yet it seemed Joe enjoyed a perfectly good time away from here. And then it struck her that it wasn't Joe she envied, at all. It was whoever was showing him the bright lights and exciting times; she envied them their time with him. Faintly ridiculous, really, that this could cause her discomfort, but she couldn't deny the emotion. And, as she drained her glass, it occurred to her that actually, it might not be envy, pure and simple. There might be insecurity in there too. How could she hope to compete?

'Can't remember the last time I went out at night,' she muttered. 'Pre Em, that's for sure.'

'I'll bet you the library has notices about babysitters,' Joe said helpfully. 'You should treat yourself.'

Tess shrugged.

'Have you met anyone, made any friends, since you've been here?'

That lovely Lisa whose invitations Tess had thus far not responded to – what would Joe make of that? She felt a bit pathetic. She could have said Mary. But actually, she couldn't – it would be contentious and untimely and she'd decided to keep Mary to herself a while longer. She could say Laura but that would be complicated and it wasn't exactly true.

'Seb,' she said, knowing she'd have to be brief because there was so little she could add.

'Seb who?'

'Seb the surfer.'

Joe's look lasted but a split second, but when Tess saw his eyes darken and focus she wondered if she recognized something – a single shot of unease.

'Seb the Surfer, eh?' Joe said lightly though he wondered whether Seb the Sodding Surfer had managed to lure Tess onto the beach, for a frolic in the waves. 'Anyway, I'm back for a week or so now.' To both of them, this came out sounding as though she should be at his beck and call. 'So – if you – well, supper and stuff.'

'Oh, OK.'

'I'll be going into the Middlesbrough office most days, but I'll be working from home sometimes. So perhaps lunch too – on those days.'

'OK.'

'A week or so,' Joe repeated, 'maybe two.'

They took inordinate interest and time with the fruit salad.

'Do you want me to ease off the renovations when you're in the house?'

'I don't see why you should – you don't strike me as a noisy labourer.'

'You haven't heard me singing along to the radio.'

'And I suppose this is when Emmeline and Wolf are asleep? So it's a case of the lesser of two evils, then? You caterwauling – or them howling and squawking.'

If it wasn't for his wry wink, Tess would have taken offence and made it known.

'Hey,' she objected, 'I can hold a tune. And Em's vocabulary is increasing daily – she knows the word for owl.'

'Isn't "owl" the word for owl?'

'You may think so,' Tess said, waggling her knife at him, 'but I think you'll find it's "wol".'

'She's very sweet, your little 'un,' Joe said and Tess had to physically sit on her hand because it would be so easy to touch his arm. 'Very sweet.'

'And actually, your dog's not so bad,' Tess said and she tipped her chair back a little to look under the table and give Wolf a nudge with her foot. 'I've grown rather fond of Wolf.' She could so easily have said, and I've met your mum and she's a very nice lady. But not tonight. Let sleeping dogs lie and all that, thought Tess, scrunching her toes into Wolf's coat.

'I'm knackered,' Joe said. 'Thanks for dinner – I'll do the honours tomorrow, if you like, if you're around.'

'Of course I'll be around,' Tess said. 'Where else would I be!'

Joe thought about this as he cleared the plates away. She could've said, where else would I go. But she phrased it where else would she *be*. It wasn't that there was nowhere she could go; it was that there was nowhere she'd rather be. Or was it all just semantics? And why was he analysing his house-sitter's turn of phrase? And why was he wondering again where Seb the Surfer fitted in?

'I really am tired,' he said. 'Goodnight.'

'I'm going to have an early night too,' Tess agreed, though she sat at the kitchen table a little while longer, gazing at the space Joe had left.

Chapter Fourteen

The thing is about flirting, Tess thought to herself as she applied a coat of mould-resistant paint in the utility room, I'm not sure I've ever really been on the receiving end, nor have I been much good at it. She considered that she'd probably just been conditioned to an abbreviated form employed as a preliminary to sex.

She thought back to student days, when it had been both the trend and peer-group pressure to drink cheap wine and pair off with someone on a Friday night. The act of being bought the wine had been the apotheosis of seduction (not least because conversation was restricted anyway, on account of the decibel level at the various college dives). But all of this was less flirting, more it was bartering. I buy you wine all evening on my student grant; you take me back to your digs to do the deed. In retrospect, the cheap wine had such a swift inebriating effect on both parties that the deed was rarely accomplished but the hangover and bravado kept that quiet.

For the first time in years, she cast her mind back to the boyfriend she had all through the third year, but even at the time she knew he was less a soulmate and more a human radiator; someone who warmed her up in the freezing shared house. They also used each other to catch up on lecture notes so they could alternate on sleeping until noon. It certainly wasn't love, it wasn't really lust. There had been sex, quite a lot of it, but it was as if they kept at it to see if it could get any better. With or without wine or spliff. Then came their finals and it was only midway through the summer following graduation that they thought perhaps the relationship had ended. In retrospect, they had merely furnished each other's lives that last year in no greater way than the Jim Morrison posters and cheap scatter cushions had furnished their spartan rooms. A distraction from the unrelenting woodchip of student digs, relief from the boredom of coursework, succour from the sudden panic of final exams, a cheap form of student exercise. Nice enough, but about as symbolic as the lower second degree they both came away with.

Then came Tess's move to London and it seemed that for a long while, the furthest flirting went was the odd person smiling at her on the tube – odd being the operative word. Then came Dick. Tess thought about Dick as she dipped her roller and worked the paint to suitable tackiness. Dick hadn't really flirted with her at all – he'd spouted some cod-Shakespearean poetry at her instead. She couldn't remember it precisely – only that he'd actually used the word 'maiden' in all seriousness. He broke off, mid-riff, from some long instrumental number on his beat-up guitar, to gaze at her as if she was a gift from the gods. He'd pointed his plectrum at her and delivered his 'maiden' soliloquy. As a rambling preamble, it worked. Some more second-rate prose-poetry, a further few chords on his guitar and bed followed. And so he came. And then he went. And Em arrived. Em, usurping utterly the love anyone else could possibly give Tess or ever elicit from her. Emmeline, her everything.

*

And though Em has remained her everything, the love of her life and the light in it, Tess quietly wondered about the recent rushes of adrenalin. As much as the love she shared with Em was primal and vast and utterly sustaining, feelings of a different type and intensity were surfacing. As the utility room walls brightened with every run of the roller and the skirting in the lounge became smoother with each rub of sandpaper, Tess thought about these swells of adrenalin; how they crested each time Joe said something like, you've missed a bit, or, would Rembrandt care for a cuppa? And she thought how, when she'd been so engrossed glossing the window frame singing along to a Golden Oldies radio show, she hadn't noticed him leaving a Mars Bar and an apple on a plate by her side – and how she'd been too thrilled to eat them. She recalled how she felt when she was carefully cutting-in along the dado and he'd knocked on the door and said, I think I hear Em – I'll go to her if you like. These little surges of adrenalin, Tess conceded, were actually good old-fashioned butterflies. But her scant experience and battered self-esteem left her unsure whether fetching a baby, or leaving a Mars Bar or calling her Rembrandt or sharing a steak was flirting, or perhaps something more. Or there again, less – just friendship or simply social grace.

She wasn't to know that Joe had told the office he'd be in afternoons only – after lunch. Nor did she know that when he was in his study, rigorously calculating forces and stresses and the risks of compression and tension, torsion and resonance; the truer challenge taxing his mind was whether it was too soon since the last cup of tea to make Tess another. And when he heard her singing, he tried to work out various ways to watch her, unseen. And how he wished he could have witnessed her reaction when she found chocolate and an apple by the white spirit! Joe hadn't really ever had to do much flirting because women had generally fallen, legs akimbo, at

144

his feet. Or fallen to their knees to unbutton his flies. Or simply fallen for him with all the sweet nothings that brought with it which, to Joe, was precisely that: sweet but nothing. There's Nathalie in France, Rachel in London, Eva in Brussels; there had been Giselle in Brazil and there would always be someone in Japan. They all come with the job. It's a perk that he's exploited – the cost of foregoing anything long-term and solid has not been a high price to pay. It's been preferable and it's been his choice. It's kept his life simple. He comes and he goes – to them and away from them and back to the sanity and sanctity and seclusion of his house.

Only now, his space here has been halved and yet somehow broadened too, by the presence of Tess. And Joe can't deny the impact it's having but he's just not sure how to calculate it. It's growing, developing, taking form – yet without him having any control over the design. The details often surprise him. There's a solidity that unnerves him as much as a fragility too. Will it hold his weight?

For the duration of Joe's visit, Mars Bars, lunch and supper, and endless cups of tea, have punctuated the days. But after a week of this, he's off again tomorrow, a fact that has been hovering like a wasp inside a window. They haven't wanted to approach it, because of the sting, so they've tried to ignore it, to pretend they're not acutely aware of it. There's been an inordinate amount of tea-making today and it's only early afternoon. But she's still painting in the snug and he's shut himself away in his study. Em is having her nap. Wolf is convinced the garden is full of rabbits that can climb trees. Joe really can't drink a sip more tea and he has much to organize prior to his departure but it seems like a good enough time to tell Tess the plumber will be calling tomorrow about the downstairs loo.

'He'll come in the morning – but take that with a pinch.'

145

And as Joe says it, he's looking down on Tess who is crouching in a corner working the sandpaper into some nook. And her jeans have ridden down just enough to reveal the top of her buttocks. She'll curse it as builder's bum but to Joe, it resembles the upper part of a heart shape. And he thinks, *pinch*. And he thinks, *nook* and then he thinks, *cranny*. And he has to turn around and tell himself to get a grip or fuck off back to his study. When he turns back, she's standing and he thinks, why the hell didn't I look for longer? And she's thinking, shit – these bloody jeans. There's an inordinate amount of eye contact and loitering for the simple information of a tradesman's impending visit.

'The plumber?' she repeats, as if the rasp of sandpaper had drowned his words.

'Yes – tomorrow morning.' He looks around the den. She's done two walls in a sludge-grey, a period colour that's perfect and, bizarrely, was the only one on offer at the small DIY shop in town. He nods his approval. He decides he'll be calling it the snug from now on, too.

'I'm just sanding down the Polyfilla,' she says. She's come over because she needs a new piece of sandpaper and it's on the table right by Joe. She has sludge-grey freckles over her cheek and a scab of Polyfilla on her chin. And Joe just can't help himself. He touches her cheek and he touches her chin and then his fingertips pause before he touches the tip of her nose. He used to have a den, out of bounds to previous house-sitters. Now he has a snug thanks to Tess.

'You're covered,' he says, 'in stuff.'

And Tess can't speak because though she didn't know about the paint and the filler she's pretty sure there was nothing on her nose. It strikes her that he just might be touching her because he wants to. She is immobilized by the possibilities this could provide. But because she can't move, when he moves away she can't reach for his arm to stop him, to turn

146

him back towards her, to raise her lips to his so that he can kiss her mucky face.

Once he's left the room, Tess chides herself. You idiot girl, he's not going to kiss you. He was just pointing out that your face is a mess.

She feels distraught and she starts sanding again, vigorously. Briefly, there are tears and when she wipes them away, she feels the sensation of salt water and sand mixed together – a combination she hates. It's not gentle on her skin and she is rough on herself.

I'm just his house-sitter, his odd-job girl, with my spattered face and ancient jeans and pasty bum. Who do I think I am that he would want to kiss *me*?

She has no way of knowing that Joe has been standing still in his bedroom, the feel of her cheek, her chin, her nose, imprinting into his fingertips. He's been standing there like a lemon for ten minutes or so, looking at an open drawer thinking, I don't want to pack, I want to stay.

It was time for another last supper and Joe had done the honours. It was impossible for roast chicken, potatoes, peas, carrots, broccoli and onion gravy not to make life seem OK again.

'What time are you leaving tomorrow?'

'After breakfast.'

'What time will you arrive?'

'Marseilles after lunch, on site near Roussillon a couple of hours later.'

'How long?'

'A week. Perhaps two.'

Tess played her fork over a pea before squeezing it down onto it, hard. 'It'll be May by then.'

'Maybe sooner,' Joe said.

'Keep in touch?'

A pause. He glanced at her. She was squashing peas again. 'OK,' he said.

'OK then.'

'And don't worry about fifty pences in the telephone jar – if you need to speak to me, just phone.' And he gamely stabbed his last floret of broccoli. 'Is that Emmeline?'

Tess was already standing. 'She never usually wakes at this time.'

'Go and check – I'll see to the dishes.'

'But you cooked – I should clear up. That's how it's been.'

'It's fine, Tess. Go.'

As Joe cleared away the dinner, he listened. The child was audibly grouchy, the soft tones of a mother's singing and cooing having little effect.

Half an hour it lasted before he heard Tess descending the stairs. Coffee, he thought, or tea. Where are the biscuits? Let's stay as we were, here in the kitchen. But when the kitchen door opened, Tess had a hot and bothered Emmeline on her hip.

'Is she OK?'

'I think so,' Tess said. 'She's not hot – I think she's just out of sorts.'

'Bottle?'

'Please – there's one in the fridge.'

Joe boiled a kettle and sat the bottle in a bowl of hot water. They both thought quietly how he'd become a bit of a dab hand.

'Thanks,' Tess said, while Em grabbed it, gave a few fractious gulps before dropping it. Tess tisked. Joe said, don't worry. Em started grizzling again. Wolf woke up and whined. Joe looked at them.

'I think I might just have a magic cure,' he said. 'It works for me when I'm fractious. Come on. Grab coats.'

'Where are we going?'

'Wait and see.'

'My grandmother used to say that. She used to say, "Wait and see with salt on." I think it was an extreme version of yours.'

'Save the family anecdotes, Tess – and get your coat, woman.'

'What's the rush?'

'Where are your car keys?'

'But I have hardly any petrol.'

'Keys, Tess – now!'

'But –'

'We're taking my car – I just need your child seat. Give me the bloody keys!'

He wasn't being rude; well, he was, but Tess didn't need to jump to the defensive because Joe was grinning his exasperation at her. There wasn't any genuine urgency, but there was a sense of excitement. Tess had no idea where they were going or what the big secret was. Five minutes into the journey Emmeline was sound asleep, rendering the excursion obsolete. But neither Tess nor Joe was going to say, well, we might as well turn back then.

They drove through Redcar and he told her how the steel industry once had its zenith here; Europe's largest single-blast furnace. He pointed out the remaining vast rolling sheds, super-stretched structures, though many were now empty.

'We used to come at night when we were kids – the sparks and the heat coming from those sheds. Molten steel, pet – as exciting as any fireworks display.'

Another industry in decline, he said solemnly. But then brightened and told her that the beach here had masqueraded as Dunkirk for a recent Hollywood blockbuster much to the amusement of the locals.

'*Atonement!*' Tess had seen it. Joe too.

Then she said, tell me where we're going!

But he just said, patience, woman.

She looked at the road signs for clues.

Middlesbrough?

She had assumed she could ably stay in Saltburn without ever having recourse to visit the city whose slightly grimy, down-at-heel reputation rather preceded it. They were driving through a strange industrial hinterland of yards and depots and storage tanks. Chemicals, Joe explained. Charming, Tess thought. It was all rather dark and desolate.

'There!' Joe swung the car to a stop, switched, off the engine and clapped his hands against the steering wheel. 'What do you think of that, then?'

From the drop of Tess's jaw and from her stunned silence, her face pressed at the windscreen, Joe deduced her reaction as precisely what he'd hoped for.

'What is it?'

'You don't know whether it's monstrous or beautiful, do you?'

'It's monstrously beautiful – but what is it?'

'Will Emmeline be OK in the car? If we just step outside for a few minutes?'

'Where are we going? I'm not going *up*.'

'Stop faffing and trust me, will you?'

She looked at him and he raised an eyebrow. She unclicked her seatbelt, glanced over her shoulder to her daughter.

'You're OK about Emmeline?'

'She'll be fine – and I will be too, as long as I'm in earshot.'

'Come on, Tess. We're the only ones here.'

Floodlit, the blue paint made the vast steel web-like structure appear luminous and contradictorily weightless.

'What is it, Joe? What's it called?'

'This, Miss Tess, is the Transporter Bridge,' Joe said. 'Tell me you have at least heard of the Transporter?'

Tess shook her head.

'Did you see *Billy Elliot*? Or *Auf Weidersehen, Pet*? It had a starring role in both – I have the DVDs at home.'

She shook her head again.

They looked up at the bridge as Joe spoke. 'Built 1911. Supreme cantilever construction with three main bridge spans. 851 feet long, 160 feet high, rising to 225 feet at the top of the two towers. 2,600 tons of steel. Two almost independent structures constructed on opposite banks of the Tees, joined at the centre over the river.'

'It's – mad! It looks so modern – but it also looks like, I don't know, like two fossilized pterodactyls!'

'It's bloody marvellous. In 1880, an iron-ore seam was found in the Eston Hills just near here and Middlesbrough turned from a small coal-exporting town with fledgling iron works into a major iron-producing area. Of course, then steel. Chemicals too. Anyway, the banks either side of the river are low, so conventional bridge design was not practical. To build at this great height allowed for the passage of large shipping traffic without inconveniencing the regular river traffic with a traditional swing-bridge.'

'But?' Tess stopped to puzzle it. 'If it's so high up, how does it work as a bridge? How do you get all the way up there in the first place to cross the river?'

'This bridge reconciled the need to cross the Tees, with the need to sail boats up it.' Joe turned the angle of Tess's shoulders. 'See there? Coming back across the river towards us? The gondola travelling above the water, suspended from those thirty wire ropes? Follow them up. The cables run on a wheel-and-rail system all the way up – *there*. Think of it as an aerial ferry.'

'Oh yes! There's a van on it – and a car.'

'Since 1911, it has crossed the Tees between Middlesbrough

and Port Clarence, in two minutes, every fifteen minutes, up to eighteen hours a day. We're lucky – soon it'll be running on a new, shorter timetable. As a bridge builder myself, over and above the fact that the Transporter provided a solution to a problem, this bridge is also a marvellous virtuoso feat of turn-of-the-century engineering. They built it – because they *could*. There were fewer than twenty transporter bridges built worldwide and all were between 1893 and 1916. Only eleven still exist and few of those are in regular use. The longest was over the Mersey – but it's no longer there. The Middlesbrough Transporter Bridge is the largest operational one in the world. It is now Grade II listed.'

'Yet it's still a working bridge. A living bridge.'

'I like it – *a living bridge*. Yes, a living, moving structure,' Joe said. 'And I love it.'

Tess knew it was a bit daft to smile at a bridge but she did so, looking up and across, up and across. Simultaneously elegant and yet somehow crude, the bridge seemed to exude a personality – like a tall, elderly well-to-do aunt with a mouth like a drain.

'In 1916, a bomb was dropped from a Zeppelin – but it fell right through the latticework and straight into the Tees. In 1940, a bomb went through the bridge's span and exploded onto the gondola – but the bridge closed for only three days. In the late 1950s, the mechanism broke down just near the shore and the passengers had to walk the plank to the bank – then the rush-hour crowds had to walk all the way up and over the top.'

'Up *there*? You'd never get me doing that!'

Joe looked at her askance but she was engrossed watching the gondola approaching with its load.

'Can we – I mean. Would it be much of a detour to – It's just that it's arriving back now. Is it expensive to cross?'

He laughed. 'Be my guest.'

*

Joe's car was the only vehicle and they were the only foot passengers in the cradle as it skimmed over the inky Tees with a clunk and a whirr.

'The synergy that I love most is that when they were planning it, they brought in a Frenchman, Ferdinand Arnodin – the pioneer of transporter bridge engineering. And of course here's me, a smoggie, now involved with the French on their bridges. And the guy who ran the Cleveland Bridge and Engineering Company who designed the Transporter, was one William E. Pease.'

'Why do I know that name?'

'Because when I showed you where the Halfpenny Bridge used to be, I told you all about *Henry* Pease, who founded Saltburn and whose white firebricks partly constructed the town.'

'This bridge is kind of your bridge too then, isn't it,' Tess said.

'I like to think so,' Joe said. 'I'm proud to be part of Middlesbrough's bridge-building heritage. The bridge over the Tyne – that's ours, also the Geordies' King Edward VII Bridge. The Sydney Harbour Bridge – that's us too. And the Menai Straits Suspension Bridge. The Severn Bridge – the first use of an aerodynamic deck. The Forth Road Bridge – at the time, the world's two longest spans. The Newport Lifting Bridge just down there. The Victoria Falls Bridge over the Zambesi. The Tsing Ma Bridge in Hong Kong. The New Lambeth Bridge in London, the Jiangyin Yangstze River Bridge in China. Then there's the Strotstrom Bridge in Denmark, the Limpopo Bridge in South Africa, the Bosporus Bridge in Turkey linking Europe and Asia – bloody brilliant bridge builders, us smoggies.'

'But is this your favourite bridge?'

'No – my favourite bridge would be the Milau Viaduct. Norman Foster truly achieved sculpture in the landscape and

153

the most profound dialogue between nature and the man-made with that bridge. But the Tranny is the bridge I love most.'

The river was crossed.

'What do we do now?'

'We could go via the Newport Bridge – that's some structure too.'

'We could,' said Tess, 'or we could just stay as we are and cross back over again. I wish Em was awake.'

'Bring her back in daylight,' Joe said. 'In fact, you have to see it for yourself in daylight. Actually, when I'm back next time, I'll see if I can take you across.'

'Across?'

'Up there.' Joe pointed and Tess looked up almost fifty metres.

'I'm not going up there!'

'Trust me. It's an awesome experience.'

'I don't do heights.'

'Heights and beaches?' He looked at her and then, as he looked away, across to the other side he slipped his arm around her shoulder. And after a loaded pause, he turned his head towards hers, leaning in closer. Their eyes locked. And Tess wondered and wondered. And wondered if she should be doing – something – too. And then he stopped and instead, he turned his gaze out to the river and he cleared his throat.

'I'd hold your hand,' he said.

It was as if a kiss hung in the air, floating above the water, left suspended like the cradle of the Transporter Bridge was suspended over the River Tees. And Joe and Tess had to climb back into the car and drive off the cradle and onto firm ground and head back home. At that time of night, it was only fifteen minutes back to Saltburn. As they turned into the drive, Tess thought back to the Transporter, calculating that the bridge would be cranking into action again one last time that night, transporting dreams across the water.

She carries Em to her cot and the baby doesn't wake. And she stands, in the soft glow of the night-light, wondering what she's meant to do now. Did he really mean to kiss her? Or was he coming in close so the sounds of the bridge and the wind wouldn't take his words away? But there was his arm around her shoulder too. It might not have been a kiss in the conventional sense but it had equal impact. And he said, trust me. And how she hopes she can.

Go down, Tess! He's going tomorrow; grab him with both hands like an opportunity you have to prevent slipping away to France. Tell him you hate heights and beaches because they both terrify you. Ask him to hold your hand as you tell him the reasons why.

'Tess?'

Tell him.

'Yes?'

'Fancy a nightcap?'

She peers over the banister and he's looking up from the hallway.

'Cup of tea?' he suggests instead because the notion of a nightcap should never necessitate such a pause.

'OK,' she says. But when it's brewed she doesn't go downstairs and he waits awhile before bringing it up, halfway. They stand there, awkwardly.

'Thanks,' she says, 'for the tea and the Transporter.'

'I wish I could show you the Milau,' Joe says.

'Maybe when you're back,' Tess says.

He laughs. 'It's in France.'

Tess feels embarrassed. 'Oh.'

France. France tomorrow. Tonight I almost kissed her.

'Anyway –'

155

'– anyway.'

And he knows he could take a step up towards her. He could kiss her then. Or he could reach up for her hand from where he's standing now. But there's a mug of hot tea between them and, over and above that, there's the look of startled faun about her now. The moment has passed. There's a flatness – just as her hair is now lank against her head, curtaining her expression, whereas on the bridge, it was buffeted away from her face revealing the dark sparkle in her eyes.

'Well – night, then, Tess,'

'Goodnight Joe.'

'Thanks for –'

'Thanks for finding a miracle cure for Em.'

He'd gone before she was up. Crept out earlier than he needed to. He'd slept badly; fretful dreams vexing him. He woke deciding it was crazy to have feelings for Tess. Absolute madness. For a start, he didn't know when he'd be back, when he'd have to go again. And anyway, he didn't know how long she'd stay either. And though she'd arrived with hardly anything visible to her name, he sensed she brought a lot of hidden baggage with her. And if she added hers to all of his, there wouldn't be room enough in the house for much else.

> *Gone to France.*
> *Will call.*
> *Take care.*
> *Joe*

Chapter Fifteen

Tess pretended not to notice that Joe was no longer there. She refused to give the answering machine more than a nonchalant glance each time she returned to the house. In the evening, either the television or the radio was on to bypass the taunting silence of the phone not ringing. She had his mobile number, it still shared the hook with the calendar on the kitchen door and every now and then she'd look at it quickly, as if checking the correct quota of eleven numbers. It was the only mobile phone number that she knew off by heart, yet she'd never once rung it. She lacked the confidence to phone just to say, hullo, how are you, how's France.

All of this was very different – the situation, the feelings – from simply missing someone. Missing someone causes one to feel incomplete, it's a vulnerable state. Tess had missed Em in a desperate, primal way when she'd been at work; a creeping, invasive hollowness that was only counteracted when her child was back with her. Over Joe, Tess did not feel fragile or gut-wrenched, she felt simply sad and alone because his company had recently enhanced her life. And though she currently kept the study door shut, as Joe always did when he was working, she couldn't create the illusion that he was in there. It seemed to her that, whichever room she was in, Joe was like an essential item of furniture suddenly gone. Nothing seemed quite right now. The time he'd spent at home recently had been so satisfying for her that it had shrunk her world, made it seem a safer and more intimate place; his presence had formed a moat and a drawbridge around her. It was a feeling of self-sufficiency. But with him gone, she felt cut off.

Strangely, though she had thought about Mary even while Joe had been home, her allegiance was now so firmly with Joe that whatever it was that prevented him mentioning his mother, was enough for Tess to respect. If there were sides to be taken, she was on his. Thoughts of Seb too, had dispersed as if they'd been but lively sparks from a bonfire – which have no real substance, not even ash. So it was unnerving, to say the least, to come across both people in quick succession a week after Joe's departure.

*　　*　　*

'Laura – she's gone again.'

'Who has?'

'Mrs S – or in your case, *Mary*.'

'Mary? You sure?'

'Just checked her room.'

'The morning room?'

'Not there.'

'Playing rummy?'

'No.'

'Sunroom? She does like the sunroom – sits herself down right in the far corner where she can gaze out to sea.'

'She's not in the sunroom. I told you, Laura – she's scarpered.'

'Well, we know where she'll be headed.'

'Doesn't make it any the less a pain in the arse – I've got

better things to do than chase through town for an eighty-year-old. She's crafty, that one. She never does as she's told. I don't know why you've such a soft spot for her.'

'She's not eighty – she's only seventy-five. It's her condition that makes her seem older.'

'Over there! Look, Laura – there she is, pegging off past Garnet Street.'

Laura had already left the room.

There was a scatter of elderly residents of the town taking the air on the elevated position of Marine Parade above the pier and beach. Laura had never become inured to their grace – their pace, the way they sat or stood, content for silent companionship, patient with each others' witterings. Mary, however, was practically jogging. It was as if the pensioners enjoying the view were acting their age while Mary defiantly was not. She appeared oblivious to the melancholy expanse of the North Sea, the majestic dominance of Huntcliff reaching out into it, the breadth of golden sands. She was walking off with a pace and purpose at odds with both her peers and the vista.

Laura always preferred to run before she could walk – because she knew it could startle the elderly lady if she approached at speed. So she'd run until Mary was in reach, then she'd walk briskly until she was abreast when finally she'd slow down and match her stride.

There she is. There she is. Between Diamond and Pearl Streets. Laura could slow down now.

'Mary,' she called in a sing-song voice from a little way off, to advise her she was all but caught. 'Mary,' she said again, gently this time, when she came up alongside her. She touched her elbow and fell into line with Mary's pace as if they were power-limping side by side intentionally. Soon enough, Laura gave Mary a quiet but insistent pull and the old lady stopped abruptly.

'I just want to go home, Laura dear,' she said with great lucidity and weariness. 'It's been so long.'

'I know,' Laura soothed, 'I know.' Then she said, Mary love – you've come out without a brolly. She passed Mary a small red folding umbrella.

Mary pulled out a patterned plastic rain hat from her coat pocket and gave Laura a look that said, you'll have to do better than that, dear.

Laura looked out to sea. A container ship almost stuck to the horizon. At this distance it looked as innocuous as a child's drawing of a generic boat. But she knew they were over a thousand feet long; she'd seen them hulking their way for fuel at Seal Sands at the mouth of the Tees. She glanced at Mary and thought how her life was like that container ship; mostly so distant that it was inconsequential though it could suddenly loom large and in pin-sharp focus and fill her mind. But it always sailed away from her until she was just an infirm pensioner, muttering to herself while she gazed out of the window in the overheated sunroom of an old-age home.

'Well – I wonder whose brolly this is,' Laura murmured because she often chose to appear less bright than she was – a ploy she used with the residents because she thought it was patronizing, intimidating even, to bandy her youth and savvy in their presence.

'Elsie's, probably,' said Mary, 'daft old bat.'

'Elsie is lovely,' Laura said.

'Or else it'll be Catherine's.' And Mary started to laugh. 'She's a one. She never knows where things are. She never knows where they belong. She forgets what they're for. Her fanny being a case in point.'

'Mrs S!' Laura protested.

'Everyone knows about Catherine's fanny,' Mary said and she had to stop completely because she was laughing so much, 'not that *she* does. She didn't know when it fell right out.'

'Mary, you're unkind – it was a prolapse. It can happen to anyone.'

'I'm not unkind,' Mary said very straight, quiet but sharp.

Laura wanted to say, I know you're not – it's your condition that's so unkind. Memory loss one day, inertia the next, sudden aggression or unpleasantness but, cruellest of all, acute lucidity every now and then. 'Catherine – Mrs Tiley – can't help it,' Laura said.

'Nor can I,' Mary said, stopping, 'nor can I.' She looked at Laura squarely. 'I may not have had a prolapse but I know something dreadful is happening to me. They're right to call me mad or doolally. I've heard them. I feel it coming. I know I try to run away – but often it's only when you bring me back again that I know I've even been.'

Laura linked arms with her and gave a little squeeze.

'Swallows is very comfortable, Laura dear. And you are a love. But I don't *want* to belong at Swallows. More than that, though, I don't want the mind I have now. It's like Babel in here sometimes.' She tapped the side of her head. 'And I'm trapped.'

'Let's get away from this cliff – there's a strong wind today. Let's follow the road round. Let's buy a fancy something from Chocolini's. Let's not talk about sad things.'

'Tomorrow – even this afternoon – Catherine might be talking about *me* because I may be talking claptrap again but of course I won't know it.'

'Let's not talk about Mrs Tiley.'

'I don't like what's happening to me, dear. It's the normal periods in between that make it so dreadful. I almost long for the day to come when I'll be permanently gaga. What fun I shall provide Mrs Tiley and the gang then.'

'Come, Mary, be kind to yourself.'

They turned into Milton Street, the jewel streets running down from Marine Parade acting as a filter to the brunt of

161

the slicing wind that can come off the North Sea at all times of the year.

'There's that girl of Joe's,' Mary suddenly said.

Laura looked ahead and saw Tess peering in through the ornamental grilles in front of the dusty old windows of Keith's Sports. 'So it is.'

'Haven't seen Joe, have we. Not for some time.'

'No,' Laura said, 'we haven't, not for a bit.'

'Dear!' Mary called ahead. 'Dear! Emmeline and mother! Emmeline and mother!'

Tess was surprised to hear her baby's name and more surprised to see who called her. She waited under the old iron and glass canopy as they approached.

'What *is* your name, dear?' Mary asked. 'Laura here thinks it's Tess but I don't think that's right. Joe's girl isn't called Tess, I keep telling her. Joe's girl is called Kate. It's been Kate for a long, long time.'

Kate? Who's Kate?

Laura could see Tess trying to compute the information.

'Not Kate,' Tess said as if it wasn't an issue, 'it really is Tess.'

'Well, I liked Kate,' Mary said indignantly, pursing her lips, which tempted Tess to say, well, Joe likes *me*.

'Chocolini's,' Laura said as if it was a password or peace offering. 'You coming, Tess?'

Ice cream was a luxury and an extravagance that Tess couldn't allow to cross her mind too often. It was, however, the perfect day for one, with May so close and the weather mild.

'Where are we going?' Mary asked.

'To Chocolini's – the fancy place you love,' Laura said.

'Would you like an ice cream, Mary?' Tess asked, clearing her throat.

'I'll have vanilla. A licky, not a cup,' Mary said. 'Kate, you are kind.'

'Tess,' Tess said quietly, feeling disconcerted by Kate, 'I'm Tess.'

She had to extend the offer to Laura. And she couldn't deny Em. And it would look very strange if she was the only one not to have an ice cream so Tess rifled through her purse and paid as quickly as she could, snapping the clasp shut when she was midway through calculating what remained. Mary and Em derived much merriment swapping a lick of strawberry for a lick of vanilla and they chuckled and conversed as easily as if they were contemporaries.

'He's gone again, has he?' Laura asked Tess, aside. Tess nodded. 'He didn't come by, you know, not this time. I don't know how, but she always knows when he's in town, does Mary. But he didn't come by this time, like.'

Tess felt compromised. She didn't want to consider that Joe might not be the dutiful son she'd like to earmark him as. But nor did she want to talk about Joe – she'd much rather ask about Kate. 'He was very busy. I don't know when he's coming home. A week or so, I imagine.' How to slip Kate in? Think of a way!

They licked their ice creams, both thoughtful for different reasons.

'You been together long, then?'

'Who?'

'You and Joe?'

'Me and Joe?' The ice cream tasted suddenly more lovely.

'You're an item, aren't you? Mary says you're Joe's girl.'

Tess knew she had a single chance, before confirming or denying this. 'And Kate?'

'Kate?'

'Mary's mixing me up with Kate today.'

'Don't worry about that, pet – she called me Hilary

yesterday, if that helps.' Only it didn't help Tess who wanted to know about Kate.

'I'm just the housekeeper. Sitter.'

The women had not looked at each other during this exchange. But they did so now. And Laura gave Tess a canny smile, accompanied by a snort which said, who are you trying to kid, hen? And Tess gave a fleeting widening of her eyes which said, don't! you're making me blush!

'You can start off as one thing and end as another,' Laura said, 'like our Aunt Win.'

Tess wondered what she meant but a slow wink from Laura suggested it was enough.

'And Kate?' Tess tried again. It sounded contrived, but at least it was out.

Only Mary had finished her ice cream. 'That was lovely, thank you, Tess.'

Much as Tess still wanted to hear about Kate, it was nicer to hear Mary using her own name again. Tess decided to leave it. She remembered how her grandmother had warned against prying. It's like sunbathing, she used to say – easy enough not to know when you've had enough and suddenly you're burnt.

So, together with Laura, she linked arms with Mary and, three abreast with the pushchair zigzagging, they monopolized the pavement all the way back to Swallows.

'Come by soon,' Laura said.

'I will,' said Tess. She turned to Mary. 'See you soon, Mary.'

'Not if I see you first, Kate.'

This time, Tess was overtly disappointed that the answering machine remained empty on her return. This time she said out loud, why don't you phone me? Then, finding herself standing stock-still staring at nothing on her way to the kitchen, she told herself to get a bloody grip and just bloody phone him instead. She took the piece of paper off the calendar hook and scrutinized the number she knew by heart.

Phone him to say what?

When are you coming home?

Why haven't you called?

Who's Kate?

What basis, though, did she have for asking any of those questions? After all, she had nothing to go on, nothing concrete at all. All he'd done was drink wine and break bread with her, leave her a Mars Bar or two. All that had happened was that he'd come in close to tell her something when they were crossing the Tees, which she'd interpreted as feeling like the verge of a kiss. And all he'd actually said was that he'd hold her hand if she didn't like heights. That's what you say to a child, isn't it. Or to anyone who's afraid of something.

She put the piece of paper back. She couldn't phone him. She could only think about him. And she found she could think about only him. She was intending to take a mug from the dresser to make a cup of tea. Instead, the photo of Joe bare-chested, in shorts and his safety hat by the unidentified bridge, caught her eye. She took it and sat down at the table. Maybe it wasn't such a long time ago. Maybe that's how he looks when he has a suntan and a hard hat. She flipped it over. It was dated just over three years previously. Above the date, the initials K.L.

Tess slumped. She felt deflated, deluded and silly – a schoolgirl crush she'd let run riot. Still, she was defenceless against stampeding thoughts.

K.L.

Bloody fucking *Kay Ell*.

Who are you, K.L.? Kate L. Who *are* you? Are you still here? Is he there with you now?

How can I *ever* compete?
How can *I* ever compete?

*   *   *

There's nothing like the unexpected attention of others to provide a timely distraction. Tess soon took herself to task, telling herself she needed a life beyond sprucing up an old house, or taking a mangy old mutt for walks whilst waiting in torment for the master to return. So she went to the toddler group at the library that afternoon and sat herself down by Lisa to sing nursery rhymes, in a circle of friendly women, babes in their laps. A group was meeting at another toddler drop-in tomorrow and Tess said, yes, OK, I'll be there. Good. Then she went to the station and looked into trains to Middlesbrough, calculating the fare against what she estimated petrol would cost. She discovered there were free t'ai chi classes and salsa dancing here in town. T'ai chi sounded good. Very balancing. But what about Em? There was always Em to think about. Tess thought about this familiar stalemate as she pushed her daughter past the bandstand near home. After the company and the decibel level and the newness of the singalong, she was pleased to have the playground to herself but she really was glad about the mums' group. It would be nice for Em. Not just for Em, for her too. Though she doubted whether her cheery little daughter ever felt remotely socially deprived, Tess had also been in the playground at busy times when she'd envied the other local mums their friendship. A wider circle would be good for them both.

A car horn beeping.

A car door closing.

'Hey!'

Tess looked to the road. Wolf, nonplussed, remained sprawled across the pavement outside the playground. By his side was Seb, waving. 'I recognized the dog,' he called. 'Haven't seen you in a while.'

'I've been – busy,' Tess called.

'Do I need a child to come in?' He looked theatrically up and down the street as if hoping to come across one.

Tess laughed. 'You can share this one?'

And as Seb came through to the play area, all brawny and attractively slouchy with his nonchalant amble, his blond hair licked into flicks and kinks by too much sea water, his constant half-smile, the premature but attractive laughter lines from grinning at the sun too much while surfing; as he came towards her, Tess thought to herself, bugger Joe and his disappearing act and his secret mother and Kate Bloody El. Bugger the lot of them.

'Haven't seen you around,' Seb said with disconcertingly steady eye contact.

'I've been around – perhaps you've been out on the waves.'

'Surf's been awesome. When are you going to let me take you out there?'

'Between you and me, Seb, you'd have more success asking me to jump out of a plane, than to surf. It's all right for you Aussies – it's in your genes.'

'What is it with you and the water?'

'It's not the water – it's the getting there.'

'The sand?'

'You could say.'

'I didn't realize quicksand was an issue in the UK.'

'Not quicksand!'

'Rip tide? Sandflies? Broken glass?' He paused. 'Jellyfish? Dog shit?'

'I just don't like beaches.'

'Piggyback?' Seb said. 'From the prom, across the beach, straight out to sea. You're thin. I'm fit.'

'Couldn't we just go for a coffee?' Tess said, not quite sure whether that sounded like she was rebuffing his offer or proposing a date.

Seb looked at her. 'You're on,' he said. 'How about now? It's teatime – excellent time for a cup of coffee.'

'Weren't you on your way somewhere? Your car is pointing up the road.'

'I was just cruising around, Tess, hoping to find someone to stand me a cup of coffee.'

'You make yourself sound like a kerb-crawler.'

'A coffee I'm happy to pay for,' Seb said, 'but not a blow-job.'

He said it so quickly it took a moment or two for Tess to register it and then he laughed at the gobsmack paralysing her face.

'So what do you say, Tess – coffee? Now?'

She looked at him. And she looked at Em who was fidgeting in the swing and starting to gripe. She'd missed her nap in favour of the singsong. Wolf was still playing dead outside the playground. Tess looked down towards the coast, and then up inland. They were equidistant from the coffee shop and her kitchen. She tried to work out if he paid for the coffee would it be a date and would she be beholden to him? Or, if *she* offered to make it, would he read this as a come-on? And then she asked herself, would either be such a bad thing?

'You could come back to the house?'

Seb's smile broadened until it was decidedly smirkish. 'I'd love to – thanks.'

'It'll have to be a quickie – I have loads to do.'

'A quickie? I told you, I'm happy with a coffee – I'm not expecting sexual favours.'

'I didn't mean –'

'You're blushing.'

'I mean –'

168

'I know,' he said, his smile now straight and kind.

'I'm just up there – leave your car here, if you like. Wolf!'

The walk home took longer than usual on account of conversation impeding the pace, yet when it came to it, Tess felt uncomfortable unlocking the door and inviting Seb in. She wasn't sure how Seb would look in Joe's space. And what if the answering machine was flashing?

It was predictably empty of messages – but this too caused her momentary regret.

'Jeez, this is a bit nice,' Seb said and his awe made him seem young and rather gauche.

'Glorious,' Tess said, now wondering whether the café would have been a better option. 'Go through to the kitchen. Can you give me a minute to settle Em in her cot?'

When she came down again, Seb was sitting at the table, his hands on his lap like a schoolboy. 'I gave the dog some water.'

'Thanks.'

'How long have you lived here?'

'I work here,' Tess said before wondering why she'd been so quick to say so. 'It's Joe Saunders's place.' Why had she, in a single sentence, changed her home back into his house? Now she was taking the picture from the dresser and passing it to Seb. 'His girlfriend Kate took it.'

Seb looked at the photo and wasn't sure what to say, really. He asked politely about Joe and was told he was an engineer who often worked abroad.

'I'm the housekeeper.'

'What a house to keep,' Seb said. 'What a place.'

'Actually, I'm more of a house-sitter,' she defined reluctantly.

'How long are you here for?'

Tess shrugged. 'I'm not sure, really. He said it's a long-term position. But it'll be for as long as he'll have me,

I suppose.' The notion of her impermanence, within this solid, steady house she'd so quickly called home, confronted her.

'Show us around, then,' Seb said.

But Tess realized she really didn't want to do that. Parameters hadn't crossed her mind until just then. A coffee was one thing. As was the gentle flirting. Ditto being on the seafront or in a playground with its public background noise. All of those were fine, manageable. But here in the kitchen, alone with a man, it was so quiet, so still – portentous almost. She could practically hear Seb think. And she thought he was probably thinking, wow, this chick has the whole place to herself.

He wasn't. He was thinking that Tess must be lonely up here on her own, cut off in such a lumbering great place; tied to it, what with the baby and the dog. And he really wanted to kiss her and he was wondering if she'd like that. And when might be a good time to try it. To suck it and see. She made a great cup of coffee and there'd been biscuits on a plate, plain digestives alternating with chocolate ones, displayed like petals.

She was returning the photo of her boss to the dresser. Seb sat as he was, watching her. He liked her bum. Her jeans were loose, sitting on hips; her waist was slim, shapely. He could already tell that she had cute tits. He pushed back his chair as she returned to the table and he pulled her right onto his lap, placing a hand quickly to her breast as he slipped his tongue into her mouth.

Tess was too surprised to do anything. And it felt so good which surprised her even more. And because it felt so good, she didn't do nothing for much longer – soon enough she was kissing Seb back.

But she didn't conjure Joe.

Nor did she think Seb Seb Seb.

She was preoccupied with the sensation of being desired, of being kissed and fondled again after so long.

With increasing enthusiasm, she responded to the welling lust to kiss back, to feel and fondle a male form. It was a feeling she remembered vividly but one that she'd tucked to the back of her mind like a holiday she knew she could not afford. Now it was at the forefront and it flowed through her blood to all the zones she'd cauterized since Dick. Since Em. The seam of her jeans was up against her crotch. Her crotch was against his thigh. Subconsciously, she was already rocking her pelvis.

I could have sex with him, right now, *Postman Always Rings Twice* style, on this kitchen table. I could strip off my top. I could unbutton his trousers and give him that blow-job. My hands are everywhere. And so are his.

It was the silent, searching look of the dog which stopped her. When she opened her eyes to sneak a look at Seb, she found her focus alighting on Wolf instead. He was sitting, head cocked, as if to say, what are you doing? Why are you doing *that* with *him*? Why can't you just wait and see?

'Can I have your number?'

'I don't have a mobile.'

'A number for the house?'

'It's not my phone.'

'Can I see you again, Tess – without the need for coffee?'

'Perhaps.'

'Are you playing hard to get?'

'No. I don't do games. My life is – complicated. My baby.'

'Perhaps I can swing by here, then? One evening? Bring fish and chips and a DVD?'

'Perhaps.'

'Look, here's my number. You call me.' And Seb slipped a piece of paper over the calendar hook so it obliterated Joe's

171

number entirely. 'I'm away for a week but please call me when I'm back. You're cute. I really like you. It would be fun. It could be good. We're foreigners in a strange land – we should get it together, babe.'

Chapter Sixteen

Tess reverberated between feeling relieved and yet miffed that Seb would be away for a week. She told herself, when she awoke the next morning, that if he hadn't gone away, she'd've phoned him that very day to say, yes, please, fish and chips and a DVD and more of that snogging. But she acknowledged that the brazenness of the thought came only because she knew to implement it was not possible. And anyway, hadn't she gone to bed the night before, early, a few hours after he left, feeling ambivalent? Seb was a nice guy, he looked good and he tasted good and he'd made her body fizz. But she had to concede he didn't measure up to Joe. Then she told herself that to harbour thoughts of Joe was ludicrous and to carry feelings for him was stupid. So that brought her back to thinking about Seb again. She wasn't sure what to think, she couldn't quite place him in fanciful daydreams – if she tried to, he appeared like a cardboard cut-out that she had to move from scenario to scenario. Whereas she frequently had to put up a No Entry sign in the places in her mind where Joe appeared enticingly whether or not she'd conjured him.

But kissing Seb had released thoughts of herself, about her self. Her body felt her own once more, finally distinct from the eighteen-month baby it had nurtured. It was back to being the sensual body of a healthy thirty-year-old. It didn't matter that she was by herself with only a dog and a toddler as an audience, post-kiss Tess felt sexy. For the first time since halfway through her pregnancy, she sought the space and privacy to invest in herself. Plying the dog and child with snacks, she sat in front of the mirror, looking and looking. Her hair now had a gloss and bounce that counteracted its need for a cut and style. Simply tucking it behind her ears, with a couple of Em's lilac slides, looked good and served to reveal the glow of her skin and the glint in her eyes. She winked at herself, she smiled at herself – and then she winked and smiled as if she was doing so for someone else's benefit.

I'm all right I am, she said quietly. She liked what she saw. It was a look she'd like to put to good use because it felt good to have.

A quieter voice whispered a thought before she went to bed that night. And the quieter voice said, if Seb *was* here you know you wouldn't have phoned him. She thought how the fun was in the memory, how there was safety in his distance. But then she wondered whether it had nothing to do with shyness or insecurity on her part – perhaps she wouldn't have phoned Seb because it was Joe she was holding out for. The friendly young surfer and the tetchy bridge builder. However, going on pure facts, if she was a sexy mama to the former and simply a house-sitter to the latter, oughtn't she to revaluate on whom her sights were set?

So, Seb's kiss hadn't actually settled a day and a night later. Certainly, it had made her body feel very good, cranking those long-dormant cogs of concupiscence back into motion. But it hadn't filtered through to her soul. And she had to admit to herself as she went to sleep that his kiss had stuck slightly in the back of her throat.

*

It had been a conscious decision of Joe's not to phone home which wasn't to say that he hadn't thought about Tess. He had. Often. And had intended to phone, early on particularly. But at the same time, absence began to do strange things to his heart – if initially it had made it fonder now with a little distance, it was also making it befuddled. Phone her and say – what? Phone to hear – what? Didn't phoning run the risk of long-distance silences? Might that not lead to those peculiar but customary snipes? He could have kissed her, that night on the Transporter, or at home later. He'd badly wanted to and he'd thought back over it since. But now he asked himself what indication if any had she given that she'd kiss him back? Of course, that wasn't a reason for not kissing her, but it was reason enough not to phone. Joe thought about it, about the kiss that hadn't happened; if it had, then what – after an impromptu kiss, *then what*?

Much as he liked impromptu and he was accustomed to impromptu, it had always been in his control, it had always been his choice and always slotted in well with his life. He really could do without any further complications. There was an almighty fuck-up on the project (they were his calculations but he couldn't work out how the error had occurred), so the straight sex on offer from Nathalie provided a perfect antidote to the problems on site. Crucial respite from daily headaches came between the sheets, between Nathalie's great legs where he could empty his mind along with his balls. He was accustomed to the way he'd set up his life, it worked for him. Why fix it if it ain't broke. He already had a broken bridge to fix and that was his priority. Tess and Saltburn, even Wolf, faded from the forefront quickly. What dominated his mind were complex issues of torsion and endless miles of steel cable. The presence of Nathalie helped him sleep at night; an orgasm being a shortcut to a few hours of dreamless brain-rest.

Then the time came when Joe was needed back in England. And that's when Tess returned to his mind, with the unexpected suddenness of a spring bulb suddenly punctuating the dark monotony of bare winter earth. It wasn't so much an image of her, but the notion of her and it sent a pang through him – not a lift, not a buzz, but a shot of emotion he couldn't readily identify. A longing to be back. A feeling that his home fires had been kept burning, that his house would be warm, that supper might await him, with its awkward hors d'oeuvres of polite conversation settling in to a relaxed main course of nattering and laughter, the likes of which he'd never known prior to Tess – certainly not in that house. Chatting with mouths full, elbows on the table, licking fingers to dab up spilt salt and excess gravy. Seconds, even thirds. And then lengthy desserts, appetite already well sated, but feeding an excuse to stay at the table and maintain the convivial communication, the comfort of company, the warmth before bedtime. He'd never drunk so much tea in his life.

It was odd, the way the desire to be back swooped through him. Prior to this trip, though he'd thought about Tess, he hadn't missed her. He hadn't spent much time thinking about those meals or about the house – he'd been far too preoccupied to do so. Anyway, over the years, he'd carefully trained his affection to steer clear of home because home had not been a constant in his life since he was old enough to leave. It had been little more than a storage facility for his belongings, a place to stay when he was in England, on a par with apartments or hotels elsewhere but without the added extras of the Nathalies and Rachels and the rest.

However, thoughts of home now came with a picture of Tess in them, Wolf too of course, even Emmeline. And no longer was that picture in a drab palette, it was a freshly painted new scene, in mould-resistant paint in the heritage colours on offer at the DIY store. His books and music

176

painstakingly alphabetized. And the kitchen ordered and always warm. Bathrooms bright. Bedrooms aired. A growing bonfire heap, piled with stuff he wouldn't miss but had never thought of ejecting. The house felt cleansed and a new side of it had been revealed. Cracks hadn't been painted over, they'd been systematically Polyfillaed and sanded smooth. New paint had released a latent energy from those silent old walls. And though Joe ridiculed himself for wondering if the pang had anything to do with homesickness, he couldn't deny that the sensation of it made him want to hasten his journey back.

He phoned.

'The Resolution – hullo?'

How could he have forgotten her elevation of his house to semi-stately! Daft girl. He now wished he'd phoned before.

'Tess.'

'Joe?'

'It is indeed. The return of the native. Almost. Tomorrow – I'll be back tomorrow.'

'Goody,' said Tess, though she quickly changed it to 'very good.'

'Must go, see you then.'

'Safe journey – see you tomorrow.'

When Joe stared at the screen on his mobile until it darkened into standby mode, he thought to himself how only Tess could say *goody*. He could visualize her, standing in the hallway wearing some crap sweatshirt, saying *goody*! Probably giving Wolf the thumbs-up. She'd be telling the dog and the baby that he'd be home tomorrow, unconcerned by their inability to reply. Joe mused on her self-sufficiency, how she seemed quite content with the one-way conversation that living with a dog and a baby surely brought with it. Who says goody these days? Nathalie says *bien sur* – and that has a whole different ring to it.

And then Nathalie came into the room. And Joe thought, home tomorrow but tonight I'm here.

And he thought, very briefly, of his mother. How he wasn't allowed down from the dinner table of his childhood until he'd eaten everything up. The kitchen of those years was a place he didn't much like. And he thought, very briefly this time, of sharing supper in his kitchen tomorrow night. A very different place now Tess had whipped through it with her cleaning fluids and ruthlessness and artistically arranged condiments. And before Joe focused on the semi-naked marvel of Nathalie he did wonder, fleetingly, who's cooking tomorrow night?

Then he blinked away thoughts of home to feast his eyes on Nathalie instead. She looked appetizing in that minuscule shimmering thing she was wearing and Joe thought, it would be a shame to let it go to waste – if it's handed to you on a plate then eat it all up.

*   *   *

When the phone rang around the time Joe was due back, Tess's spirits plummeted as she anticipated a delay or, worse, cancellation. She'd already shopped – dinner for two despite it decimating the contents of her purse. And she'd scrubbed, hoovered and spritzed; flinging open all the windows so that the keen spring breeze could breathe into the house from the woods over the road. But the phone continued to ring and Tess knew it could only be Joe which meant there was a problem. Reluctantly, she answered it, eschewing her more usual formal greeting for a simple hullo.

'*ullo?*'

It wasn't Joe. It was just some foreign *'ullo*. Hurray! It's not Joe! Joe *is* coming home, Joe *will* be here any minute. Joe is on his way.

'The Resolution – can I help you?'

'Joe Saunders – he is there?' A French woman. Tess took exception to the way she pronounced his surname. Sow – like a female pig. Sow'n Dairs. She also objected to the slightly accusatory tone – *he is there?* Even a thick accent and scant English wouldn't preclude such a caller rephrasing it as, may I speak with Mr Saunders? or, hullo, is Joe Saunders there?

Why the presumption? And how about a little less familiarity? And just as Tess was about to wonder who on earth this woman was, she suddenly thought, oh Shit, is this *Kate*? But she quickly summoned her schoolgirl French and appeased herself that Kate is not a name indigenous to the Gauls. This must be someone from the French office, that's all.

'He hasn't arrived back,' Tess said and she made sure her voice was warm because then this woman could report back to Joe how amenable the lady at his house had seemed. 'I'm expecting him any minute. May I take a message?'

There was a long pause. 'Who are *you*?'

Tess was taken aback that the question had been asked of her before she'd had the chance to pose it to the caller. But more disconcerting was the inflection. Someone from his office wouldn't have asked. They'd've said who they were instead. Zis is Marie-Claudette from ze office. Zis is Celestine from Le Pont du M. Saunders; I av a fax for Mr Sow'n Dairs.

But here was a voice demanding to know who Tess was. This accusatory but undeniably sexy French voice wanted to know what she was doing there. This voice was probably expecting her to say, I'm Tess the house-sitter. I walk Joe's dog. I work for Mr Saunders. I'm taking his messages for him.

'This is Tess,' she said instead, slowly and clearly, as if she considered the question slightly preposterous and somewhat impertinent.

'Tess – who?'

179

Tess thought about it. She didn't need to give her surname to answer that question. If the conversation was ever to have any comeback, Tess could just claim her intention had been lost in translation. 'I'm Joe's Tess,' she said.

There was a snort. 'Well, *Tess*, please when Joe arrives, you will tell him he leave his BlackBerry at my apartment.'

'BlackBerry. Apartment,' Tess said as if she was jotting it down.

'You tell him he leave it *here*. In my bed.'

And there was no time for Tess to be stunned into silence or to think, shit, shit, parry back – quick! or even to repeat it as if she was taking notes, because the caller had hung up. The grandfather clock tocked but time had stopped for Tess. He has a girlfriend. The notion, the reality, slammed into her with such force that she sat down hard and fought for breath. With the air silent but still charged, she wanted to shout, to vent, to wail, but Em had come toddling up to her, striking a stab of reality. What Tess wanted most was something she just couldn't have. She couldn't have Joe. She couldn't even have ten minutes all to herself, to think, to brood, to practise a soliloquy in front of the bathroom mirror. Just ten minutes, that's what she wanted. In fact, she'd settle for five. But Em allowed her just a few seconds.

'What is it, Em?'

The toddler could only grouch back her inability to explain.

Eventually, Tess found out that grapes would appease her daughter and, as she peeled and deseeded them, she snatched back moments to reflect. The outcome was somewhat melodramatic.

I am here and I am taking messages for Joe. I'm here because he isn't – and that's the point of me. That's my job.

She tried briefly, unsuccessfully, to equalize the score by deciding that the caller was some landlady who goes in to clean the apartment when Joe leaves.

A French version of me.

She doubted it, though. But, worse, she doubted herself now.

Tess put herself on autopilot; singing row-row-row-your-boat, letting Wolf out and then back in again, hanging out a white wash, going to the toilet. She knew it was ridiculous but everything she did was underscored by a silent chant. Stupid French cow, stupid French cow. French Sow. Sow'n Dairs. Joe leaving his phone in an apartment was one thing. In this woman's bed, with her velvety guttural emphasis on the possessive pronoun, was quite another. Who is she? Is she Kate? *Can* you be French and be called Kate?

But I thought he wanted to kiss *me*.

* * *

So Joe arrived back with Tess wanting to belt him. And she knew if she told him about the call straight away, she might very well do that. But she bit her tongue so she could just soak up a little of him first; absorb the warmth from his expansive smile, fill her ears with his voice, come close to him so she could brush by, accidentally on purpose, as she went to make tea, collecting a little of his physicality like it was magic dust that could seep through her clothes, through her skin and deep into her, carrying with it a cure. She just needed a little time to act as though she was fine, time to enjoy the ritual of making two cups again. Just five more minutes of him asking her this and that. Time to glance over at him leaning casually against the wall, or relaxing at the kitchen table, or giving his head a scratch, stifling a yawn, having a stretch. The hair on his stomach. How long had it been since she'd seen that? She'd only seen it the once.

'What's for supper, then?' he asked. 'I'm looking forward to a home-cooked meal.'

Tess felt peculiarly triumphant – as if he'd been underfed or poorly nourished whilst he'd been away. Ha! Kate's obviously a shit chef! But then Tess thought, shit! I bet they eat out every night in romantic little bistros. And then she thought, why am I fretting? Why does this hurt? She could neither justify the feelings – yet nor could she deny them either.

It was only when she began to cook, with Joe wittering on in a friendly, anodyne way, that Tess was consumed with an invasive sadness. An intense and private remorse that there was indeed nothing going on. Because Kate was real. And Tess had been so happy to delude herself with daft little daydreams this last fortnight. Must get a grip. Must not be sad. What would my grandmother say? She told me to cook with love. She said, happiness is like seasoning, tiredness dulls flavours, anger turns food sour but sadness can kill a dish completely while love can flavour a dish to perfection.

So Tess added a lot of garlic and a pinch from every herb jar to counteract this. She didn't have the stomach to taste it. But Wolf gazed up at her expectantly and Joe kept saying, wow, smells great, when do we eat? And she kept thinking to herself, who am I cooking for? *Who* am I cooking for?

They ate. It was easy enough to laugh when Joe said something funny, to smile when he smiled at her, to be captivated by his bridge talk and appalled at the extreme hassles of the particular project. But it wasn't easy to strike up the conversation herself.

'You're not very chatty, Miss Tess,' he remarked, thinking she'd say, oh, I'm just tired – Wolf/ Emmeline had me up in the night. He certainly wasn't expecting the monotone response when it came.

'Miss Tess?'

'Kate called. She has your BlackBerry.'

It made no sense.

'Kate?'

'Yes, she called – about half an hour before you arrived home.'

'My BlackBerry?'

Tess sighed. 'Yes, Joe, your BlackBerry. You left it at Kate's. At her apartment. In her *bed*.' And she scraped back her chair and dumped her plates beside the sink and walked out of the kitchen saying she was knackered, she was going to bed, goodnight.

Joe remained at the table wanting to laugh and groan simultaneously. Laugh because there was something so compelling about Tess when she was stroppy – the effect it had on him was the polar opposite of that which she intended. He just wanted to stop her and tuck her hair behind her ears and cup her face in his hands and call her a mad woman and tell her she was extremely attractive when she was pissed off and kiss her. But he had to groan because he *had* left his BlackBerry in France; groan because Nathalie *had* phoned here and got Tess and from Tess's reaction and the fact that she reported the sodding thing was in her apartment *in her bed*, Nathalie had obviously made it plain to Tess that though this wasn't a business call, she meant business. Groan because why did Nathalie call herself Kate? Groan because it complicated things with Nathalie – he didn't want to have to explain away Tess but nor did he want to relinquish the easy sex. Not yet. And how the fuck could he call Nathalie anyway – she had his BlackBerry and the only record he had of her number was in the bloody thing. He knew he should have synched the bloody thing with his computer. And then Joe realized in all of this there were more groans than laughs. He'd been travelling all day, for God's sake. He was tired, he had a lot on his mind far more pressing than angry lovers changing their names and petulant house-sitters stomping around his home. More groans than laughs, then – that was *not* what he wanted in life, it went coarsely against the grain of all he'd spent the last twenty years cultivating.

Bedtime.
The difference between men and women.
Oblivion in an instant for Joe.
A sleepless night for Tess.

Chapter Seventeen

She was either going to have to say, sorry about last night, or persuade herself that she was entitled to her displeasure and thus manufacture a moral high ground to stomp around on today as well. Had she not been so tired, the former would have struck her as the right thing to do as well as the simplest and most sensible. But her lack of sleep made her crotchety and that made it easier to opt for the latter. She'd passed Joe in the hallway. He'd said good morning cheerily enough but with an audible question mark too. She'd smiled curtly before clattering around in the kitchen, giving an almighty sigh as she removed to the utility room Joe's kicked-off shoes. She also gave Wolf short shrift for darting around her legs with the slinkiness of a silverfish, his trademark display of affection which on all other days Tess would trip over and laugh at.

Joe was nonplussed, wondering quite what had happened to strip this girl of her artless sweetness, to have triggered instead the thunderous demeanour she was hurling around his house. He was about to suggest a cup of tea when he heard the front door slam and glanced from the window to see Tess marching off down the driveway, the wheels of the buggy skittering over the gravel as if she was making it travel faster than it was able.

Fresh air didn't seem to have lifted her mood or smoothed the furrow to her brow when she returned. She declined his offer of a sandwich and, later, she called downstairs that she wasn't hungry when he'd announced, for the second time, that supper was ready.

In her room she sat by the open window, trying to combat the mouth-watering drifts of lamb chops and sautéed potatoes filtering up from the kitchen by switching on the radio so she could concentrate on a sound other than her hunger pangs. She gave it an hour, then she eased open the bedroom door, leant over the banister and listened for sounds of activity. Hearing none, she descended the stairs, craning until she could see that Joe's study door was closed. Downstairs, the kitchen was in darkness and from the gap between study door and floor, she could see the light was on in there. She walked softly, quickly, over the flagstones in the hallway and once in the kitchen, she switched on the light in the extractor hood over the cooker – because the main light buzzed when it flickered into life. She'd meant to suggest to Joe that he consider replacing the strip lighting with something less harsh. What did it matter now? She opened the fridge door. Two lamb chops under cling film on a plate. She didn't take it to the table, but ate them then and there, using her fingers, too hungry to chew properly, swallowing mouthfuls that caught in her throat, sucking at the frills of meat left clinging to the bone.

'Can't resist my cooking, hey?'

She spun. Joe was standing there leaning against the door-frame in his usual casual stance. Her first thought was to say that the chops were tough, leathery even, but the implicit nastiness shocked her.

'Ta,' she said instead, plucking an apple and biting into

it smartly. She made to leave, winking at Wolf as she went but avoiding Joe's eyes. The problem was, he was blocking the doorway. She realized this halfway across the kitchen, by which time it was a little idiotic to retrace her steps, go through the utility room, through the boot room, out to the garden, circumnavigate half the house and enter through the front door. She did, though, momentarily consider it. No, she'd just have to stand her ground and keep moving.

'Excuse me,' she said, when she was in danger of treading on his socked feet.

Joe moved but as she passed, he caught her arm – he didn't hold on to it, he just caught it for a moment before letting it go.

'Tess, why are you being so stroppy?' he said to her back.

'I'm not,' she said, without turning.

'And petulant.'

'I'm *not*.'

'You are. You are being stroppy and petulant. What's up?'

'Nothing.'

'You're being stroppy and petulant and uncommunicative. I don't like it.'

This was too much for her to tolerate without eye contact. She spun around.

'Go to hell!'

'Shall I add "insulting" to the litany, then?' Joe's arms were folded but no longer in a relaxed way; his eyes had narrowed, he appeared taller, older, stern.

She said nothing, just stared at the space between them.

'And aggressive – that goes on it too. For fuck's sake, Tess, if I've done something to upset you, will you please have the courtesy to tell me what?'

The deeper and darker Tess's mood became, the more difficult it was to haul herself out. If she was mad at Joe, she was also livid with herself. She'd gone beyond the point of being able to say, sorry about that – I'm just being a silly moo. She was now hopelessly trapped in the vortex of her own bad temper.

And then she looked at Joe and she knew why. What she saw she couldn't hate, she couldn't even dislike – what she saw was what she wanted. That's why she was hurting. The nearly kiss. The loaded silences. The eye contact lasting that exhilarating moment too long. The banter. The teasing. The making time to be – together. She had thought she was wanted too. But that was then, she told herself, that was way back then. That was before the reality of Kate. Before his phone in her bed. She felt caught between the strange dichotomy of mourning the kiss that never was, and outraged at Joe's duplicity. Only a quiet side of her, which she was too preoccupied to hear, wondered if she was entitled to feel either.

'Tess?'

She turned away.

'Oh, for God's sake,' he said. 'Grow up.'

She swung round to face him, as if she was about to land a punch. 'You should have said something about Kate, you know. Because – you were going to kiss me on the Transformer Bridge. You *were*. It's not nice for me – I'd been looking forward to you coming back, idiot that I am. Don't you play with me, Joe Saunders, don't you *dare* play with me.'

Her eyes might be bristling with indignation but her voice was wavering and Joe hadn't the heart to correct her transformer bridge to his Transporter Bridge or say, don't you mean *toy* with me?

'Tess, can we please sort this Kate business out? Why do you keep harping on about someone called Kate?'

Fury scratched itself across Tess's face. 'You're going to deny it? Oh, come on, Joe. Tell me to my face that your phone isn't in the bed of some girlfriend in France?'

188

Joe gave himself a moment. 'I am not in a relationship with anyone.'

'Forgive the semantics,' Tess said. 'Your phone is in the bed of some woman you're shagging, then. Go on then – deny it.' Yet as soon as she said it, she suddenly dreaded the confirmation.

Again, Joe paused while he organized his response. 'Look, I don't know why you think it's any of your business but OK then, there is a woman in France who I –' He paused. Whom he what, exactly. 'There's a woman in France – it's not a relationship. But yes, I sleep with her – it's just casual.'

Tess looked appalled, as if she'd just been winded. He was not going to feel guilty – which wasn't to say that her visible distress didn't unnerve him.

For Tess, it wasn't the specifics of Joe's consensual fuck-buddy set-up that had stabbed her (she'd had to broaden her outlook when she met Dick); it was Joe referring to Kate as *a woman*. She felt a girl by comparison, diminished somehow. She couldn't imagine any man referring to her as a woman, despite the fact that she was a mother. She felt suddenly small, unappealing, defeated by Kate and her grown-up, no-strings womanly sexiness. She was acutely aware of standing in this man's kitchen with a sulky pout across her face, and stupid Winnie-the-Pooh socks on her feet, her figure swamped and denied by her shapeless hoody and her slack jeans. She felt ashamed of herself and she wished she could look up at him and tell him so. But if she looked at him, he'd look at her and all he'd see was her flushed face and the socks and the sweatshirt and the hair that desperately needed a cut and could do with a wash too.

Joe wanted her to speak to him and he wanted to say something to make her feel a little better. 'Tess, if it helps, she isn't Kate – she's Nathalie.' His tone was gentle. He thought the information would appease her – if she thought she had the wrong name, she might think she had the wrong end of the stick too.

However, Tess's hands fell so sharply to her side that when they hit her thighs it sounded as though she'd slapped herself and hard. 'Great, so you've got more than one on the go.' She could cry but she fought to glower instead. 'One for love, one for sex – and me to bandy about in some fucked-up game?'

'*Game?* What on earth are you on about?'

Do not cry. Don't you bloody dare cry. 'You *were* going to kiss me on the bloody bridge!'

Joe paused. This was true.

'You were going to kiss *me*. You could've, you know.'

She sounded defeated and she looked broken.

Was he meant to reach out for her? Look at her, having a silent battle against tears – he could hear it in the brittle croak of her voice. He could so easily put his arms around her, coax that crumpled face up to his lips. Plant the kiss that had germinated that night on the bridge. But he really didn't want to kiss her now – not with her like this.

'I was, Tess. You're right – that night I really did want to kiss you. And it wasn't just a heat-of-the-moment thing. I was about to kiss you on the bridge that night. And when we got back – I could've done so then too.'

'But you didn't!'

'Because you gave me no signs of reciprocation.'

Tess stamped with frustration. It was so true. He was absolutely right and her indignation came from Joe's perception. It was maddening. The sides of the hole she'd dug herself were crumbling and she could not work out how to clamber back to normality.

'Well! I'm bloody glad I didn't. We wouldn't want you *three*-timing Kate, would we!'

Joe closed his eyes, placing fingers against his temples as

if to keep his temper in check, or to protect himself from further onslaught, or to guard against the threat of a headache of blinding proportions.

'I do not know a Kate, Tess.'

'You're lying – I've seen the photo!' Tess was not going to listen to him or think before she spoke.

'The *photo*? What photo?'

'This one, idiot!' And Tess darted back in to the kitchen, snatched the photo off the dresser and brandished it at Joe. '*This* one – look. K.L. See! *K.L.* – and the date on the back and smiley loved-up Joe on the front.'

Joe took the photo from her as if he'd never seen it before. He turned it over and over; from the photo on the front to the writing on the back. Then he looked at Tess but she gave him no chance to speak. She was on a mission to have her *coup de grâce*; a little girl power over Kate and Nathalie, a swipe at Joe for saying she'd given the impression she didn't want to be kissed when she had.

'Anyway,' she said, 'I don't need the photo to know about Kate. Your mother has told me all about her.'

'My *mother*?'

'Yes, Joe. Your mother. You know – the secret one you keep squirrelled away at Swallows. I thought I was seeing ghosts – someone lurking outside the house at weird times. And one day I confronted this little old lady loitering in the garden and what do you know, she used to live here!'

'You met my mother?'

'More than met – I visit her now. I've had her here for tea, for a little sit-down. I drove her back to Swallows. I bought her an ice cream. I chat to the other biddies. So yes, I know your mother, Joe, and *she* told me all about Kate.'

Joe said nothing. But he needn't have said a thing for Tess

to know in an instant that something was very wrong. He was no longer looking at the photo, he was looking utterly poleaxed. She saw that this had nothing to do with Kate or Nathalie or Tess – his expression then had been one of wry bemusement. Now something far more fundamental, something darker altogether, striated his face. He turned his back on Tess and walked off, whistling for Wolf who didn't give her even a glance as he trotted after his master for a late-night ramble.

Tess sat by herself for a while trying to figure out what had just happened. She felt no triumph, she just felt panicked. When that subsided, she experienced surges of dread and remorse. What had she done and what could she do? Was there anything she could salvage from the jagged twists of the horribly crossed barbed wires? She tried to tell herself that she'd saved herself future hurt by exposing Joe's duplicity, or even triplicity. But then she pointed out to herself that, in doing so, she'd also forfeited the possibility of ever having that kiss and being able to return one. And what was she to think about his reaction to his mother? She couldn't work that one out at all. By the time she went to bed, though, she deeply regretted her tirade. If only she'd shut up about Kate and Nathalie. If she'd just shut up instead of flying off the handle, then there could have been room for her in Joe's life. Her more involved presence might have furnished him with enough to decide there was no room for the other two. But then she told herself her high self-regard was ludicrous. And so her low self-esteem slid back around her like a constrictor.

I'm just his house-sitter.

And beyond that I'm just a single mum who has run away from a mess of my own making that I fear I'll never be able to clear up.

The look on Joe's face when she told him about his mother.

She might have made a fool of herself venting about the other women. But the look on his face when she told him about his mother. She had been wrong but she had no idea how to make it right.

They met again, in the kitchen, the next morning. Tess shuffled in meekly, fussing quietly around Em. Wolf was spread out in a deep, twitchless sleep, as if he'd been up all night and his battery was dead. Joe was at the stove, cooking a fry-up.

'Breakfast?' he asked and Tess tried to analyse his tone of voice. It sounded normal really, friendly even.

'Um –' She didn't have an appetite. She didn't have words, either. 'OK.'

'The works?'

'Thank you.'

Five minutes later, a loaded plate was laid before her. She looked up at Joe who was looking down on her, his expressionless face somehow contradicting the gesture of making her breakfast. Actually, he wasn't expressionless, he was closed down, shut off – as if he was giving her breakfast and nothing else.

She looked at the eggs, sunny side up, a little of the browned butter flicked back over the white – Joe's forte. She'd lauded it when he first cooked her one. He'd said, why thank you, ma'am, and it had made her laugh. The morning after, he'd cooked her the same again, and in front of her place setting was a silver salt and pepper set. She'd seasoned her food and held her cutlery with her little finger stuck out at a theatrical angle and that had made Joe laugh. You are a one, he'd said, flicking the tea towel over his shoulder, rolling up his shirt-sleeves to wash up. You are a one, Miss Tess.

He'd been whistling that morning. Never had eggs tasted so lovely. She'd eaten her breakfast listening to him, watching his back as he washed up. The way his shirt caught over his shoulder blades. How it would feel to rest her face between them.

Now look at him – an awful lot to see, nothing coming back. Tess looked down at her plate, thoughts racing to say the right thing.

'Joe?' She forced herself to maintain eye contact though she'd rather slip under the table and lie alongside Wolf. 'I'm very, very sorry.'

She tried to analyse the quick shrug Joe gave her. Reluctantly, she had to admit the answer it gave was that whatever she said, the damage was done.

They ate in silence. Tess cleared the plates. When she turned from the sink, Joe had gone from the kitchen.

She loitered around the house and garden, playing with Em though her mind was elsewhere – a failing that any toddler won't tolerate and will counteract with whingeiness.

'Sorry, baby girl. Mummy's been naughty. Mummy needs to make things better. Silly, silly Mummy.'

Em called Tess silly and Tess didn't know whether to laugh or weep.

Joe didn't want tea – she'd twice knocked on the study door to offer it.

'There's a doorstep sandwich for you, on the kitchen table. With pickle,' she said later. But by the time she came back downstairs from settling Em for her nap, the plate had gone and the study door remained resolutely shut. In the early evening, while running a bath for Em, Tess heard the crunch of tyre on gravel and she hurtled to the window to watch Joe drive away. She darted down to the kitchen. Back through to the hall. Upstairs to her bedroom. No note. Nothing. Just gone.

She was devastated, incapable of doing anything for the

rest of the evening apart from sitting downstairs in the drawing room, in a tiny huddle on the capacious sofa, her lolling arm perfectly placed to run Wolf's ears through her fingers, an action conducive to contemplation.

Have I screwed things up?

or

Did I have a lucky escape?

but

Why didn't he leave even a note?

and

Where has he gone?

but

When will he be back?

and

What should I do?

but

Can I do *anything*?

'I need to build a bridge,' Tess told Wolf. She felt so tired, too tired to go upstairs to bed even though she was now cold, down here. 'I need to build a bridge but I don't know how.'

She stirred and woke. From the stillness and the silence, it was obviously very late. She felt discombobulated and stiff-necked from her slump on the sofa. Very cold. And suddenly in a panic at the looming presence of someone else in the room.

'Sorry – I didn't mean to wake you.'

'Joe? No, it's OK.' Tess scrabbled to sit herself up. 'I must've dozed off – what time is it? I'm—'

But Joe interjected. 'I'm off.'

Tess stared at him. 'Off?'

'France. Elsewhere.'

Words careened around Tess's head while she frantically

tried to arrange them into sentences. Practicalities – when where how long. Declarations of regret – I shouldn't have said what I said in the way I said it. Proclamations of intent – if you kiss me now I *will* kiss you back. Naggings of insecurity – France? Oh shit that means Kate and Nathalie. A need to make amends. I'm sorry, Joe, sorry for – it's just, it's just.

But before she could formulate a single sentence, he delivered answers to questions she hadn't yet prepared.

'My mother has dementia,' he said, 'early-onset dementia after a fall and a stroke almost two years ago. She is safer at Swallows. Even before the dementia, she wasn't living here. She hadn't for quite some time. And the dementia might cause her to think this place is still her home, but her dementia does not mean that she is now somehow welcome.'

Tess opened her mouth though she knew she was speechless.

'I'll be gone for a few weeks,' Joe said flatly; he glanced across to Wolf and then looked at Tess. 'You are welcome to stay here in that time – but it would probably be best if you look for a position elsewhere.'

There was a lump that was threatening to obstruct her breathing, but the dryness in her mouth made it impossible to swallow; as if the sides of her throat were coated with sandpaper, rasping together. Joe made to leave but hovered in the doorway and looked back over his shoulder, directly at Tess.

'There is no Kate, Tess,' he said. 'The initials K.L. on the back of that photograph? They stand for Kuala Lumpur. It's a commonly used diminutive – *Kay Ell*. I was involved on a project there. The photo was taken by Taki Kanero, a colleague and great friend of mine. He's in his fifties, a lovely man with a wife and two – no, three now – children.'

Chapter Eighteen

As soon as the seatbelt sign went off, Joe unbuckled, reclined
his seat, closed his eyes and willed sleep. But this was not
possible, partly because the level of organization required for
his impromptu return to France had left him wired, partly
because his fellow travellers in row 12 were two elderly ladies
yaketting away fifteen to the dozen. He might not be able to
sleep but he could certainly make it look as if he was and
avoid a flight's worth of pleasantries. Countering the steady
motion of the plane, his mind whirred like a small tornado,
plucking elements of the preceding days and swirling them
in an eddy with his plans for the next few days. Tess and
Nathalie and his mother chased each other round and round
his mind's eye, while the Transporter Bridge and the bridge
in KL and the new bridge he was returning to, vied for his
attention; the khaki water of the Tees running into the clearer
navy of the Sungai Klang, both running dry on reaching the
lush valley landscape of his bridge in progress. Oh, for God's
sake, couldn't he just think of one thing at a time? More to
the point, couldn't he just empty his mind completely? He
tried to cue in to the sounds of the plane, the pressurized
cabin, the chirruping chit-chat in row 12, the drifts of people's

conversations in the neighbouring rows, the clatter of the trolleys being prepared for their pedantic passage up and down the aisle. He found he could not. His mind was preoccupied and in his mind's eye, the spiral of women had slowed down and it was thoughts of Tess that solicited him first.

Taken on its own, Tess's rant about the other women – even the fictitious Kate – could have been quite flattering, really. Certainly, it fed Joe's ego but more than that there was something quite nourishing about the strength of Tess's feelings towards him, about which he had hitherto been unsure. He thought about this as the plane settled into its altitude. He recalled her ire, the way her eyes darkened with glinting indignation and her jealousy carved itself in the twist between her eyebrows, the purse of her lips. The contortions of her face relating directly to the intensity of her feelings for him. He thought of her brandishing the KL photo with furious triumph, ignorant of the prosaic truth behind the picture. How he could have laughed; how he could do so right now. She'd been so sure, she had kept it until the perfect moment – her trump card with which she could indict Joe, have him fall to his knees, have him entreat her. Plead, even. Kate was then, I don't love her, she means nothing – it's you I want, Tess.

Actually, he had never had a girl called Kate. He didn't even know a Kate. Silly old Tess, in such a tizz. The creeping redness around her throat, the change in her voice, her fiery face. She'd actually stamped. The hand not holding the photo had been in a fist. But she hadn't been rendered ugly and he hadn't felt repelled at the time. Even now he was still struck how all that infuriated him about her colluded with all that he liked and together, they welded an attraction for a woman who was complex, colourful, real.

Now Nathalie – she wasn't remotely complex, her underwear was colourful and his time with her existed outside reality.

There was an element of playing at a laissez-faire situation between broad-minded consenting adults. No chit-chat, no pea-squashing, no seconds of custard or endless cups of tea. No gentle teasing, not much laughter. Time spent with Nathalie was about constructing a reality where life was refreshingly uncomplicated, nothing to argue about, little to discuss, no need for extraneous chat – just a fantastic glut of sex which made them feel so good about themselves. What attracted Joe to Tess was what also irritated him about her – the gamut of emotions brought about by the slightest thing. Now he thought of Nathalie, attractive, available, aloof – no demands, just sexual abandon on tap. Nathalie made him feel all man; Tess made him feel fantastically frustrated.

Up at 36,000 feet, with the sensation of putting life at ground level on hold, Joe could think about it all whereas driving to the airport had been another matter. He had been rushing. He had been fuming. He'd spat out loud in the car, you stupid little cow, Tess, you stupid girl. But now, thinking of Nathalie, Joe had to wonder why the hell she'd laboured the point of his bloody BlackBerry being between her frigging sheets. She'd altered the dynamic, unbalanced their equilibrium, and potentially screwed up their zipless fucking. Her sudden possessiveness; his loss.

Women, thought Joe at 36,000 feet, an hour into his journey, bloody bloody women. He opened his eyes to see the air hostesses and their drinks service. Were they any less complicated? Their highly trained smiles and tolerance, their skilled deportment, trolleying up and down the aisles in high heels making light of the trials of turbulence. What were they like on terra firma, he wondered? At home, did they fly off the handle at their partners allowing imagined demeanours to become real? Did they wave innocent photos, exclaiming S.F! S.F! Who the fuck is Sarah Fanshaw? Did their partners have to say, shh, silly, I don't know a Sarah Fanshaw but that photo was taken in San Francisco? Did they phone their lover's home number and, on hearing a female voice, decide to spin out details of his phone – my bed? How about the elderly ladies sitting next to him – would they invent some golden girlfriend expressly for the purpose of sabotaging their son's independence and happiness?

Women – they're never the same. Joe had always loved this about them and, for that reason alone, had indulged himself in more than one at a time. Now, on the plane to France he thought no two are alike – but they're all too bloody similar, whatever their age or nationality.

He gave the charming hostess a what-the-hell smile and ordered himself a Scotch and soda. He took a sip; the taste was immediately reassuring and it settled his gut quickly. As he sipped, he tried to conclude the situation still rampaging in his head. The Nathalie phone call would have been enough in itself for Tess, and for him, without the added complication of Kate. If it had been only the Nathalie phone call, it was very likely that he would have taken Tess in his arms and said, she means nothing to me – it's you I want. But Nathalie alone was not the problem. The woman who complicated everything wasn't Nathalie, nor was it Tess and of course it couldn't be Kate. It was his mother.

Spoiling things again, he thought. She's bloody spoiling things again.

Then he thought, the stealing back to the Resolution is a relatively new thing of hers, but how stupid of me to think I could hide her away. And he wondered if he'd been unfair on Tess – who'd told him about her family when he'd asked though he'd fobbed her off when she'd asked him. They're not around, he'd said of them, and he knew he'd made it sound like they were dead. Up at Swallows, he could deal with his mother because the surroundings were neutral and help was at hand. Why hadn't he told Tess that his senile mother lived down the road and up the cliff and she might appear at the kitchen window every once in a while and could Tess possibly take a bunch of flowers if he was away for more than a two-week stretch? Swallows: the best care, close to home, that money could provide. He'd asked himself, on many occasions, whether he was paying more to feel less guilty. Then he'd chide himself – why feel guilty when the harm was done to him? Are the senile absolved of blame in the way they are released of memory and sense of self? Joe was still unable to balance his anger at his mother with his pity for the dreadful affliction befalling her. The unresolved emotion was apt to churn inside him at the slightest prompt. And that's what had happened when Tess brought her up.

Joe felt restless, confined, cramped in his mind and his body. He needed fresh air, the space to unwind, the privacy to shout, to shadow-box, to chuck a rock or swear excessively. The plane was certainly not helping but another Scotch would. He twisted around in his aisle seat; the neat, navy-clad bottom of the air hostess was just a little too far away now for him to order another drink.

'They don't hang about, do they?' said one of the elderly ladies sharing his row.

'They have the whole plane to do, Milly,' said the other, 'and now the drinks aren't for free, they have to do all the *money* too.'

Joe smiled vaguely without facing them full on.

'I'll say you wanted some peanuts with your Scotch,' said Milly.

'I'll say he wanted a double,' said the other.

'I can offer you a Murray Mint,' said Milly and her fingers faffed with a packet and Joe felt it would be rude to say no even though he knew that accepting a mint would invite conversation.

'Business?' said Milly.

'Pleasure?' said the other.

'A little of both,' Joe nodded and suddenly he thought, sod England and Saltburn and all who are there – Nathalie doesn't know the details but she knows she has amends to make and she'll know the perfect way to do that. Finally, Joe had a solution: brain rest in France from the head-fuck at home.

'A French lady friend, is it?'

'She comes with the job,' Joe said, not caring if the women detected his tongue in cheek because he was consumed by an image of Nathalie coming – her gasps and groans, the way her body would tauten, the way she stretched and arched herself worthy of any porn film.

Milly bristled at his rather vulgar turn of phrase.

'Gracious,' the other murmured, 'it's not just the pension and the paid holidays – they think of everything these days.'

Joe looked at her and he liked her wry smile so he chinked plastic cups, though his was empty.

'Is she French, then, your lady friend – your *chérie*?' she asked, nudging Milly when she spoke the single word of French.

From nowhere, Joe wanted to ask them, do you have sons? He wanted to ask, do you have a good relationship with them – now? Did you – when they were little? Do they have lady friends, your boys? He wanted to ask, how old are you? Are you well? He wanted to say, my mother is nearly seventy-five – only seventy-five – but she has dementia and I pay for her to stay less than a mile from where I live because she made my life a misery then and I won't let her make a misery of it now. He wanted to say, I don't mean to punish her – I just want my life to myself.

'I work in France, on and off,' he said instead, 'and there's an on–off woman there too. It's been easy and enjoyable and has suited me just fine. But now there's a girl back home – and it's complicated everything.'

'Whoever said life should be simple?' said Milly.

But the other lady said, 'Funny how you call the one in France a woman and the one back home a girl.'

And Joe thought, it is odd that I should do that – not least because the girl at home is older than the woman in France, and a mother herself.

'I'd say it's make-your-mind-up time,' said Milly. 'It can't be fair on anyone to be carrying on like this. Not least yourself.'

Joe was about to clarify the situation – but then he thought, why? What's to clarify anyway? Nathalie – and all the other Nathalies I provide myself with – they are what I know, what I've chosen; they have suited me perfectly over the years. Why break the habit of a lifetime? Never in a million years could it work out with Tess. Anyway, she'll probably be gone by the time I'm next home. Gone – for good.

'Can I buy you ladies a drink?' Joe asked, seeing the trolley returning.

*   *   *

Tess spent two days wandering about slightly stooped, often clutching her stomach as if she had some gastric bug. She felt ragged. She felt wrung out – as if the pain of losing Joe before she had even had him was being fed through a mangle together with the gut-wrenched dread of being potentially homeless and jobless. When she was in the house, she'd trail her hand wherever she went; touching the walls gently as if they were animate, clasping the banister as if it was a helping hand, pressing her cheek against the closed door of Joe's study as if to detect a heartbeat, her fingertips trailing the undulations of the dado as if reading for positive messages in Braille. When she went out, it was for short trips only – requisite fresh air for dog and child. She felt depleted of the energy required to walk far, to tackle the hill back home. She ate toast and Marmite without tasting it. She didn't drink enough water and had headaches because of it. She couldn't sleep at night and felt half-hazed by the afternoon. She didn't think of Seb at all, let alone wonder if he was back from wherever he'd been. She didn't think to call Tamsin. The only person she could think of was Joe and she couldn't very well call him though she begged the phone to ring and be him.

The day he left, when Em slept after lunch, Tess shut Wolf in the kitchen and went to Joe's bedroom. There, she lay on his bed and inhaled into one pillow while placing another one lengthways along her back. With eyes closed and her dreaming head on, she could almost conjure the sensation of another body. She let tears blot into his sheets and she whispered out loud to the room, as if her words might somehow travel through the ether to him. Sorry, she said. She said, please come back. She said, please let me stay. I do not want to go, she said, and I so want you to come back.

With so much time spent in the house in voluntary exile, Tess developed imaginary conversations with Joe, honing gesture and expression in front of any reflective surface she passed, rehearsing as if she might have the opportunity to perform them. She would cast her eyes down before looking up at him and she practised diverse apologies and manifold ways to express them. Perhaps touch his arm for emphasis. Have him feel touched. Not to save her skin – though the thought of leaving the Resolution was so abhorrent that she refused to touch upon it again – rather, she wanted to say sorry because it was simply warranted. She knew she hadn't just picked up the wrong end of the stick – she'd made an impetuous grab and had clung on tight, refusing to loosen her grip despite the stick she'd swooped on being riddled and rotten. She'd made a reality of Joe's past and present that were so far removed from the truth they now precluded any future for her with him. He'd done nothing wrong: not kissing her on the Transporter Bridge was no crime. He was doing nothing wrong – having a French fuck was not illegal. To be estranged from his mother was a shame, but no sin.

Kuala Lumpur. Kay effing Ell. What an utter fool she'd made of herself and what a shambles she'd made for herself. So there was no Kate. No Kate at all. It was now glaringly logical that a batty old woman could fabricate a non-existent person, whether wilfully or otherwise. What an utter waste of worrying. But if there was no Kate, now there was no Tess, no Tess at all either – and she was entitled to worry about that. How could she make amends – and was it possible? Hadn't he told her to go? But wasn't it a crime to let wholesome daydreams go to waste? Wasn't there some Richard Bach adage that proclaimed we're not given dreams without the power to fulfil them? She scanned Joe's bookshelves. No Richard Bach. She wasn't surprised.

Tess found herself by the phone often; staring at it, looking at all those numbers there for the dialling, listening thoughtfully to the dialling tone as if hoping to detect a secret message. She cursed herself for cutting up her SIM card – how she'd love to compose a text message to Joe that, despite the brevity and abbreviations of the medium, would say so much.

Pls 4giv, me so sorry, me silly, me vv embrssd – truth is i think i love u. Txxx

But no doubt her contract was suspended now because the direct debit would not have gone through. She thought about pay-as-you-go, or going to an Internet café and sending an email, even if it necessitated the cost of a trip to Middlesbrough. However, she had no email address for him – but that was OK because she couldn't bear the thought of Joe accessing his BlackBerry from that Frenchwoman's bed.

She could write snail-mail – but where would she send it? And what exactly would she say? What was it that she really wanted to say? Of course she wanted to say sorry because she was very sorry – but the apology she wanted to give wasn't entirely altruistic. She wanted to elicit a particular response. If she could deliver the best sorry in the world, then Joe might be moved to say, don't go, Tess, don't leave. I'm coming back Tess, put the supper on. Stay.

She felt impotent and it made her feel small and unattractive. And then, perversely, she'd make herself feel even smaller, even less attractive, by thinking about Nathalie; taunting herself that at this very moment, Joe was probably with her. Bugger the crisis on the bridge. They were in his bed having fun. His BlackBerry on vibrate, placed on her stomach, on her thighs, up between them. Laughing and kissing and being intimate and sexy. Look at her amazing figure, at her stylish apartment. She knows all about Kuala Lumpur – she's been there. Well-travelled, high-heeled, sophisticated woman that she is. See how elegantly she dresses for some amazing job. Watch her undressing so seductively in front of entranced Joe. Why *would* he want Tess when he can be in France and have No Strings Nathalie?

The fabricated images sickened Tess more than the reality of her current situation. However, by forcing her mind to dwell on imaginings, she was able to postpone figuring out what on earth she was going to do. Not just about Joe – about everything. There'd be no pay-as-you-go phone. No train to an Internet café in Middlesbrough. There was no money for such things, there was only a small amount left now, earmarked for Em of course.

Chapter Nineteen

For a girl who hated the beach, Tess did a very good job of burying her head in the sand. Five days on, she hadn't contacted Joe nor had she made any attempt to look for another job. In fact she'd gone to greater lengths finding reasons to stay. Lisa she liked very much, meeting up with her and a couple of other mums almost daily. The friendships soon extended to tea and coffee at their houses where chat deepened and Tess told them that yes, she used to live in London but no, she wouldn't be returning – home was here now.

She found herself saying the same to Tamsin whom she finally phoned, spur of the moment and reverse charges from a call box near the station. Listening to the dialling tone, she was ready to confide, to ask advice, to be honest. When Tamsin answered, Tess found herself steering clear of anything to do with her situation. She didn't want to invite Tamsin to ask her what she was going to do. She couldn't tell her what had happened – it would just sound too ludicrous out loud.

I can't believe you thought Kuala Lumpur was Kate Someone-Beginning-With-L, you numpty.

Why on earth did you have a go at Joe for not kissing you?

You told him about his *mother* – are you mad?

He's admitted to having this woman in France? Well, what are you hanging around for?

Don't bloody phone him, Tamsin would say. She'd say, pack up your stuff and come back down here. You've done your potty Northern sojourn, now it's time to face reality. Tamsin would tell her, you're not in some Channel 4 documentary about starting a new life in some far-flung place, you know. You ran away to a seaside town in the North-East. Now you've been sacked. So come back, Tess, come back to what and where you know.

But Tess didn't want to risk Tamsin saying any of this, so she made everything sound peachy and she kept the conversation short enough so she had time and energy to phone her sister. The more upbeat she'd been on the phone to Tamsin, the more reality hit her once the call ended. She had no option other than to phone Claire and it was one call she didn't dare reverse the charges; she couldn't risk antagonizing her sister before the conversation was underway.

After pleasantries, the predictable pause. Then, the purpose of the call, which Tess requested in a voice akin to the wringing of hands. Joe had left without paying her and her funds had dwindled alarmingly. She needed her sister to help and her sister made it a horrible thing to have to ask. But Tess did ask, and after an extravagant sigh, her sister responded.

'For God's sake, Tess, how long do you actually spend physically *house-sitting*? Surely you can do something else in between?'

Be nice, Tess thought, don't take offence. Claire wants to be humoured – like the last time I had to ask.

'I did think about it – and there's a waitressing position at Virgo's which is a lovely place, it does all this gluten-free food too.'

'Even better – they probably give you a free gluten-free meal per shift too.'

'But Claire, the problem is Em. I looked into making arrangements for her – I scanned the local paper and the notices in the library but I worked out that what I'd be paid against what I'd pay out for childcare, would be so negligible as to be not worth it.'

'You were in that situation in London.'

'I know.'

'So in other words, you've made no progress at all with your life have you.'

'But I have! I mean, you're right of course, on a practical level – but to live like this here, in Saltburn, is much better for Em than living like this *there* – back in London.'

'A change of scenery does not change a situation, Tess. God. Look, I'll pop a cheque for a hundred pounds in the post – OK? But don't bloody ask again – not till your birthday or Christmas. It's not that I can't afford it, it's that I feel I'm not doing you any favours. You've got to drag yourself out of this pit, Tess. You've been in it for long enough. I know about things like this – it becomes habit, to wallow.'

You? Claire? Know about *this*? When you've been provided for and kept in the manner to which you so swiftly became accustomed as soon as you met your husband? You with your joint bank account into which you put no funds? Your rich, devoted husband providing you with a chequebook and a credit card, support and approval, for your every whim?

There was so much Tess could have screamed out in her defence – but she didn't dare, not during this phone call.

'It's easier said than done,' she said quietly instead.

'What about Child Benefit?'

'It's a standing order into my bank account.'

'Well then!'

'But my bank card—'

209

'Christ, Tess. I mean – *honestly!*'

Tess had to swallow down hard – on her pride and on tears. 'Claire – please help. I won't ask again. I'm only asking you now because—'

'God! Come on then – give me your address,' and the tedium in Claire's voice could so easily have reduced Tess to tears. If she wasn't so desperate, if she had more pride, if she felt more up, if Joe hadn't left, she might just have said, stuff your bloody money.

'Your address, Tess? I have to pick up the kids.'

'Could you not send cash?'

'Don't be ridiculous.'

'But if you send a cheque the bank will just swallow it whole.'

'For God's sake, Tess, how can you *live* like this?'

'Because at the moment, I have no choice.'

'Don't be so defeatist. Life is what you make it.'

'All I wanted was to make a good life – but things didn't go my way.'

'Well, change bloody direction then.'

'That's what I'm trying to do.'

'I can't send cash in the *post*.'

'Could you perhaps send a postal order?'

'Do they still do such things?'

'Yes, they do.'

'You need to do *something*, Tess. Seriously. It's pathetic.'

'I have been trying. For over two years, I've been trying. I continue to try. Why do you always imply it's something I have the power to change?'

'Oh, come on – don't do the feeling-sorry-for-yourself act, or absolving yourself of responsibility. You can't be blameless in this situation and therefore there must be something you can do – something other than holding the fort for some old fart, dusting his doorknobs and putting out the rubbish. Why don't you get a proper job?'

'I just said why. Anyway, this is a proper job – and it's board and lodging too.'

'Well, why not ask Lord of the Manor to pay you more? Do his ironing or cooking or something. You'll still have time for his doorknobs and dusting.'

'He's not here often enough.' Tess held the receiver against her chest and rested her forehead against the glass. Oh Joe, you're not here nearly enough. Please, please come back. Please, please let me stay. 'Please, Claire.' She tapped her head against the glass and closed her eyes. 'I'm –' begging you.'

'OK. OK. Give me the address. I'll sort it tomorrow. I've got to go, Tess. *God.*'

*   *   *

The relief of banknotes. The feel of their oily, parchmenty surface. The smell of them. The Queen's face, benevolent. The novel sensation of closing her wallet with the notes inside causing a slight resistance when she folded the leather, like a foot in a door; something in there at last. Thank you, Your Majesty.

Tess bought Em a shiny foil windmill and she treated them to soup at Virgo's. She had a window seat. Every mouthful was ambrosial after all that Marmite and toast. One of the mums she'd befriended walked by and waved. Life didn't seem so bad when there was good food in one's stomach and money in the pot and a friendly face waving, hey, Tess. And then the sun came out and Seb sauntered past just as she dunked the complimentary biscotti in her cappuccino.

On the other side of the window, Seb made the universal gesture for sipping a hot beverage, to which Tess shrugged and smiled and nodded that he could join her.

'Hey there, stranger,' he said, lowering his voice when he

saw that Em was sleeping. 'If I'd waited by my phone, I'd be fossilized by now.'

In her need over the last few days to suspend reality, Tess had forgotten about Seb's number on the calendar, about his trip away, about his previous offer of fish and chips and a DVD. 'I'm sorry, Seb – something came up. It's been really full-on recently. I was going to ring – tonight.'

'Yeah, right.'

She reddened; it sounded stupid and flagrantly untrue. But because he'd nobbled her so sweetly, she could scrunch her napkin and chuck it at him.

'I *was*!'

'Baby's asleep,' Seb noticed. 'That means I don't need to watch my language. So – what a day, what a fucking awesome day.'

His eyes were a little watery, the irises vivid, the whites a little bloodshot as if he'd just come out of the sea.

'Nice waves?' Tess tried. 'Swell swell – or whatever the correct surfing terminology is?'

Seb laughed. 'Nothing to do with the sea – though I was out first thing. No – you are looking at one rich fucker.' He leant back in the chair and patted his puffed-up chest.

'How so? Is that why you went away? You were only away for a week.'

'Yeah, and I've been back a week too. No – I went to see rellies down in Cornwall – you know, we trade surf every couple of months. It's an awesome day today because of a nice fat insurance payout that's come my way.' Seb said it as if it could have happened to anyone in the town that Tuesday morning. Apart from Tess, it seemed, who looked confused. 'A couple of years ago I was in a car crash. My friend was driving. I sued him. The money came through today.'

'You sued your friend?'

'Yep.'

212

She baulked.

Seb laughed. 'He's a lawyer – he told me to. It was his idea.'

'And is he still your friend?'

'Still a lawyer, still my buddy – despite the fact that I now set the alarms off when I go through airport security on account of the metal in my back and leg. Anyway, do you want a cake to go with your coffee? Lunch is on me.' Seb gave a rather fey wave.

'I can't eat another thing,' Tess said.

Seb leant back in his seat and looked at her. 'Will you keep me company, then?'

How nice to be asked. Tess looked at the milky foam clinging to the coffee cup and nodded.

He talked with his mouth full. He was ravenous, slightly hyper, pronging his food a number of times before it stuck to the fork. He had mayonnaise on his chin. He made her laugh and he did a lot of laughing himself. He insisted on paying for her lunch and she thought it would be rude not to accept though she was happy enough to go Dutch. They loitered on the pavement, Tess fiddling her feet along the line between slabs, Seb making small talk in unfinished sentences.

'Thanks for lunch then.'

'Pleasure, Tess, my pleasure. I was thinking of – I'm not working this afternoon. I don't know – do you want to go for a walk?'

Tess looked at the buggy as if it was as cumbersome and inappropriate as a pair of high heels. 'I can't really,' she said.

Seb didn't look at the buggy, or at Tess's feet. He just looked at her face and gave a disappointed smile. 'Another time, then.'

Tess nodded. 'Sure.'

He paused, as if he was about to sneeze. 'Like – Friday night?'

'Night?'

'A date, Tess. Not a walk. I'm saying let's go out on a proper date, on Friday night – babysitting depending, of course. What do you say?'

Tess found she didn't feel like backing away behind her customary reticence. She felt like staying exactly where she was, with the sunlight squinting her face into a grin, buying a little time to mull the offer. And when she accepted she realized the first person she'd be telling – and soon – was not Tamsin for advice, but Lisa for a babysitting favour.

'Phone me if there's a problem,' Seb said, 'otherwise, I'll see you right – *here*!' And he stamped his foot as if marking the spot.

'OK,' Tess laughed, 'unless you hear from me, I'll be right – *here*.' And she nudged his shoe out of the way so she could tap hers on the precise place on the pavement.

'Cool.' He smiled and he lingered and then he executed a strange bounce on the spot, which tipped his body forward and enabled him to kiss Tess lightly on the lips, regain his composure and saunter off before she could quite register just what had happened. A little way off, he cast a glance over his shoulder to find Tess standing stock-still. He turned, walking backwards for a couple of steps. Then he pointed to the auspicious paving stone with a broad grin before turning again and strolling away.

Tess thought, he's just kissed me. Kissed me for a second time. With more intent than the first time though it was quicker and more chaste. She thought, I've been asked on a proper date. She thought, Seb's fun and good-looking and he's just kissed me and asked me out. And she thought, I must phone Lisa straight away. She walked briskly back up to the house, phoned Lisa who sounded happy to supply the favour and Tess found that, with not much arm-twisting, she was telling Lisa that yes, it was a *date* and that the guy seems really nice. Yes, good-looking too – in that windswept surfer-boy kind of way. From Australia. Our sort of age. Perhaps younger, actually. No, not a toyboy – we might be mums but surely we are not old enough for toyboys, are we?

Unable to sleep, it was only when Tess went down to the kitchen for a glass of water and caught sight of Seb's number on top of Joe's, that she realized she hadn't thought of Joe since Seb appeared at the window of Virgo's. A good eight hours of respite, she calculated. Tamsin would probably say this was no bad thing.

Wondering what to wear wasn't a problem – finding the time to change at all was. Tess prioritized Em – writing a list of likes and dislikes, a timetable of what Lisa could expect and when, and adding Seb's mobile number on every page. The likelihood was that Em wouldn't stir, but as Tess would be uncontactable unless Seb's mobile was in signal, she wanted to cover all options. Apart from her work days in London, she'd actually never left Em before, not in nineteen months, certainly not for her own leisure. She had not been out in the evening, let alone on a date, in all that time. During the afternoon, she started to feel that the whole thing was a little self-indulgent. By early evening, though, she couldn't ignore a frisson of anticipation.

Lisa arrived. Em was asleep. Wolf was fed and had been out for his ablutions and was now prostrate at the foot of the stairs. Lisa marvelled at the expanse of hallway before narrowing her gaze to focus on Tess, looking her up and down.

'What are you wearing?'

Tess looked at her clothes. She was wearing what she always wore.

'Is that what you are wearing *tonight*?'

Tess paused. 'I'm not sure.'

'Well, off you go and get sure – Mary Poppins is here.'

'Oh, about that – here's a list.'

Lisa flipped through the pages, which she then rolled up and used as a truncheon against Tess's arm. 'A list? It's an encyclopaedia! Have you forgotten my son is the same age as your daughter?'

'I know – I know, it's just I haven't—'

'I know – you said. I'm teasing. It's fine.' And Lisa gave Tess's arm a little stroke. 'So show me around, show me everything. It's like Buckingham Bleeding Palace compared to my place. Oh fuck – look at that dog.'

'He's harmless.'

'He's huge. He looks so—'

'Shh! You'll hurt his feelings.'

They stared at the great lumbering bulk of Wolf, twitching in his sleep, the pads of his paws looking like dirty pebbles, his coat appearing to have been stolen from a hobo, his over-sized tongue looking synthetically pink amidst all the wiry grey and matted brown. 'It won't suddenly turn on me when you've left, will it?'

'He's a *he*. And no, he won't. He's soppy and gorgeous.'

They had to mountaineer over him for Tess to give Lisa the guided tour.

'My place – including the garden – would fit into the entrance hall. I can see why you'll not be leaving anytime soon. What's he like – the chap who owns it?'

Tess tried to counteract the pause with a light tone of voice. 'Oh, he's fine – not here much.' She ignored Lisa, looking at her askance. Lisa was starting to remind Tess of Tamsin, which both amused and unnerved her.

'This your room then?'

'Come on in,' said Tess, 'help me find something to wear.'

After assessing all the clothes Tess owned, Lisa looked at her. 'You're in serious need of a shopping trip, pet.'

216

'I need to win the lottery first,' Tess said.

'So, it's jeans or that denim skirt with the stain?'

'Yes – and that polo neck or any of those T-shirts. It's what they call a capsule wardrobe.'

'It's what I'd call my biggest nightmare.'

Lisa looked at the clothes thoughtfully. Then she looked at Tess. She thought of her own husband, happy to babysit while she nipped to Yarm to shop. She thought of their cosy but smart two-up, two-down in which he was always tinkering – replacing the plastic sockets with smart chrome, building a breakfast bar, putting in low-voltage lighting, glossing all the sills, skirting and doors. Their home, their castle. A lucky couple – completed eighteen months ago with the arrival of much-wanted baby Sam. She thought of her husband now, babysitting so she could help out her new friend. Happy enough with his takeaway pizza and a couple of tinnies and some crap on telly he wouldn't dream of foisting on her. Bless him.

'What's he like, then – tell me again?'

'As I said, he's – he's not here much.' She paused to dwell on a mental image of Joe, lovely, painful. 'He's in his forties. He's funny and moody and you could say handsome. He builds bridges. He took me to the Transporter and told me about the Halfpenny Bridge.'

Lisa didn't take her eyes off Tess.

'I wasn't talking about His Nibs – I was talking about Seb.'

Tess gave Lisa an exaggerated silly-me look.

'Oh, *Seb* – like I said, he's – nice. Charming. Chatty. Sporty.'

'And you've had one snog and one quick kiss-with-subtitles?'

Tess laughed at this. 'On paper – yes.'

'What does that mean!'

'It means both times I sort of suddenly found myself in the process of *being* kissed.'

'Did you kiss back?'

'The second time was so fast.'

'The first time then?'

Tess remembered her tongue taking over instinctively because her mind was too slow to react. She nodded.

'Right then, lady,' Lisa said and before Tess could express any opinion, Lisa had taken off her own skirt (it was cute: vivid blue, corduroy, A-line, just above the knee) and stood waiting in her tights, arms crossed, while Tess put it on.

'Suits you!'

'Do you think so?' Tess moved this way and that in front of the mirror, slightly in awe of what she saw.

'Look at yourself, Tess – look at the pins on you! It's a crime to hide them. Do something with your hair, though. Get your slap on. You can take my lippy with you – it's only from Boots but it's called Honeytrap and with you in that skirt, it'll do what it says on the packet.'

Borrowing some shapeless old jogging pants off Tess, Lisa went downstairs. Tess sat in front of the mirror and said, hair, what am I going to do with you?

Mascara helped. And a carefully mussed-up ponytail that took ages to perfect completed the look. She sat there a while longer than she needed. She felt displaced all of a sudden – as if dates were hugely adventurous even risky pursuits undertaken by other more qualified people. She thought of Em. And tried not to. She thought of Wolf and tried not to. She didn't let herself think of Joe. She said out loud that she would borrow Lisa's sure-fire lipstick, if the offer still stood. She looked at herself in the mirror and said, you look stupid, you don't look like you. But then she heard Lisa hiss from downstairs that Tess was late, to get a move on or risk being stood up.

*   *   *

She was late but he didn't stand her up. He was waiting for her at the specific paving stone and he took her to the pub at the bottom of Saltburn Bank. It used to be a dive, Lisa had told her. Minging, she said. But now it was the place to go, all fancy decked verandas speckled with little bright blue halogen lights, woodwork painted in New England colours. Lisa had told her, you don't go to the bog there any more – they've *restrooms* now with polished granite and all. It had a commanding position too, with 360-degree views and an interrupted vista out to sea, hence its new name, the Vista Mar. Tess had never seen it by night. Swish for Saltburn. Then she thought, she hadn't really seen Saltburn by night either – only when passing through by car on the way to the Transporter Bridge.

Stop it! This night has nothing to do with Joe.

'Loving your hair,' Seb said. 'What are you drinking?'

'Wine, I think.'

Eye contact, Tess, eye contact.

They stayed until last orders. Somehow, she managed to elicit plenty of details about Seb's life without revealing too many of her own. Tess's grandmother always said she was a good listener, for Tess though it usefully precluded too much personal exposure on her part. Her grandmother would have deemed him easy on the eye and Tess would have agreed with her on that one. He was easy to listen to as well, especially on account of his accent. She still had no desire to surf by the end of the evening but his adventures on the waves were entertaining in their own right, as were his tales of Australia and his relatives' acres in Cornwall. Two ex-girlfriends of any note, one or two rebound flings, a couple of good-time girls this last year. Nothing serious. How about you, Tess?

'Oh, my family live abroad.'

'Do you visit?'

'We're not close, really.'

'And work?'

'I'm house-sitting at the moment.'

'Taking a breather?'

'I suppose so. Though I find it very satisfying. But I needed a change of scene.'

'Wise. And men? If you don't mind me asking?'

'You are nosy, aren't you? Nothing very juicy for you – no one special, really. The teenage sweetheart who was eventually more like a brother. The college boyfriend who I graduated on from once I'd graduated. One one-night stand which was one too many. Em's father, of course – but I wouldn't know how to begin to describe him.'

'A wanker?'

'Seb!'

'Special?'

'Unique is probably a fairer word.'

'How so?'

'He's a free spirit. He's in the wrong decade – he needs San Francisco at the height of hippydom.'

'Shirks his responsibility, does he?'

'Not intentionally.'

'Sorry – tell me to shut up if I'm prying and we'll talk about the weather.'

'Let's talk about the weather, then.'

'You don't want to talk about him, do you?'

'Well –'

'Do you know how I can tell? It's because you've gone a bit twitchy – here, on your lips, just *here*.' Seb's fingertip stayed against Tess's mouth and his eyes bore through hers.

'Shall we go?'

'Go where?'

'Back to mine?'

Her mouth was twitching again, she could sense it.

220

'There's a bottle of white in the fridge,' he said as if surely that could seal the deal.

'I mustn't be too late.'

'Just a glass of vino back at mine, Tess, not a pyjama party.'

A compact, modern, second-floor apartment on the other side of town.

'Furniture isn't mine.'

She didn't think it was.

'It's all in with the rent. Not bad really.'

Bathroom could be cleaner. Yesterday's paper open on the sofa. An odd shoe, kicked off in front of the TV set. Washing-up to be done. The housekeeper in her thought, he could make more of an effort. The girl in her said, he's a boy! give him a break! so what if there's a lads' mag peeping out from under that chair and a *Little Britain* DVD out of its case on top of the speaker? Then she thought, that's an unopened bottle of wine and it isn't plonk. She rather thought he'd put it in the fridge with a wink and a wish before he came out tonight. She told herself, you're on a date, he asked you and in his own sweet way, he's planned for the evening to unfold.

'It's nothing like your place,' Seb was saying, motioning her to the sofa while he set two glasses of wine on the coffee table, 'but it's home.'

'It's not my place,' Tess said, because she didn't want to be distracted by thoughts of that beautiful old building, of Em and Lisa and Wolf. Joe. She needed to concentrate on the veneer coffee table and the very white mantelpiece that surrounded no fireplace, only a slab of marble. This was her, here and now, and if she didn't make the most of it, what would have been the point of Lisa's skirt and Tess's sheaves of notes and the lipstick and the hairdo and finally, finally, making it out all on her own. 'Cheers.'

'Cheers.'

221

They sipped self-consciously and Tess glanced around for a clock.

'I mustn't be late.'

'You won't be. It's only a ten-minute walk.'

'Fifteen after all the wine I've consumed!'

'You drunken slag,' Seb teased and it made Tess giggle which made Seb think, now's my chance and he put their wineglasses down and reached for her. His mouth found hers and his hands honed in on what they'd fancied all evening long. Tess liked the way he kissed, the way he sucked her lips, she liked the taste of another tongue and the way it rudely probed her mouth as if asking personal questions. The feeling of her breasts being fondled was tantalizing and she found herself thinking, you can use your mouth, Seb, if you want to. He took her hand and led it down to the bulge in his trousers and though initially he had to grip her wrist and move it for her, when he let go she continued. The reality of a stiff cock was suddenly exciting to her and she felt her hips starting to gyrate instinctively. His hands were travelling up her thighs, politely spending non-focused attention there before surreptitiously working her tights down.

'Oh, for fuck's sake,' he said, laughing, as he hoicked her legs akimbo and peeled her tights away. Suddenly, he was pressing his mouth against the gusset of her pants and inhaling ravenously. Tess felt strangely paralysed, her body saying, yes please, more; her head saying, you really should be going now. It was like reading a book at bedtime, looking ahead for a convenient place to fold the corner of a page and call it a night. But, just like an easy read, she kept passing over line breaks and full stops for others further on. One more kiss, then I'll go. Actually, I'll just take my bra off – just for a minute or two. But actually, he's fingering around inside my knickers and – God, that feels good. Perhaps it would be really nice to come before I go.

He had a finger pulling her knicker elastic aside, his tongue slipping into the space this created, his tongue licking through the folds of her sex, dabbing at her, lapping her up. She didn't want to look at the ceiling and turning her face one way gave the disruption of the TV set on with the volume off. Turning the other gave her a faceful of pastel swirls of the upholstery. But if she looked down, she saw a blond, tousle-haired man called Seb busy with his tongue between her legs and that sight was too specific. She shut her eyes to focus on the feeling alone. She just wanted to concentrate on the tremors building in her body from her sex being licked so well. Was it horribly self-serving to close her eyes so that it didn't matter who was doing it? By now, she just wanted to come, to have a man make her come, to come on the mouth of a man.

Her hips were rocking hard to facilitate her orgasm which came in a gush of such intense pleasure that it wracked her body and her voice rang out in the soundless room.

And then it all ebbed away. The throbbing, the sound of her, the presence of him.

'You can open your eyes now,' Seb laughed but it took effort for Tess to unscrunch them. When she did, she needed to concentrate on the buttons of his shirt. She didn't want the bigger picture. She wanted, really, to leave. She felt emotional, a bit drunk, confused how her body could have been so sure when her mind was still wanting to mull it all over.

Black buttons on a navy blue shirt.

'My turn?' He sounded shy, hopeful. The thought hadn't crossed her mind.

And Seb was suddenly straddling her, unbuckling, unzipping, whipping it out.

How long since she saw a cock? The sight of it, of Seb's strong surfer's legs, of the way he was breathing, stroking her hair, grabbing her pony-tail, helped to put thoughts of

223

heading home to one side. She played with his balls and fingered the length of him, kissing her way up the shaft, and tongue-flicked lightly over the top before taking him in her mouth, sucking him all the way down. She shifted so that she could use her hands too but she couldn't get comfortable. Her neck was a bit cricked and her jaw was locking and when she opened her eyes she saw her shoes and suddenly she longed to be on her way. Come on, come on. Come.

'Can I come in your mouth?'

No, Tess thought suddenly. I do not want you to come in my mouth.

She pulled away, hoping for the sake of her conscience and his ego that she looked a little bashful, apologetic.

'That's OK,' he was saying. 'I guess a full-on shag is out, then?'

She giggled. Dear Seb, so easygoing, funny, kind. She wished she felt more.

He sank back into the sofa and drew her to his chest. She watched his hand slide up and down his shaft. She tiptoed her fingertips over his stomach and down to his arm and along his hand, which he gladly accepted. He was close so she took over. He was clenching his fists and his teeth, his eyes screwed shut, his legs tensing, his pelvis thrusting as he spurted over his stomach.

He panted with the triumph of having just run some race. He pulled her to his chest and stroked her hair. She listened to his heart beating fast, then settling.

'When can I see you again?'

He was looking down at her, his gaze intense.

Tess suddenly felt enormously tired, too tired to think about the answer so she nodded and smiled and let him kiss her gently. He went to the bathroom and by the time he was back, she was dressed, her shoes on, standing by the door insisting there was no need whatsoever for him to escort her up that steep old hill to the house.

The moonlight and the solitude are soothing. Tess thinks how you don't get this quality of darkness in the city. The woods to her left appear to have a depth ten times that in daylight. They are eerie, not malevolent, but she feels tiny and cold. No traffic. No people. She can hear the sea and it sounds brutish – as if it is on best behaviour during the day. The chill air sobers her up and she finds her pace increasing when the house comes into sight. One of the things she has grown to love more than anything is the opening of the gate and then the closing of the gate. Home and safe.

Lisa arrives in the hallway just as soon as Tess is inside and has shut the door.

'How was it?'

Tess's new friend in Tess's cruddy old trackie bottoms. Lisa is all expectant and she's grinning away.

'Fun,' says Tess, with a nod and a smile. 'I had fun.'

'Fun *and*?' Lisa is digging with a wink. 'Any – shenanigans?'

'Well,' Tess pauses. This reminds her of a long time ago, sharing juicy details with Tamsin, the look on a friend's face of excitement and anticipation – and praise. 'We did go back to his for a glass of wine.'

'A glass of wine *and*?'

'And – a bit of a fumble.'

'A fumble!' Lisa all but cheers. 'A *fumble* she calls it!' She pauses. 'Did you?'

'On a first date?'

'Not sure I'd have your self-restraint, pet. But good on you. Will you see him again? I'll gladly babysit. You just let me know.'

Tess nods. 'Thanks *so* much, by the way.'

225

'As I said, any time,' Lisa says, gathering her stuff, and she gives Tess a little hug because she's really glad this lovely girl was paid some attention tonight. She deserves it, thinks Lisa, good for her.

'Thanks again.'

'Happy to help.'

'See you at playgroup next week?'

'Perhaps before. How about tomorrow morning? Pop over to mine for a cuppa?'

Lisa has gone. Em has been checked on. Tess is sitting at the base of the stairs hugging Wolf who is at her side. She glances left. The answering machine still says zero. Something inside sinks a little.

Chapter Twenty

Joe didn't hear his phone the first time. He was on site, with trucks coming in convoys and an irate foreman jabbering at him fifty to the dozen. Joe's French was quite good as long as he was given time to translate what was said and formulate the appropriate reply. It didn't help that the man was from the Ivory Coast and his accent was different, more twangy, yelling and gesticulating at breakneck speed. Joe beckoned him into the site office, offered him a seat and tea. He took off his hard hat and motioned for the man to do the same. Being bareheaded and sharing a cup of tea, albeit in a prefab office but with the door closed, created a more genial atmosphere between them and when the latter took off his helmet, he let go of his aggression too; allowed himself a sigh and a stretch and a moment or two just to hold the mug and blow meditatively. Joe noticed how he held it genteelly, as if it was bone china. The ritual of taking tea provided both men with respite from their dispute, until their mugs were empty at least. He offered the man another cup, which was gratefully accepted. Joe found him pleasant to trade details with and they bantered amicably about their home countries and the French until an insistent buzzing in

Joe's pocket interrupted them. He took out his phone and glanced at it. A voicemail. Six missed calls. Joe assumed half would be from the UK office, one was probably Nathalie confirming their dinner arrangement, another could well be from Belgium – he'd sent a message saying he'd be a day or so late. He scrolled to the missed numbers only to find all six were from the house, from home.

Filling the kettle, Joe tucked the phone under his chin and dialled his voicemail. What could be so important it warranted six calls successively from Tess? Had she found a new job already? Suddenly he found himself hoping not. He couldn't deny the tiny knot of tension hitting him between the shoulder blades as connection to his message service was made. He glanced at his watch. Nearly lunch-time here. An hour earlier in Saltburn. And suddenly Tess's voice in a tone he'd not yet heard. Not the temper in which she'd seethed at him. Not the shy voice of when she hovered outside the study, or the soft sing-song tones reserved for Em. There was none of the chattiness he'd been able to elicit after a glass of wine, or the playful indignation she employed to respond to his teasing. And it wasn't the comedy voice with which she communicated with his dog. She sounded panicked, half sobbing, and all she said was, Joe, please call me, as soon as you can.

'There is a problem – in the UK – at my home. Do you mind?' Joe replenished the man's tea who gave him a sympathetic look, pressing his own phone to his chest in support before leaving. Joe dialled Saltburn. If Tess didn't answer in her daftly formal trademark way, he'd know that something was seriously amiss.

It was ringing.

There was a clatter.

'Joe?'

'Yes – it's me. I'm sorry – I've only just picked up your message. Is everything OK?'

There was silence.

'Tess?'

'Joe.'

'Yes, Tess. What's up?' He had no idea how to decipher the pause that followed. Usually, he never noticed if he was in one country calling another. But the distance today was palpable. 'Are you crying? Tess?'

'It's Wolf.'

Joe went stone cold. Not Wolf. Let the house be on fucking fire – anything – but not Wolf. He was going to have to ask – God, he feared it but he had to – and quickly. 'Is he dead?'

Tess was clearing her nose, it sounded like static on the line. 'No. But he might not pull through. He was hit.'

'Where is he now?'

'At the vet's. He's having an operation – they're going to try.'

'What happened?'

'I don't know. I found him – at the side of the road.'

She was sobbing and her unabashed emotion both touched and frustrated him because he really needed details, facts, however hard. He needed them so he could feel some control and to judge how to react. It was as if his emotional capacity was pressed up against a dam of emergency common sense. He assessed he was in a different country on a Saturday lunch-time. There was nothing he could do this minute, this afternoon and probably not for the next few days either.

'OK,' he said.

Tess didn't sound OK at all.

'Are *you* OK, Tess?'

She sounded distraught. 'You should have seen him, Joe. Poor Wolfy, poor little guy.'

Suddenly a swell of tenderness swept up and over that dam of Joe's. He thought of his dog, of Tess, of her affection for Wolf, of his affection for her and for his dog. And he thought, who but Tess could call a thunking old hound like Wolf *little guy*? But she was right; it was a pertinent distillation.

'I'll try and come back,' he told her, 'as soon as I can.'

'Joe – don't,' Tess said. 'The vet – she said she'd call. And I said, should I call you and she said, yes, she thought I should but she said – she said she really didn't know. So she said just to wait in for her call.'

'Will you phone me as soon as you've spoken to her?'

'Of course I will.'

Out of the window, Joe could see the man, still holding his mug of tea, still having time off his gripe. He was about to say goodbye when he stopped for a moment.

'But are *you* OK, Tess?'

She took a while to respond.

'Poor Wolf,' she said. 'You should have seen him, Joe, you should have seen him.'

Joe was walking across the town square, late for supper with Nathalie, when Tess finally phoned him. He'd tried her a couple of times during the afternoon; both times she'd hurried him away, saying, I thought you were the vet, go away, I need to keep the line clear. He had checked his phone regularly, simultaneously relieved yet also perturbed at no missed calls, trying to chivvy himself that no news could potentially be good news. How did Tess know where the vet was, he wondered, not knowing if the number was in the scrappy notebook by the phone. How did it happen? Why didn't they stop, the bastards? How could you not know if you hit a dog like Wolf? Such thoughts underscored his day like the constant threat of inclement weather.

Actually, it was a fine evening, when late April masquerades as mid-May and dusk decides to fall a whole lot later than yesterday. He'd showered at the apartment; his phone on the edge of the sink, angular and black and masculine alongside the feminine scatter of Nathalie's cosmetics. She wears too much make-up, really, Joe thought, sniffing a lipstick. She over-eggs the pudding sometimes, Joe thought, unscrewing the mascara wand and thinking, how the fuck do women let bristles like that so near their eyeballs. He thought how every time he'd stayed here, she'd always been the first one up, off to the bathroom to paint what she believed to be the prettiest picture for Joe. But he had seen her barefaced and thought it was a pity she'd never believe him if he told her that make-up masked a little of her beauty. In his eyes, at least.

Come on, *phone me.*

Summer was tangibly close because in the square the old boys were settled at outdoor tables, playing cards or chess or chequers, with bottles of *pastis* to hand. Women were wearing their cardigans loose around their shoulders and there were bare legs where, even a week ago, there had been boots and tights. He entered the restaurant, shaking hands with the proprietor and going over to the table to Nathalie.

'You are late, Joe.'

'I've had a day of it.'

'Of what?'

'It's an expression. How was your day?'

'It was good – but it is not good that you work on Saturday, no?'

'It's not good, tell me about it.' Joe drained his glass of beer. 'And the men aren't happy – but we can't leave the materials because they will set. We've broken the back of it. Perhaps I won't go in on Monday.'

Nathalie raised an eyebrow lasciviously and chinked glasses before calling for fresh drinks. No sooner had they arrived, than Joe's phone went and he leapt from the table to rush outside.

He never usually answers it if it goes out of hours, Nathalie thought. Or he takes the call with a roll of his eyes and only

231

half an ear. She looked outside, he was pacing, his head bowed, biting his thumb, listening intently. So maybe this isn't work, thought Nathalie.

'He's going to be OK, Joe.' Tess sounded triumphant and exhausted.

'Halle-fucking-lujah,' Joe said.

'They could save his leg – but not his tail. He broke two ribs but his jaw didn't need pinning and his back is fine. He had to have lots of stitches and the vet said he looks worse than the injuries are – on account of having to shave his fur here and there.'

Joe listened.

'I can collect him – perhaps as soon as the day after tomorrow, would you believe. He just needs to be nursed and kept quiet.'

Joe listened.

'I can't tell you how horrible it's been.'

'I'm sorry I wasn't there.'

'I'm glad you weren't,' Tess said and he could tell from her tone she wasn't being remotely objectionable. 'You're his master,' she said. 'I wouldn't want you seeing your boy like that.'

'He's lucky to have you,' Joe said. And then he thought about it. 'Thank God you were there.' And he thought about it some more. Then he didn't think, he just spoke. 'Thank you for being there.' Pause. 'Stay put, Tess,' he said. 'Don't go.'

She thought about that as she replaced the receiver. Where else would I be, Joe?

Nathalie was pouting.

'He's going to be OK.'

'Who is?'

232

'Oh – I didn't tell you. My dog was run over – they thought he wasn't going to make it. But he is. That was the call.'

'I am pleased for you and for your dog,' said Nathalie, who'd seen a picture of Wolf and had wondered why English people so often ignore basic tenets of taste by choosing things so overtly vulgar. She'd only been to England once – long before she'd met Joe. The hairstyles of elderly ladies, the apparel of teenagers, the types of dogs, the combinations on menus, the men who worked as builders – they were all guilty of the same crime: the cult of the vulgar. 'You were speaking to the vet, just now?' She checked her watch and raised an eyebrow. The English and their pets.

Joe was engrossed in his fish soup; the relief of the good news had unleashed his appetite which he had neglected all day. He glanced across at Nathalie who was regarding him levelly.

'No, it wasn't the vet – it was Tess.'

Her expression didn't change and he now noticed a haughty pinch to her lips, which he didn't like. 'You spoke to her,' Joe said, 'when you phoned the house.'

'She is your –?'

'She was my house-sitter,' Joe said.

'Was? This is the past tense? She is no longer?'

Joe spooned soup. 'I don't know.'

'But she is still there, at the house?'

He didn't bother to nod. Obviously she's still at the house – she phoned me about my injured dog.

'You are fucking her?'

Joe had learned not to be startled by Nathalie's bluntness so he didn't rise to it. He didn't like her tone or the implication and her jealousy was as unbecoming as it was flattering. So calm and controlled and cold, compared to Tess's uncontained indignation. Nathalie's eyes burned dark with possessiveness; Tess's cheeks had simply turned puce.

Should he answer? Could he be bothered? Couldn't he just

233

enjoy the meal and drink to Wolf's good health? The soup was wonderful but he fancied more *rouille* and he looked around for the waiter.

'You are fucking this woman Tess?'

Joe looked at her. He could easily take his mind off the stress of the day by playing Nathalie. But he didn't want to. 'Actually I'm not, Nathalie.'

She didn't look as though she believed him.

'I don't know what you are pushing for,' he said.

She shrugged sulkily. And after the meal and a bottle of wine at her apartment, she fucked his brains out.

Before Joe went to sleep, as Nathalie trailed her fingertips over his biceps, his chest, she propped herself up on her arm, her other shoulder back a little to display her breasts to their best advantage and she asked him again.

'If she is no longer your house-sitter, what is she still doing at your house?'

Joe thought about it. He thought how, whenever he thought of his house, Tess populated whichever room sprang to mind. She hadn't found a new job, had she? He had asked her not to go, to stay. What was she doing right now? Pottering around, shifting his things from room to room, shunting his furniture from here to there? Making toast in the kitchen? Checking on her baby? Sanding, painting, tidying? Writing labels for jam jars? Other nights, quite possibly any combination of the above. But he thought she was most likely tonight to be mourning the huge space Wolf's absence would have created.

'She lives there.'

Nathalie asked him again if he was fucking Tess.

He pretended to be asleep because he really couldn't be bothered to validate her question with even a one-word answer.

Chapter Twenty-one

Seb was disappointed that Tess hadn't phoned, disappointed but not despondent. She hadn't phoned him the time before either, after he'd sat in the kitchen of the big house and pulled her onto his lap for that snog and fumble. He'd given her his phone number then, tacked it onto the kitchen calendar himself, if he remembered rightly. He liked to think himself an easygoing bloke, so he was happy to wonder whether Tess simply hated using the phone. After all, his dad did and Seb never doubted his affection. Whenever Seb phoned home long-distance, which he did weekly, if his father answered Seb had come to expect little more than, hullo, son, I'll just pass you on to your mother. Some people just aren't phone people, Seb thought as he checked with his boss at the surf shop if he could take an hour for lunch. As he headed up the bank to Glenside, he rationalized that he couldn't really be disappointed because Tess hadn't actually let him down, let alone blown him out – she said she'd call after all, she just hadn't called *yet*. He liked her; he'd enjoyed her company in the pub and he'd certainly liked the stuff back at his place afterwards. He was just hoping for an action-replay sooner, he fancied a bit more of that indoor sport. So, he decided to facilitate it – and save her a phone call – by taking an early lunch hour and popping by to arrange another date now.

He really didn't need his fleece on. He pulled it over his head as he walked along Albion Terrace and tied it loosely around his waist. Not bad to be out and about in a T-shirt. Mind you, it would be May in two days. What does she do in that big old house all day, he wondered? Fancy choosing a job in Saltburn that had nothing to do with the beach and actively enforced periods of time indoors. He often marvelled that he was actually paid to do what he did. The job in itself – and the ability to be in the sea most days – was rewarding enough. Meeting someone like Tess was an unforeseen bonus – he'd been here a few months and was intending to stay for the British summer before heading home for the Australian one. He had assumed early on that, other than grandmothers and midriff-baring teenagers, there were few females in the town of his own age and standing. Well, the few he'd seen had rings on their fourth fingers and usually a toddler or two in tow. But then, along came Tess. Toddler yes, ring no, midriff – now he'd seen it – in better shape than most of the teenage contingent of town. There was also something encouraging about a fellow out-of-towner. You could say things like, *you know – that place around the corner from the station, off the street where the dodgy pub is*, with no shame for not knowing specifics. You could share a private joke at the expense of the locals without it being treason. You had common ground – finding out how each other came to be here and whence each other came.

Here he was, at the house again, the gate closed – but wasn't it always? Yes, he thought it was. Anyway, no harm in trying the bell. He rang and waited and thought the hollow reverberating clang sounded incongruously Addams Family for Saltburn. He was enjoying an image of Tess dressed up as Morticia, when she opened the door in jeans and a grey top.

236

'Hey – just thought I'd pop by – just fancied a stroll during my lunch hour.' He paused. 'Good weekend? It was nice to see you on Friday – I was wondering if we could, you know, do it again?'

Tess twitched her lip and for a split second Seb thought, shit, she's going to blow me out right now, and he started to back away with an easygoing shrug.

'I'm sorry – I said I'd call, didn't I?' And while Tess was relaying the details of Wolf's accident, Seb was thinking to himself, thank you, God, it wasn't me – it was just the old hound.

'So you'll call, will you – let me know how the old guy is doing?'

'Of course,' said Tess, as if Seb's visit had been in Wolf's honour all along. 'I hope to have him home from the vet's in the next day or two.'

'Right,' said Seb, 'well, I suppose I'd better head back to work, then.'

Tess thought to herself, you ought to invite him in for a cup of tea or a glass of water at the very least after he's tramped all the way up the bloody hill to see how Wolf is. 'Would you like something? Before you go?'

Yes, he bloody well would. Her hand was on the front door, but he was over the threshold and, with little more than a subtle lean, his mouth reached hers. And once again, Tess found herself being energetically tongued. His hands, today, focusing on her bum. He stepped away and gave her a lascivious wink. 'Phone me, babe,' he said. 'We can pick up where we left off.'

I only meant would you like a glass of water or a cup of tea, Tess said silently as Seb walked off down the drive, turning every now and then to salute or wave to her.

'He is such a lovely bloke,' said Tess. 'I wish I liked him more.' She stopped. 'I don't know what to do.' Suddenly, she was aware that she was alone in the kitchen. She'd been talking out loud forgetting that there was no longer a dog to raise his head and thump his raggedy tail against the flagstone floor at all she said.

The call Tess and Joe were waiting for came after surgery hours a couple of days later, on the Thursday evening, five days after the accident.

Tess phoned Joe directly. They'd been speaking daily. Though Wolf had been taken off the critical list, the calls had continued and had veered off at tangents. Wolf, still the reason for the call, was no longer the purpose of the call. The calls were an exercise in bridge building – Joe forming the support on one side in France, Tess forming the other back in England; Wolf was what they carried, he was the span between the two. The material Joe and Tess were using was mundane chat – and it was proving to be long and flexible. How's the weather with you? they'd ask after the update on the dog. What's Emmeline been up to? Any troubled water under the bridge? It's over a valley, Tess – I told you. Oh sorry, I forgot. Well, you've had other things on your mind. I know – I'll call you tomorrow, if you like. Please do. When's a good time? Any time, Tess – if I see it's home calling, I'll always answer. OK then, I'll phone tomorrow. Good – speak then.

So, Tess phoned him on Thursday evening. Nathalie heard the phone, saw it on the bookcase, but glanced away as if the thing was of no consequence. She increased the volume on the television. She had grown used to these daily calls between Joe and Tess. She took comfort in imagining this house-sitter cum veterinary nurse being square in fashion sense as much as physique. Just some dull, dowdy girl no doubt with a bit of a crush on Joe. He probably barely noticed her. Nathalie told herself to fear nothing – not least because Joe was rampant at the moment, absolutely insatiable.

'Joe! Your phone!'

He came through, a towel around his waist, little trails of water dinking and darting mercurial paths through the hairs on his legs. It was Tess. If he asked Nathalie to kill the volume, he'd be obliged to take the call right here. If he didn't, he was at liberty to go back to the bedroom, or out onto the balcony – though standing there in just a skimpy towel might be unwise.

'*Chien*,' he said to Nathalie who nodded at the television and didn't touch the remote control.

Joe took the phone back to the bedroom, answering it as he went. 'Tess?'

'Joe – it's me! He's coming home – the vet phoned. He's coming home tomorrow. I can go and collect him after surgery hours!'

'Slow down, woman – say it again?'

So she did, with exactly the same flurry of triumph and relief. 'What a clever little chappy, hey! Fixing himself in only five days. The vet said he surprised them all. She said she'd write a paper about it! He has to have antibiotics and he'll have to wear one of those flowerpot contraptions around his neck to stop him chewing his stitches. And his dressings will have to be changed – I'm supposed to be doing that last bit, but that's fine with me.'

Joe decided not to interject; he was enjoying absorbing the information and energy.

'Shall I phone you, Joe – when he's back? When Wolf's home again, safe and sound?'

'You do that, Tess,' said Joe. 'Promise me you'll do just that.'

Tess was enjoying Friday morning very much because later that day she'd be bringing Wolf home and it was a lovely day already, balmy and bright. Spring seemed very last season

239

though the month had only just changed. She and Lisa had met in the playground with plans to feed the children up at the house afterwards. Lisa was extracting the details of Seb's impromptu visit earlier in the week and telling Tess to get herself a bloody mobile phone soon.

'You can't construct a relationship in the modern age without the power of the text message,' she said. 'Most of which I will insist you forward to me, of course.'

'Who said anything about a relationship!' said Tess.

'You need to be contactable at all times,' Lisa said.

'Be his beck-and-call girl?'

Lisa laughed. 'I'll bet he has a great line in dirty texts, love. You must ring him – you will, won't you? He'd be great company while you're dog-sitting.' Lisa pushed Sam's swing and said, wheee! wheee! before turning to Tess in giggles. 'You could phone him, Tess. Phone him and say, hey, Seb, fancy coming over to do a little babysitting, doggy style?' Her raucous glee was infectious.

'You dreadful woman,' Tess laughed. 'The very thought of it.'

'The thought of it? The thought of a nice buff surfer's bod? The thought of a lad obviously hot for you? Yes – you're quite right, Tess. Dreadful thought – dreadful.'

Tess stuck her tongue out and then returned to pushing Em, thinking about the thought of it. Not so dreadful, really. Perhaps she ought to call him, once Wolf was settled and doing well.

Sam was fidgeting to leave his swing for what Lisa and Tess described as 'the boingy thing', but Em objected when Tess tried to coax her out of hers. She didn't mind, she'd always found pushing a swing comforting and meditative.

So when Joe strolled down the hill, under the auspices of filling the fridge but with a private hope of coming across Tess perhaps out for a walk, that's what he saw – Tess pushing the swing, enthralled by some daydream or other if her beatific smile was anything to go by. She'd lifted her face to the sun, she was miles away according to her expression. Joe observed them: Tess and Emmeline, happily lulled by the catharsis of peaceful playground simplicity. He thought, Tess is not wearing a hoody. He thought, her hair has grown longer. He thought, I like the way she's wearing it loose. He thought, shall I back away now and just surprise her at the house – or shall I make myself known, stop and say hello?

His decision was made for him. Tess sensed someone looking at her. When she turned and saw it was Joe her hands fell away from the swing so that when it came back, it knocked her firmly in the stomach. But she didn't seem to notice. She could only stand stock-still, mouth agape as she looked over to him. The swing touched her again, just glancing against her body this time. And then it slowed, as if it was tired, as if that's the end of the ride. And Tess didn't appear to hear Em's protestations. But Lisa did – and Lisa looked at Tess and thought, what's she looking at? And she followed Tess's gaze and alighted on Joe and Lisa thought, who the bloody hell is that?

'Who the bloody hell is that?' Lisa asked as Tess walked past her, Em flailing her discontent in her mother's arms. But Tess didn't notice and Tess didn't answer Lisa. She just walked straight over to Joe and they stood there, either side of the railings for a suspended moment. Lisa watched them greet each other – him lowering his head a little as Tess raised hers a little. She saw how Tess smiled, that Em had reached out and Joe had given his finger to the baby, putting his other hand gently, briefly, on Tess's shoulder as they spoke intently to one another.

Lisa thought, Jesus, Tess, *I'll* get you a bloody mobile phone – if ever there was a time to text you to say you dark horse, you dark dark horse you. You never told me you were in love with this Joe bloke.

*   *   *

'I was just strolling down to pick up some food.'

'I was just in the playground.'

'I know – I saw.'

Tess rolled her eyes at herself but Joe just laughed.

'Do you want to join me, Tess? You're probably more aware of what we need.'

'Yes, sure. Oh – I mean no. I can't – I didn't bring the buggy.'

'I see.'

'Lisa – my friend over there, with the little boy with the curly hair – we meet here.' And then Tess stopped. She didn't want to tell Joe about her previous plans for lunch in case he said, carry on, don't mind me. The truth was, much as she had grown so fond of Lisa, Joe was back. Joe was here and Wolf would be coming home and everything else would just have to wait.

'Lisa,' said Joe vaguely, looking back to the playground.

'She's lovely.'

'Well, what do we need?'

Tess thought about it. I need *this*, she thought, I've missed this.

'Oh – just pick up what you fancy.'

'I'll see you back at the house,' Joe said, doffing an imaginary cap. 'Back at home.' He headed down the hill and Tess and Em walked back up it slowly towards the house. She passed Lisa in the playground, now chatting to another mum. Lisa motioned to Tess the universal gesture for 'phone me'. Tess's response was an expansive, double thumbs-up. Lisa thought, poor old Seb – you don't stand a chance.

*

242

Back at the house, Tess gazed at Em who seemed unaware of her mother's state of heightened excitement. Tess dropped to her knees, though the cold flagstones met her, giving her daughter a gentle prod in her rounded little tummy.

'Em,' she said in a whisper, 'Joe's back. Joe's come home. And Wolfy's coming back too and by tonight, everything will be back to how it should be.'

Em held onto her mother's probing finger. Tess touched Em's nose. 'Wish us luck,' she said, 'wish us lots of luck. All of us.' Em said the word that only her mother knew was 'nose' and Tess took time out from her grown-up ponderings to complete the points of the face with her daughter. Yighs. Years. Mowf.

'Clever Em,' said Tess, scooping her up and hugging her close. She stood, silent and still. Please let today be lovely.

'Quick! We need to tidy!' and Tess scooted off from room to room, flinging up windows, plumping cushions, straightening furniture, checking for dust, her every move shadowed by Em.

Joe returned, laden with shopping.

'I thought we'd do a simple lunch,' he told her, busying himself putting stuff away because Tess was standing peculiarly motionless in the kitchen holding Emmeline's wrists, who was standing barefoot on the table. 'Then we can have a celebratory dinner to toast the return and the speedy convalescence of the Wolfmeister.'

He laid out cheese and crusty bread, some celery sticks and fresh tomatoes, a jar of chutney. 'Excuse me, Emmeline,' he said as if Tess wouldn't know that her daughter was in the way but he ended up having to lay the plates and cutlery at the other end of the table and moved the food accordingly. He looked at Tess. 'You all right? Hungry?' He nudged her and broke the trance.

243

'I'm starving,' she said, as if she'd just come into the kitchen.

And there they were once again, eating together and chatting away.

'I can't believe you're here,' said Tess. 'Wolf is going to be thrilled.'

'Wolf won't know what hit him, hey?'

'God knows what hit him, Joe – but I wouldn't be surprised if it was a steamroller. No one stopped – can you believe that?'

'Perhaps they didn't realize.'

'How can you not realize if you hit a dog the size of Wolfy?'

Joe glanced at his watch. 'So we can pick him up at six?'

'*You* ought to be the one to pick him up,' Tess said quietly. 'It should be you to go.'

Joe thought, that's thoughtful. He found his gaze lingering until Tess made a sudden move and said, tea?

'Thanks,' said Joe. 'I'll do a couple of hours' work, then.'

Tess made him a mug of builder's tea. A KitKat too – he hadn't seen those when he'd put the digestives away. 'I keep them in the fridge,' she told him, 'in the door – where the eggs could go. But it's a trade secret – KitKats taste better chilled and eggs should be kept at room temperature.' She opened the fridge for emphasis, then pointed to a little wire basket which he remembered seeing in the box in her room, now on the dresser with half a dozen eggs in it. When they both looked at the eggs they couldn't help but catch sight of the photo of Joe in KL right next to them. They'd forgotten about all that. If they started talking about it, they'd have to confront the other stuff too, like mother Mary. It had been easy and lovely thus far. It was a special day. Neither wanted to sabotage it. They glanced away from the photo and stared at the eggs before taking their cups of tea and proceeding with their separate afternoons.

'Any washing?' Tess knocked at the study door and used her hushed tone. 'I'm doing darks.'

'There's a heap on my bathroom floor,' came Joe's disembodied voice. 'Help yourself, if you really want to.'

'Oh, I don't mind,' Tess said to herself as much as to Joe as she climbed the stairs, 'I don't mind at all.'

*　　*　　*

Tess had so wanted Em to stay awake for Wolf's return – a welcome party befitting him – but though Joe had left before six, over an hour later he was still not home and Em had dozed off. Tess went from window to window, craning a view in any direction. Like a magical omen, the weather was so warm today she'd been able to keep many windows open. At this time of evening, with birds busy singing the glories of the day just gone, the light golden and mellow and promising all good things for tomorrow, the breeze a little fresher but still benign and the dimensions of the house's windows – broad, tall sashes – allowing it all to sweep through the house, the division between outside and indoors became wonderfully indistinct. I ought to change, Tess thought. And then she thought, Wolf won't mind. And she didn't think Joe would mind either.

She went downstairs and opened the fridge. At the playground, she'd asked Joe to buy fresh liver for Wolf. It was there. So was a fresh trout and, by the looks of things, various accoutrements for a fine dinner. She rummaged around. Fresh dill. New potatoes. Where did he find the asparagus? She looked in the freezer: luxury vanilla ice cream. It all made her smile, and it made her hungry too. No good staying in the kitchen, she'd only pick. She went back to the hallway where, in the side return, which was simply an aesthetic space with no prior function, she'd made a parlour for Wolf. His blankets, a cushion, his favourite rubber toy and one of Joe's moccasins. On a tray, his bowls and underneath it all, newspaper to guard against accidents. She'd said to Joe that Wolf could feel part of the action here, without being in the thick of it. He won't want us tripping over him if he does his usual splay halfway across the kitchen floor, she'd said. And they'd both looked pensively back into the kitchen, the expanse of flagstones looking bare and cold without Wolf lolling about in his trademark sprawl.

She glanced at the grandfather clock though she knew the real time bore no relation. She gave the pendulum a swing, as she often did, like she'd seen Joe do. She thought, they must be back soon.

'He's a soldier, this one,' the vet says to Joe.

'He certainly looks like he's been in the wars,' Joe says, stroking what he can of Wolf. 'Don't you, old man? You brave old boy. Poor lad.'

'I have every faith in him,' the vet says, 'and in my skills.'

'He does look a state,' Joe says affectionately.

'He was no oil painting before,' the vet laughs. 'Were you, Wolf?'

'No, you're right.'

'He'll be a conversation starter – you won't be able to go two steps without someone asking all about it.'

'Well, it'll make a change from being stopped and asked, what the hell kind of breed is *that*?'

'Exactly – he'll have a whole new notoriety and a new following too,' the vet says. 'Now, in addition to the appointments we've made, I'm going to have the nurse show you how to change the dressings – and what to look for in the tail stump particularly.'

She watches Joe shift. She thinks he's gone a little pale but she can't be sure because she likes a sunbed herself and everyone else round here always looks pasty to her.

'I'm not very good at – stuff,' Joe says. 'Call me squeamish.'

'Well, Wolf needs you to be good at – *stuff*,' the vet says. 'It's straightforward enough.'

Joe doesn't look convinced.

'Perhaps Tess could take charge,' the vet says. 'She's a capable young woman, that one.'

Joe thinks about this and the vet regards him for a moment, a little quizzically. 'Do you know how she brought him here? Have you heard? Did she tell you?'

Joe looks confused.

'Thought not,' the vet says. 'Well, I'll tell you. I was actually out in Saltburn on an emergency. She phoned the surgery and asked where we were exactly. The nurse said, Marske and Tess said, where's that – she thought we were in Saltburn. She was given road directions but she said she couldn't come by car so the nurse said, grab a cab, they'll know where we are. So I'm driving out of Saltburn and I came across this sight – some poor girl pushing a galumphing great hound in a kid's buggy while she somehow carried a small child at the same time. She must have done nearly a mile like that. Needless to say, I picked them up. She was frantic.'

'She could have killed him,' Joe says, 'lifting him, transporting him like that – surely?'

'She probably saved his life, actually. She had him swaddled tightly in a towel. It stemmed the bleeding. It was good for shock. She was killing herself to bring him to us.'

Joe thinks about Tess's car, how it had sputtered into his drive on that first day. About the boxes that were to be left in the boot. He remembers her saying it was low on fuel. He remembers her saying she'd driven his mother back to Swallows. He thought back to how they'd taken his car to the Transporter Bridge. Tussling with the child seat, narking at each other, laughing.

*

247

Joe pulls into the drive, turning a slow, careful arc in contrast to his usual gravelly spin. He's seen Tess dart from the drawing-room window, reappearing at the window by Wolf's new quarters. Now she's gone again. He opens the car door and by the time he's eased Wolf carefully onto the ground, the front door has been opened and Tess is standing there, her hands to her mouth. Joe lets Wolf set the pace and he finds himself tottering a little in sympathy. He thinks Wolf is like a very doddery old gent today. Usually, as soon as the car door opens, Wolf has bolted out to careen around his estate as though he's been incarcerated. Not today. Joe looks over to Tess. She takes her hands away from her mouth, crouches a little and opens her arms, like he's seen her do to Emmeline. He can see that she's too choked to speak and that Wolf can't wag in reply because he no longer has a tail, he has a stump swathed by a bright green bandage. All he can do is keep going, wearing the vast white plastic lampshade around his neck like a ludicrous bonnet. He has a bright blue bandage around his foreleg and as he hobbles closer, Tess can see shaved areas and stitches here and there.

They are by her now. She's on her knees, trying to cup Wolf's face in her hands though she has to delve right inside the lampshade to do so.

She looks from Wolf to Joe and back again.

'You know something,' she says and Joe is listening though he knows she's speaking to the dog, 'you look a whole lot better than you did last week, little guy. You look like Wolf again – just in some crazy fancy dress costume. Welcome home, daft dog. Welcome home.'

Chapter Twenty-two

Tess sat up in bed, in the dark, with the curtains open so she could sense the black nothingness of a countryside night uncorrupted by streetlamps or sirens. She pulled her knees up and linked her arms around them under the quilt, laid her cheek against them – it really felt as though she was giving herself a hug. To smile in the dark felt somehow safe; as if she wouldn't be tempting fate if she couldn't be seen. She pondered the reasons for her contentment; it wasn't as if specific things had been said or any overt gestures given – it hadn't been a special evening, if special is defined by specifics. On the contrary it was the lack of specifics – it was instead the things in general that made it so affirming. No declarations of intent, no mulling over what had passed, no discussion of the issues that had arisen – yet no active avoidance of them either. It was just an evening during which they had both been at their ease.

She went over to the window, pressing her face against the glass, looking out into the night garden. They probably could have gone over the whole Kate business and likewise, they could have talked through the issue of Mary. But these things seemed somehow trivial compared to the bigger picture of enjoying the here and now, of feeling comfortable in trading chit-chat and falling into step alongside each other again.

Do you think it needs pepper? No, not really. I think I added pepper too early in the cooking – did you know it loses its potency? No, I didn't. Oh yes – it does, that's why you should always add pepper right at the end. I heard that a squeeze of lemon juice added at the end really brings out the flavours without adding its own. That's news to me – I'll try it. I wonder if Calpol works for dogs. What's Calpol? It's children's paracetamol – it's strawberry flavour. You know, Tess – the vet's given him pretty heavy-duty meds. I know – but they look horrible whereas Calpol is pink and sweet and soothing. Poor old Wolf. Yes, poor old thing. He seems OK in himself, don't you think? All things considering, yes. And he loved the liver. He did, didn't he? He won't want to go back to Pedigree Chum! It'll cost you a fortune, Joe. So you're sure you don't mind being head nurse then Tess? Not at all – though I wouldn't have you down as squeamish. I can't even deal with splinters. Actually, I've become much more capable with all that stuff since becoming a mother, I used to be an utter wuss before that. Are you saying I'm an utter wuss? Yes, Joe, I am – can you pass the water, please?

Replaying the minutiae again a couple of times, Tess thought how the ease of their communication was as important as the topics themselves. And they weren't topics, really, not in the sense that they were deliberately chosen for interesting discussion. Joe and Tess were two people who, when together, could just talk. Banter, blether, chinwag, natter – when they were together, there was no shortage of what to say. She opened the window. It was chilly and there she was, in the draught in a vest and knickers at God knows what time. But it was invigorating and grounding and the physicality seemed to imprint this specific night on her soul. She thought, here I am. I'm still here, at the Resolution. I'm here on the night of the day that Wolf and Joe came home. She breathed in the air, it was sharp and bracing. She ran her hands lightly over her arms, liking the sensation of goosebumps against her fingertips, enjoying the feel of her touch on her own skin. Could she remember her sister stroking her arms when she was little? Or did she just make up that memory? She wasn't sure, knowing full well how it is easier to invent a past than acknowledge memories that aren't particularly happy. And, for a moment, Tess regretted that it was hardly the kind of thing she'd ever ask Claire now. But she bolstered herself with thoughts of Em, sound asleep in her very own room just yards away. And she smiled when she remembered those very first months utterly alone with the baby, feeling that the world could collapse around them and they'd be OK, in fact they probably wouldn't even notice. Week after week in a cocoon of insane exhaustion softly lined with utter awe, when the baby would be in her arms and she would stroke and stroke and stroke.

The pull to Em was intense and Tess left her room to check on her daughter. She didn't touch, she just gazed, thinking to herself, oh God, I love her so much I could roar. And then she thought, I'd better not, I'll wake the household. And then she thought, I must nip down and check on Wolf. It was gone one in the morning. She last checked on him a good two hours ago, just before she went to bed. And as she descended the stairs, she thought to herself, I've just spent two hours really happy.

The first creak on the stairs glided into whatever it was Joe was dreaming about so he didn't notice. The second creak broke his sleep wave. The third woke him up. At the fourth he thought, what's she doing? And because all was then quiet, he deduced she was now downstairs on solid flagstones, rather than upstairs on the uneven corridor. She's checking on Wolf, he thought. He looked at his clock. It seemed to him that he'd been deeply asleep for far longer than two hours. He thought about yesterday; how he'd decided in the small hours that he'd return to the UK. Everything then dovetailed so seamlessly it just served to affirm that he was doing the right thing. No one gave him a hard time, the flight was there – cheap too and fast. He'd really wanted to see Wolf, and actually, when he thought about it now, he'd had a real urge to be home. Not homesickness – he wasn't pining – more it was a drive, a draw that there was one place that he should be and he was going to go there without delay.

And he'd come back and the house had been empty. He hadn't expected Wolf, of course, but he'd imagined Tess. The empty building, though echoey and still, was full of them – Tess, Wolf, even Emmeline: the folk that made his house work. That make my *housework* – he laughed at this, recalling the little jammy handprints low down on the kitchen door, Tess's bizarre arrangement of what appeared to be verge-side grasses in a stained old bottle she'd found God knows where which unbeknownst to her had left a ring mark on the mahogany console, the scatter of buggy and boots and rusk crumbs in the entrance hall. But then he thought to himself, that's unfair of me, the house has never seemed so bright and homely and fresh.

It was colder here than in France. Not because the weather was that different this time of year, but because in France he spent his time in a modern apartment with communal, regulated heat and also a body in the bed. Here he was in a high-ceilinged stone building over 130 years old, with windows that didn't close and gaps under the doors. He left his bed and pulled on boxers and a T-shirt. What's she doing down there? he wondered. Perhaps I'll go and see.

Tess thinks she knows the stairs pretty well – which treads cause a cacophony of creaks, which ones have a milder groan that won't wake Em or make Wolf bay. However, she's not aware that those have woken Joe. Down in Wolf's sickbay, she's not aware that Joe is making his own way down, that he knows a route along the stairs that is utterly soundless, a route he perfected during his childhood in the silent watches of the night when he'd creep soundlessly downstairs and stand by the front door and wonder how to run away.

Joe, though, is far from Tess's mind just now. As he makes his silent passage down the stairs, she's already engrossed in tending to Wolf.

And the sight of her causes him to crave invisibility.

Appropriately enough, there's a full moon for Wolf. It's sufficient for Tess to nurse the dog without the need for artificial light. Joe sees how the moonlight glances off the flagstones and reverberates from the white walls to bathe everything in soft silver. She's sitting on her heels on one of the blankets, with her back to Joe, bending forward, whispering to the dog.

Tess in a vest and knickers. A plain white vest and white cotton knickers. Between the two, as she leans forward, a small but compelling ellipse of skin – like a shy, pink smile. He thinks, that really can't pass as a camisole and panties, that really is just a vest and knickers. No frills. The simplicity, combined with the light and the time of night, is peculiarly stunning and Joe is perturbed how aroused it's made him. She's sitting on her heels and she's leaning forward and her bum, demurely covered in white cotton, is really so peach-shaped that Joe has to admit the cliché is both perfect and yet does her an injustice. The soles of her feet under her bum. The pads of her toes, becoming rounder as they become smaller, like little buds. Shoulders bare and shapely, as if carved from alabaster by the lick of moonlight. Her hair she has scrunched up to keep it away from her face, inadvertently revealing the elegant curve of her neck for Joe.

What's she doing exactly? Joe wonders as he watches her soak a flannel in a bowl of water, her face in profile. It strikes Joe that, unseen, Tess's prettiness can reveal itself. It's as if it hides when she's in company, as if she draws it into herself and says, don't come out until no one's looking. Like that day when he watched her hanging out the washing. Like this morning, when he saw her in the playground. Like this evening when she thought he was engrossed at the stove but he turned and just looked at her while she was busy writing some list or other. And like now – her features in profile as delicate and defined as a Victorian cameo silhouette. But what's she doing with that flannel, dipping it in the bowl, wringing it out a little? Whatever it is, he's pleased for her to continue because he gets to see the sweep and delineation of her arms.

He must have shifted because Wolf has clocked him and has made a brave attempt to voice a greeting. Tess turns quickly – but she settles because it's Joe, it's only Joe.

'Sorry, did I startle you?' he whispers, walking over.

'No,' she says, 'I'm used to far stranger creaks and shadows when you're not here.'

He comes to stand by her, looking down on her and his dog. She looks up and sees boxer shorts and looks away quickly. His knees are at her eye level and she's never seen his legs bare and they are athletic with a smattering of dark hairs. She drops her gaze and sees his feet; they are shapely and strong and she is pleased she's dipping the flannel in the bowl because otherwise she'd be tempted to trace the tendons of his foot with her fingertips. He squats down, one arm relaxed over his knees, his other hand down on the floor for balance.

'What's with the flannel?'

'Well, don't laugh – but I wondered if Wolf was thirsty but

feeling a bit incapacitated to drink from his bowl. So I'm just dipping the flannel and doing a bit of a drip and sip for him.'

'Seems he is thirsty.'

'Actually, he probably just likes the attention. I'm a muggins.'

'You're Florence Frigging Nightingale, my love.'

And Tess's heart lurches and she thinks, oh, call me 'my love' again.

'I was awake anyway,' she shrugs, 'so I just thought I'd pop down and see how he was doing.'

'A model patient, I'd say.'

'Nothing seeping or bleeding. His nose is nice and cold and he feels good and warm. I just wish he had his tail to wag.'

'That tail,' Joe laughs. 'The number of times I cursed it – one wag and oops! another glass broken, or another pile of papers scattered to the floor.'

'He whacked me with it one time,' Tess tells him, 'hard across my thigh. It hurt!'

Joe pauses. 'Thanks, Tess – seriously.'

'Oh God, Joe – it's the least I can do.'

'You're not blaming yourself, are you?'

'No – but that's not to say I wish I'd loitered when he went out for his pee.'

'The vet told me – about how you took him there.'

She looks down and doesn't comment.

'Thank you,' says Joe.

Wolf gives a grumble, as if he's been happy to listen to them witter on but he's tired now and could they go.

'Sleep's the best medicine – that's what my grandma used to say,' Tess says and she sits up off her heels and stands. And now it's Joe who's low, looking at her feet and thinking, you've painted your toenails since I last saw them. They are pale turquoise and they remind him of Tess's sense of humour.

255

At his eye level, her thighs. He decides it would be prudent not to look higher – he's only in his boxers after all.

'Well, night then, Joe.'

'Night, Tess,' he says without turning – he doesn't want to lose his balance. He's still squatting down. He's not as young as he was, you know. It's not just his floorboards that creak. Especially when flagstone chill has just infiltrated his limbs. He waits a moment or two, listens for the sounds on the stairs before he rises. He smiles at Wolf and turns for bed.

Ethereal, like a ghost, Tess is passing along the landing after the first flight, the white of her vest and pants almost luminous. He's now reached the top of the stairs; his door is a little way down the corridor, in the opposite direction.

'Night then,' he says, holding onto the newel post.

She's about to climb the stairs to her floor.

She turns. 'Night, Joe.'

And motion fails them at first because they find themselves rooted to where they stand, facing each other at either end of the landing, yards apart, both of them in the direction opposite to the one they'd intended to go. And then suddenly, motion liberates them, releasing their bodies without them having to think about putting one foot in front of the other. They have no awareness of bridging the distance of the landing. All they know is that they're gliding, they've floated in close and their lips are going to touch any second now. Joe's fingertips have found her jaw, her neck, and Tess's hands have alighted on his forearm, the centre of his chest. There's less light up here than downstairs, it's diffused but it's sufficient for them to see eye to eye, for Joe to dip his face as Tess raises hers, for their noses to gently nudge against each other until their lips whisper the overture of a kiss.

*

Then they have no further need of moonlight or sight because touch takes over. As the kiss deepens, as lips part to welcome in tongues, so featherlight fingertips change to probing, clasping, all-feeling. His hands hold her close in the small of her back, then flow up to her neck, along her collarbone, her cheek, her head, his fingers snagging on her scrunched-up hair. Her hands are sweeping up his arms, over the dip below his biceps, the rise and run of his shoulders, the strong curve of his back and up and over the band of muscle either side of his spine. She can sense his erection and drops her hand to touch it fleetingly through the cotton of his boxers. They pull apart and stare at each other; in this light their eyes are uniformly dark and glinting, in this light there's a sheen on their lips from each other's kiss.

Tess in a vest. Tess in a vest. Tess's nipples springing behind that vest. Joe is transfixed by them, he puts his hands over them and just keeps them there. In the cup of his hands, he can sense how her breathing quickens and it makes her breasts swell and fit themselves perfectly into his palms. He breaks off to kiss her again, holding the back of her neck and pulling her in close and sinking his mouth, his tongue down deep. Tess in a vest. He's as enthralled by the sight as by what the white cotton keeps out of sight. He tugs the vest down, not at the shoulder straps, but from the neckline. He pulls the cotton down until it's looped underneath her breasts and they are exposed. They are round and perky and, as he caresses one he sips the nipple of the other between his lips. And while he does so, Tess takes his head in her hands and pulls his hair through her fingers and she closes her eyes and thinks, I could stop right here for ever.

He takes his mouth away from her breast and kisses her again. Then he speaks, without breaking the bond between their lips, and it means she can actually feel his words as she hears them.

'Will you sleep with me, Tess? Can I take you to bed?'
He takes her hand and leads her to his room.
She thinks, he sleeps with his curtains open.

He pulls his top over his head to reveal a torso that is manly but not intimidating. He sits on the edge of his bed and pulls her between his legs. He lifts her vest off and takes a moment to just look at her before he starts to kiss her stomach. His hands travel up and down the backs of her thighs, his tongue-tip dips into her belly button. He's feeling around to the fronts of her legs, up to the undulation of her waist, higher to her breasts; down again. As they lie down, they don't take their eyes off each other and they fold themselves into each other and wrap the covers around them. Tenderness and lust inter-mingle. The soft stroking soon enough leads to the ripping down of knickers and boxers and condom pack. Their breathing is audibly short, the instinct is primal and Tess suddenly wants to roll on top of Joe, open her legs and welcome him in deep. She cries out. It's insanely exquisite. Joe is abandoned to the pleasure, moving into her, tasting her, feeling her sex closing around him, sucking him deep as she comes, pulling his own orgasm out to mingle with the receding throbs of hers.

They stay there, fused, exhausted and exhilarated. They are spent and speechless but they continue to kiss. Joe and Tess have discovered they kiss each other with the same ease with which they talk and they find there's so much to say.

Chapter Twenty-three

Tess was woken by the dawn streaming in through the uncurtained windows of Joe's bedroom the next morning, pestering her face and diluting her sleep. She lay still, listening to a bicker of birds outside, to Joe breathing rhythmically next to her. She was lying in the crook of his arm, her face fitting the jigsaw dip just inside his shoulder. Her field of vision was filled with flesh and it was a novel sight indeed, one that she wanted to pore over. A little chest hair, a dark brown nipple, a couple of paler-hued moles. The steady rise and fall of his ribcage, a prominent collarbone. Without moving her head, she raised her eyes. Bristles on his jaw. She smiled – his morning kisses would be less smooth than those last night. His other arm was above his head and along the pillow and she gently took her hand and whispered it over the hair in his armpit before gently laying her arm along his chest. She didn't want to wake him, she just wanted to steal a little private time to look at him and to snuggle herself into the clarity and joy of the precise moment.

But then she heard Em. At first, just the happy little noises which made Tess feel wonderfully replete, as if there were no further gifts that could better her life just then. She was lying in a grand old *bateau-lit* bed, in a room with a view, in a magnificent old house, in the arms of a man for whom her feelings were intense, while listening to the jolly ramblings of her beloved young daughter. However, Em soon tired of being unanswered and so she made sure she wasn't unheard and her chatter turned to complaint and soon enough to hollering indignation. And for the first time in Em's life, Tess thought, shut up. Tess thought, I don't want to come to you, you'll have to wait, I want to be *here*. I want to lie here for longer; I don't want to share myself. I'm not coming.

Em was *not* having *that*.

Tess was not sure when the transition came but she found the impetus for leaving the bed had little to do with the fact that Em wanted her, more that she didn't want Joe to be irritated. Tess's needs and Em's need were colliding. She was going to her child not so much to comfort her but to keep her quiet.

'Em,' she protested as she scooped up the child, 'couldn't you give Mummy a little peace and quiet? Some Mummy time?' She changed the nappy. 'Some grown-up time?' She didn't look at the baby directly. 'Some time for Mummy and Joe?'

From lover to mother, Tess could feel the shift. What was the way back? Plonk Em somewhere safe with a glut of rice cakes and sneak back into Joe's room? Impossible.

Tess went to her room and dressed while Em pulled out the contents of the bottom drawer. What am I meant to do now? Tess wondered. Do I go back to his bedroom with Em in tow? Take him up a cup of tea? Do I wait for him to surface? If he wakes and I'm not there, is the connection gone?

'Was it the heat of the moment in the dead of night?'

260

Tess asked forlornly. 'Em – not that. No, naughty Em. Give it to Mummy. Good girl.'

'Woof.'

'Yes, let's go and see how Wolf is feeling this morning.'

As they made their way down one flight of stairs, Tess cast a longing look down the corridor to Joe's room, before they descended the next flight. Dear God, let him wake up and want more.

Em didn't appear to notice the surgical lampshade contraption encasing the dog's face, nor the fact that his tail was now a fraction of its original length and the stump was sheathed in a wedge of bright green bandage. She didn't pay much attention that his foreleg was bandaged in blue to the elbow and that he was currently standing a little splayed and drunken like a newborn foal. Em just knew that the dog was back and that made her happy so she toddled over and grabbed her usual handful of coat that rose in a coarse roan tuft at the base of his neck.

'Careful!' Tess said, because Wolf looked as though he could be toppled but she saw that the dog was unconcerned. In fact, she thought he probably appreciated this gesture of normality more than the solemn visits from the midnight nursing staff who used to be his master and his master's house-sitter.

'Breakfast?' she asked.

They looked at her beseechingly.

She made them all eggs. Two for Wolf, hard boiled, which she fed him by hand because the walk to the kitchen had obviously been a bit much for him as he was now standing like a wind-hammered scarecrow and staring at the tiles. Em, meanwhile, stabbed buttered Hovis soldiers into a soft-boiled egg. Tess's egg remained unbashed on her plate, with triangles of toast and a mug of tea.

And then Joe came in and said, morning all, and he sat down, pulling Tess's plate over, tucking into her breakfast, mashing the egg onto the toast and taking hearty swigs of her tea.

'Morning,' she said, trying not to let a grin spoil her mock indignation. She made more toast, boiled another egg and guided Wolf to the back door. As she stood in the porch, watching Wolf dodder off for his ablutions, she put her hand on her chest and felt how her heart pounded. This was one of the best mornings in her life so far – and she hadn't a clue what to do next. Ultimately, Wolf solved the dilemma for her.

'He did a wee!' was what she announced even though she thought it was probably the stupidest thing to say.

But Joe just laughed. He'd finished his breakfast, or her breakfast. He rose from the table and took his plate to the sink. On the way back, he touched Em's curls. And then, as he passed by Tess, he put his hand on the back of her neck as he went, his touch gentle but emphatic, and he said, I'm going to have a shower. And there she stood, transfixed by the significance of his touch for long after she heard the tank belching out the hot water.

She turned to Em. 'When you're a teenager,' she told her, 'and someone touches you like that, you'll be saying to me, Mum, I'm never going to wash again.'

But then she thought to herself how Joe's touch hadn't make her feel like a teenager, actually it had made her feel like a woman.

She turned to Em again. 'When you were a baby, you'd go down for an after-breakfast nap, you know. For a good hour.' She tapped Em on the nose. 'And that's when Mummy could have a really long shower.' She listened to the sound of Joe taking his. 'More's the pity,' she said to Em.

After dressing Em, Tess checked Wolf's dressings and as she did so, she wondered about the day ahead in view of the night just gone. Was she meant to loiter for Joe – might they spend time together today? Or was she meant to proceed with the day alone, and was last night just an anomaly? Her heart hurt at the thought of that. She scrambled around her memory for evidence to say otherwise.

But he wouldn't have touched my neck in the kitchen! He could have just said he was going to take a shower! In fact, he needn't have said anything!

But what was she meant to do? And why did it demand so much thinking and fretting? That can't be a good sign. She felt anxious.

In whose hands was it, to carry today what was formed last night?

Or was nothing formed – was it just a shag?

It hadn't felt that way to Tess. In her opinion, they'd made love.

'But who am I to judge? It's been a long, long time for me.'

'What has?'

Tess started and turned from squatting by Wolf in the hallway. Behind her, Joe was leafing through the post.

'What's been a long, long time for you?'

She was stuck how to answer him. She couldn't think of anything clever, or even plausible, to say and the truth wasn't an option because it felt too risky to lay herself bare at this time in the morning.

It's been a long, long time since I nursed a dog.

It's been a long, long time since I saw that much post.

It's been a long, long time since I last saw my father.

It's been a long, long time since Em and I had an ice cream.

It's been a long, long time since I felt this way, Joe – happy and frantic and alive.

It's been a long, long time since I last had sex and, come

263

to think of it, I don't think I've actually been made love to before.

As if. She wasn't going to be saying any of these things.

She felt suddenly shy and stupid. And because she felt shy and stupid, she sensed she'd gone red. So there she was, actually aware that only two minutes previously she'd been deeming herself a woman to whom Joe had made love, but now she was just standing there like a gormless, blushing teenager. She really didn't dare glance at him, but her body conspired against her and her eyes met his and he raised his eyebrow quizzically. All she could do was shrug at him. But he answered that with a wink; an easy, affectionate wink. And she thought, oh God, what shade of red have I gone now? So she said to him, I'm just going to take Em out for some fresh air, do you want anything? And he answered with another wink, this one unmistakably lascivious. And she thought, if I don't go right now, my face will look like beetroot and there'll be no more winking from Joe.

She meandered around town, absent-mindedly pushing the buggy here and there while focusing on her recollections of the night with Joe and trying not to taunt herself with what if it was a one-off. The girlfriend in France sprang into Saltburn out of nowhere. Not a girlfriend – a casual, sex-only set-up totally off Tess's moral radar. The thought of it made her shudder and she felt intimidated by it. Too shy to ask about it. She'd strolled right to the other side of town and suddenly she felt too far away, out of range, out of sorts. She began to walk home at some pace, feeling that she'd ventured too far and been gone too long. It was as if the further away she was from Joe, then the less vivid she felt herself to be. Like a cordless phone, she mused, taken too far from its base station.

'I can't believe I'm comparing myself to a cordless phone.'

It didn't cross her mind that she might come across Seb, or that she could pop in on Lisa, or phone Tamsin reverse charges from that phone box over there and say, Tamz, you'll never guess what I did last night. Just then, to Tess, her *genius loci* centred around herself and Em and Joe and the house. Saltburn was irrelevant. She didn't notice what colour the sea was today, or what was going on along the beach, or how many people were on the pier, or how crowded the café was. She wasn't even aware, really, that she was in Saltburn with its Lisas and Sebs and shops that were now her locals. Her focus was fixed on a place she hadn't known existed until last night. It was a new location, one she was desperate to explore, one she felt compelled to return to and quickly. So she arrived back breathless from both the fast stomp uphill and the anticipation of regrouping with Joe.

He was in the kitchen making doorstop sandwiches. Wolf was in his toppled-scarecrow stance nearby, globs of liver in a semicircle around him. Tess assessed the scene and she felt a calm joy seep through her.

'Oh, you cruel, cruel man, Mr Saunders,' she said and she delighted in the return of her larkiness. 'How can the poor dog reach the liver with that thing around his neck – it's as long as his face, you divvy.'

Joe looked at her. And then he looked at the dog and the liver. He looked at her again.

'Did you just call me a *divvy*?'

But he didn't give her time to answer, he walked over and slipped his arm around her waist and pulled her in very close and pressed his lips against hers. His eyes were shut tight. She could see that. Hers closed when he licked along her lips and eased his tongue into her mouth. Then Em walked by and gave Joe a bit of a shove, and he and Tess pulled apart though Joe kept his arm around her. And at exactly the same time, Joe and Tess said, no! Don't eat that, Em! That's for Wolf.

As the evening progressed, the pleasure of sharing their space transformed into an almost agonizing thrill about the potential to make love again. How do we go from here, nattering over supper, to the bedroom? they both wondered. How do we move the conversation from who's washing up and who's drying to let's go to bed and whose room? Should I ask her – or should I wait for her to say she's calling it a night? Is he going to say something – he's been reading that book for bloody ages.

'I think I'll check on Wolf.'
    'Do you want a hand?'
    'It's OK, Joe, I have it down to a fine art.'
    'I'll say.'

'Tea, Tess?'
    'Yes, please.'
    'OK.'

'Anything on the box, then, Joe?'
    'Ten o'clock news – shall we see what the world's up to?'
    'All right.'

'I'll just check on Wolf again – take him out for a pee.'
    'Do you want a hand?'
    'No – we're fine.'

'Cup of tea, Tess? A nightcap perhaps?'
    'No – I think I'd better go to bed. Look at the time!'
    'Bloody hell, you're right.'

*

It's bizarre. Neither of them fears rejection by the other – from the frisson that has underscored their waking hours today, they are both confident they wish for the same thing. Yet there they are, in separate beds on different floors both behind closed doors. And it's late now; really it's time for sleep never mind anything more active. But there she is, wide awake in bed and horny too. She's stuck, though, as if she's acutely aware that there's some finer point of sexual etiquette of which she's ignorant. And there he is, in his bedroom, standing by the window chiding himself for not reaching for her as she left the sitting room, even though that was over an hour ago. Her arm, her slender arm, the downy little hairs revealed only when the light catches them – her arm had practically brushed his when she left the sitting room. Why hadn't he put his hand out, pulled her onto his lap, kissed her and whispered something about coming to bed – or perhaps kissed her and found there was no need to say a thing? In fact, why the need for bed, per se – now Joe is torturing himself with images of him and Tess in naked abandon on one of his capacious sofas? It could have been so easy! But he's in his bloody bedroom, on his bloody own.

'I've never had this problem before,' he cusses. 'I've rarely had to ask, even.'

I'll go to her room, he thinks. I'll just bloody well go to her room and knock on the door – and then I'll go right in.

Tess is thinking much the same thing. She hasn't had the thought about the sofas. The only place she's kicking herself for not being in, is Joe's arms. She has silently opened her door. She has hovered on the landing. But the route to his room, in the thick silence of the night, seems now to be a chasm over which there is only a precarious rope bridge. And she just doesn't think she's brave enough to test how strong it is.

So she goes back to bed.

And Joe goes to bed too because he sees it's almost two in the morning and he tells himself she'll be fast asleep by now.

It's five thirty a.m. Tess's dream is interrupted by a soft knocking. It's very strange, because the entire dream, in all its banal and convoluted detail, has been leading up to this moment of the sound of knocking. She opens her eyes and waits and there's the knock again. And she turns in bed and looks at the door handle and wills it to turn. It does. For a moment, she wonders whether it is telepathic kinetic energy – and she sincerely hopes not. It isn't. The door opens and in walks Joe. He sees she is already holding the quilt open for him and he tucks down beside her, their hips already starting to move in a gentle rhythm, their hands already reaching for each other, their lips already magnetized.

He whispers in her ear. 'If I know Emmeline, we have a whole hour before she wakes.'

Chapter Twenty-four

It was beautiful. It was beautiful because it could be played out against a backdrop of early summer, which had arrived now for good in a burst of bluebells and the clement weather scenting the air. The crocus might now have gone and the dog violet was on its way out, but primula sprang a chorus of yellow and cream alongside the proliferation of wild bluebells and tangle of wood sorrel. It was also beautiful because it was so private. The house – their castle. No one need know they were there. It was the perfect stage-set on which they could play out the happiness they felt. And, because it was so private, and they felt so happy, so it became all encompassing. There was no need to venture further afield than the perimeter of the grounds. They allowed nothing to trivialize their time together – no unnecessary excursions from the house, nothing as base as thoughts of work or worries about money. No unwelcome visitors encroached on the space they constructed. Well, one did but Joe told the bloke that no, Tess wasn't in and yes, he'd pass on that Seb had called by, though he had no intention of doing anything of the sort. The phone went unanswered. Well, Joe let Nathalie ramble on his Blackberry voicemail but he didn't return the call.

He likened the building of their relationship to the construction of the Brooklyn Bridge. The East River was too far to cross in a single span in 1883 so the towers were to be built in the river itself. To reach the bedrock through 24 metres of silt and sludge, a caisson was built – a watertight box on the river bed in which the miners could work safely. The caisson itself would go on to form the foundation for the massive tower to grow above. That was how it felt to Joe – he was willingly inhabiting a hermetically sealed space in which home life with Tess, even with Emmeline and Wolf, could develop and flourish. This time together, this safe and private caisson, would become the bedrock on which their relationship could prosper.

So she made a large batch of scones. And he made porridge for everyone. They drank wine and tea and had hot chocolate at elevenses. She sewed on his loose buttons and he tinkered with her car. She gave his bathroom a spring clean and he put the border up properly, permanently, in Emmeline's room. It was as though they were playing house, as though they were practising Happy Families and the more enjoyable it was, the more viable and real it felt. With Wolf improving by the hour and Em sleeping through the night and the constant pleasure of each other's company – whether chatting in the kitchen, or sharing quiet in the sitting room, or combining their bodies in bed, or being intrinsically aware of each other while they slept – it ceased to feel like playing or acting, it all felt pretty effortless. And because reality was apparently so easy to construct, the euphoria they felt became the norm, just a regular emotion, a state they were determined to cherish and maintain.

This was not the time to say, Joe, tell me more about your mother. Nor did Joe feel it appropriate to ask Tess why she'd left London in such a hurry. She didn't dare think about the French fancy with the BlackBerry in bed and he wasn't going

270

to waste time wondering about some bloke called Seb who knew where she lived. Instead, he said, show me how to change a nappy, then. And she said, why don't we paint your bedroom. And they sorted out the larger shed in the garden and she found out he was just as wary of spiders as she was.

They'd kiss under the humming neon strip in the kitchen, as well as in the moonlit garden and of course in the thrill of a cool, dark bedroom. And late one night Joe said, Tess! I didn't know you'd do *that*! when she sucked his cock and swallowed. And early one morning she said, Joe! I didn't know I could do that! when he made her come twice in quick succession.

They grinned at Em when they broke away from one embrace in the courtyard to find her chortling and clapping. And they praised Wolf when he managed to wag his bandaged stump in response to Tess and Joe larking about with a tea towel and the water spray she used when she did the ironing. And when she did the ironing, Joe came up behind her and put his hands lightly on her waist and laid kisses up her neck and breathed in the scent of baby shampoo from her hair. And when he was doing *The Times* crossword, she sat herself on the edge of his tub chair and slipped her arm around his shoulders, laying her head against his to help him think. It's *clipper*, she said – 10 Across is clipper – *trim shipshape*. And he said, you're not just a pretty face, you know. And then he said, you don't actually know how naturally pretty you are, do you? He said, it's one of the things I love about you – you and your appalling hoodies and crap jeans. But Tess didn't hear the jibe about her clothes; her head was filled only with the sound of Love.

A week later, however, the phone went when they were in the kitchen debating whether 7 Across could be *lummox* because that meant 5 Down could be *Achilles*. They listened to the ringing for just a second too long to ignore.

'Perhaps you ought to get that?' said Tess.

'You're probably right,' said Joe.

It was only a phone call but the intrusion seemed a shrill and portentous disruption to their self-imposed isolation. As Joe went to the hallway to answer the phone (thinking, hang up, hang up) Tess sat alone in the kitchen, unable to do the crossword, unable to decide who would be an acceptable caller. Listening to Joe, it did not take her long to deduce it was only the vet. With a lurch, she realized they'd missed Wolf's appointment.

'God, I'm so sorry,' Joe was saying. 'We could bring him down this afternoon? Five sounds good. We'll see you then.'

Joe returned to the kitchen. 'I clean forgot about Wolf's appointment – I wrote it down somewhere.'

'You lummox,' said Tess, thinking to herself, he said *we* – he said *we* could bring him down. He said *we'll* see you at five.

So they all piled into Joe's car.

Driving through Saltburn it felt as if they were returning after quite some time away. There seemed to be more people around and, after days of fine weather, more colour too. There were children on bikes and teenagers in T-shirts and pensioners without headscarves or hats. Some of the shops now ventured their wares outside, promoting them in racks and baskets on the pavement. The milkshake booth was open on the lower prom and there was quite a queue. The cliff lift was in operation. The pier was packed, the sand was speckled with families and the windbreaks looked like colourful punctuation marks.

Joe had to carry Wolf into the surgery because Tess's coaxing hadn't worked; in fact the dog's quaking and whimpers had started in the car when they headed out of Saltburn towards Marske. This, in turn, set Em off but the pair of them yowling and resisting merely made the grown-ups roll their eyes and laugh.

The vet was pleased with Wolf's progress. The bandages were changed (Em was invited to choose and went for orange and mauve) and the dog was extravagantly praised. Finally, the plastic collar was ceremoniously removed and another appointment made for a week's time.

'I won't be around,' Joe said, 'but Tess'll bring him in.'

This torpedoed through Tess like a bolt of lead. Quickly, she forced herself to concentrate on a packet of organic dried pet food because her eyes were smarting at the thought of Joe's departure. She didn't know when, exactly, it was to be. But what she did know was that he would indeed go. And soon. Where? Where was he going?

Stop it! He's still *here*.

As they walked back to the car, she slipped her hand into his, giving him little surreptitious tugs to slow the pace.

'I *will* have to go,' he told her the next day, as if he'd been conscripted.

'But not tomorrow.'

'Not tomorrow,' he said, as if the notion was preposterous, 'but by midweek.'

And though she was about to put her arms around him just then, he quickly set off swanning around the garden, picking up anything he came across. Twigs. Leaves. A peg – as if it was a pressing job earmarked for precisely that moment. He kept his face turned.

'Belgium,' he said, 'then France.' He was putting the items on the garden table, arranging them into a pointless pattern as if it was all part of the chore.

Tess knew she couldn't afford to comment because the

273

sharp pressure at the base of her throat would reveal itself as a telltale crackle to her voice. She couldn't comment because the notion of Joe's indisputable departure suddenly stripped her of confidence in their closeness. France! she goaded herself, you know who's in France. All she could do was stick a banal smile on her face and busy herself too, picking up the odd leaf or peg or plastic bottle top that Joe had missed on the lawn. How she had felt herself blossom this past week – now she could sense her petals closing; furling themselves tightly around her core.

Joe wanted to be able to say, I'll try and come back most weekends. But he knew he couldn't because actually, he just didn't know when he'd next be back. He also wanted to be able to go over to her and take the garden debris from her hands and raise her face to his and let a thoughtful kiss say it all. But he couldn't do that. Because he found that he was already walking to the house under some ridiculous pretence of checking if his Gore-tex boots were there or whether he had left them in France. It wasn't about the boots; he knew that. It was about feeling bizarrely and horribly awkward in the presence of the girl who'd recently made his life seem wonderfully straightforward.

Tess was able to snatch a moment by herself in her room. Em was happily engrossed watching *Story Makers* and Tess had asked Joe, who was reading the paper in the same room, whether he'd watch Em while Tess ran her bath. With the bath running, she had taken herself into her room and stood in the centre, her face in her hands. She had to acknowledge it wasn't simply that she wanted him to stay because she loved being with him and she'd miss him. It was that she didn't want him to go because she didn't know where it was he went and she suddenly feared where it was that might lead. What if, when she was out of his sight, someone else sprang to his mind?

They'd co-existed in this wondrous world in which she'd so easily believed that they had discovered some kind of super-reality. Now, standing alone in her room, she wondered whether they'd simply constructed a hermetically sealed fantasy. She went to check the bath. So much noise, for such a slow system. She had the temperature just right and she added bubbles before sitting herself on the edge in a deflated slump. In a rush of masochistic taunts, she goaded herself that she was just a bloody house-sitter and skint single mum with no hope in hell of the sort of happiness she'd kidded herself was so real and feasible during this last week.

Over the next two days, Joe and Tess tried their best to recapture the spirit of togetherness but the spectre of his departure hung over them in a pall they just couldn't shrug off. Even Em being unbelievably cute and Wolf managing to clown around rather unsteadily didn't bolster them much. They weren't gloomy, certainly they weren't snappish or uncommunicative; it was as if the soundtrack of life in the house was now in a minor key whereas before it had been a veritable symphony in C major. The colours of their aura were in subdued hues rather than the dazzling primaries of the days just gone. The sex was still good but it was more inward and the eye contact lessened.

After a final supper, over a last glass of wine and the crumbs of Stilton and Jacob's Cream Crackers, Joe finally broached the immediate future.

'What'll you do, Tess?' he asked. 'What have you planned when I'm gone?'

She thought about it. She actually hadn't thought about it at all. She'd been too involved in the present.

'Well,' she said at length, 'it'll no doubt revolve around playgroup and the vet.'

Joe nodded. 'Thank you,' he said, 'not just from Wolf – from me.'

'I guess I'm going to have to find a bit of work.' She said this more to herself.

'Work? Why?' He paused. 'Tess,' he said, 'my last trip – what I said about you leaving –'

She shook her head, signifying he needn't say more.

He reached for her wrist and squeezed it.

'Joe,' she found herself saying. 'What you said – about the lady, in France –'

But this time he shook his head, signifying she needn't say more and he squeezed her wrist again for emphasis.

'OK?' he said, a little sternly.

'OK,' she said, a little shyly.

They paused with their empty glasses and dabbed at microscopic remains of cheese.

'So why look for work?' Joe said at length. 'Surely there's still plenty here that could do with your magic touch?'

She looked desperately uncomfortable and it took her a while to respond.

'Because I'm a bit broke.'

'Shit,' he said, 'I'm so sorry – I completely forgot. I must owe you two months?'

'I didn't mean—'

'No,' Joe protested, 'that's crap of me. Hang on.' He left. And then he returned. He sat down and opened his cheque-book.

'*Miss Tess,*' he wrote. Then he paused. 'Tess – I don't know your surname.'

Tess felt enormously tired all of a sudden. Too tired to tell him her surname, let alone request cash instead of a cheque.

'Are you OK, pet?'

'I don't know. I feel odd. I think I'd better lie down. Stilton does this to me sometimes.'

It wasn't true, but Stilton did make Tamsin come over all funny and just then, to appropriate her close friend's condition provided Tess with a much-needed connection to her past. She touched Joe's shoulder as she left the table. He made to take her hand but she was already beyond reach.

He could only make out the top of her head from the depths of his duvet when he went to bed much later. It seemed to him that she was fast asleep.

She woke and wondered if there was any way she could avoid the goodbye, short of running away. But there was a baby to feed and a convalescing dog to attend to. And there was so much to say, if only, if *only*, she could muster the courage. She had to get up and get the day moving because what else could she do.

In the kitchen, on the table, was the cheque. It was made payable to *Miss Tess* and the biro had been left on top of it. It was for two months wages' with something on top. She didn't want to accept it at all, really. She wanted to dispense with this particular dynamic with Joe. Boss and house-sitter – where could that leave love? Two months' pay – with extras. Were those last week? But she needed the money, God knows she needed it. However, the same old problem remained: relinquishing a cheque to her fetid bank account. It was like a bog. A cheque would be sucked down until the surface closed over and it looked no different from before. However, asking her sister for a postal order was one thing. Asking Joe for cash again was another. It didn't make her feel cheap; it just made her feel poor. And that decimated her self-esteem.

'Morning,' he said, suddenly behind her, a gentle smack to her bottom. He noticed she was holding the cheque.

'Everything OK?' he asked. She nodded. 'I don't believe you.' He crossed his arms and looked at her askance. 'I know you, Tess,' he said.

And Tess thought, but Joe, there's stuff about me you *don't* know. Secrets I don't want to share.

'I'm fine – honestly – it's just the last throes of that bloody Stilton.'

Joe thought to himself, but I know you, Tess – we've shared Stilton on previous occasions with no adverse reactions.

She was hiding something and he wasn't sure he liked it.

'I'd better make tracks, really,' he said.

She nodded whilst fixating on a recount of the eyelets in his shoes.

He lifted her chin with his thumb. 'Bye.'

He kissed her and oh how she kissed him back.

'Bye,' she said eventually, when it really was time for them to pull apart.

Chapter Twenty-five

Lisa and her husband were taking Sam on the miniature railway to the Italian Gardens for a picnic. With May in full swing, the weather was glorious. They only lived a stone's throw away and doubtless lunch would be a far easier affair to have at home – but she'd found it fun to prepare a picnic. Sam had a new baseball cap with NYFD embroidered on it. She'd bought it on a trip to Coulby Newham and though she knew it wasn't the genuine article, if Sam looked cute, what did it matter. The hat, high-factor suncream, the picnic – it all filled Lisa with joy that summer was undoubtedly here. The train rolled away on its short journey with a satisfying clicketting along the narrow-gauge tracks and Lisa thought how she'd be perfectly happy taking the little train to and fro all day.

'Is he all right?'

Lisa's husband jolted her back to reality.

'He keeps saying "oof" – sounds like he has tummy troubles.'

'Oof.'

Lisa turned this way and that. 'Where's Oof, Sammy? Where's Oof?'

'Lisa?'

'Look, Sammy – there's Oof! There's Oof! Oof all better!'

'Lisa – what the –?'

'Stop the train!'

'You can't stop a miniature railway, you daft bint. What's this oof business?'

'It's Wolf – Tess's dog – the one who was hit! Look, there he is. Christ alive, he looks shite. Tess! Tess!'

But Tess, who had adopted a similar gait to Wolf, appeared not to hear.

Lisa put her little finger and thumb in her mouth and gave out a raucous whistle.

'I didn't know you could do that.'

Lisa put her index and middle fingers in her mouth and whistled shrilly through them.

'Nor *that*,' her husband marvelled.

She poked her tongue out, then rolled it vertically from side to side.

'Bloody hell.'

Lisa laughed. She hadn't managed to catch Tess's attention but her husband was captivated.

They alighted at the gardens and then doubled back on themselves, through the meadow between the river and the tracks, looking for a suitable spot to picnic. It was also the direction where Lisa had last seen Tess. She laid out the lunch with only half a mind on the job while she glanced around her every few seconds.

Her husband flicked a cheesy puff crisp at her. 'Go on – go and see if you can find her.'

Lisa didn't need asking twice and she marched off, leaving her husband to tut, women! to their son.

It didn't take her long to catch up with Tess, on account of how slowly Wolf was moving. Em squealed when she caught sight of Lisa, Tess stood still and grinned, Wolf continued on his lope, unaware of the action behind him.

'You!' said Lisa, not sure where to start.

'Me,' Tess said with a mixture of pride and embarrassment.

'Where the – excuse me, Em – fuck have you been!'

Tess shrugged.

'Feathering some love nest up at the big house?'

Tess drew an arc in the grass with her foot.

'You old *slink*!' but Lisa was obviously delighted. 'That bloke –'

'Wolf!' Tess called. 'Wolf!'

He turned like an old jalopy doing a six-point-turn and ambled back.

'Wolf,' said Lisa, giving him a rub, 'you must have a tale to tell, old thing.'

'Actually,' said Tess, 'he has no tail to speak of.'

Lisa looked at her then smiled broadly. 'That's good, that is – clever, very clever. You're not just a pretty face, are you, love?'

Tess had a good look at her shoes, and Lisa's, before raising her face. 'That's what Joe said to me too.'

Lisa put her sunglasses up on her head even though it made her squint a little.

'So – this Joe, then. Does this mean Seb's not getting a look in?'

Tess visibly paled. 'Bugger,' she said. 'Seb.' She paused. It sounded too crass and heartless to say she hadn't given him a moment's thought – but that was the truth.

'The thing is,' said Lisa, 'I'll bet that, when Seb came courting, your mind still wandered to Lord of the Manor – even if you didn't want it to. But when Joe was back, I don't reckon the Surfer even made it to the shoreline of your mind.'

Tess thought about this. 'You're right,' she said, 'and God, you have an amazing way of putting things.'

'I'm not just a pretty face either, you know.'

They laughed.

'Have you eaten?' Lisa asked. 'We've a picnic – if the trolls haven't troughed the lot. Come on.'

281

So Tess and Em and Wolf joined Lisa's family for lunch. The picnic was set out in the triangular meadow, bridges for Poohsticks at either end, the steep haul of the woods as a backdrop, the river and miniature railway as soundtrack. The grass was lush, long and glossy, not yet put upon by the main brunt of the visitor season. It was the first time that Tess had properly met Lisa's husband and she found him amiable. She liked the way he was with Lisa and with Sam. He gave Wolf some chicken and he sprang Em's curls between his fingers. He also seemed genuinely interested in his wife's new friend which Tess found affirming.

'And what's next, then?' he asked, when she'd given him a room-by-room inventory on her work at the house.

'Well, I'd like to do the attic rooms – but there's so much stuff there and none of it's mine, so I can't chuck it out without Joe's say-so.'

'You'll have to put it on hold, then, till he's next back.'

She nodded.

'When'll that be?' Lisa asked.

Tess ran her fingers through the grass like she did Em's hair. She wanted to appear blasé and not crestfallen. 'I don't know.'

'Didn't he tell you?' Lisa said, indignant, ready to chide the bastard when he next sprang a surprise visit at the play-ground.

'He doesn't know either,' said Tess.

'Oh,' said Lisa and her husband.

'I need to find something else to do – I need to top up my income.'

'What can you do?' Lisa's husband asked.

'I can sing "Wheels on the Bus",' Tess said, a little lacklustre. 'I can puree a carrot to perfection. I can change a nappy in the dead of night without being fully awake.' She thought to herself how much pride she took in her ability to do all these things, but how lame they sounded out loud.

'Did you work – you know – before the baby?'

Tess thought back to that distant land that she'd lived in prior to Em arriving; rough terrain that had turned so hostile. Strangely enough, Lisa had never asked her about it directly; as if she considered Tess's life in London and her life pre-Em to be of no consequence to their friendship. But, while Lisa piled coleslaw on Tess's plate and her husband topped up her juice, Tess was so embroiled in her sudden memories that she might as well have been sitting on concrete paving slabs in London, as in a field near the sea.

'I can't open this flaming box,' she heard Lisa say and, as she glanced to see Lisa handing her husband a box of cheese biscuits, she thought about the boxes in her car.

'Before the baby, I was a beautician,' she said.

Lisa's husband had almost forgotten what he'd asked. Lisa was now all ears.

'Beauty? What – like nails and the like?'

Tess nodded.

'And facials?'

She nodded again.

'Did you do waxing?'

Tess nodded.

'Can you wax me within an inch of my life?'

Tess laughed and then she nodded.

'Ace,' said Lisa, '*ace*.'

'But it all went a bit wrong,' she said. 'Very wrong.'

'What did you do?' Lisa asked, imagining some plucking session ending in a lawsuit.

'I set up a business,' Tess told them because just then, in this meadow, amongst friends who'd fed her and her child and her adopted dog, she felt they'd support her whether or not they sympathized. 'I set up a business – organic potions and lotions. I took out a loan. I bought pots and pots of the stuff. And – well – now I'm a house-sitter in Saltburn, flat broke.'

Lisa wittered on about all bank managers being bastards, that it wasn't Tess's fault, that it was an outrage that small businesses failed, that she mustn't be demoralized, or blame herself, just blame the recession and the flaming bastard bank. Meanwhile, her husband dunked cheese biscuits into the glob of hummus left on Tess's plate and ate thoughtfully.

'You've still got some of your stuff then? Your potions and lotions?'

Tess nodded. 'It's all I use my clapped-out old car for, at the moment. A storage depot for three boxes of pots and tubs.'

'So – why not have a Tupperware party?'

Lisa butted in. 'You daft bugger, it's not those types of pots and tubs – it's organic potions and lotions. Didn't you hear her?'

Her husband gave Tess a look which said, I love my wife but dear God, is she annoying.

'I *know*,' he said very slowly to Lisa. He turned to Tess. 'My mum used to do Tupperware parties – at the house. Her friends would come and they'd natter the evening away over wine and cheese. She never did the hard sell – the stuff was just there, like a silent member of the party. But everyone used to buy something to take home.'

Lisa was looking at her husband in awe.

'I've got it!' she said. 'We'll do it at mine – I'll invite everyone I know and you can flog us your stuff. You can do little mini treatments – you know, a quick hand massage with your handcream.' She looked triumphant. '*Try before you buy*.' Tess cast Lisa's husband a glance that said, thank you – thanks so much. 'You could sell your stuff and yourself – people can take home a list of what you can do. We must get you a mobile. They can phone you and say, ooh, can I book a facial and can I order two tubes of your whatever it is you have in tubes that's good for faces, Tess.' Tess was laughing. 'Next week,' Lisa was saying, 'we'll do it at ours,

284

one day next week.' She turned to her husband. 'You're all right to watch Sam and Em then?' She turned to Tess before he'd answered. 'Hey – you can tidy his eyebrows instead of paying him babysitting. Look at them!' She snuggled up to her husband and fiddled with his eyebrows. Tess smiled and looked away. She thought to herself how there was something really lovely about being party to another couple's intimacy. Being in the presence of love, when she herself was in love, was a wonderful place to be. She looked around her. What a truly lovely place for a picnic on a warm Sunday in May. Wish you were here, Joe – you could be regaling us about the Halfpenny Bridge because it used to be just over there, didn't it – I remember you saying so.

Tess felt horribly lonely that night, tired too, but she couldn't sleep. The loneliness nagged at her thoughts and sat heavy in her diaphragm. She wished Joe hadn't left her a message on the answering machine but he had, stumbling over his words a little, saying 'anyway' a number of times. He sounded simultaneously right there, yet so far away. Should she have phoned him back? She went through the pros and cons and allowed the lame excuse of Belgium being an hour ahead not to. She was tired. She'd caught the sun on her forehead and her upper arms. She'd caught sight of the boxes in her car boot when she'd returned that afternoon. Lisa and her husband might have filled her head with their good ideas for her future but for Tess it served as a reminder of the bad ideas of her past.

I'll sleep on it, she told herself, I'll let it lie for a couple of days, then I'll think about what to do. She wondered whether she could change her name on Joe's cheque to Lisa's – and have the cash from her. It wasn't illegal and she was sure it wouldn't be a problem for Lisa. But God, it was grim to have to consider it.

Chapter Twenty-six

'Hullo.'

'Hullo.'

'It's me – it's Tess.'

'I know it's-you-it's-Tess because it says so on my mobile.'

'My name comes up?'

'It says *Home.*'

They let the sound of it hang for a moment.

'Everything OK? Wolf, Emmeline – you?'

'Very OK, thank you Joe. I just thought I'd phone to say hi. I missed your call yesterday, or the day before.'

'Day before,' Joe confirmed because yesterday he'd found himself glancing at his phone from time to time, trying not to wonder if it was odd that Tess hadn't called back.

'Well,' said Tess, 'I must be costing you a fortune, phoning you abroad from your phone at home. But I just wanted to say hullo.'

'It's lovely to hear from you. Phone any time.'

'You too,' said Tess.

Neither wanted to say goodbye just yet, but how to truncate the pause was another matter.

Joe glanced from the apartment window. Nathalie would

be back soon. 'I'm sorry I had to leave when I did, Tess – and I hope to be back really soon.'

She didn't want to say goodbye just yet, but she couldn't find the words to say that she really would like him to come back soon, too. 'Where are you now? What are you doing?'

For the first time, Joe asked himself what the fuck he was doing in Nathalie's apartment.

'Joe?'

'Hullo – I'm still here.' But I shouldn't be *here*. 'I'm just looking out over the little town square, thinking about supper.' Though masking the truth had wiped away his appetite and his stomach was now quite full with leaden remorse.

Tess looked outside too, a little absent-minded, as if she was expecting to share Joe's point of view. It was closer to his than she could know and a similar lurch of dismay hit the pit of her stomach. She hadn't looked out onto some square in France but she was looking out and watching Seb coming through the gate.

'There's Em,' she hurried, though she hated to implicate her daughter. 'I ought to go. Bye, Joe. Bye for now.'

She couldn't pretend she wasn't in because Wolf had been outside anyway and was currently limping over to Seb. In addition, all the ground-floor windows were open and Radio 4 was drifting out to the garden from the kitchen.

'Seb!' She opened the door before he'd rung the bell.

'Hullo, stranger,' he said, placing an easy kiss on the side of her mouth, his hand in the small of her back. 'How are you doing? The dog's soldiering on, I see.'

'Yes, he is,' Tess said, coming out of the house so she could move away from his touch. It was late afternoon, still warm, the light was honey-hued.

'What are you up to?'

Tess felt flustered by the question. 'Nothing!'

'Want to do nothing together then?'

'Oh. Well – I mean, I'm about to start the whole bath-time, sing-song, bedtime palaver.'

'Want a hand?'

Tess felt discomfited by both Seb's offer and his relaxed demeanour which, with his kiss and his touch, was verging on the intimate. She fidgeted for her response.

'I can sing "One-two-three-four-five".' And he did so.

Such a nice guy. He really was. It confused Tess – had there been no Joe, there very well could have been Seb. After all, on paper he was a better match and a surer thing – younger, more even-tempered than his itinerant rival, for a start. Tess looked at him, singing away, and she nodded her head to his tune. But it didn't help. It had nothing to do with what Seb had to offer, what he was so keen to give – but it had everything to do with what was missing for Tess, what she had with Joe. The connection – quintessential, unfathomable, addictive.

Now, Seb was singing "Row Row Row Your Boat".

'Em is a little crotchety.' Another lie foisted upon her daughter.

Seb pulled Wolf's ears gently through his fingers. 'OK,' he said at length. 'So how about later – later tonight, or later during the week?' He scoured her face while she trawled around the diplomacy section of her mind for something to say that could be kind but not misconstrued.

Seb, though, was too nice and Tess was just too slow. 'You look a little tired,' he pre-empted. 'Let's do it later in the week. I just wanted to call by to see how you all were.'

Tess's relief wore itself as an expansive smile, easy to misread.

'Thursday?' said Seb. 'Friday?'

All Tess could think was that tomorrow was Thursday so she found herself saying Friday though she felt sure this was the wrong answer.

'Vista Mar – eightish?'

She could only nod.

'Just give me a call if there's a problem with babysitting.'

She nodded again and let herself be kissed goodbye. How had her reluctance to have him even help with bath-time resulted in an unwanted date in two days' time? But he was gone now, and it was done. She called Wolf to come in. She shut all the windows and closed the door.

'Can you talk?'

'Can I call you back in half an hour?'

On the rare occasions that Tess sought advice, any delay was potentially detrimental to her ability to listen let alone absorb guidance and therefore half an hour was too long for Tess to wait for Tamsin. So she picked up the receiver and dialled.

'Can you talk?'

'Course I can – you all right, chuck?'

Lovely Lisa, thought Tess. Lovely, lovely Lisa – my up-here Tamsin.

'I'm fine – just in a bit of a muddle.'

'Go on.'

'How do you let down someone that you really quite like, who's a lovely person, who's done nothing wrong apart from being not the right one?'

'How do you know he's not?'

'Because I know, for all I'm worth, that someone else is.'

Lisa thought about it. 'And that someone is Joe – am I right?'

'Yes.'

'And Seb is the one who's not right – right?'

'Right.'

'Doesn't sound to me like you're in much of a muddle at all – sounds like you're pretty clear.'

'It's still awkward though.'

'What's the story exactly, Tess? You can give me the gories – I'm unshockable. I've seen the pile of porn my husband thinks he's secretly stashed in the loft.' Lisa winked at her husband who looked aghast at his wife's revelation.

'I'm in love with Joe,' Tess said.

'Tell me something I don't know,' said Lisa and Tess felt a sudden mix of pride and embarrassment.

'You done the dirty deed with him, then?'

'Yes.'

'*Before* you had your rummage with Seb?'

'No.'

'Well, that's something – it's not as if you're doing the dirty on Seb then, is it? You've not done anything immoral, have you, pet? You've not seen Seb for a while anyway, you'd not promised him marriage and babies. It's just circumstances, Tess. That's all.'

'The thing is, Lisa – I know all of this – the problem is I just don't know what to say to Seb.'

'You must have a few pat one-liners up your sleeve?'

'Me? I've only ever been on the receiving end, Lisa.'

'Like?'

Tess thought back to being dumped. 'Oh, you know – *It's not you, it's me.* And – *I'm not ready for this.* Or there's always – *I think we should just be friends.* They're all awful, Lisa – they were horrible to hear and I don't want to say them. Not to Seb. Not here. Big words in a small town.'

Lisa thought about it. 'Can you think of a way of telling the truth in a nice way?'

'What – *Oh hi, Seb, the thing is I feel dreadful because you're great and gorgeous but actually just recently I got it together with someone else?*'

'Sounds bang on to me.'

'But I've stupidly said yes to meeting him on Friday.'

'Why did you do that?'

'Because I was taken off my guard. Can I just phone to blow out Friday and tell him all this at the same time?'

Lisa wasn't sure about that one. 'I'd say no – you ought to meet as planned. It's fairer. He's a nice lad, isn't he – he's around, he could become a friend. This may not be such a big deal for him anyway – thought about that, Tess? Perhaps he likes you because you're an outsider too, you're pretty and single and good company. Maybe he simply fancies you because you are *there*. But what do I know? What does your mate Tamsin say?'

Tess looked at the grandfather clock and, though of course it wasn't telling the right time, she could see that she'd been on the phone for over ten minutes. 'I haven't spoken to Tamsin yet.'

Lisa was touched. 'Best call Tamsin too.'

'I will,' said Tess, 'and I reckon she'll say what you've said.'

'And will she then say, tell me about Joe, or does she already know all about him?'

'She doesn't know a sausage.'

'I see,' said Lisa, touched again. 'So, Tess – tell me about Joe.'

Tess turned her back on the clock and sat down. It was the first time during the call that she laughed. 'I love him, Lisa – it's as simple as that. I want to be with him – no one else, from now on, just Joe. I want to stay put – I've found my home.'

'We'd better get your career here up and running then, pet.'

'My career?'

'Unless you want to be a fat old housewife like me? You're better than that, girl.'

'Lisa, you are *not* fat and you're younger than me. What a weird thing to say.'

'How about next Tuesday – at mine?'

291

'Tuesday?'

'Kick-start it.'

'Kick-start what?'

'Your career, pet. You bring those boxes in the back of your car, Tess. And make a menu of what you have to offer. Just you wait and see – the eyebrows and stiff necks and hairy legs and undernourished skin of Saltburn need you.'

Chapter Twenty-seven

So, there's Tess wanting to do the right thing by Joe and by Seb. And here's Joe with his head between Nathalie's legs. Because he's not quite sure what he's doing, he's keeping his head buried right where it is, doing the thing he's sure he does very well. Now he's here, he's making the most of it, giving a sterling performance, but nevertheless he's not quite sure how he came to be here. His head has been full of Tess, now his face is full of Nathalie. And yet he left England in love with Tess and he arrived in France with the emotion intact. With his forehead resting against the aeroplane window, the taxi window, even the window of Nathalie's apartment, he's daydreamed frequently back over the specifics of his time with Tess; conjuring images of her, recalling her physiognomic quirks, replaying the little things she says, the sound of her laughter, remembering the feel of her, the taste. He couldn't wait to phone her. He willed her to call him back sooner than she ultimately did. And when she did, it gave him such joy to hear her voice, to envisage exactly where she was. Yet now he's all ears to the sound of sex with Nathalie.

Nathalie is writhing and moaning. The French accent is a boon because she sounds nothing like Tess. Whereas Tess responded to his touch and their coupling with small gasps and excited, hastened breathing, Nathalie is all extravagant moaning and throaty panting. She tastes different from Tess too. The whole feel of her is different as well. Nathalie is leggy and toned but that amount of conscientious grooming has added a hardness to her body of which Joe had never really been aware until he'd slept with Tess. Tess is smaller than Nathalie, lithe of limb from pushing that buggy uphill and hoicking the toddler about but there's a softness to her figure too. Her deportment may preclude Nathalie's elegance but Tess is still feminine, even with the hoodies and jeans and haphazard hair. The salt scrubs, the firming creams, the hours at the gym, the frequent lymphatic massage all ensure Nathalie's sculpted form. High heels and high skirts enhance the line of her legs, low-cut tops complement her décolleté, jewellery sets off the sweep of her neck, aubergine nail polish presents her hands to their best advantage; her posture is perfect and to walk behind her is a feast for the eye.

Tess, though, doesn't have the time for any of that, nor the inclination as far as Joe can make out. She's fit because the demands of her day have made her so, have given her curves and dips in the right places. But hers is a real figure, too, an everyday one – a bruise on her shin, a bit of a spot on her chin, an inconsistent blush of suntan across her chest, a little fuzz under her armpits, nails it would be daft to grow. But tatty trainers don't detract from the fact that her ankles are slim, her calves are shapely and her knees are nice. That funny old floral tea-dress, not as shapeless as it would seem when it softly alights, tantalizingly, on the swell of a breast, the curve of a hip, the roundness of her bottom. And when her body is swamped from view underneath those oversized T-shirts and hoodies, the fabric might as well be transparent now because her figure has become so legible to Joe. Perhaps it is unique to Tess – because though Joe has slept with many women, it's been a revelation for him to discover that, between skin and structure, there's this enticing layer of softness too. Tess's buttocks, her stomach, the fronts of her thighs, the backs of her arms – even as Joe bucks and humps into Nathalie, he surges at the memory of sweeping his hands over and over Tess's body.

But he really is here, in France. It surprises him to find he's had his eyes screwed shut. Usually he gorges on the view. Here he is, gripping Nathalie's arms as she straddles him, as she lowers herself down, screws herself on deep and tight and rides herself to a loud orgasm. What the hell is he doing here?

Before he falls asleep, Joe reckons all of this – whatever is going on either side of the Channel as well as deep inside him – is an essay in feeling. He reasons that, the thing is, he really likes sex and he's good at it and he's been lucky because his bedmates have always been enthusiastic, accomplished and permissive. With Nathalie tonight, it's been just as fun and harmless as it's always been because it's only sex, it's just a mutually greedy exchange of fluids. It's always been thus between them. Those contractions and spurts and spasms of physical relief. She knows where he's coming from. She also knows where not to go – not that she has any true ambition to go there. As long as Joe comes to her, she's always fine about when he goes again. Because he always comes back for more – why wouldn't he, when no strings can feel so good. Joe considers how the feeling really is purely physical when it comes to Nathalie. And he considers how it has nothing to do with Tess; it really has nothing to do with her at all.

But then Nathalie turns in her sleep and as she does so, she inadvertently jabs the side of Joe's leg with a sharp toenail. The feeling adds a sudden, pointed dimension to Joe's contemplation. He realizes how this concept of feeling over which he's been musing carries with it another factor he's never confronted – that there's more to Feeling than the purely physical. He likes the feel of sex, of a horny woman bringing him to orgasm – whether she's Nathalie, Rachel, Giselle – it's never really mattered to him who. The apotheosis of the sensation comes from his balls – he'll admit that he thinks with his dick but he also prides himself on being pretty thoughtful with his cock. His women have never complained, they've always hollered for more, more, more. But here's the thing: when it comes to Tess, Joe has experienced something novel – it's not about the feel of her, it's about the feelings he has for her and for the first time he's been confronted by a gamut of them – cerebral, emotional and physical. That's why sex with Nathalie during this recent trip has been like it's always been, but that's why he continues to think of Tess. Because Nathalie and Tess might both be very good, in their very different ways, at emptying his balls, but only Tess has filled his soul.

Joe glances across at Nathalie. She is beautiful, stunning in fact. Her physical attributes – if measured on some worldwide objective scale – far outshine Tess's. But it strikes Joe that it wouldn't matter to him in the slightest if he never saw her again. And then, just before he falls asleep, it strikes him harder how truly he longs to be with Tess.

Chapter Twenty-eight

All this is actually worse for her than it is for me.

She's blustering over her words like a novice surfer floundering in the spume.

I could make it easier for her; I could let her know that I'd already got the vibe that if she was hesitant at first, latterly she's been reluctant. I will be telling her that it's no big deal, I'll tell her I'm cool and that of course we can continue as friends – but I'll just let her stumble through her reasons a little longer because she's cute; all wide-eyed and lip-chewing and touching my arm every so often. And anyway, it's only half nine (not that she didn't spend the first hour and a half fixating on chit-chat) and I've still got a pint in front of me.

What makes it all right – bizarrely – is knowing that it's because of another bloke. It makes it easier on the old ego, really. If she was single, and simply not that into me, that might have dented my pride a bit, knocked the old confidence, mangled the machismo. So it's weird but though some lucky sod gets to have her and of course I wish it were me – it's OK, I'm cool. I like it that she's a one-man woman. I wouldn't want to be her bit on the side when the other guy's abroad. But she's not like that. Which is why I like her.

Bless her – now she's rattling off cliché after cliché:

It's not you, it's me.
    I really hope we can be friends.
        You're a great guy – it's just that . . . you know –
           I really hope I haven't led you on.

Don't you worry, Tess, I'm not going to go home and slash my wrists; I'm not even going to go home and wallow in Radiohead. I certainly won't be avoiding you when you go for your strolls along the pier. I'll still say, hey, fancy a coffee. I'll still want to grab a bite at Virgo's or Camwell's. I may even come on up to the house if I haven't seen you for a while. But for now, I'm going to stay right here with you, sitting on the fancy decked terrace of the pub looking out to sea, drinking beer and, by the time you've finished your soliloquy I'll most probably have finished my pint and I'll suggest another round and we can just sit here and shoot the shit as friends do. Just as soon as you've finished – and surely you can't have that much more to wring your pretty hands about.

*   *   *

See? That was a cool evening in the end, wasn't it? You relaxed and we had a laugh. You finally stopped crinkling your eyebrows and picking your nails – a couple more glasses of wine helped, as did watching those pissheads streaking into the sea. And you were positively effervescent when you were telling me about Lisa setting up this thing for you at her place next week. I liked talking about myself too – I liked it that you seemed genuinely interested. I liked your questions. It was

298

fun swapping dog stories. How the fuck did you get me telling you that if I have kids I like the names Ben and Ali?

But you still won't tell me why you won't go on the beach. Never mind – it's my mission now, with or without the reason behind it. I'll get you paddling before long. Not least because the weather's turned for the better, that's for sure.

Best of all, though, was just now – when we gave each other a peck on the cheek goodnight and you gave me a second hug and I said, I guess a shag is out of the question and you laughed and laughed and laughed.

Chapter Twenty-nine

'Bloody wish I could come – it sounds like fun.'

'Well, no doubt you still have drawers full of my creams from when I collared you into buying them first time round. But I too wish you could come, Tamsin – couldn't you come and visit anyway? Soon?'

'Actually, I only have a couple of pots left – they made good Christmas presents last year. And yes, I'll come up – when I fancy an ice cream.'

'It's not just ice cream we do well here.'

'*We? We?* Dear God, woman, you're starting to sound like a tourist guide.'

'If – scrap that – *when* you come, you'll see what I mean and you'll see for yourself what all this means to me now.'

'Christ alive, you'll be dropping the "r" from "bath" and "laugh" and "plaster" next.'

'And I'd love you to meet Joe.'

'You'd trust me not to burst into song? You know how I like a bit of "Bridge over Troubled Water".'

'I had you down as more of a Red Hot Chili Peppers girl.'

'I am – but you can't go wrong with a little Simon and Garfunkel every now and then.'

'It's *Gar*. *Gar*funkel. You always put the stress on *funkel*.'

'Stop being such a purist – have you really phoned me to nitpick my rock 'n' roll pronunciation? Stop laughing! I'm pissed off! I could be – I don't know – washing the cat, instead of talking to you. I'm serious!'

'I miss you, Tamsin – I really do. I wish you were coming tonight. You'd like Lisa. She's daft.'

'I like Lisa because you like her enough to turn to when I'm not around.'

'Lisa said just what you said about the Seb thing.'

'And did she say, "see – told you it would be fine,"' after the event, just as I would?'

'Of course she did.'

'Knowing there's a Lisa makes me feel better about you being up there in Madsville-on-Sea without me. You're not on your own any more, are you – with or without Joe.'

'You're right. I didn't think of it that way – I do have my own, small burgeoning community now. With Lisa as kingpin.'

'And what does she have to say about Joe? Tess? You still there?'

'Yes – still here. I was just thinking. She's like you, Tamsin. She revels in all the details, romantic or saucy. She's just like you – I reveal things, in all seriousness, and it sets her off into fits of giggles.'

'But does she also tell you to tread carefully?'

'Yes.'

'And what about Madame Mysterious and BlackBerry-*sur-Lit*? Do Lisa and I speak as one on that front?'

'Yes.'

'And? So? Did you ask Joe? To clarify – to assure you?'

'It wasn't like that.'

'What do you mean? You did ask? He did tell?'

'The time we spent together was so – I don't know how best to describe it. It was so all-encompassing, it was so

301

sustaining. It's clichéd to say it but it felt so real. So, I feel pretty good that I'm to him as he is to me. There's a connection between us, Tamsin. I don't need to ask – *directly*. Now you're the one who's gone quiet.'

'Two things, really, Tess. Firstly, I love the sound of Joe but you have to know that as your best friend I do not want you to be hurt. And my experience says that if you jump into love head first, you risk a fast fall and injury. Secondly, if it's so real with Joe, where's the reciprocal exchange of information? Why haven't you been clearer with him about what happened? Why haven't you confided in him? Confessed? Can you expect him to give himself to you if you're keeping stuff from him? Do you know the whole Joe if you're not showing him the complete Tess?'

'Tamsin.'

'I don't mean to burst your bubble, babe. Truly I don't. I want it to work out for you – even if it's on the other side of the world or wherever Madsville-on-Sea is. If your feelings run as deep for him as you feel that they do, then go for it, Tess. Show him all of you. Is that not the greatest gift we can bestow on those we love – our totality? See what he thinks. If he's the man you feel that he is, you'll be so pleased you did. If you're the girl of his dreams, he'll take all you give him and treasure it. It's the fundamental difference between a pretty-enough sketch and the beautiful, finished, whole picture.'

''Kay.'

'Don't go sulky.'

'I'm not.'

'You know I'm right.'

'I know. You are.'

'But here endeth my sermon – and it just leaves me to say I *wish* I could be with you tonight – get trolleyed on Thunderbird or Special Brew or whatever's the drink *du jour* up there.'

302

'You snob!'

'I'm teasing.'

'I know.'

'But I wish I was coming.'

'Me too.'

'And I do want to meet Joe.'

'You will.'

'I'll look at my diary.'

'Promise?'

'Promise. Oh, by the way, I'm sending you twenty-five quids' worth of M&S vouchers – I won them in a raffle at work. Do they have M&S Up North?'

Tess replaced the phone and looked at Em.

'Your Auntie Tamsin is one in a million, you know.' And as she licked her thumb to wipe away some smear or other off her daughter's chin, Tess suddenly rued the fact that the distance between them meant that Em would probably not recognize her godmother when she finally made the trip to Saltburn.

As she pushed the buggy and matched her pace to Wolf's improving limp, Tess thought, not for the first time, if only I hadn't been so hasty in cutting up my SIM card – there were photos on it I could have shown Em of her Auntie Tamsin.

She laughed.

There had also been a fair few of herself and Tamsin that were certainly *not* for Em's eyes.

'Your Auntie Tamsin – when are we going to entice her up here?'

She bought mince from the butchers on Dundas Street (they added a little bag of tripe for Wolf), and bread from the bakery opposite the station clock tower (Em was given a

303

taster of bun). She crossed over to the small, perfectly stocked deli and bought herself a box of amaretti biscuits and it was while she was wedging the box into the folded hood of the buggy that she became aware of frantic waving outside the shop window. It was Laura – lovely Laura from Redcar who worked at Swallows. It struck Tess that she had last seen her a month ago, when no one dreamed of going out without a coat on.

Their greeting was warm – but it had to wait until after Laura had squatted down to make much of Em.

'How are you? I'd begun to think that you'd buggered off back South.'

Tess laughed. 'Not a chance.'

'What happened to Wolf?'

Tess relayed the saga.

'I wonder how Mary will react. If she's up and sparky, it'll upset her – if she's in one of her fogs and she doesn't recognize him, well, that'll upset me.'

'How is she?' Tess was tentative. Her conscience ricocheting between her loyalty to Joe, her own curiosity and a genuine concern for the elderly lady.

'It's been a shame you haven't popped in,' Laura said but she said it so brightly that Tess felt far more guilty than had it been said accusatorily.

'Wolf,' she shrugged, 'Em. Time – it's just flown.'

'Well, don't be a stranger.'

'I won't – I'll call in soon.'

'She scarpered a couple of times – headed off in your direction, but they caught up with her before she'd made it to the bandstand. I've been off work – had the flu.'

'How are you now?'

'Well, I'm happy because I lost a few pounds – but I still feel a bit *flat*.'

Tess regarded her. 'Laura – are you around this evening?

Would you like to come to this – thing – my friend Lisa is doing at her place?'

Laura looked at Tess. 'What's a *thing*?' She knew whatever the thing was, she'd go. Devil Worship. Silent Meditation. 'Is it an Ann Summers party?'

'Nothing as exciting as that – it's just some stuff of mine.'

'Stuff? What kind of stuff?' Laura couldn't imagine – she certainly didn't think Tess had worldly goods for sale.

'Well – some organic skincare I used to produce and sell. Down South. Before I came up here.'

'Smellies? Ace!'

'And I'll be giving mini pedicures, and hand massages, and neck rubs, and if there's time, eyebrow shaping.'

Laura was scanning Tess's face as if she didn't quite understand. She was a plain girl, with overly plucked brows and a figure that could benefit from less snacking, but her eyes always shone kindness and when she smiled a natural femininity emanated.

'I used to be a beauty therapist,' Tess explained, 'in a former life.'

She's nervous. She's looking at herself, giving herself a sharp word for being such a silly mare. She doesn't doubt her ability to shape brows and neaten nails and undo knots in the neck – though the last time she did any of those was in London a lifetime ago. She isn't worried about her products, which Lisa had taken from the boot of her car to display in her home for this evening's event. What disconcerts Tess is that she'll be out in the open, the centre of attention – a place from which she's always, always darted to the safety of the periphery. The thing is, she says to herself, the thing is all the women tonight will be going to have a great time and they'll be looking to me to assist this.

Can I do it?

Was I ever much good?

My business failed, after all. The Next Jo Malone I certainly was not.

'Tess?' It's Lisa's husband, downstairs. 'You ready, pet?'

'Just coming.' She gives Em a quick shrug, which belies the emotion in her eyes – part excitement, part terror. She looks at her daughter, all snuggly in her night-time babygro. But Tess had to cut the feet off all of them last week, because Em's legs have grown and though Tess justified, why buy new when you can mend and make do? It still pained her to resort to scissors. And now she thinks to herself that tonight has a proper purpose – if she makes a little money, she can treat Em to something nice and new.

'Coming,' she calls down again and she lifts Em onto her hip, slings the bag of baby essentials over her shoulder, and makes her way downstairs.

Her first thought is, Christ, with this decibel level, Em will never settle. Her second thought is, pour me a glass of wine – this looks fun. Her third thought is, they don't look half bad – and this she directs at the assembled women as well as her wares. The jars and tubs and tubes are well displayed, laid out over a black cloth on a table to the side of the room. They look rather good – the matt white containers, with deep pink glossy print that, though costly at the time, even now Tess is pleased she insisted on.

A glass of wine is put into her hand and, a sip or two later, she feels able to focus. Laura has come – brilliant. And there are the mums from toddler group. That *has* to be Lisa's sister. Oh my! She's even roped in the lovely young waitresses from Camwell's. And isn't that the lady from Chocolini's? Bloody hell – there must be at least twenty people here!

And Lisa's husband, who has just popped his head round the door, catches Tess's eye, gives her a wink and the thumbs-up.

'OK, girls,' Lisa announces whilst bashing a teaspoon against her wineglass. 'Some of you know her, some of you don't – but you've probably all seen her around. So this is Tess and she brings her skills to Saltburn from London where she worked in a top salon.'

Lisa knows Tess will be cringing. Tess is actually more than cringing; she's concerned that Lisa's gross distortion of the truth will have some horrible karmic backlash. So much so, that she is actively shaking her head at the gathered women – all of whom simply laugh and raise their glasses.

'Also tonight, Tess has brought with her some amazing creams and lotions. They're exclusive and the edition is very limited – once it's gone, it's gone. So stock up, girls.'

Tess thinks, Lisa you're wasted here – with your skill for spin and your ability to make bullshit smell so sweet, you should work in politics.

'Aren't they?' Lisa is talking at her.

'Sorry?'

'The creams – they're from organic ingredients.'

'Yes, they are paraben free, hypoallergenic,' says Tess and she can't do anything about her voice, which has the aural equivalent of a rabbit caught in headlights. But then she glimpses Laura engrossed in one of the tubes that is being circulated and suddenly her voice is so confident it could see her to a job on a shopping channel. 'Rosehip is a powerful cell regenerator. It's excellent for softening wrinkles and treating scars or stretchmarks. Calendula – the posh term for marigold – is a wonderful soothing multipurpose ingredient. Great for babies' bums. I chose Tunisian neroli rather than French because it is cultivated and harvested with no agro-chemicals. Neroli is the essential oil from the bitter orange tree and for centuries it has been used for its powerful anti-depressant, balancing, sedative qualities. Its fragrance is divine. Eucalyptus is famed for being antiseptic, clearing, stimulating.

Geranium is brilliantly soothing and balancing. Moroccan rose is similarly soothing but also uplifting. Open it!' she tells a lady she recognizes but can't place who is examining a tube of All Over You body cream. The woman twists off the cap and squeezes a little cream onto her hands. She coos and offers her skin for the others to smell. The murmurs of appreciation and the clamour to sniff and dab and try, allows Lisa and Tess to grin at each other and chink glasses.

By the end of the evening – and it's way past eleven when the last guest has left – Tess has shaped three pairs of eyebrows, given everyone either a mini hand or foot massage, advised one lady about the best way to deal with milia, painted Lisa's toenails and forbidden everyone in the room from shaving against the hair growth or using their husband's blades. By the end of the evening, there's only enough of her creams to fill one box half full. Lisa set the prices before Tess had a chance to say, don't! you can't charge that – it's fraudulent! But Lisa said, shut up, Tess – you don't know what you're talking about. And now, with the counting over the three-figure mark, Tess concedes to herself that a little bullshit goes a long, long way and that next time Lisa tells her to shut up, she won't question why. She feels almost flush – two months' wages, tonight's unexpected windfall, the vouchers from Tamsin. She can manage the next few weeks quite well and it is a great concept.

'You must take a cut,' says Tess, peeling off two twenty-pound notes.

'Don't you bloody dare,' says Lisa and actually, she looks grossly offended.

'But Lisa –' Tess pauses. If she released her lips from the pressure of her bite, she could have a good old sob. 'Why have you done all this – for *me*?'

'Exactly,' says Lisa, '– for *you*. Don't you go getting teary, pet. Just take your cash and your stash and bugger off home. I'll see you tomorrow – playground, ten-ish?'

'But Lisa –' But Tess sees that Lisa's eyes are a little watery and she knows it's not the wine because she knows by now, that wine doesn't have that effect on Lisa's eyes. It just makes her even more noisy.

'Well, thank you – thank you so much.' And Tess hands Lisa one of everything. Helping Hand handcream with cocoa butter. Face It facial oil with neroli and rosehip. All Over You body cream. Smooch lip balm.

'Thank you very much,' says Lisa and for a minute or two, the women try and out-thank each other until Lisa's husband says, girls, girls, it really is time to take Tess and Em home.

Chapter Thirty

The vouchers from Tamsin arrived the following morning. Tess kept saying, are you sure you'll be OK, Wolf, but this was for her own peace of mind really. Once in a while, each day, Tess felt compelled to hear her voice, employing a tone that was grown-up and conversational, because though she no longer felt lonely sharing the house with a dog and a small child, there were times when she could feel cut off. Most days, though, there was someone to meet or a group to go to but still the big house on the hill could seem so self-contained from the community at large that Tess could feel quite isolated. Of course, she would not entertain such an emotion as being negative; instead, she'd speak conversationally to the dog or the child never yearning a reply but just to hear her normal voice. Em was still of the age at which a sing-song voice was most appropriate and Wolf – well, Wolf was a dog. A lumbering, limping old thing at that, who frequently got under Tess's feet but answered her frustration with big doleful eyes, gruffles and sighs as he mooched about the ground floor of the house in his motley coat of hessian and thatch. That morning, Tess kept asking him if he'd be OK – not because he seemed under the weather because his strength and mobility were greatly improved, but because she wanted to leave him at the house while she went on a shopping trip. We're going to Middlesbrough, she kept whispering to Em as if it was on a par with absconding for a spree in Harvey Nichols. But it was not the destination which was the thrill, it was feeling justified to eschew the tabletop sale at the church for a trip away from Saltburn, the opportunity to buy something new, even frivolous for Em; for Tess to afford to be able to dress her child in clothes that were first hand and full price. She'd bought a top and trousers combo for Em from the nearly-new morning at the library the other week, only to be stopped a day or so later by someone telling her how much her own daughter had loved that outfit first time around. More recently, Lisa had passed on a brand new sunhat with a ladybird motif saying Sam was scared of ladybirds, then an unopened pack of socks, saying they were a bit girly for boys.

Lisa had offered to accompany Tess when they met in the playground earlier in the morning but Tess had declined, fumbled for a reason which Lisa had generously fathomed and so told Tess, oops, can't come, forgot my ma-in-law is popping by. The truth was that actually, Tess just wanted to feel that she could make this shopping trip unaided and unassisted.

Not counting the night-time trip to the Transporter Bridge, this was Tess's first trip to Middlesbrough and only her third excursion from Saltburn. She allocated herself enough cash only for transport and perhaps a cup of coffee and a cake – the remainder she'd carefully squirrelled away, having counted and recounted it first. The wherewithal of the trip was Tamsin's vouchers and, though they had arrived just that morning, Tess heaped an imagined urgency upon them as if they had a sell-by date of tomorrow.

Are you sure you'll be OK, Wolf? Want a wee?

*

Tess laughed to herself that she was probably more excited about the train journey on Em's behalf than her daughter was herself. Marske. Longbeck. Redcar East. Redcar Central. She read out the names of the stations on the way and pointed out anything she thought remotely worthy. Look, the sea. Still the sea. Chimney, Em. Big smelly factory. Lots and lots of rooftops. Children, Em – oh, defacing a fence with a spray can. A dreary industrial landscape; vast pipes running alongside the tracks, factories of corrugated steel ominously windowless. Smoke, steam, belching silently. But over there! The Transporter Bridge! She could just see the top of it – like the upper parts of a rollercoaster with unseen excitement beneath. Moments later, she noticed that the filigree ironwork at the station appeared to be picked out in Transporter Bridge blue.

Middlesbrough. After the domestic scale of the local shops in Saltburn, the stores in the city seemed like countries in their own right. Tess felt oddly intimidated by the size, by the crowds, by the nose-to-tail traffic. She told herself, Christ, girl, you lived in bloody London for a decade – this is Camberwick Green in comparison. But actually, she could no more downplay Middlesbrough than she could talk up London. Before she set foot in the shop, she'd already decided she wouldn't be prolonging her trip with a search for coffee and cake.

Em came away with new, big-girl pyjamas, a set that comprised a pinafore, T-shirt and cardigan, a pair of jeans from the sale rail, two pairs of leggings and two tops that were buy one get one free. Tess hadn't seen the sign saying *All Childrenswear – 25%*. It happened to be the last day of the offer and when the sales assistant handed Tess further vouchers as change, Tess thanked him as if he'd blessed her personally. She went round the department again and spent the remaining vouchers more frivolously, on a book called

My Mum and a soft plush snake, so floppity Em could practically wear it as a scarf. It was lurid pink and yellow but being able to buy it gave Tess such pleasure that she found herself stroking it as she queued to pay. Silly Mummy, she giggled to Em, silly old Mummy. Em, though, was soundly asleep in the buggy.

Tess felt quite high, but stronger than the urge to browse for longer, was the pull to take the train back so she could unpack the purchases and revel in owning them. Then she'd phone Tamsin to thank her profusely – no, better still, she'd write her a card. The little gallery on Milton Street near the station had some lovely cards – if Em was still sleeping when they arrived back, she'd buy one before going home. Tess settled into the train and watched the city peter out. She knew she was absorbing the details with a mother's eye again – she almost bounced on her seat when she saw the llamas near Redcar – but Em still slept and the journey passed in silence. It was difficult to sense the sea with houses so close to the track that their interiors were visible and industrial works appearing to stop the spread of countryside. At Marske, a shard of sea became visible over the proliferation of bungalow roofs. Finally, the relief of country-side stretching flat to the sea cliffs. Soon, the gentle dichotomies of Saltburn: the busy allotments against the open land, the caravan park against the Victorian turrets near the coast.

The sea quite took Tess aback – she had no inkling until she saw it again how much she took it for granted, how she had grown used to it being there. That great mass, whose colour changed from grey to green to platinum to black, always providing light and a big sky and a breeze of varying strength which could stiffen her clothes or mist through her hair or lightly dust her skin with salt or even threaten to push her right over. Seeing the sea again, Tess thought about the sensation of the city encircling her and she knew that it was nothing to do with the traffic or the rush and scamper of the busy streets, it had instead everything to do with the lack of sea.

I'm daft, she thought.

If Tamsin could see me now – grinning at the North Sea.

But Tess had an answer up her sleeve for Tamsin.

I'm soothed by the sight of the sea, Tamsin, because it means I'm nearly home.

She bought a card from the gallery – a set of four photographs showing the Halfpenny Bridge in the various stages of collapse. Tess imagined Joe there as a ten-year-old and she felt a pang of longing that decided her to phone him before she rang Lisa just as soon as she was home. Leaving the gallery, she saw Laura ahead of her, approaching arm in arm with an elderly lady as if they were the best of friends. Momentarily, Tess was disappointed that it wasn't Mary. She waved and called to Laura who waved and said something to her charge. They could not increase their pace and Tess felt it would be overtly rude to increase her own so they made a slow, smiling passage towards each other.

'Hullo.'

'Hullo, Tess. Mrs Tiley, this is Tess. Tess, this is Mrs Tiley.'

'Pleased to meet you.'

'And you, dear.'

'And that there is Emmeline, fast asleep.'

'We've been out shopping, Laura. M&S in Middlesbrough.'

'Good for you.'

'The sales are on.'

'I don't want to know! Thanks for last night, Tess – it was good, it was a laugh. A nice bunch – and I love your stuff. I used the All Over You cream after my shower this morning. Mrs Tiley – Tess here is ever so clever. She makes her own creams – you know, for hands and the body. But she also does beauty – you know, manicures and the like.'

314

'Do you, dear?'

'Well, more then than now, really.'

'Look at the state of mine. The days before dishwashers, you see. Mind you, though we worked our hands we did try our best by them. We used – oh, what was it called? We'd rub each other's hands and do each other's nails. What was it called?'

'Mrs T – we'd best be making tracks now.'

'Nice to meet you, dear.'

'And you.'

'See you soon, Tess – give Em a kiss from me when she wakes up.'

'See you soon, Laura. I'm glad you enjoyed last night.'

'It was a laugh. You should do another soon.'

'Palmers Cocoa Butter,' said Mrs Tiley.

'Ah,' said Tess, 'Palmers. You can't beat it.'

Tess let the pair pass before she headed for home, going via the Everything Shop and putting a few essentials onto Joe's tab as he'd insisted she must. She picked up the pace to make light of the hill. But then she slowed down and soon enough stopped altogether. It wasn't the gradient. She was tired from the excursion and the excitement – but not that tired. What was it that was perplexing her so? It took a while to pinpoint it. It was Mrs Tiley. It was her hands. It was the notion that, in her youth her hands were fair, that the domestic drudge of hands that do dishes had ravaged them. It was the image of Mrs Tiley and her friends as younger women, rubbing in cocoa butter and doing each other's nails. Most likely sharing a gossip and a giggle. It was the knowledge that those flaky nails and papery skin had had no attention for years. Tess turned and retraced her steps, muttering under her breath, you'll be OK for another half-hour or so, won't you, Wolf.

*

315

'Laura? Someone to see you. It's that lass who came up here once or twice – with the little 'un. I'll see to Mrs Lee.'

Laura smoothed Mrs Lee's hair the way she liked because she knew it would not cross Di's mind to do so. Then she left the sunroom and walked briskly to the front door. There stood Tess and wide-awake Em who was wrestling with the harness of the buggy like Houdini in a tizz.

'Hullo again. Well, good afternoon, Em.'

'Look, Laura – this might sound a bit far-fetched but I was thinking. I mean, I know last night was fun – but I have a few more pots and tubs and there's not enough for another evening. And even if there was. Well – even if there was. The thing is, I was thinking – after meeting your Mrs Tiley – I'd like to do something. I'd like to do *something*. I wanted to ask you if you thought they – your residents – might like me to pop in one day and do manicures? Pedicures?'

Laura regarded Tess whose words were spilling like an ice cream float when the vanilla has just been added. Effervescing. A bubbling over of sweetness.

'I could be a volunteer,' Tess said. 'I want to do *something*. Something I'm proud of.'

'Tess—'

'I mean, I am properly qualified.'

'I'd have to put it by the boss, of course.'

The bright mood across Tess's face faltered. 'Would they need references?'

Laura looked confused. 'But you *are* qualified?'

'I am.' Tess was reticent. 'I am. Of course. It's just – and I know the salon would give me a glowing report – but it's just I don't want them to know I'm *here*.'

Laura looked unsettled. 'You in some kind of trouble, pet? Is that why you suddenly appeared here?'

'Not trouble as in bad stuff, Laura – I promise you. I just –'

Em was jabbering and Laura was obviously all ears and just

then, Tess did not want to compromise a lovely day, or diminish the energy her idea had given her. 'It's nothing. It's fine. They can phone for references. Nothing happened at work – they were always pleased with me. It was other stuff that was crap.'

Laura still looked concerned. 'You just showed up here, didn't you – you didn't know a soul. You didn't even know Joe, did you – when you first arrived?'

'No, you're right. I didn't.'

'But you're saying there's nothing – you know – dodgy?'

'Nothing dodgy,' said Tess, hoping an avoidance of the whole truth couldn't be classed as a lie. 'Well – perhaps you'll think about it anyway,' she said. Her face had fallen flat and so had her voice. She pulled herself together and said goodbye before pushing the buggy and heading away.

Mary was in a chair by the window overlooking the front. She watched them go. She raised her hand but she wasn't noticed.

Laura did think about it. And she spoke to her boss about it before clocking off that evening.

'She'll have references, will she, Laura?'

'Oh yes – she worked in a posh London salon.'

'Oh?'

'In the West End. Oxford Street I think – same as Selfridges.'

'Oh?'

'But I'm telling you, I was at an evening she hosted and she's good – she's really good. I'll say it'll not be long before she's up and running here in Saltburn – a little salon perhaps. *Beauty by Tess* or the like. I think we should give her the go-ahead.'

'And she'll bring her own stuff, will she?'

'Yes – you should smell it. It's grand. All posh and organic and pure and all.'

'And she doesn't want paying?'

'No.'

'Why not?'

'Because Tess is nice – she's a good girl. She told me she wants to *do something*.'

'Give a bit back, perhaps, to the Olds? A volunteer?'

Laura nodded.

'Well, shall we see how the Olds take to her? A trial, like?'

'Shall I check the references, then?'

'If she passes muster with you, Laura, she's OK by me. You're a good judge of character, you are.'

Wolf was fine.

Em was dressed to the nines.

Tamsin was cordially thanked by card.

Lisa was regaled with the list of purchases and the discounts garnered.

And then Joe was phoned.

'Hi, it's me.'

'Hey you.'

'Is it OK to phone – is it a good time?'

'It's fine – I'm just finishing off for the day. It's been busy – but the progress is amazing. I've taken photos – I'll show you them. Tess?'

'Yes?'

'You OK?'

'When?'

'When what?'

'The photos – when might I see them?'

'Soon. Soon. You sound low. Tess? Sorry? I didn't quite catch that?'

'I just said that I'm looking forward to seeing you again, that's all. Hullo – Joe?'

'Yes?'

'You still there?'

'Yes.'

'You OK?'

'I'm looking forward to seeing you again too, Tess. I'm working on it.'

Chapter Thirty-one

Both Nathalie and Joe were well aware that it was the first time he'd used the premise of a headache. In fact, it was the first time that he'd turned down sex. Moreover, Nathalie hadn't even managed to perform much of an overture before Joe turned away from her in bed and said, Christ, I have a killer headache. She lay there thinking, the guy works too hard. He lay there thinking he'd like to be at home. The somewhat alarming proximity of another woman's nakedness caused him to avoid specific thoughts of Tess (though, after their phone call, he'd thought of her intently) to nurse a general homesickness instead. He'd been away for almost two weeks. He was needed in Brussels. They wanted him in the States – which could wait, but not for long. He couldn't quite leave France just yet. A couple of days' time, perhaps. He might only manage a fleeting visit home – but he would gladly rejig all those pressing commitments to facilitate it.

Hours later, Nathalie moved in her sleep, her leg pressing up alongside Joe's. He remained still for a moment before inching away from the contact. The next morning, when he woke, he found her arm lolling across his stomach. He lay still for a while, then glanced over to her; she was sleeping.

Gently, he picked up her wrist and moved her arm away from his body. With a stroppy fidget of her limbs, she placed it back. Whether she'd been asleep before, he was now unsure. What was certain was, though she said nothing and her eyes were closed, her hand was very much awake, travelling down his body to tickle her fingertips up and down the tumid shaft of his early-morning erection. Now she was awake and his eyes closed. She encircled his cock, first with her hand, then with her mouth before climbing aboard and sinking her hot wet sex straight down on him fast. He kept his eyes shut as they fucked and, as he came, he cried out to himself, Tess, Tess, Tess.

Nathalie thought Joe had kept his mouth shut because he was gentlemanly about his morning breath. Because Joe was a very good kisser. She always enjoyed the way he kissed her and she always judged herself on the voracity of his tongue, the persistence of his lips, the imaginative uses to which he could put his teeth.

He left the bed to shower.

'I see you later, Joe.'

'*Allons*,' he replied.

*   *   *

'You seen much of Joe, then?' Laura asked conversationally over her shoulder as she led Tess through the hallway to the morning room.

'Not for a fortnight.'

'Busy, is he?'

'Very. He's still abroad. But we speak – daily if we can.'

A sly grin filled Laura's pause. Then she put her work face back. 'He phoned here a couple of days ago – Mary hadn't a clue who he was. He always seems more relieved when she's like that than when she's, you know, *together*.'

'Oh?'

'Odd that – it's usually the other way round with families of our residents.'

Tess would have liked more time to mull this over, more time to speak to Laura even though during such conversations they both trod a diplomatic and formal two-step around the subject. But Laura was already holding open the door to the morning room and saying, now, ladies, what a treat we have for you today.

Tess looked around the room. She was unsure how many of the residents were actually looking at her. There were five ladies and she noted Mary was one of them, as was Mrs Tiley. The other three she knew she'd probably smiled at previously though her awkwardness would have prevented her from looking at them more intently then. She turned to Laura and spoke in a low voice.

'Should I –?'

Laura smiled at her and clapped her hands in a merry rhythm. 'Good afternoon, ladies. You may remember Tess when she's popped in before – well, you probably remember Em better. Isn't she a doll? Hasn't she grown?' The ladies cooed and clucked and Tess remembered one of them by the way she held out her hands to Em, rubbing her fingers together as if to entice a cat. Em toddled over to her and allowed her curls to be stroked.

'Ladies,' said Laura again, 'our Tess here is a very skilled beautician.' She savoured the word as if it brought with it the pleasures of the trade itself. 'She's going to come to you, one by one, and offer you a manicure – or you can request whatever you like. You know – for your hooves and paws.' Chuckles wove through the room in a happy ripple. Laura turned to Tess, sotto voce. 'Start wherever – I'll be on hand. I'll keep an eye on Em – though it's good you brought her.

I don't trust this lot not to get all uppity and queue-jump each other's facials.' Laura observed Tess casting shy glances to the five residents. 'Why not start with Mrs Tiley,' she suggested. 'After all, she was your – inspiration – wasn't she? She's part of the reason you're here today.'

'That does feel lovely, dear.'

Tess liked to work with minimal conversation – she always had. That wasn't to say she wasn't talked at. A towel (one of Joe's fluffiest) was across her knees and a pair of hands in her own hands rested lightly in her lap. She had been engrossed in Mrs Tiley's hands, sensing the tendons and bones, thin but still strong beneath the fragile surface which carried the age spots and veins and a crackle of skin over knuckles and joints, like the map of a long life.

'It's not Palmers Cocoa Butter, I'm afraid,' said Tess.

'Well, it's lovely stuff, dear.'

'Thank you.'

'Mrs Tiley, I'm going to shape your nails today – buff them too – but I shan't varnish them. Can you wait till next visit? I'm going to rub in a little almond oil. They're very dry, your nails – they need a nice conditioning before we put polish on.'

'Whatever you suggest, dear – it's not like I've anything fancy in my diary.'

'Would you like me to leave the almond oil with you, Mrs Tiley? For you to use yourself?'

'No, dear – don't do that. I don't want to do it myself – I want you to come back again, you see.'

Tess looked around and saw Em and Laura explaining to a frail old lady whose neck seemed unable to support her head, the intricacies of the plastic *Teletubbies* musical wind-up portable TV that was one of Em's most treasured possessions though it cost 10p at the tabletop sale. Even from the tragic angle at which this lady's face was restricted, Tess could deduce a smile. Laura caught her eye and backoned her over.

'This is Mrs Ellsworth, Tess – we call you Mrs Ell, don't we, Mrs Ell?'

The lady appeared unable to move her head much at all, not even to nod, but Tess found if she dipped hers to a similar angle, they could establish eye contact. And, once she'd sat down on her stool and put her towel across her lap, she could actually look up into Mrs Ell's face and converse quite naturally.

'Would you like a manicure, Mrs Ell?'

'A manicure you say? What a treat.' But her hands remained curled around a handkerchief held close to her chest. Gently and slowly, Tess reached for her hands, unfurling them and bringing them onto her lap. She was stunned. Mrs Ell's finger-nails were beautiful and needed no improvement. She told her so.

'I like to keep myself nice,' Mrs Ell said.

'Would you like me to paint them? I have these polishes.'

Mrs Ell gave a little laugh and a sigh. 'That colour there – we used to call that Wild Cherry in my day and it was my favourite shade.'

Tess looked under the bottle. It was called Bloodsucker these days. She didn't think Mrs Ell need be party to this information. 'Would you like Wild Cherry today?'

'Shall I tell you why I liked it so?' She was whispering. Tess looked up and gave her a covert nod. 'Because my name is Cherry. Well, it's Cheryl. But when I was a young thing, they all called me Cherry. Not here, though – here they call me Mrs Ell, which I don't mind. Because I'm eighty-four, love – I'm almost eighty-five years old and it's the right age to be called Mrs Ell, or Mrs Ellsworth, because I'm a grand old dame now, aren't I? And it's a bit of respect for Mr Ell who passed on five years gone. But today, between you and me,

I'd very much like a little Wild Cherry if you please because I'll let you into a little secret – but it's a secret, mind, and not for sharing – I'd snare the boys with my Wild Cherry nails.' Mrs Ell broke off to check Tess was all ears – and from the unbroken eye contact she could tell that she was. 'I'd paint my nails in that shade and go off to the dances in Marske and Redcar and here in Saltburn too when the Zetland was a fine hotel, the finest. It's flats now, you know. Well, they'd woo me, they would, and they'd say what beautiful hands I had. And I'd say "Wild Cherry" and they'd say, what a name, what a name for a nice young lady to have. And I'd laugh and we'd dance – we'd dance the night away.'

They waited in silence for the base coat to dry.

'Happy days,' Tess ventured as she rolled the nail-varnish bottle between her palms.

'They were wonderful!' Mrs Ell declared.

'Mrs Ell, would you like to try my foot spa – while your nails dry?'

Mrs Greene chose In-the-Pink for her nails and she and Mrs Tiley started a chorus of 'Pink, pink, to make the boys wink'. It didn't matter to them that Laura and Tess caught each other's eyes as if to say they hadn't a clue what they were singing about. Em liked it and did her wiggle dance, which made the song last longer. Mrs Greene had a go with the foot spa too when Mrs Ell's nails were dry.

'She rubs your feet,' Mrs Ell said to Mrs Greene though Tess was right there. 'She rubs your feet after the machine's finished with them. And with her fancy creams too. Lucky old toes.'

Mrs Hansard seemed reluctant for a manicure and she shirked away from the notion of the foot spa. In my day, she said, people put electrical things in water to kill themselves. But she didn't want not to have Tess; Tess just needed to work out what she could offer.

'My shins, love, they're very dry. They can be very sore, you know.' She rucked her skirt up a little and, even through thick beige stockings, Tess could see what she meant.

'I have a wonderful balm, Mrs Hansard,' Tess said. 'It's very mild but very nourishing. Here – would you like to have a smell? Do you like that?'

'It's lovely dear, very nice.' She let the folds of her skirt drop back down, smoothed the material at her lap and clasped her hands loosely together.

'It's OK, Mrs Hansard. We don't have to do your shins, if you don't feel comfortable.'

'It's not that, dear. It's – something else.' She leant in to Tess, her breath sweet–sour, a little like tea that has stood for too long. 'I hate them.'

Tess sat back on her stool from the force of animosity in Mrs Hansard's steely voice. But Mrs Hansard was still leaning.

'My whiskers,' she hissed at Tess, 'I *hate* them.' With a surreptitious look left and right, the lady then lifted her chin a little and turned her face this way and that.

Tess was cautious not to downplay them, nor make too much of them either.

'Mrs Hansard,' she said quietly, 'my tweezer skills are unsurpassed. I'm just as good with whiskers as I am with eyebrows. Would you like me to – see to them?'

She soaked a flannel in warm water and laid it lightly over the lady's chin. This she repeated four more times. Then, she chose There There lotion (with tea tree in it, to soothe, she explained), poured a little onto cotton wool and swept it over Mrs Hansard's face. Swift and businesslike, Tess set to work with the tweezers and, after Mrs Hansard had inspected the results in the mirror, she then gave Tess the go-ahead to treat her shins.

Tess hadn't meant to save Mary until last but that was the order that had transpired. Mary didn't seem to recognize Tess,

326

though she'd been in deep conversation with Em. Tess thought, therefore, that she ought to call her Mrs Saunders.

'What would you like?' she asked her. 'A mini facial and your nails done?'

'My hair,' said Mary.

'I don't really do hair, Mrs Saunders, I'm terribly sorry.'

'Could you just brush it, do you think? The girls here – they're so rough. Mind you, from the looks of them, they've never had a comb near their hair.' Tess glanced at Laura who rolled her eyes.

'I don't have a hairbrush with me, Mrs Saunders, but if someone could fetch yours, I'd be pleased to brush your hair.'

'Never mind about my hair,' Mary snapped. 'I'll have polish, then.'

'Would you like to use the foot spa too, while we do your hands?'

'No.'

'Would you like to choose a shade of varnish?'

'What's that one called?'

'Purple Prose.'

'What's that one called?'

'Tangerine Dream.'

'What's that one called?'

'Um. It's called Red-in-Bed.'

'And that one – what's that one called?'

'This one is, well, it's called Kissy-Kissy.'

'I'll have the one about bed, then.'

There was a bitterness scorching Mary's voice that Tess found upsetting. Polite conversation was met with curt one-word answers so Tess depended on her creams and fingers to provide the soothing. Eventually, it worked. Not immediately, not while she was massaging Mary's forearms or pulling on her fingers gently, twisting her own fingers

327

around them. The lift in Mary's spirits came when the massage was finished, when her hands were on Tess's lap, her nails base-coated and twice painted with Red-in-Bed, the non-chip, shine-protecting top coat drying.

'My husband hated polish,' Mary said. 'He'd tell me it made me look like a tramp.'

Tess didn't know how to reply because her immediate response was, your husband was my Joe's dad.

'You don't polish your nails, do you – do you not practise what you preach?'

'Well, Mrs Saunders, I don't really lead the lifestyle that warrants fancy nails – what with looking after a house and a dog and my little girl.'

'How is Wolf?'

Tess worked at not registering surprise. 'He's well.'

'Is he on the mend, then?'

How did she know? 'He is recovering very well.'

'My son told me about the accident.'

Tess nodded while she blew gently on Mary's nails. 'It was dreadful. Wolf's a lucky boy.'

'He's a dog.'

'He's a lucky dog.'

'My boy is lucky,' said Mary, 'my boy has you.'

* * *

Joe saw that the caller was Tess. How he'd love to speak to her. Have a little chat. Listen to her voice blather on about the minutiae of life in Saltburn, which Tess was the first person, in Joe's experience, to make sound fascinating. He'd love to wile away a good half-hour talking bollocks and making her laugh and allowing her voice to cross the Channel, travel down the land mass of France and set itself within his smile. But not just now. And not on the phone. Not here, whilst he was sitting on Nathalie's couch, using her laptop to explore flights home.

* * *

Tess felt deflated. She didn't want to leave a message. She'd so love to have spoken direct with Joe. He was the person off whom she most wanted to bounce her ideas. And she wanted to open up to him, she liked to think that she might have said, Joe, I just want you to know I did something today of which I'm really proud. And perhaps she'd say, but I'm not sure, what do you think, Joe – how do you feel? Would she have said so? She liked to think she might.

'What am I thinking, Wolf – he'd be very cross with me. Let down, too. He was cross enough the first time. Now he might well see it as betrayal.'

She was tired even though she'd had an unbroken ten hours' sleep. Yesterday had been such an involved afternoon at Swallows; followed by a milkshake on the pier with Lisa yaketting twenty to the dozen about what her sister had done with her sister's best friend's husband, the slink. Tess had gone to bed early, longing for Joe to be home. She felt so lonely on waking this morning. And she hadn't hoovered upstairs since last week. And there were still the garden sheds to sort out. But the to-do list was nothing compared with the what's-done list. Yesterday, at Swallows, Tess had experienced a surge of awareness that she was doing something that made a difference and, for the first time, she sensed that her own skills actually had some value.

But she was also aware that what's-done could cause conflict with Joe – and she didn't know how to reconcile that with the enormous sense of purpose, the boost it had given her. She had to put that on the to-do list. Lisa had ticked her off for using her own products when it was now clear that they could make her money, but Tess was adamant that this was what she wanted to do with her remaining stock.

The doorbell went.

Wolf shuffled over ahead of Tess.

It was Mary. And Laura. Laura linking arms with Mary in the way she had with Mrs Tiley too. Affectionate and supportive. Lean on me, easy how you go, don't stray too far, Mrs S.

'Hullo, dear,' said Mary.

'Hullo, Tess,' said Laura.

'Tess,' Mary said to herself, as if reminding herself of some etiquette.

'Tea and biscuits?' Tess offered.

'We've come to see Wolf,' Mary said.

They all inspected him with great interest.

'I think we will have that cup of tea,' Mary said to Laura before leading the way into the kitchen.

They didn't stay long, just long enough to let another layer of top coat dry over Mary's Red-in-Bed once she'd finished her cup of tea.

On their way out, Laura turned to Tess. 'Same time next week, then?'

'Same time next week,' said Tess.

'Or – I know it might not be convenient – but how about Friday? This Friday – day after tomorrow? You were the toast of Swallows after you'd gone. The other residents are clamouring for you.'

Tess beamed. 'My pleasure,' she said. 'Of course I'll be there.'

The phone call came late into the evening. It was Joe.

'Hullo, Miss.'

'Hullo, Mr.'

'I'm coming back.'

330

'Joe! Really? When!'

'Day after tomorrow – only for the weekend. But better than nothing.'

It was only after the call had ended that Tess twigged that the day after tomorrow was Friday. And that she had no idea what time Joe was due back. But she was expected at Swallows just after lunch. She couldn't cancel her commitment, not even for Joe.

Chapter Thirty-two

It felt to Tess as though she had three eyes – not that she needed the extra one in the way she often muttered about needing an extra pair of hands; more that she had acquired one from necessity that Friday afternoon. She kept one eye on the time (each hour, that day, carried potential significance), one eye on the job in hand (there were to be five pairs of old frail hands in hers today) and one eye she darted to and from the doorway at Swallows. She kept her ears peeled too, as if expecting the bell to ring and Joe to come through the doorway and discover her there. Swallows might very well be the place in which she felt she might find herself – but that wasn't to say she wanted Joe to find her here. She was stuck between wanting to provide and not wanting to betray. For Tess, the loaded anticipation was akin to imploring the TV programme to finish so she could scoot back to bed before her dad came up, none the wiser, to check on her. It was similar to the urgency when filching from Rebecca Varley's maths book in Year 9 as Mrs Butcher approached to collect their work. Tess filed nails, bathed feet, organized eyebrows and blitzed whiskers. As she worked, she thought quietly to herself. If I told Joe, and told him why, he might well be OK about it. He might even reciprocate with the history behind his personal why-nots.

'It's probably better to reveal than conceal when it comes to love,' Tess said quietly to herself while using the pumice gently on Mrs O'Sullivan's corns. Mrs O'Sullivan was dainty: white-haired, a white cardigan, an old gold necklace carefully laid around the collar of her blouse. Tess liked her spectacles: they were old-fashioned, styled with a little swoosh at either edge, like tiny wings or ticks of approval. The frames seemed to be embedded in the bridge of her nose, her skin appearing to overlap the fake tortoiseshell. Tess wondered whether she'd ever had a different pair, she wondered how long it had been since Mrs O'Sullivan had had an eye test, she wondered whether it was something Swallows offered. Or whether, at this age, it was a given that sight deteriorates and if the glasses fit, why fiddle. Mrs O'Sullivan, according to Laura, was also deaf as a post. So it came as some surprise that she should respond to Tess's quiet personal aside.

'Don't do that, dear.'

Tess looked up sharply but there was nothing about Mrs O'Sullivan's expression to suggest anything untoward. 'I'm sorry – is it sore?' She inspected Mrs O'Sullivan's corn.

'Not *that*, dear. I wasn't referring to my trotters. I'm referring to you – I'd advise you to keep a little back.' She was smiling intently at Tess, a glint to the diluted blue irises of her eyes.

'Conceal and not reveal?' Tess said, her voice intentionally low to check the legitimacy of Mrs O'Sullivan's hearing.

'You give a man everything – you have nothing for yourself. And anyway, they tend to die before you and you end up burying everything with them. Then you're stuck in old age wondering, where has it all gone and what do I do now with so little? You end up like me.'

'I'd be quite happy to end up like you, Mrs O'Sullivan.'

'Only on the outside,' Mrs O'Sullivan said. 'Not bad at all for my age and the life I've had. But you wouldn't want to be me on the inside, dear. I'm just waiting, now, waiting to go.'

Tess tutted. She thought about it.

'Isn't love about sharing everything? Isn't secrecy anathema?'

She held Mrs O'Sullivan's foot between her two flat hands, as if clasping a prayer.

'No,' Mrs O'Sullivan said, 'it isn't.' Her bluntness was oddly compelling but Tess didn't want to continue the conversation; she'd never done more than pass the time of day or the state of the weather with clients. For Tess, for some time now, other people's wisdom and their informed advice had served not to benefit her but to magnify her own shortcomings. She needed to return any conversation to a more anodyne level.

'Laura is quite convinced you are deaf, Mrs O'Sullivan – or at least, hard of hearing.' Mrs O'Sullivan looked at her blankly. Tess was about to lean closer, and repeat herself, when she saw that Laura had come into the room again, with a jug of iced water and a round of glasses. Everyone was 'pet' to Laura, whatever their age or mood. When she came to Mrs O'Sullivan, she asked very loudly, water, pet? but Mrs O'Sullivan kept her eyes trained on Tess as if she hadn't heard a word.

As Tess introduced herself to the next resident, she wondered about Mrs O'Sullivan. She felt flattered but unnerved too to be party to Mrs O'Sullivan's deceit. Why had she feigned to be hard of hearing? Was it to have a secret last laugh of some kind, or was it to cling to privacy now her life was condensed into a small cupboard, a chest of drawers and communal sitting rooms in a residential care home? Perhaps, though, she was just an awkward old mare – a term Tess had baulked at on hearing it used, albeit affectionately, by a member of staff.

'I am Miss Edmondson,' the next lady said, 'and I don't think you'll have much luck with my nails.' She held out her hands, so gnarled by arthritis that her fingers were contorted at a severe angle to her hand, like wind-blasted trees on a hillside.

'How about the foot spa and a nice soothing hand massage?'

'If you like, dear.'

Her response forced Tess to consider how, for many of the residents, visits such as hers simply passed the time. What else were they going to do on a Friday afternoon? Sit in their chairs. Like the rest of the week. Waiting. She brought something new to the sitting room, whether the service was truly required or not.

'I think you'll like it,' Tess said. 'I think you'll like it so much, you'll be putting in a request before my next visit.'

'Will you be bringing your little girl?'

'Em? Yes. She likes it here.'

'Is your husband—'

But Tess was used to cutting short such a sentence. 'Oh, I'm not married.'

'Oh. Are you on your own, love?'

Tess paused to ponder this and, when she had the answer, she savoured it before assuring Miss Edmondson that no, she wasn't on her own, not any more.

'Nice to be looked after,' said Miss Edmondson, 'by someone you love.'

If it wasn't for the buggy, Tess felt she could have skipped all the way home; not metaphorically, but in proper, school-girl, ground-covering leaps. She'd agreed with Laura to continue with twice-weekly visits, on Tuesday mornings and

Friday afternoons, and Laura had shown her a secure cupboard where she could leave her foot spa and other items. Again, Laura had told her, you're good at this, Tess – you shouldn't do it for free, you know. But again Tess had replied, I know I know – but I want to.

After this second visit, she realized why the work was so satisfying – it was because the clients were way past vanity. Certainly, through the power of nail polish or the precision of tweezers, the ladies looked better for Tess's expertise. But more to the point – for them and for her – they *felt* better; a response clearly legible in the increased levels of chatter when she left, than when she had arrived. For Tess, there was more job satisfaction to be had here than from the hasty thanks and desultory tips that came her way in the London salon. And because there was no charge, and they were free to avail themselves of her skills, she felt no servitude to them. She liked making them feel nice, and she liked listening to them. She had to admit, though, that it wasn't the good Samaritan in her which had unleashed this urge to bound all the way home with a big grin on her face, it was that Joe was coming back. Maybe he's there already.

She waited.

Actually, she didn't wait; she busied herself tidying and cleaning and preparing food for all the inhabitants of the Resolution. Her ear strained for the crunch of tyre on gravel and her body fought the magnetic pull to any window which looked out onto it.

But he didn't come.

By eight thirty she was really hungry and though she dithered for a while, she phoned his mobile. The sound of the overseas ring tone made her sit down heavily. He was nowhere near here. She was just about to ring off when Joe answered.

'Sodding flight cancelled, trying to buy alternative.' He was speaking like a text message. 'Phone you when I know.'

She had to have a moment, did Tess, to realign her disappointment. She couldn't be pissed off with Joe but that wasn't to say she couldn't be utterly cross with the situation. Remaining in a lumpen sulk by the phone, she swore at the French, at air travel, at Joe's job, at her own romantic fantasy. Then Wolf came to see her, towering over where she sat, and the attention was welcome at first until the threat of his viscous drool, currently swinging from his mouth like the chain on a crane, motivated Tess to pull herself up and pull herself together.

The chicken would keep until tomorrow. The potatoes, peeled and ready to be roasted, could stay in a bowl of water in the fridge. She bit into a raw carrot and decided to cook the rest for Em. It would give her something to do while she waited to hear from Joe.

He phoned soon after, he had a new flight, he'd be in very late, he'd eat on the plane, don't wait up, Tess.

She wanted to – she'd planned how she was going to greet him. But ultimately she didn't because she simply couldn't stay awake though she went to bed as late as she could manage. She woke at one in the morning and darted to the window to see if Joe's car was in the drive.

It wasn't.

She rested her forehead sadly against the windowpane and she thought to herself, it's just not fair. He was meant to arrive yesterday but he's not even here yet.

She went back to bed but couldn't settle. It was heading for a quarter to two when she next looked at the clock. She was starting to feel sleepy again, but not so sleepy that she couldn't leave her room, check on Em, go down a floor and settle herself into Joe's bed. She rued the taunt of the notion that they could have had hours together between these sheets by now, if he'd arrived yesterday as planned. But his bed felt the best place to be, it made him seem real and far closer than a daydream away.

He was on his way, and at some point today, he'd come into this bed and fold himself around her.

Bloody four-hour delay. Bloody Manchester – what sodding destination was that for a sodding detour? Why couldn't they have been rerouted to Newcastle at the very bloody least? Fucking air-traffic controllers. The total bloody bastard wankers.

Joe didn't swear often which meant that, on the occasions he did, it was enormously resonant and gratifying. Nothing quite like fulminating at the top of your voice in a hire car while belting away from bloody Manchester to travel east and north. He could have made a short detour to Teesside to collect his own car but as he'd be back at that airport tomorrow evening, there seemed little point. And the hire car was quite nippy. And he was enormously tired.

He couldn't contain a groan of relief when he finally stilled the engine on the driveway of his home. It was gone three in the morning. He sat and peered at the looming mass of the house; there was little moonlight but its shadowy bulk was benign and downstairs the hall light was on, emanating a sense of warmth. It seemed such a long time ago that Tess had asked him if he minded her keeping that particular light on – because he usually switched every one off. No, he didn't mind. But he asked her, do you not feel safe here? To which she replied, oh, I feel safe, all right – I would just hate to trip over Wolf.

She's in there.

They all are.

Sound asleep.

He could imagine Tess saying to Em earlier, Joe'll be home soon – stay awake, baby girl, so you can say hullo.

And then a little later on she'd have said, where the hell is he, Wolf?

And later still, bastard air-traffic controllers, Wolf, he's still in bastard France.

And much much later, night night, Joe, wherever you are.

Well, he thought, I'm here now and it's too bloody late to call out, honey! I'm home!

He'd planned to do it. The thought had made him chuckle – imagining himself flinging open the front door and making like Jimmy Stewart or someone. Joe couldn't remember the last time he'd actively daydreamed but he'd enjoyed that one. He had envisaged Tess, perhaps barefoot, dancing down the stairs laughing at his announcement and floating into his arms. He'd spun her round in his mind's eye, twirled her two, three times while she buried her face in his neck and then kissed him and kissed him and kissed him. And Wolf had been there too, lolloping around. As had Emmeline; squawking in delight whilst grabbing fistfuls of his trousers.

Not to be. Not at this time of night. Not this trip.

He saw to his joy that Wolf no longer required his convalescence quarters in the hallway and the dog gave him a rapturous welcome in the kitchen. Then Joe went upstairs, straight into his en-suite to strip off and give his face and hands a good wash. He suddenly hadn't the energy to go downstairs and fetch his bag to retrieve his toothbrush. There was toothpaste by the basin and he squeezed a little onto his finger just to refresh his mouth. He took a good rinse of water and then, with his lips to the tap, a long drink. How he loved the water here. He switched off the light and stood still in the darkness. Should he tiptoe in to Tess? It was so ridiculously late. Could he minimize the creak to her door just so he could see her? It was so bloody late.

He crossed into the bedroom; sat on the edge of his bed

thinking, Jesus Christ, I'm seriously tired. And then he realized that Tess was there. Asleep and still and silent and soft. Slowly, carefully, he settled himself under the covers. He didn't turn to her and reach for her; he simply lay there sensing her. When his eyes adjusted to the darkness, he rolled onto his side and peeled back the sheet. She was facing away from him and in the little light there was she looked carved from alabaster; the sinuous line of her back, her hair pulled away from her neck. He watched the rise and fall of her breathing. Carefully, he pulled the sheet up over her again and moved himself against her so that she was enfolded within him, his arm over hers, his hand holding her wrist, her feet tucked on top of his. He hoped not to wake her, but his need to soothe himself after the rigours of his journey, to feel himself back into his home life, was stronger. After a nightmare of a day, he was back in the place he wanted to be and the night was now magical.

She stirred. 'Joe?'

'I'm home, Tess. Shh. Go back to sleep.'

Chapter Thirty-three

There was a fair amount of cash, in mostly low and obviously used notes. It wasn't a fortune but the amount was certainly surprising, not least considering where it was hidden.

You don't *keep* money under a mattress, Joe thought as he regarded the notes under Tess's. You *hide* it there.

It was perplexing. It wasn't like coming across someone's diary – one would sense that it was private and above board. But cash? And talking of boards, what was he to do with the large piece of plywood he'd brought into her room? It was propped against the door, next to the mattress he'd upended against the wall. He went to the window bay and sat in the Loom chair.

Very nice to find you here, he'd said to her when they woke in his bed earlier that morning.

Don't flatter yourself, boyo, she'd replied. It's only because my back's been a little sore – that bed in my room is a bit slack.

He knew what she meant – the morning he'd crept in alongside her, they'd been rolled into a squash in the centre of the bed, much like an overloaded hammock. This morning, while Tess was showering, he thought to himself, I know, I'll surprise

341

her; I'll do a little estate-maintenance of my own. There are a couple of sheets of ply up in the attic – I'll strengthen the bed base for her.

And now she was downstairs preparing lunch and he was upstairs trying to do a good turn but he'd found a problem bigger than the knackered bedsprings.

Why would she hide her money? he wondered. What's wrong with the local bank? It was then that memories of details – insignificant at the time – drifted into his mind where they became evidence of something amiss. He remembered how Tess had not wanted her wages by standing order. In fact, she'd requested cash from the start. He looked again at the money. It was around two months' worth of the wages he paid her, plus a hundred pounds or so more. But hadn't he written a cheque last time – because now he remembered putting only Miss Tess on the payee line.

Why didn't he know her surname?

What had she been crying about, in secret, that time on the landing?

Who doesn't have a mobile phone, these days?

And what was that stuff with the sister?

Standing there, looking at her money, Joe realized with some concern that there was obviously quite a lot he didn't know about the girl he thought he knew off by heart. And yet – he loved her.

But, if he didn't have the full picture, what was it that he loved? Carefully selected highlights she'd chosen? A medley of her best bits? And if he found out more, what then – would he still love her? And if further information could alter how he felt about her then wouldn't he rather just not know? Because the love feeling was good, it was really good. So why have anything jeopardize it? They could just play house each time he came home. Intense, hermetic periods of time where they could live the rosiest life complete with child and dog and the seaside.

Is it better to have secrets than the truth?

Isn't Nathalie a case in point?

He'd hardly been true to Tess – but a secret that tormented him was better than the suffering the truth might cause her.

The sound of Tess coming upstairs jolted him from contemplating his morality, but it did not give him enough time to right the mattress and move the sheet of ply.

'Joe?'

Conflicting feelings of guilt and of being aggrieved kept him pinned to the chair.

'Joe?'

You're going to have to answer her.

'In here.'

He said it the moment she opened her bedroom door – and the moment she opened her bedroom door the sheet of ply fell away from it and fell to the floorboards in such a slap and clatter she never heard him answer her. However, the whack of ply against oak boards was nothing compared to the far sharper slap Tess felt she'd just been given around her face on seeing the mattress off, her money there and Joe sitting staring right at her.

It was horror and embarrassment and outrage, shame and fury simultaneously. Her face crumbled at the weight of so many emotions and immediately, Joe felt wretched. He hadn't suffered emotions anywhere near as intense when he'd come across her money. He'd felt slightly indignant, a little peeved – but mainly he'd been just curious.

'What the –'

But Joe didn't want to hear her swear. 'I was going to ask you the same thing,' he interjected.

She was speechless, glancing at the money as if it had betrayed her, as if it had called to Joe, under here! under here!

'It might look like I was barricading myself in your room,' Joe said. 'Actually, I only came in to strengthen your bed.'

He watched her stare at the plywood and saw her figure out that he was telling the truth.

She slumped down to the floor, rested her arms on her knees and sunk her head against them, her mind a racket of hurried sentence-starters. She concentrated on the weave of her jeans, because that's what filled her field of vision. A tiny voice, the sensible one she didn't hear too often, was telling her that this was her opportunity, this was a timely chance to try a little honesty, to reveal not conceal, whatever Mrs O'Sullivan made of that. Because who was Mrs O'Sullivan anyway – didn't Tess's grandmother always subscribe to a problem shared being a problem halved and hadn't Tess trusted her grandmother more than she'd trusted anyone else in her life?

She stared at the denim. Around the knee it was paler, a slight fur to the stressed surface. It would no doubt split before too long; after all she did spend an inordinate amount of time on hands and knees being a horsey to Em or scrubbing Joe's floors. Hopefully, torn jeans would come back into fashion. Or had they never really gone out? She wasn't that concerned with sartorial trends any more; in London in the salon, she had the chance to peruse *Grazia* on a weekly basis. It hadn't crossed her mind to buy a copy since she left and came here.

'Tess?'

Joe's voice. Joe in a chair just over there. All the money behind her. Perhaps an opportunity lying ahead, if she chose to take it. But Tess no longer liked risk. She could instead just blank out everything and simply focus on the weave of her jeans.

344

'Tess?'

She looked up and he looked across at her and she gave a shrug and said, Christ, Joe – you have no idea.

And just as she wished, he comes over and sits next to her on the floor, their backs supported by the side of the bed.

'No idea,' Joe says. 'You're right. I thought the only people who kept their money under their mattress were daft old chaps in Ealing comedies.'

'I have to keep mine there,' Tess tells him and she's really pleased when he gently stills her hands from worrying the denim around her knees. 'I have to keep my money with me – now that I have some. I can't take it to the bank. I'm in a bit of trouble.'

But just as Joe's about to say, tell me, a clatter and howl point to trouble of a more pressing kind elsewhere in the house. They belt out of the room and charge downstairs with urgent cries of Em? Emmeline? Not in the sitting room, nor the drawing room, front door shut – thank God – but all is eerily quiet. And when they enter the kitchen, they see why. Seemingly nonplussed and apparently uninjured, Em is sitting on the floor. Wolf is sitting gingerly some way off, looking at her reproachfully. They are surrounded by everything in the kitchen that was previously within reach of a toddler.

'She probably clonked him with one of the containers,' Joe says. 'That's why he howled.'

Tess doesn't comment. He glances at her and sees that she is desperate to bite back laughter.

'You're wanting to come across all stern and cross, aren't you?' He nudges her. 'It's our fault really – trying to have a deep and meaningful, relationship-defining heart-to-heart upstairs whilst leaving a toddler and an old dog to their own devices downstairs.'

'Look at the mess!' Tess says.

'It's only cornflakes.'

'And rice.'

'And clothes pegs.'

'And every pot and pan you own.'

'And all the tea towels you like to iron.'

'And soap pads I bought specifically because they colour coordinate with Wolf's coat. I'm joking, Joe.'

'No, Emmeline, yukky. You don't have to suck a dishcloth – let's go and get an ice cream instead.'

The money remains upstairs, uncovered. The mess is left in the kitchen to be dealt with later. They all need fresh air and a change of scene and they've all lived here long enough to know that there's little an ice cream beside the sea can't fix.

Joe treats them. Emmeline and he both have strawberry but Tess has a milkshake of inventive flavour combining – chocolate, ginger and malt. They stroll along the pier; the tide is well out beyond it and families have appropriated slithers of the vast beach as their own behind colourful windbreaks. From the pier, those further away look like a spatter of paint against a beige sand canvas. There are jet skis in the water, canoes too and the ubiquitous surfers. Tess casts a quick thought to Seb but then she thinks, well, if he's here then he's here – it's his town too. But the surfers are too engrossed to do any people-spotting on the pier.

They stroll to the end of the pier and back again and when they reach the amusement centre they turn and simply walk back along the pier more slowly this time. Tess has finished her milkshake. Joe is trying to enjoy his ice cream without Wolf's doleful glances distracting him. Em's in her own little world.

'The thing is, Joe,' Tess suddenly starts, 'it wasn't that it happened quickly, it didn't take me by surprise, I didn't wake up one day and think, shit, I'm stuffed – it was the *severity*

346

by which it snowballed. It was the horrible power of the momentum – it just grew worse and worse and worse.'

After a day of airports and stress, Joe had been enjoying the fresh air and mellow pace of his town, the humbling scale of the sea, the magnificence of Huntcliff Nab glazed by sunshine, dominating the section of sea from which it rises so staunchly. The scars and striations of coastal erosion, the rutways carved into the bedrock from the old alum and ironstone industries, combined to resemble hieroglyphs carved into the cliffs. He had assumed they'd leave Tess's issues on the base of the bed with her cash, to return to them later. He turns to her. She looks a little lost.

'Sorry?'

She sighs. 'Oh well,' she says, 'what the hell.' Then she stops the ice-cream cone reaching his mouth. 'I love you.'

It's momentous. She could now say nothing and just rest her head against his chest and wait for his response. But she doesn't – because she didn't say it for him to say back to her. It's her prologue. So she doesn't notice that the ice cream still hasn't reached his mouth because he's stunned and still. And she doesn't see the sparkle in his eyes as he looks at her intently. She's looking out to sea. She's taking a deep breath – not of sea air but of courage because she's decided to talk her heart and she has a lot to say.

'I'm broke, Joe. I'm so broke. I don't honestly know what I'm going to do. I owe thousands of pounds. My bank account is frozen. Everyone is chasing me – three companies in particular. In addition, I owe money to my sister, my friend Tamsin – and my old landlord. I have four credit cards maxed out. I can't afford to fill my car let alone tax it next month. I have nothing to my name apart from what I brought with me to Saltburn. And I'm thirty and it's humiliating and pathetic and what kind of a mother does it make me?

'And yes, I ran away. I ran away because it was so bloody

347

grim in London. I ran away, really, to hide from them all. Not from my sister or Tamsin – but from the demands and the aggression: the letters and phone calls and the bailiffs who kept coming to the front door. I ran away and hid here.

'And here, all these months later, I am. I came out of my hiding place and found the place I loved and the life I want to lead. But that doesn't mean I've solved a bloody thing. I hide my money under my mattress. I don't know what I'm going to do. It's irrelevant that there's a recession worldwide. Last thing at night, first thing in the morning and intermittently through the day I think of the mess *I'm* in. It's pathetic.

'But do you know something? No one points out that borrowing money is exactly the same thing as owing money. They hide that in the small print of gaily-designed leaflets that positively invite you to take money. They make it sound like they really want to give it to you. Take a loan! Have a small-business account! We'll help! We support enterprise and initiative! Have another credit card! Transfer your balance to this one, to that one! No interest for the first six months! Phone us if you find it difficult to pay! We'll help – we're hear to listen. We're the caring, sharing, listening, friendly, lovely lovely bank!

'Bollocks, Joe – it's bollocks. You phone them because you're finding it difficult to pay and then they start phoning you, for being difficult because you can't pay.

'I've been over it in my head so many times. It seemed such a sound venture – my own little business using my skills as a trained beautician with the growing trend for all things organic. So I did some research into oils and bases and emollients and I dreamed up lovely creams and lotions and sourced a wholesaler to manufacture them. The products were lovely – I have a tube of It's Balmy for you. It's perfect for after shaving.

'Oh, what was I saying? Oh, so I found a company to

produce my recipes, then I found another who'd supply the containers and I found someone to design my website and I spent a fortune on advertising and I spent so much time and energy and more money on marketing and publicity. And I called it Made With Love. And I was so very, very proud – proud of my products and proud of me. And now it's the bloody albatross around my neck. There's a very dark, threatening cloud never far away, Joe.

'I don't know where or at what point precisely I fucked up – but my profit margins were never going to be big enough and also I couldn't pay quickly enough. I'm convinced that those companies who lent me money knew that from the start but chose not to advise me. So the manufacturer stopped production. Then I persuaded them to produce another batch – with promises of funds within twenty-eight days. I couldn't make money if I didn't have the product to sell, could I? But then the company who did my containers refused to let me have any more because I hadn't paid them – however, I couldn't pay them until I sold some more creams but I couldn't sell cream if I had nothing to put it in. So it all went belly up. And fast. That part happened very fast. And my job in the salon was soon not enough to pay the rent let alone cover the minimum payments and provide for childcare for Em. And then the bailiffs came knocking. Banging. Believe me, they all look like they're related to the Krays.

'So that's why I ran away, Joe. I ran away from all of that but believe me, I sense it inching a slow, menacing path back to me.

'They'll still be looking for me, Joe. They'll be hunting me down. All those horrible letters – threatening and harsh. They'll be arriving every day at the flat I used to rent. The bailiffs won't have gone away. And I fear if I even set foot in a bank, some vicious vacuum will suck every penny from my pockets. My overdraft is terrifying in itself – but the bloody fines they heap upon it have made it horrific. I stopped opening my statements – the whack of interest just adds insult to injury. I never really worked out what credit card interest rates were all about because I never imagined I wouldn't be able to pay off my bills in full from the money I'd make when it was Made With Love.

'I used to have to park my car at least a street away, Joe, so there was no incriminating evidence for debt collectors outside my front door. I'd answer the phone in a stupid American accent so I could say I wasn't in right now, so I could tell them to leave me a message and I'd have me call as soon as I was home.

'But I want you to know that the money under my mattress, that's all honest. It's from you and from this crazy beautiful evening Lisa organized where she basically sold most of my remaining stock single-handedly. And Tamsin sent me M&S vouchers she won in some work raffle and it was the first time I felt I could spend on Em. I don't want to have to cut the feet off her babygros just to sneak another few weeks' wear out of them. I don't want to compromise on proper shoes for her. I want to be able to provide the best for her, every step of the way. I've let her down. I hate myself for it. I'm an idiot. I was stupid. I'm a failure.'

She is sitting heavily on a bench along the pier. Her cheeks are crimson but everything else about her ghostly pale. She's fiddling with her nails, her leg is jigging, her feet are turned in and she's shaking her head at herself. Wolf is gazing down onto the beach, desperate to make merry with the dogs down there. Em is in her buggy, blissed out and dozy from a glut of homemade strawberry ice cream.

Gently, Joe puts his arm around her shoulder.

'The way I see it is there's good debt and bad. It's not as if you blew the lot on booze and betting. And you obviously don't have a shoe or handbag addiction.'

Tess manages a small smile before she shrugs, deflated. 'I'm still in debt and the people I owe don't give a fig for the morality behind it.'

'I like the sound of your business.'

'It's kind of you to say so – but it's over. I can't even say it was good while it lasted because it never really began. It certainly never took off. Eve Lom and Liz Earle never lost any sleep over me.'

'So you ran away. It was brave of you.'

She looks at him. 'I'm a coward and an idiot and a failure.'

'No, you are *not*,' he says and his tone is very straight. 'You're beautiful and strong and you've been through a really tough time. You didn't run away because you didn't want to stay and face the music – it seems to me you ran away because you ran out of options.'

'I've fucked up.'

'It wasn't entirely your fault.'

'Joe – it's easy for you to be so sweet.'

'Why? Because I have a well-paid job and a roof over my head and I pay my credit cards off in full each month?'

Tess shrugs.

'I haven't had to confront what you've had to confront, Tess. Even running away from London to Saltburn-by-the-Sea was a gutsy thing to do. And to change your lifestyle diet to the humble pie of house-sitting? Yet to be so even-tempered and to have such pride in your new life? And to make such a difference to my life – such a difference to how I see the Resolution?'

He gives her a hug and when he speaks it is with genuine amazement. 'And all the while you've managed to raise a beautiful, healthy, happy child? And nurse an ugly, limp-along old hound? And make new friends?' He gives her shoulder a little shake.

'You're an inspiration, Miss Tess. And I love you.'

'I'm in deep shit.'

'Doesn't mean you're not amazing.'

'You're just being nice.'

'Is there anything wrong with that?'

'In my case – it's deluded.'

'Bollocks – they might be collecting debts but don't you dare let them come after your self-esteem.'

'What am I going to do, Joe?' She's clinging to his hands, to his words too. She'll do whatever it takes and whatever he suggests because he's told her he loves her and she cannot feel poor in the face of that.

'We'll think of something, pet,' he says. 'You and me – we'll figure it out.'

Chapter Thirty-four

'If I told you I'm going to take Wolf for a hobble along the beach, would you come?'

They'd remained on the pier for a while in affable silence, Joe's arm still around her, Tess's head resting against his shoulder. She felt drained and depleted but aware that what had been siphoned out was the bad, creating room to be filled with better things now. Initially, she didn't want to talk figures with Joe – she hadn't with Tamsin or Claire for whom the fact of her impecuniousness sufficed. But Joe made it clear that he was asking not out of curiosity but so that he might know how best to advise. It was his maturity, his calmness that she felt she could lean on, as much as his shoulder. So she did tell him, darting her eyes to and from his as she did. He didn't bat an eyelid; he just nodded which gave the outward impression of it being no great drama though privately he baulked, bloody hell, Tess – *how* much?

'Will you let me help?'

'Help?'

'I have money.'

'No! No!'

'I have a friend.'

'A friend?'

Joe knew a chap, he told her, his old friend Andy – they'd been friends since childhood. He'd been at Joe's birthday when the Halfpenny Bridge was demolished. Andy had left Saltburn, but only for Stokesley twenty minutes away where he worked as an independent financial advisor.

I have no finances for him, Tess said. Andy will have advice for you, said Joe.

'Oh God – go bankrupt?'

'Not necessarily.'

And then Wolf had seen a game of dog frisbee underway on the beach and he'd started turning circles perilously close to the pier railings, barking with all his might, and Joe had turned to Tess and kissed her on the forehead and had said to her, if I told you I'm going to take Wolf for a hobble along the beach, would you come?

But she looked at her lap and looked forlorn.

'OK – so how about this. If I asked you very nicely,' said Joe, 'if I said I'd hold your hand, would you come for a walk on the beach with Wolf and me?'

'Why don't I go back and make lunch, Joe. I'll see you at home.'

It'll come, Joe thought to himself. It'll come.

It wasn't merely to avoid a walk on the beach that Tess headed for home, it wasn't a burning desire to fix lunch, it was also a need to mull over the morning privately. For Tess, there was a sense of relief, undoubtedly – not because it felt as though her problem had been halved let alone solved; rather, that she no longer had to keep secret from the person she loved a huge part of herself which, it transpired, wasn't as loathsome to him as she'd feared. In fact he wanted to *help* – and this notion was eye-opening. Tamsin had only ever been able to offer

354

comfort, Claire had only ever been scathing. Joe, though, had ideas.

When she arrived back, she went to her room and transferred the money to a drawer in the dressing table and then, plonking Em on the chair saying, stay! in the voice she used for Wolf, she manhandled the sheet of plywood onto the base of the bed and replaced the mattress. Again, in the voice she used for Wolf, she said, come on! to Em and they tested the bed with a good bouncing.

He loves me, Tess said. Did you hear him, Em?

'I'd've moved it for you,' Joe said of the ply, when he returned. 'Is it OK? Does it do the job?'

'It's brilliant,' Tess said.

'And will you be sleeping there tonight then?'

She was at the stove, checking corn-on-the-cob, and he'd come up behind her, his hand on her waist, his mouth at the soft kiss-shaped area between her hairline and her ear.

'Mr Saunders,' she protested, 'not in front of the children.'

Joe looked around. Em appeared far more interested in some cornflakes Tess had missed right under the kitchen table. He snuck a kiss.

'What's your surname, Tess?'

'Adams?'

'Oh. *Adams*. Tess Adams.'

'Didn't you know? Did I never tell you?'

'Nope. I don't think I had the chance to ask. You might remember that you were so intent on rebuking me for Wolf when you turned up here, that formal introductions were overlooked.'

Tess winced at the memory but she grinned at the same time. 'And you never gave me your house-sitter's pack.'

Joe raised his eyebrow in a don't-push-it kind of way. 'Anyway,' he said, 'since then, there's never been a time when

I've needed your surname. Apart from when I tried to write you a cheque – but of course, if you'd told me from the start that you were destitute and on the run –'

Tess thwacked him with a tea towel. 'I'm not on the run – I just ran away.'

'By the way – what did you do with that cheque?'

'Lisa cashed it for me. I've confided some of this to her.'

'So you're a money launderer too?'

She flicked him smartly on the forearm with the tea towel and told him to bugger off until lunch was ready.

At supper-time, Joe suddenly disappeared between courses and Tess sat at the table listening to the clatter and rummage drifting through from the study. It was only fresh fruit for dessert, it could wait. She was arranging Cadbury's chocolate fingers into a starburst on a plate, boiling the kettle for coffee, when Joe came back into the kitchen. He looked very pleased with himself.

'Here!'

Like a page presenting something precious to royalty, he walked towards her holding in front of him a box.

'It's for you.'

It was quite a large box, of a size that could take a pair of boots. But it was sturdy – in lacquered wood of a deep red-brown hue that darkened to black along the edges. There was a keyhole. Solemnly, Joe handed Tess a small key and nodded at her. She slipped it into the lock and turned it with a satisfying click. He whispered for her to open it and with great anticipation, she eased up the hinged lid. The interior of the box was lacquered too, jet black. The box, though, was completely empty. She stood looking at it, wondering what to say, wondering if Joe thought some trinket or other was in there.

'It's for you,' he said again.

She looked at him, hoping that her bewilderment looked more like gratitude.

'Thanks so much,' she said.

'I thought it would be useful to you – a nice bit of lacquered, lockable home-banking if you like.'

Tess looked at the box anew, opened the lid and assessed the interior with fresh, informed interest. It had the space for a lot more cash than the quantity of notes currently in the dresser drawer upstairs. She imagined filling it to the brim. She'd like to be able to do that.

'It's an amazing piece, isn't it?' She closed the lid and stroked the surface.

'It was given to me – and now I'm giving it to you. I never really knew what to keep in it. But it's got your name written all over it.'

'Thanks, Joe. I love it. I'll treasure it.'

'Your personal treasure chest!'

'It's beautiful. What's the story behind it? Where's it from – you said it was a gift?'

'My great friend Taki gave it to me. When we finished the job.' Joe paused, tipped his head and gave Tess a wry smile. 'In Kuala Lumpur.'

Tess stared intently at the box. Then she looked up at Joe and turned a sheepish expression in to a blatant smile. 'And would that be Kay Ell, Joe?'

'KL,' Joe grinned back.

She glanced over his shoulder, to the dresser, to where she could see the photograph of bare-chested, beaming Joe propped up against the upturned cups.

'God, I was a mad woman, that day.'

'You were a bit.'

They paused, standing there with their hands on the lacquered box.

'Seems a long time ago,' Joe said, 'all of that.'

'It does, doesn't it,' said Tess.

'Wanting – so much – to kiss you.'

'The Transporter Bridge.'

'I feel, I don't know – different, *changed*.'

'A lot of water under *our* bridge?' Tess smiled.

'And would that be a beam, arch or suspension bridge? Cable stayed?'

'I don't know,' said Tess, 'but what I do know is it's sturdy – and I trust it now to carry me, however much baggage I might bring.'

That night, though Tess said my bed or yours, they chose Joe's room – but no sooner had Tess got into his bed than she left it again. She returned a few minutes later and sat beside him. He appeared happily engrossed in *The Life of Pi*.

'Here you are,' she said, 'this was my It's Balmy cream.' She slid the tube down the open pages of his book. 'Calendula and geranium, mainly. Very nourishing.'

He inspected the packaging approvingly, hoping that she hadn't noticed on her cleaning blitzes that he was a soap-and-water man who had one everlasting bottle of Neutrogena that did for everything. He unscrewed the top and took a quick sniff before replacing it.

'No, silly,' Tess laughed, 'you can't tell like that. Here.'

She took the tube from him and squeezed out a little of the cream and rubbed it between her hands briskly.

'You should always warm it between your palms – not your fingers – first.'

Joe nodded as if he was taking notes.

'Close your eyes,' she told him and she smoothed her hands over his face in quick, deft strokes before using her fingertips, her thumbs, the heels of her hands to massage the cream in.

'Sit forward,' Tess whispered and she took herself behind him, opening her legs so he could rest between them, his head against her chest.

'Ever had a facial massage before?'

Lightly, she traced the shape of his eye sockets and nasal bone, adding more pressure for his jawline and cheekbones, then she rolled the fleshy areas between her thumb and fingers and eased the tighter area of his forehead by moving the skin up and into his hair. She lay her fingers softly against specific points on his face and then, just perceptibly, increased pressure into a push-and-release action which, when she took her hands away, made his face feel both utterly relaxed and also rejuvenated. Joe couldn't help but give an involuntary swoon.

'Nice?'

Joe was beyond answering, he felt semi-hypnotized and it was a state he was happy to inhabit for as long as it was on offer.

'I'll give you a proper facial,' she said. 'Massage – combined with an exfoliate, tone, emolliate. Tomorrow, perhaps – before you leave.'

But for now, she finished. She knew well enough that to prolong facial massage was not a good thing. The nerves of the face have a sensitivity that, when overstimulated, transmit the sensation as negative, as an irritant. Joe hadn't moved. She rested her hands lightly on his shoulders, travelled them down his upper arms and gave his biceps a little squeeze.

'Earth to Joe.'

He mumbled in response. She thought to herself, so what if I'm done with the facial and we're so tired. She thought to herself how fulfilled she felt, sitting up in bed, taking in her arms the man she'd taken into her confidence that morning. She stroked him and pressed her lips against the top of his head, closing her eyes as she felt herself respond to the feel of his skin which itself was reacting to her touch.

She looked down at him, his chest, his stomach; she watched how his breathing increased when her hands changed location or when she altered the pressure of her touch. She saw a quiver from under the sheet, the evidence of his increasing arousal.

He's not asleep, the bugger, he's not asleep at all.

The knowledge of his hardness, tantalizingly masked by the sheet, itself aroused her and the mood of her touch changed instinctively. She shifted position so that she could bring her face around, close to his, and she homed in on his lips, first with the softest sweep of her cheek, then her lips, her tongue. And suddenly he was responding and the trance her touch had instilled was replaced by a wide-awake urgency to look and taste and feel. They rolled and thrashed about, gluing together any parts of their bodies that could fit. Fingers were interwoven, legs plaited together like rope, mouths fused, torsos melded, eyes bored into one another; voices echoed the same lustful rasp.

He pulled her on top of him, her sex a tantalizing inch or so beyond the reach of his cock.

'Don't close your eyes, Tess. Don't take them off me.'

As she eased herself down on him, the pleasure was so exquisite that her body felt as though it was about to liquefy, as if it was beginning to melt into his.

'Don't close your eyes, Tess.'

His hands coaxed her upright, held her steady at the waist. She watched him, as his eyes alternated between travelling all over her body and fixing on her eyes.

'Move with me,' he whispered.

As hard and as hot as he felt, so she felt wet and soft. Sitting astride him, matching his bucks and thrusts, her eyes played a charged relay with his. The intensity was unlike anything Tess had imagined or Joe had experienced. Her mouth was so moist it felt as if it was mimicking her sex; he slipped his finger into her mouth and it might as well have been his cock, so titillating was the feeling. When he took his hand back to her waist, a thin thread of saliva seeped out from her lips like a liquid kiss. The perfect baseness of it, the feeling of it reaching his chest, released a torrent of lust in Joe that saw his hands leap for Tess's breasts and she in turn clasped her own hands over his. Abandoned to the imminence of orgasm, they were helpless not to close their eyes. But only for a moment. Hearing Tess's voice gasp as she was about to come, hearing the sound of himself moaning, Joe opened his eyes.

He'd never come with his eyes open. Previously, the sensation had carried a selfish intensity, a lack of concern for the actuality to focus inwardly on his own gratification, more often than not fleshed out by some private fantasy. Now he wanted to give, to feel her come and to watch her, to sense her pull himself out of himself: spunk, love, voice, feeling.

He soaked in the sight of her as she soaked up the sensation of him.

'Open your eyes, Tess. Let me look at you.'

In the small hours, Tess awoke. She was lying on her back and Joe was lying on his side very close. His arm was across her stomach, his breath whispered over her shoulder, warming her skin on his exhale, chilling it on the inhale. She lay there and waited for sleep to return but something was preventing it. It had been such a full day. Days with Joe were usually replete with colour and detail anyway, but today's had had an added dimension. All that honesty. Being able to vanquish the fear that her life would tumble down if she revealed the foundation of her troubles. And, with Joe's support, finding the confidence to gather her dignity and confide what she had assumed she would have to hide.

Now, in the stillness and the silence, she thought about secrets.

How choosing not to share information needn't be classified as a secret per se – but to actively keep from a loved one certain facts that define you, no matter how bad you perceive them to be, undermines the core of that love. Tess's level of debt and the way it had been accrued wasn't so much a secret as a huge humiliation she'd kept private. But when she'd revealed the unglossed details to Joe, he hadn't told her off nor had he run off. He'd listened and empathized and suggested practical solutions and best of all she believed him. He'd stayed close, in fact he'd moved in closer. And now, they were closer still.

It was big, for her to tell, for him to hear, for them as a couple to share. But it had brought an increased sense of closeness and though it was still a very real problem, it wasn't as terrifying to her any more. But now she was aware that she was lying there unable to sleep because there was something else she hadn't told him, something he'd never find under her mattress or in a drawer or in the boot of her car. She could keep it hidden – but now she no longer wanted to. If you keep the truth hidden, you show only the lie.

Joe was deeply asleep, the pattern of his breathing told her so. He was so tired. After they'd made love, he'd said, that'll send me to sleep with a smile on my face. And he'd promptly done just that. She looked at him now. Would he mind? Would he mind being woken? Would he mind what she was going to tell him? She wondered whether she'd mind – if it were Joe waking her to confide something that defined him?

'Joe?' His face registered nothing. 'Joe?' Nothing. 'Joe!' A stir. 'Joe?'

'Hmm?'

'Might you wake up a while? I wanted to talk. There's something I want you to know.'

His eyes opened and he lay there blinking as if unsure whether he'd just heard her through his sleep or whether he'd been dreaming.

'Yes?'

'Joe?'

'Yes?'

'Are you awake?'

'Yes?'

'I wanted to tell you something. A secret. Another one. Something I want you to know.'

She turned towards him and rolled in close.

'There's some stuff you just don't want other people to know because you know you can't change it. But you know you can't obliterate it either so you keep it secret, determined that no one will ever be party to it.' She paused. 'Are you awake now?'

'Yes, I am. Go on.'

'Like my – money problems.'

'Yes – but you needn't shoulder all that alone any more. We'll find a way.'

She was worried he was going to drift off to sleep so as she stroked his shoulder, she give him little nudges.

'I know – and I can't tell you how much safer I now feel. But Joe, you see there are secrets and there are *secrets* – don't you think? I kept my debt secret from you without having any reason to actually *lie* – I just hid it. But I wanted to tell you another secret – one I *have* hidden from you behind a lie.'

'You've *lied* to me?' He couldn't think what about.

'Yes. But if there are secrets and secrets – then perhaps there are lies and *lies*. Some stuff we lie about because the real facts are so brutal. I've grown to feel that I tell lies better than most people tell the truth.'

'What are you talking about, Tess, what have you done?' He was wide awake now, but gentle: tucking her hair behind her ear soothingly, rhythmically, as he puzzled her words.

'I haven't done anything – apart from not tell you the truth

363

about something I've kept secret from everyone in my life. Everyone. So far, I've spun the same story to you too. But now I want to undo it – maybe not for them just yet, maybe never, but for you certainly I do.'

'What's this all about, Tess?'

'It's about Em.'

'What about Emmeline?'

'About her father.'

'What about her father?' Joe was a whirl of thoughts but he couldn't get a handle on any.

'It's untrue – what I told you, about him.'

'How so?'

In the scant moonlight of muted silver highlights in the bedroom, he could detect a crestfallen look to Tess's face, a heavy silence about her.

'What is it, Tess? Is he not – you know – her real father?'

'Oh, he's her real father all right,' Tess said. 'It's just much of the stuff I've told you about him that isn't real.'

When one awaits the truth from an untruth, the thought of what that might be is often remote from what transpires. For this reason, Joe didn't bother himself too much with thoughts of Em's father being a homicidal axe-wielding drug-addled maniac. He just kept his eyes trained on Tess, encouraging her to forego the lengthy silences and bring to light what was currently in the dark.

'He's a sod, really.'

Her voice was so hollow it filled Joe and he wasn't sure how to respond – he sensed not to use 'why' just yet.

'I rather remember you describing him as a gorgeous, useless, beautiful, crazy dreamer,' he said.

'He's none of those things. Well, physically he is very beautiful. On the outside.'

Joe waited a moment again. 'What did he do, Tess?'

'I knew him for six weeks – that's true. The bit about him

364

singing me those crap songs is true too. He seduced me – well, actually I was desperate to sleep with him because he was such a renowned free spirit and my ego goaded me to attempt to be the one who could inspire him to settle down. How ridiculously clichéd was that? Thinking back though, he groomed my ego in the first place – not just by singing for me, but by saying stuff like, "Jeez, Tess, a girl like you could get a guy like me to change his ways." That's quite intoxicating, really, for a girl like me – who hadn't been lucky in love. A girl whose father left and there was nothing she or her mum could do to have him change *his* ways.'

She paused.

'And?'

'Well, Dick and I had this crazy few weeks of music and candlelit crappy flats with mattresses on the floor and batik hangings on the walls. And he kept on with the lyrical bullshit – which at the time seemed to me the most sublime poetry I'd ever heard, of course.'

'And then?'

'Then I found out I was pregnant.'

'It was his?'

'Oh, Joe – of course it was his. I may be hopeless but I'm not like *that*.'

'Sorry, pet – I didn't mean it that way. I'm just trying to guess, that's all.'

'When I told him I was pregnant –' She paused and her shudder was visible. She took two long, measured breaths.

'The thing is – about secrets and lies, Joe – that this is a memory I've banished behind a reasonable lie for so long that I haven't had to confront the truth. I tucked it away – though I couldn't diminish the hurt.' Joe touched her cheek gently with the back of his hand. 'Dick's response was not what I was expecting. His face didn't even drop – let alone register a single emotion. The first thing he said was, "You're joking," and the second thing he said was, "Get rid of it." It wasn't a question. Or a suggestion.'

Although she had paused again, Joe was so shocked he couldn't catch up with his thoughts to grab a couple and form them into something worthwhile or comforting to say. He searched for her hand under the covers, found it in a clench and gently unfurled it.

'He was vile,' Tess continued. 'He said if I kept *it*, not to expect any support on any level from him. Kids, he said, weren't part of his game plan. He asked me who the hell I thought I was, dumping this on him. He called me a sly bitch, too. He told me to get out of his face. He said, "Do what you want, honey, but I'm out of here." Anyway, the long and the short of it is I haven't had any contact since. None at all. So there you have it, the unexpurgated truth – there's nothing more to tell. All the rest was lies – all of it. His free spirit, his world tour, his penniless but cosmic heart. I fabricated it all so I could keep the hideous truth secret.'

'Jesus, Tess,' Joe held her tightly against him. 'Did you not tell me he already had a child?'

'When I met him, he said he did. But I don't even know if that's true or whether it was the sort of kind-to-animals-and-kids line a guy might spin to get a daffy girl like me into bed.'

'Oh, Tess.' Joe kissed the tip of her nose, her forehead, and he thought to himself, if I was to describe her to someone, I'd probably say I'm in love with this strong, lovely, daffy girl. He brought himself up higher in the bed, higher than Tess, so that her face was in line with his chest; as if he wanted her to sense that he was very much a man compared to this immature wanker of whom she'd just spoken.

'I haven't seen him since. For a while, during my pregnancy, I imagined him fronting up, guitar over his shoulder like a strolling troubadour, having found himself on the road to Damascus. Later into my pregnancy, I let go of this image and just hoped for a call or a card or a letter or something. Then I had to let go of that. When I was in labour, I did wonder if magically he'd show up – which was why, stupidly, I'd said, no, Tamsin, I don't need you. In fact, I told her Dick was on his way. But he didn't come, of course, I gave birth to Em alone. Well, that's a lie – there was this lovely midwife from Ghana called Angel. I don't know where Dick was that night. I couldn't get hold of him. I don't know where he is now, either. But I wouldn't try to get hold of him. He does not know when Em's birthday is.'

There was no more hair to tuck behind her ear so Joe just moved what was there already so he could repeat the soothing process.

'But, Tess,' he said, 'I'm not sure why you did him the courtesy of lying – of investing qualities in a bloke who's obviously a total cunt.'

Tess never used the C word and it quite took her aback, not least because she could sense Joe's intense indignation.

'Why didn't you just tell those close to you what was going on – the truth? They'd've flooded you with support and sympathy. At the very least you'd have had someone's hand to hold during labour.'

Tess looked up at him. 'Because, Joe, what would that have made me? How little worth would I have to hear out loud? Reality made me feel so bad – and a bit of a lie, a secret, could make me feel a tiny bit better.'

'And did it?'

'Not really.'

'Because you've had to shoulder the truth, the secret *and* all the loneliness yourself.'

Tess didn't respond.

'I've heard you cry, Tess,' Joe said gently. 'I've seen you

cry all alone, when Emmeline is asleep. Outside her room, dissolved into a huddle on the floor.'

Tess nodded reluctantly and concentrated on Joe's Adam's apple because she didn't want to cry now. 'I haven't wanted to wake her – yet there have been times when I've so badly wanted the cuddle.'

'You know you never have to ask,' Joe said. 'I'm telling you now – you never have to ask.'

She swallowed hard on the surges of emotion: relief, sorrow, comfort, love.

'That's what's been so tough – my secret fight not to let Dick's rejection negate me, deny me what I believe about myself and, most importantly, Em. That the gift of a child could be rejected – well, for me that's the worst thing. You see, I think I'm –' She struggled and then she shrugged within Joe's arms. 'I think I'm nice. Nothing special – but *nice*. I think Em and I are a pretty good package. It's tough to figure out why we were discarded. Was it our fault? My fault? Is there something *wrong* with me? It's difficult not to judge yourself by someone else's reaction – even if your sensible side is pleading with you to be reasonable.'

Joe felt very thoughtful. He wanted to soothe her and he wanted now to reveal how much he felt for her. But as phrases filled his head, he thought they sounded too much like a contrived response.

'You're not nice,' he said at length. 'I mean, you *are* – but you're a lot more. So I don't ever want to hear you say that you're nothing special. You're extraordinary. You've turned my life around. And you and Emmeline are the most perfect package ever to arrive on the doorstep of Resolution House.'

Tess stayed very still while she absorbed his words. 'I suppose if Dick had indeed been the man of my lies – then Em and I would currently be living in some dive with too many joss sticks and too much Jim Morrison.'

Joe laughed. If she could find humour now, in the immediate aftermath of her revelation, then she'd be OK.

'But what do I tell Em – when she's older?' Tess's voice was so small.

Joe thought about it. His voice was bold. 'The truth, Tess. Parents have an absolute duty by their children to always tell the truth.'

Chapter Thirty-five

'Resolution House. Good afternoon.'

'Hullo. Is that Miss Adams?'

'Yes?'

'I was given your name by Joe Saunders.'

'Oh. Well, I'm afraid you've missed him – he left yesterday. He's abroad, now. You can reach him on his mobile.'

'Er. He just reached me from his mobile. He's in Belgium, right?'

'Yes?'

'Well, Miss Adams, he asked me to call you.'

'Oh?'

'This is Andy – an old friend of Joe's. He mentioned me to you, I believe. And now he's mentioned you to me – and I believe I can help.'

'You're the financial bloke – who watched with Joe when the bridge came down?'

'Er – that'll be me, yes. I'm phoning to make an appointment for you.'

'Oh.'

'I'm far less scary than the dentist – I promise.'

'Oh.'

'How about this week – Thursday? Have you any plans – say, after lunch?'

'Um – no. I think that's fine.'

'I'm in Stokesley – on the main street, just along from Boyes. Hullo?'

'The thing is – how do I get to Stokesley from Saltburn?'

'Oh – I forgot – you're not local. Well, it's an easy drive – it'll take you twenty, twenty-five minutes.'

'But. Well, my car isn't very – *well*.'

'I see. I'm not sure about public transport – I'm sure there's a bus, though.'

'OK – shall I find out then, and give you a call? My friend might know. She *is* local.'

'OK. No – actually, not OK. I promised Joe I'd look after you. Look, how about I come to Saltburn? It's been ages since I saw the old house.'

'Did you know it well – when you were a child?'

'Oh yes. The Doctor's House. Spooky old place, don't you think? Joe was always round ours.'

Spooky? How could anyone find this place spooky?

Tess was bemused.

So the house creaked and groaned a little and the refreshing breeze that some of the door and window frames let in would probably be slicing draughts come the winter, but this house was a place that filled Tess with a sense of security; it felt safe and sturdy and the bricks seemed to breathe benevolence. Perhaps this Andy bloke didn't know Joe as well as Joe thought. Perhaps she should phone Joe and say, are you sure about this guy? But then she thought about the effort Andy was going to, to secure a meeting with her and she felt that actually, this said a lot about his opinion of Joe and the friendship they shared which had spanned decades. And he'd promised Joe he'd look after

371

Tess – which suggested to her that Joe had told him she was worth looking after.

She didn't see Laura when she went to Swallows the following day, which was a shame because she'd mentioned to Lisa having them both round to dinner. But she did see Mrs Tiley again, who told her that, gnarled and time-ravaged her hands might be – but actually, Tess had made them feel so good that she rather thought she would like a bit of polish today. They chose vivid scarlet.

Mrs Corper initially opted for a pink so pale it was all but transparent. Tess though, persuaded her otherwise. 'If you're going to have varnish, you may as well go the whole hog, Mrs Corper. Polish and be proud.'

'You'll be waxing my fanny next, dear.'

Tess was so stunned that she didn't notice a glob of nail varnish fall from the brush directly onto her jeans – and her good jeans at that.

'We listened to a programme on the wireless – didn't we, Hilda. It's all the rage, dear – some leave what they call a landing strip. Some have it trimmed into shapes and dyed – you know, hearts, flags. A sort of topiary. They interviewed one lady – well, *lady* is probably being a little too charitable – anyway, she has her derrière bleached. All the rage, dear, a fad – didn't you know? By the amount you're blushing, it seems that you didn't.'

'She'll be thinking old dears like us shouldn't say fanny,' Hilda chuckled to Mrs Corper. 'She'll be worrying that finding out about the crack-and-sack wax popular amongst the queers will finish us off.'

'You mustn't call them queers, Hil. You have to call them *the gays.*'

'Well, that's quite ridiculous – what am I going to use for gay in the normal sense?'

'Colourful, jolly, I suppose.'

The ladies looked at Tess who was sitting there, mouth agape.

'We were young once, you must remember,' said Mrs Corper.

'Footloose and fancy free,' Hilda laughed.

'It wasn't just your feet that were loose, Hil,' Mrs Corper said with a jauntily raised eyebrow that Tess decided she'd offer to shape a little.

'Now now,' said Hilda. 'You wouldn't want me dragging up mention of Steven Hunter, would you?' She turned to Tess and whispered rather loudly. 'She was the talk of the town after *that* little episode with *him*, believe me.'

Tess concentrated on Mrs Corper's nails but she thought to herself how enjoyable it was listening to their banter. 'You've been friends a long while?'

'Sixty years, dear.'

'That's amazing.'

'Do you have close friends, yourself?'

'I do indeed. I have Tamsin back down in London. And I have Lisa here.'

'Nice to count your dearest on one hand, I always say. And what does your husband do?'

'Oh, I'm not married.'

'How very modern of you.'

'Do you call him your *partner*? Or your lover, perhaps?' Hilda eavesdropped.

'Or your *beau*,' said Mrs Corper. 'I've always liked that one.'

'Better than boyfriend – that's dreadful.'

'What does he do, then, the man you're not married to?'

Tess looked up. She looked up and away as if she was thinking about her beau. Actually, she was looking straight at Mary.

'He builds bridges,' Tess said, projecting the information boldly into the room. Another resident raised her head. Mrs Corper and Hilda clucked and nodded their approval. Mary, it appeared, didn't hear. But there again, she hadn't registered Tess's presence in the room at all that Tuesday.

In the evening, sitting on her own eating an omelette, Tess could so clearly envisage sharing the highlights of her day with Joe. Making him laugh as she relayed the humour and wit and wisdom of the pensioners. She felt suddenly bemused, and rather sad, that in reality this appeared not to be possible. He'd all but banned her from talking about his mother, hadn't he? There was some mammoth issue, some dark secret, that he didn't seem prepared to share with her. And she thought, he knows everything about me now. And she thought, I wish I could coax more from him. And then she thought, is this an imbalance and if it is, will our bridge not stand steady? Then she thought, I must stop talking in metaphors. But she did think, I wish Joe would tell me more, I wish I knew what happened.

And then she sat in the drawing room with a cup of tea and thought how all she had told Joe had brought so much benefit – to her individually and to them as a couple. What she had considered an unspeakable secret, a necessary lie that she'd have to tolerate like an insidious cramp, had been not just diffused but obliterated by sharing it.

But what if the health of the relationship suffered because a secret was uncovered? Could that happen too? She thought perhaps a fine line could be drawn between privacy and secrecy; the former a right, the latter a risk.

She glanced at the time. She'd give him a call soon, just to say hullo, goodnight. She had to tell herself however batty Joe's mother was now, however undeniably tragic the circumstances of dementia were, it was clear there was murky history with her son and bad blood between them. Tess knew Joe was entitled to his feelings and his privacy however harmless the poor old dear appeared to be to Tess. Whatever acrimony existed between them, she had to admit it had nothing to do with her. Perhaps she was just plain nosy.

When Mary made her way to the Resolution the next afternoon – with Laura trailing her a respectful distance behind, having phoned to forewarm Tess, Tess considered how she just couldn't like Mary less on account of Joe being estranged from her. Something had happened at some point during Joe and Mary's life together – but to Tess she was a senile old lady now, who was compelling because she carried such sadness and introversion around with her; hauling it from Marine Parade uphill all the way home. Turning up at the Resolution with her history heaped upon her, weighing her down, like a caryatid with its stone. Whatever her feelings for Joe, Tess found she was still drawn to the woman. Perhaps she reminded her a little of her grandmother. Perhaps she was a link with Joe when he was gone. She didn't want to write Mary out of her life just because Joe had. But if she didn't, she ran the risk of writing a lot of trouble into her blissful story with Joe.

Chapter Thirty-six

'Andy? It's Joe – how are you doing?'

'I'm good, mate, thanks. How's it in – where are you?'

'Belgium – this week.'

'Building?'

'Pitching – costs and forecasts. Listen – and I don't want to overstep a line – but I was just calling to see if you managed to meet Tess?'

'I did.'

'Well, that's a relief – I wondered if she'd bottle and bolt.'

'So did I – but she didn't. I went to the old house – it's changed, Joe. I wouldn't have recognized it – I certainly don't remember it being so light.'

'That's because it was always dark – very dark – when we were kids.'

'She's nifty, isn't she?'

'She is,' Joe paused. 'She's great.'

'How long have you been together, then?'

'Funny thing is, it's difficult to tell. Looking back, since the moment we met really, back in March. It was cold then, it seems a long time ago. But anyway. You managed to sit her down? Listen – just tell me to back off if there's some kind of client confidentiality.'

'Well, it seems you know her precise position – she kept saying, "Joe knows." I've been through the options with her and I'll make an appointment with an insolvency practitioner I know. It's between bankruptcy – and she burst into tears when we spoke about that – or an IVA which is an Individual Voluntary Arrangement. An IVA has more flexibility than bankruptcy. It's thought of as "second-chance legislation" – it provides help with a wide range of debt problems. Each IVA is unique to each set of individual financial circumstances.'

'Will it help her?'

'Undoubtedly. Bankruptcy lasts a year but there is still a social stigma attached to it and Tess seems appalled by having to file – even though I pointed out that it is a good option considering she has no assets or significant income.'

'An IVA?'

'An IVA allows for payments to be made over five years. All legal action is dropped, calls and demands are stopped. On the whole, it's a better option for creditors too. Debts are consolidated into a single contract with one monthly payment – at the end of the IVA period, the remaining debt is written off. The administration costs are lower than bankruptcy and the debtor does not face the same restrictions as those imposed on bankrupts. She could even have a bank account – but with no overdraft. IVAs were set up to be less stressful than bankruptcy – though both are pretty depressing, I have warned her. She's absolutely determined to settle her debts.'

'Between you and me, can I still pass her cash, then, for her house-sitting?'

'I didn't hear that.'

'I said – can I still—'

'Joe, I can't *hear* that – OK?'

'Ah. I see. OK.'

'The trouble is, you need to be in employment to do an IVA – you can even continue to trade and access trade credit if it helps you pay off your creditors. So it's a bit of a shag that her work is voluntary at the moment.'

'Well, it is and it isn't – she volunteers what she wants to do to the old house and then I pay for the materials.'

'No – I mean the other stuff.'

'Oh – the face creams and things. It was her friend who organized that evening. Sounded more like a casual one-off than a regular thing. It was cash, for sure – most of it was under her mattress.'

'I didn't hear that either, Joe. No – I mean the voluntary work she does at the old folks' place.'

Joe paused.

'Joe?'

Still he paused. Then: 'I can't hear you. Line's gone a bit – I'll call you when I'm next – Cheers, Andy.'

'She's a great girl, Joe – you've struck gold with her.'

'I can't hear you,' Joe said quietly and he ended the call.

Voluntary work?

Why didn't he know about that?

At an old folks' home?

Shit.

Penny's dropped.

Why the –

Pretty quickly though, Joe decided not to let the penny drop. Instead, he picked it up and put it in his pocket, intending to take it home with him that weekend so he could hand it over to Tess and say, hey, does this belong to you? If Tess had been so open with him about issues she'd previously closed off from her entire world, then in all probability there was nothing untoward about this old folks business.

There were plenty in Saltburn, anyway. The Endeavour – the next house but one – had been converted into such an establishment.

But why hadn't she mentioned it, he wondered as he checked the hotel room and puzzled over which country his brown shoes were in – he was sure he'd brought them to Belgium. He reasoned that during his last visit home, they'd talked about so much else of such great significance that there probably hadn't been the time or an opening for Tess to mention a bit of voluntary work she'd picked up. As he checked out and hailed a cab, he did wonder – she wouldn't hide something from me, would she? She wouldn't be doing the very thing – the only thing – he'd asked her not to do, would she?

By the time he arrived at the airport, he'd decided that no, Tess wouldn't do that. There might be stuff she might not want him to know – she might have had secrets but she wouldn't be secretive, she wouldn't be deceitful. Not with him. She loved him too much. He'd never felt anything like it.

But then Nathalie accosted his mind's eye.

As did Rachel in London.

And Eva in Brussels – after all, hadn't he phoned her when he'd arrived, just to say, hi, I'm back in town? She was out of the city and now Joe had to admit to himself that though he'd felt relieved at the time, hadn't he also felt just slightly disappointed too? As he waited at the gate to board, he did contemplate the finer points of secrecy and deceit and he thought about the stuff he wouldn't want Tess to know. Settling into his seat, putting on his safety belt, he challenged himself about it all. He asked himself, what would you have done, had Eva been around, had you had dinner with her, had she suggested coming back to your hotel with you? He answered himself: you'd've said to yourself, where's the harm – no one need know. You'd've said to yourself, it's only sex;

it has nothing to do with my feelings for Tess. He asked himself, what'll you do when you're next in France? But he feigned not to hear himself. He focused instead on the journey he was embarking on. Back home. To Tess. One thing he was sure about was that he never thought about the other women once he'd left their countries – but he thought about Tess all the time.

Tess, Tess, top of my list.

There shouldn't be a list really, he told himself. Everyone else should be gone from it. Why haven't I struck them off?

As the plane taxied, Joe closed his eyes. They felt sore from all that sudden introspection. He opened them again only once he was back on British soil. It struck him, as he drove from the airport and headed for home, that he'd booked the flight on the spur of the moment because he wondered if he might catch Tess out. He imagined turning up unannounced and coming across her in the act. Only now did he ask himself why he wanted to do that. Was it to make himself feel better? Or was it far more complex than that? The act he envisaged intercepting was hardly on a par with what went on with him behind Tess's back. Why was he rushing home with sabotage in his mind? He had to pull in to a lay-by and think about that one. He rummaged around in the glove compartment and found half a tube of soft mints. There was a sour taste in his mouth. He thought, maybe I'm trying to pre-empt it all coming tumbling down – like they did with the Halfpenny Bridge. He thought, maybe I'm going to destroy this relationship myself before it reaches the danger point of implosion, does more damage, causes greater hurt. Because that's what relationships do, don't they? Proper ones – not the casual set-ups I've hitherto organized for myself far from home turf.

He drove off, keeping in the slow lane. He knew he'd never been in love before because he'd actively avoided it; he'd organized alternatives where the fun and his independence were not compromised and where his emotional security could never be undermined. He had never wanted to live with someone or do the family thing. In his experience, it was not the path to true happiness but a shortcut to pain and loneliness.

But wasn't he now living with the girl he was in love with? They shared a home, didn't they? Their love was not conditional on how much time they could spend together at home. Their love bridged distance and time.

*　　*　　*

Tess was beside herself. She was clambering all over Joe in much the same way Wolf used to do before his accident. He was intending to go to Swallows that very evening – but it could wait. Anything that might disrupt this flood of harmony and happiness could bloody well wait.

'If I knew you were coming – I'd've, I'd've –' She laughed and burst into song. '*If I knew you were coming I'd've baked a cake.*'

She put her arms around his neck and leant back so she could take a long look at him. Then she came in close, standing on bare tiptoes, kissing him over and over. 'I'd've gone to the shops at the very least – there's not much in the fridge.'

'My feeling is you quite liked the surprise, missy. But next time, I'll furnish you with my flight times, then. I'll phone you en route, if you like.'

'No! Don't! I love it! I *love* it!'

'We could just do fish and chips for our tea?'

'Yes!'

'Or we could have –' Joe looked into the pan simmering on the stove, '– orangey mush?'

'That's Em's – and it's organic sweet potato and butternut squash mash.'

'I said mash.'

'You said mush!'

'I love the way you feed Emmeline. Where is she by the way?'

'Out there – look.'

They looked out into the garden where Em was busy decanting water from a selection of receptacles into a large washing-up bowl.

'I love it that Em can mooch about, safely on her own. That I can potter about – and every now and then I look up and she's happy in her own little world. But you can pop out there for me and tell her it's supper-time. If you like.'

'We call it "tea" round these parts, Posh Totty.'

Tess watched Joe go out into the garden. Her adrenalin was still up from his arrival and yet she felt utterly grounded. And proud – all this way to see her! And that lovely comment about her maternal skills. She thought, whatever he says to me, I believe. She thought, Grandma always said to accept a compliment and now I really understand what she meant. Compliments, Tess had previously thought, oughtn't to be trusted. A compliment from Joe, Tess decided then and there, could be taken at face value.

She watched from the window as he strolled over to Em, stooped and tapped her on the shoulder most formally. Em looked up and seemed nonplussed by his arrival on the scene. He offered her his hand and they had a rather solemn handshake. Then she offered him a jug full of blue soapy water and he pretended to take a good glug before he dropped to the grass and rolled around as if poisoned. Em peered at him and slowly emptied a beaker of the water all over the seat of his trousers. Inside, Tess clasped her hand to her mouth. Oh God, he's *soaked*. She was about to tap on the window, shake a responsible finger at Em, but the peels of Joe's laughter stopped her. Let them have their quality time and their private joke, Tess thought. And when she heard them make their way to the back door, she busied herself at the stove.

'Emmeline is ready for her tea. And I'm ready for a shower.'

'Goodbye,' said Em.

'Goodbye,' said Joe, matching her gravity.

While she stirred the pan, Tess silently sang out, oh, I so love you both.

Fish and chips it was.

'So, what have you been up to these past few days?'

'Well, I saw Andy.'

And once Tess had finished telling Joe all the ins and outs of IVA it seemed to him too forced to say to her, and what else, Tess, what else have you done, where have you been, who have you seen? Actually, he was avoiding it, he knew he was. He didn't want anything to threaten the idyll. Wasn't it worth all that travel for this? Wouldn't it be a waste of a journey just to instigate conflict?

The next morning, though, the need to rumble Tess rose like bile in his throat. It was a hateful feeling and he loathed himself for it. He had to do it, though, despite being aware that he only half understood the personal drive behind it. He didn't really want to catch her out, or endanger the tranquillity she brought to him; certainly he didn't want to upset her – but there again, he didn't really want to go to Swallows either and see his mother. But he was just going to have to do both. To prove something or other to himself. Quite what, he didn't really know. But the task to find out had been looming like a portentous shadow from the moment he'd woken.

He had her.

He knew her facial expressions absolutely and was thus

able to note her momentary look of panic, in reality little more than a flicker across her eyes, when he said he was just off out, just had a visit to make and no, he wouldn't be taking Wolf.

Tess felt fear fill her mouth with silence while her conscience screamed at her to tell him, tell him about Swallows, tell him it's all above board – tell him it's a good thing, nothing to hide, you've discovered a really good thing you can do. However, she was tongue-tied, hiding her alarm behind Em's wriggling little body as they waved Joe off.

Shit, what's the number for Swallows? Laura gave it to me. I don't know where I put it. Lisa! She has Laura's number – they swapped them after the Made With Love evening. Phone Lisa.

Both numbers were somewhere in her pocket diary which she belted up to her room to find, almost tripping over Em on her way down. She'd practically forgotten about Em. She wondered for a moment who to phone first. She chose Swallows. Only Laura wasn't there and Tess had no idea what to say to the lady who'd answered whose voice she did not know. She thought, I'm hardly likely to say I think the son of one of your residents may be popping in, please could you make sure that neither the staff nor any of the residents mention the girl who's been coming in twice weekly doing the beauty treatments. As she dialled Lisa's number, her fingers slowed and she replaced the receiver before the call connected. It didn't matter if Lisa did have a number for Laura, what could Laura do about any of it anyway? Tess knew she wouldn't ask her even if she turned up on the doorstep this very minute.

She kept telling herself, I haven't lied to him, I've just kept it quiet. She kept telling herself, I haven't done anything wrong.

But she kept answering herself back.

You've done what he expressly asked you not to do. You've let him down. You've betrayed his trust.

'Hullo, Mr Saunders – well, this is a surprise.'
  'Flying visit – as usual.'
  'I'll see where Mum is, shall I?'
  'Thank you.'
As the matron bustled off, Joe looked around the spacious hallway at Swallows. It really was a lovely building – airy and elegant and not institutional in the slightest. And it was fragrant too. It was one of the best. He shuddered, recalling some of the establishments he had visited. He looked around him, alighting on the noticeboard. Bingo on a Wednesday evening. Sing-song on a Saturday. Walking Club every morning 9.30. Church on a Sunday. Bridge on a Monday. And well, would you look at that, Tuesdays and Fridays Heaven at Home.
  Look and feel years younger! Let our skilled beautician pamper you!

I wonder who that could be.
  As if I didn't bloody know.

'Yes, it's a full week for those who take up all on offer.'
  Matron was back, standing alongside Joe.
  'Bridge, bingo and a sing-song?' said Joe. 'Isn't that admitting you're old?'
  'We have poker evenings too, every once in a while. And we tried a Debate Evening – but it almost ended in fisticuffs. Mum's ready – she's in the sunroom. Please follow.'
  He wanted to talk about the notice about the beautician but the matron was bustling him along.
  It was when Joe was at the door of the sunroom, when he peered in to see her sitting by the window, that he realized

he hadn't actually come here to see her at all, he'd only come for proof that Tess had been. He didn't much want to take a single step further, but he could hardly turn and go now. He took a deep breath and inwardly squared his shoulders. He walked over and sat down.

Eventually, Mary turned to him.

'Hullo, Mother.'

'Mother? No no, not me – I'm Miss – do I know you?'

'Yes, you do. I'm Joe. I'm your son.'

'Try her – over there. She's always waiting for her son to come.'

Joe looked around the room. The elderly lady, clock watching. He'd only ever seen her watching a clock, whichever room she was in. He turned back to his mother.

'It's a lovely day out there.'

'Isn't it. I do love France. People rave about the British seaside – but of course, you just can't depend on the weather over there.'

'This is Saltburn.'

He expected her to argue that it wasn't. But it seemed she hadn't heard him, or she hadn't the energy, or there was something far more interesting out of the window, or in her mind. He'd stay a little longer. At least she didn't know him today. They sat quietly; every now and then a sigh or splutter or mutter about a cup of tea elsewhere punctuated the thick silence of the room.

'Do you like it here?' Joe asked.

'Oh, it's lovely. I've lived here all my life, you know. The only way I'll be leaving is in a box.'

'Do you have many visitors?'

'Oh yes, lots and lots.'

'Family?'

'Friends – my family has all gone.'

'Who comes to visit you?'

A vague look swept over his mother's face as she tried to find names for the multitude of imagined visitors clogging her mind's eye in an unruly, faceless mob.

'Don't worry – I'm sure you're very popular.' He tapped her hand. And then he looked at it. Her fingernails were bright red. He hadn't seen her with nail varnish for years. Not since he was much younger. He didn't like it then and he doesn't like it now.

'Look at your nails,' he said.

'Ah, that's the girl who visits here now.'

'Visits?'

'She comes in with all her paints and potions. This colour is called Red-in-Bed.'

'I see. What's her name?'

'Red-in-Bed.'

'No,' said Joe, 'what's *her* name?'

'Sorry?'

'What's her *name?*'

'Who?'

'The girl.'

'What girl?'

'The *girl*, Mum – the girl who does your nails.'

'The girl. Who does my nails.' Mary looked at her hands and then looked out to sea, her lips moving over silent words like the little bibbling waves that lap tirelessly at the shoreline. 'I don't know. Miss Someone or Other.'

'Tess?'

'Tess who?'

'The girl who does your nails?'

'I don't know if she is called Tess,' Mary shook her head the way a child might. 'I don't know what her name is, actually. But I do know she brings her little girl with her. Dear little thing. And I do know that *her* name is Emmeline.'

Joe sat for a moment longer. 'I have to go.'

387

Mary looked up. Even frail and puckered, he knew that face off by heart but he could see there wasn't a flicker of recognition in her eyes. Not today.

'Goodbye.'

'Well, goodbye, love. Thank you for your visit.' Mary turned to one of the other residents – a lady Joe didn't recall – whose hair was like candyfloss but whose skin was peppered with cruel brown tags.

'Ellen, dear – you can have him back now. So kind of him to spend time with me. He's a canny lad, your boy.'

Joe sat himself down on one of the cliff benches just over the road to collect his thoughts. He wanted to rant, bloody little bitch. Conniving cow. But that wasn't right. Tess was none of those things. He wanted to spit, stupid old bag. But he couldn't bring himself to talk of his mother like that.

Why did Tess go there? Of all the bloody old-age homes in this sleepy old town, why choose Swallows? She knew how he felt – they'd had that one, solitary confrontation about it. So why betray him? What was so bloody compelling about Swallows?

'What's she hoping to gain that would be worth losing what we have?'

Laura was walking by, for her afternoon shift.

'Joe! This is a surprise.'

'Isn't it just.'

His response took her aback. Charming Joe Saunders? Whose visits were fleeting and sporadic but whose phone calls were regular? Sat there, on a bench, with a cob-on? Laura did what Laura did best, she sat herself down next to him, with a cheery huff of how that hill was going to kill her, the hotter the summer became.

'Is everything all right, then? Is Mum not so good today?'

'Oh, she's fine – she's off being someone else today.'

Well, then, thought Laura, why is Joe not content – he's usually far happier to find her like that than her *compos mentis* narky self.

'I hope you noticed her nails.'

'Of course I noticed her nails.'

Laura did not have Joe down as the snappish type. It just made her want to try harder to lift his mood.

'That's your Tess, of course – she's brought a lot more than just fancy polish to Swallows.'

Joe turned to face her. She couldn't read his expression so she turned her gaze to the sea as she prattled.

'She's a lovely girl – but of course it's Em who's star of the show.'

'She doesn't talk about it.'

'Who? Em?' Laura laughed. Then she tapped Joe's knee. 'Well, that's Tess for you, isn't it? Bet she hasn't told you how we offered to pay? We'd still be happy to – but she's insisting on there being no charge, like. And using all her own lovely creams too! She won't let us even cover the costs of those. And do you know, Joe, just yesterday when she came – well, she'd run out of organic whatever-she-called-it, that she'd use on the feet. Something special it was – smelt gorgeous – all minty. Anyway, it's finished – she'd used up her last tube on the ladies. No more available. So you know what she did? She turns up with a bloody great big pot of Vaseline and a roll of clingfilm and she says to the ladies – she says, "This is just as good as any of the fancy stuff you can buy." And they had such a giggle as she slathered their feet with Vas, wrapped them in clingfilm like chicken about to go in the fridge. Then she plonked their feet, all swaddled up like that, in tubs of warm water. They all sat there in a semicircle – they did look a picture. But what do you know, Joe – there's a lot of nice soft tootsies at Swallows now.'

389

Joe, though, didn't want to know.

Joe had heard quite enough.

Tess is awaiting Joe's return like a child who has broken something precious but feels compelled to remain next to the mess.
He's been gone a good hour. How she hopes it has indeed
been *good*. She hears the crunch of footsteps on gravel. She's
round the back, with Em and Wolf. The dog knows it's Joe
and gives a joyful bark but his attention remains on Tess and
the pegs, one of which she throws into the bushes for him to
find. She's lost a lot of pegs that way – today, over the months
– but it's been worth it for the comedy Wolf has provided.
She manages to laugh at Wolf while to herself she's murmuring,
shit shit shit, what's he going to say, what should I do, shall
I just act dumb, shall I witter on fifteen to the dozen and talk
about a picnic in the woods or a walk to the river?

'Joe! You're back! Hi! Nice – time? I was thinking about
a picnic to the woods or a walk in the river?'

Joe walks over to her but stops abruptly just beyond reach.

'When people hide stuff from the people they say they love
– you have to ask yourself, why would they do that, why
would they have secrets? What kind of person does that make
them?'

Tess's eyes scour Joe's face as if it's a map she cannot read
because she's lost and in a panic. 'Joe – I—'

He's looking over the top of her head. 'When someone you
love does something you've asked them not to do, you have
to ask yourself, do they actually love you?'

She raises her face. 'Joe – I just—'

'Then you ask yourself, do I actually love them?'

'No! Don't say that! I just—'

'Couldn't you *just* respect my feelings – my past – that
some things are *just* none of your bloody business?'

'But – I—'

390

'You're like a squatter, Tess. An emotional squatter. Wheedling your way in.'

He's about to turn on his heels, he's planned to strop off into the house and pack and be gone, travel off into the old life he knows and trusts. Tess, however, has different ideas. He's watched her, standing silent and mortified. He's seen her bite on her lips as if doing so might close her tear ducts, he's seen her bite even harder when it's obvious that doesn't work. He's watched a fat, oily tear snake a slow passage down the side of her nose to the corner of her mouth.

But it is Joe who is left standing there, because suddenly Tess has gone. Without a word, she has walked off. Through the gate. He doesn't know in which direction. But she's run away. She's gone.

Chapter Thirty-seven

For the first time in his life, Joe had sole charge of an infant. Well, there had been times, just once or twice, when he'd amused Emmeline – or she'd amused him – while Tess had been busy running the bath or making supper or clearing up some mess or other. But that had only ever been for a matter of minutes.

He peered at Wolf and he peered at Emmeline as if to assess whether they'd been party to the words that had passed between him and Tess before her sudden exit. But, out in the garden, it seemed they were both still captivated by the pegs. There was washing yet to hang out and though it struck Joe as wholly bizarre, he found himself pegging it out. Then Emmeline inadvertently twanged herself with a twig and Joe found that she was in his arms and he was hushing her not quite knowing if he was doing it right, or what he was meant to do next, or when the crying would stop.

'Mummy?'

'Back soon,' Joe told her.

'Iggle Piggle?'

Joe looked at her. She knew what she was talking about but he hadn't a clue. 'Iggle Piggle to you too.'

'Iggle Piggle?'

'I don't –'

Emmeline was pointing to the house.

'Is Iggle Piggle in there, Emmeline?'

She nodded vigorously. He gave her his finger, which she grabbed in her fist, and he let himself be led to the house. He looked through a small pile of books on the kitchen table and asked her if Iggle Piggle was in one of those. Apparently not. He was set to follow her upstairs when she stopped at the sitting room. He cast a cursory look around, peered under the coffee table and looked behind a cushion or two. There were no toys or books that he could see. 'No Iggle Piggle in here either,' he said. She started to cry. 'We could read a different story? Does Emmeline have another book she likes?'

'Iggle Piggle,' the child sobbed.

'But I don't know where it is.' Joe looked at Wolf who was doing his Charlie Chaplin thing with his eyebrows. 'Let's find another book.' He scooped up the baby who arched her back and kept pointing a flung-out arm back to the sitting room. He took her up to her room and she stood on the rug, runny nosed and tearful, while Joe went through all the books murmuring, Iggle Piggle Iggle Piggle. Nothing. He held up each of her toys in turn and asked her if they were this Iggle Piggle. Categorically not. Still she cried and still he tried. Is it a song? He attempted to put the words Iggle Piggle to a tune. This made her throw herself to the floor in sorrow. He slumped down next to her.

'I'm sorry, Miss Emmeline,' he said. 'I'm not a mummy or a daddy and I don't know who or where or what Iggle Piggle is.'

'Mummy?'

'Back soon.'

'Mummy?'

'Back soon.'

'Mummy.' She'd sat up hopeful – now she was distraught. Joe pulled her onto his lap, rocked her, placed thoughtful kisses onto the top of her head. 'Mummy back soon,' he said, 'I hope. Mummy make it better. Mummy make everything better.'

He thought about this.

Hadn't Tess already made a lot significantly better? Was it really her, making everything worse? He wondered, was it really Tess's remit to make everything better? Wasn't it his?

'Let's go and see what's on television, shall we?' Joe said to Emmeline. 'Then I suppose I have to think about your lunch. And mine.'

He carried her downstairs saying a theatrical yuk! when she wiped her snotty nose against his shoulder which made her do it again and again each time he said it. He put on the television and went to the Kids home page and told himself off for sounding like an old fuck for querying the number of channels available to the children of today.

'Is CBeebies good?' he asked, not expecting a reply. 'I've heard of CBeebies. Look here we go, something called *In the Night Garden*. Does Emmeline like *In the Night Garden*? Oh look – there's a channel further down with *Tom and Jerry*. Joe likes *Tom and Jerry*. Who is *Ben10*? What'll it be, Emmeline?'

He looked at her; she appeared to be as squashy as the cushions against which she was sitting. Teary and expectant, she was evidently looking at him to save the day.

'Mummy back soon, Emmeline,' he murmured, selecting a channel. 'Do you watch by yourself or do you have a grown-up with you?' He regarded her, so tiny. 'I think I'd better stay.'

He sat beside her and put the volume up. And Emmeline screamed out, Iggle Piggle – but she was no longer crying, she was ecstatic.

Joe looked at the screen.

'Is *that* Iggle Piggle? That *thing* is Iggle Piggle?'

Good God, he thought, bring back *Listen With Mother*, all is forgiven. But then he thought, I never got to listen with Mother. And then he thought how nothing had been forgiven. And then he gave himself a shake to bring him back to the present and he lifted Emmeline onto his lap to watch *In the Night Garden*. And he felt very proud of himself. They'd got there, he and Emmeline. And he thought, come back, Tess, please come back.

If finding Iggle Piggle had flooded him with a sense of relief, then knowing he was going to have to change Emmeline's nappy consumed him with a sense of terror. Halfway through *In the Night Garden*, he thought to himself, what's that smell? By the end of the programme, he knew exactly what it was and what he was going to have to do about it.

'You're going to have to help me with this one, Emmeline,' said Joe. And they muddled through, the two of them. Joe only came across the baby wipes after he'd been through half a roll of toilet paper and two flannels. And he'd learned that if there was to be a next time, he'd be rolling up and bagging the soiled nappy immediately, or else Emmeline would slap a limb down straight into it – which is precisely what she'd done. And he had no idea that baby lotion was so runny. Nor that it probably wasn't for bare bottoms when he discovered, later on, a tube helpfully called Happy Bum Nappy Cream. But however unconventional his changing technique, Emmeline was clean and dry and Joe felt rather pleased with himself as he escorted her downstairs for lunch.

'Baked beans? Will that do? What do you have it with? Toast? I've seen Mummy make you toasty soldiers – will that be OK, for lunch?'

She ate everything and Joe found this so satisfying that he had beans on toast for his lunch too.

'Now I know you have a snooze after lunch,' Joe said, clearing up yoghurt and wondering to himself how a child could derive so much pleasure from such dreadful stickiness. It was as if Emmeline had taste buds on her cheeks, on the bridge of her nose; it was as if her hair acted as straws through which she could suck up the stuff.

'Yuk, don't put those fingers near me, young lady.'

Which of course she did, much to her amusement.

And Joe thought, I could have backed away just now, I could have taken myself beyond reach quite easily. And, as he took Emmeline from her clip-on high chair, he thought to himself, is that what I've done? Have I backed away and taken myself beyond Tess's reach?

He settled Emmeline for her afternoon nap. He said to her, 'Mummy home soon, hey, Emmeline, Mummy coming home soon.'

He only appeared to remember one children's song so he sang her 'When the Boat Comes In' in a Geordie accent before tweaking her curls and leaving the room as quietly as he could. He hovered in the hallway for a few minutes. Listening for Emmeline. Looking at Tess's door.

With Emmeline asleep, Joe turned his attention to Wolf.

'What am I doing, old fellow? Me – changing nappies and singing songs?'

His dog had no answer.

'Let's go and check the washing on the line, shall we – see if my pegging has held.'

He wasn't sure what to do with the remainder of the afternoon, so he told himself to Think Like Tess and he decided on fresh air and ice cream once Emmeline woke up. He changed another nappy, which didn't really need changing but it felt good to do a better job of it second time around. Then, he prepared to go out. It was like the Memory Game – he closed his eyes and envisaged Tess bustling about organizing what she needed and placing items in the base of the buggy. What was usually there? A beaker – definitely a beaker. What was in the beaker? Diluted juice, he seemed to remember. Half and half. Nappies and a nappy sack – look! they're there already. What else? He glanced outside at the weather. It was a beautiful day. He saw sunblock in the pocket of the buggy hood and slathered Emmeline all over before putting the bottle back. Drink. Nappy. Sun protection. Wipes – wipes would be good. And while he was in the kitchen retrieving the packet from the kitchen table, he saw an unopened pack of rice cakes and thought it prudent to take them. He packed it all into the base of the buggy, plonked in the baby – and spent a further five minutes struggling with the straps and clasps. He almost forgot Wolf's lead. He just about remembered his front-door keys.

At first, he thought he might just about manage the distance to the playground and five minutes on the swings. But then he thought, bugger the playground – this child needs sand between her toes. How could she ever have been to the beach if her mother had some ludicrous pathological fear of the place? Saltburn – all this time and never once to the beach? It's mid-May. It's warm. It's a perfect day for the beach.

No voice cautioned him that he was doing to Tess exactly what he'd perceived her to have done to him. Not respecting her wishes, however dark or daft the reasons behind them might be.

I don't do beaches. She'd said it so many times.

I don't do beaches or heights.

*   *   *

397

'I really really hope that Mummy is there when we arrive back,' Joe said as they trudged back up the hill towards home, late in the afternoon. 'Not because I can't manage,' he said, tipping up the buggy so he could talk to Emmeline and pull a face at her and make her whoop and flail her sandy hands at him. 'Not because I haven't had fun.' He stopped and waited for Wolf to catch up. 'I just really hope that she's there.'

*   *   *

Tess would have turned up much, much earlier of course but Tamsin said not to. Tamsin said, go around to Lisa's. So Tess went to Lisa's and Lisa wouldn't let her return for a good long while either.

'It's the longest I've been away from Em,' Tess said, by mid-afternoon.

'Bollocks it is,' Lisa cried. 'You used to go to work all day – remember?'

Tess was stunned. 'Bloody hell,' she said, 'I'd actually forgotten all about that.'

They'd talked over endless cups of tea in Lisa's back garden – about family, about jobs, about childcare, about Saltburn. And they talked about Joe.

'You did the right thing, pet,' Lisa said. 'If he'd have stormed off first, he'd be halfway back to some bridge somewhere. Just let him cool down. You won't have lost him.'

'Promise?'

'As much as I am able.'

'And then? After I've let him cool down?'

'And then – let him stew. Silly sod.'

'And then?'

'You go back – and wait and see what he has to say. And then you say stuff and he'll say stuff and then there'll be kissing and happy-ever-after.'

'You make it sound very easy.'

'I don't mean to. It won't be. But I do think that's the logical outcome – but the timing's crucial.'

'Can I tell you something else, then – while I'm waiting?'

'Course you can.'

'I had some advice about – well, you know – my situation. I know I've shied away from telling you too much and I've probably glossed over what I have told you. But anyway – there appears to be a way out, a legitimate one.'

'I'm all ears.'

'A friend of Joe's is a financial advisor. He came to see me – and he was so kind. He's going to set up a meeting for me with an Insolvency Practitioner. About whether I can avoid bankruptcy by choosing this thing called an Individual Voluntary Arrangement. Lisa – it may just allow me to settle my past debts and give me a future too.'

Lisa listened thoughtfully. 'So – will it enable you to set up again? You could do the same skincare recipes under a different name, perhaps?'

'Well, I could,' Tess faltered. 'But you know what, Lisa, I don't know if I'd want to. Not just because my confidence has had a knock – just that it's not something I think I want to do any more.'

'Salon work?'

'No – not salon work either.'

'I mean, have your *own*.'

'I don't want my own salon.'

'What then? Seems a shame to let your talent and training go to waste.'

'But it wouldn't – I like doing my voluntary work. I just don't like the trouble it's now got me into.'

'Listen to me, love – it hasn't got you into trouble. The problem's with him. It's not your problem. And if he's got any sense he'll see that if he shares it with you, rather than blames you, then the problem won't be as big. Like you did with him – with yours.'

'I know. But he said—'

'Men – they're bastards, the buggers! They don't know how to argue properly. They just lash out with stupid one-liners.'

'But lashing out hurt. What he said – about me being an emotional squatter.'

'Sticks and stones, Tess, sticks and stones. Didn't they use just sticks and stones to build the earliest bridges?'

Chapter Thirty-eight

Oddly, for the first time the hill didn't feel particularly taxing. In fact, Tess had to consciously slow herself down. Then she realized this might be because she was unusually buggyless. What a novelty that was. She quickened her pace, hoping she'd be arriving back just in time to bath Em and she had strict instructions to phone Lisa whatever the time should she need to. She'd walked in time to a mantra – *I haven't done anything wrong! please let me explain!* Her grandmother had been a great believer in marching rhymes – but hers had never had any personal dimension. As she walked, Tess remembered journeys home from school with her grandmother, both of them chanting, *Left! Left! I had a good job and I left!* It never mattered to her that schoolmates saw, heard and sniggered. A quarter of a century later, she was stomping up the hill in time to *I haven't done anything wrong! Please let me explain!*

The gate. She took a deep breath. The drive. Surreptitiously, she scanned the windows, relieved to see no face or faces looking out for her. Once again, she wished she still had a mobile. She could text Lisa or Tamsin – or send the same text to both – Shit! wish me luck! Txxx

The front door. Its usual groan. Tess stepped inside. The hallway was inviting and cool after the hot walk home and she slid off her shoes and stood still, settling her bare feet into the undulations of the stone slabs. The kitchen door was open but she sensed the room was empty. Tess knew Wolf well enough by now to be able to detect his presence in a room even if she couldn't quite see him. The sitting-room door was shut so they couldn't be in there. Were they in the garden? She'd already closed the front door as quietly as she could and she wasn't sure whether she wanted to go to the effort of easing it open again. Then she heard the pipes start up their clangorous objection to the hot water making its spasmodic journey from tank to tap.

They're upstairs, Tess thought to herself. Joe's running Em a bath. And for a moment, the notion of what he was doing allowed Tess to feel bolstered that maybe, just maybe, everything could turn out just fine.

On the first landing, Joe's bedroom door was open and she was helpless not to pad along the corridor to look inside. Her heart plummeted at the sight of his holdall on the bed all zipped up. Suddenly, the fact that he was doing the family thing of bathing a baby carried little weight. Nor did it matter to Tess any longer that Lisa and Tamsin both thought Joe owed *her* the apology and explanation. She simply didn't want him to leave and, just then, she thought if she could say sorry and tell him why, then maybe she could persuade him to stay. She felt anxious; adrenalin coursed through her body in erratic surges, like the hot water in the pipes in the house. As she trod the stairs up to her floor, all attempts at planning a soliloquy failed. She couldn't even remember her marching rhyme though it would have little impact on her faltering footsteps now. She couldn't remember what Lisa had said that made so much sense. And she didn't know if she trusted herself not to burst into the bathroom in sobbing disarray.

But she didn't. Because she heard Joe's voice first. And it was so calm, sweet and focused yet conversational, that it settled her nerves.

'Bath-time for you, Miss Emmeline,' she heard him say.

They weren't in the bathroom – she could see that. The door was open and Tess looked in and thought, he's used too much bubble bath. They were in Em's room. She made a slow passage towards the door, which she could see was ajar. It opened as she approached and Em appeared with her trade-mark chattering waddle, naked except for her nappy. Joe was just behind her. And Wolf was behind him.

'And here is Mummy,' he said, as if he'd been expecting to see Tess right at that moment all along, as if he'd told Emmeline that this was precisely what was going to happen. But he couldn't meet Tess's eyes, keeping his firmly fixed on the top of Emmeline's head.

'Em,' Tess said as she scooped up her child, 'your nappy's on back to front.'

But Joe turned very obviously to Wolf and he said, 'Didn't I tell you I thought it went the other way round?'

Tess couldn't meet Joe's eyes either. 'I'll do the bath,' she said and she bustled down the hallway to the bathroom, leaving Joe and Wolf glancing at each other on the threshold of Emmeline's room.

She couldn't avoid it any longer. Her baby had fallen sound asleep a full ten minutes ago. With an extra kiss to her index finger, which she transferred to Em's cheek, Tess left the room. She went to hers. She sat in the Loom chair and looked out of the window. Wolf was mooching about outside and Tess thought that from this almost aerial perspective,

403

he looked like something hiding under someone else's coat. The sound of Joe's low whistle called Wolf to attention and it also made Tess leave the chair and tuck herself to the side of the window. She eased herself forward, millimetre by millimetre until she could just see him. Was he on the verge of leaving? Was his holdall now in the car? Was he taking Wolf with him? Though she could very well have continued to watch, unseen, she needed to verify the urgency of the evening. She left her room for a fleet-footed visit to his and all but rejoiced on seeing the bag still on the bed. She wasn't sure where to go next: upstairs, downstairs or outside. What she knew was that she wanted to talk and she wanted to listen and neither of those could be accomplished with the protagonists so far apart. She was not going to run away and she was not going to allow him to do so either. Warily, she went outside the long way round – exiting through the utility and boot rooms off the kitchen. She walked to where she had last seen Joe and Wolf. It was light, the evening sky was clear and the breeze had dropped. Wolf gruffled conversationally, seeing Tess before she saw him or before Joe saw her.

'Oh, hullo, Wolf,' she said as if he'd appeared from nowhere.

'Hi,' said Joe.

'Oh,' said Tess though she knew it sounded contrived, 'hullo, Joe.'

'I –' he stopped. 'Had a nice day.'

Tess nodded. 'Fine, thanks.'

'I meant *I* had a nice day,' said Joe. 'Sorry about the nappy.'

'Well, it seems to have done the job,' said Tess. Then she said, 'I see you're all packed.'

'Yup,' Joe said, 'I'm just about ready to hit the road.'

'OK,' said Tess.

'Right,' said Joe and he walked past her and into the house. She stood outside and looked at Wolf.

404

'Shit,' she whispered. He butted his snout into her hand and managed to unfurl the tight clench of her fist to give her a sweet lick.

'Right then,' said Joe.
    'OK then,' said Tess.
    'I'll be in touch,' said Joe.
    'OK,' said Tess.
    And that was it.
    He shut his car door and drove off, leaving the gate for Tess to close.

*   *   *

He made it to the airport. He put his car in his usual long stay. He queued to check in. He checked in. Hand luggage only. He was going back to Belgium. He wasn't entirely sure why. They didn't need him there. It was simply the place he'd come from and it was as if he wanted to retrace his steps, to rewind the last twenty-four hours so he could do it all differently a second time. He made it to the gate. They were boarding the plane. And that's when he thought, no, I'm not doing this. I'm not bloody doing this.
    And he apologized, over and again to the airline staff and the security staff, telling them how sorry he was about all of this, and how much he regretted inconveniencing them – but he'd just been made aware of a family crisis that only he could sort out. He was escorted from airside back to the landside, by a burly official who really didn't seem bothered whether Joe spoke or not. But Joe spoke. Joe could not shut himself up. Joe only hoped he wouldn't run out of energy or words by the time he arrived home.

Chapter Thirty-nine

Tess wrote to Joe. She wrote pages and pages. She started off on two sheets of A4 that were on the kitchen table and had crayon daubs by Em on one side only. Then she continued on the blank scraps of paper she used for shopping lists and to-do lists which she'd taken to keeping in a cone-like furl in one of the mugs on the Welsh dresser. When these ran out she rummaged through the drawer in the table on which the phone stood in the hallway and ripped out the back pages of two of the address books. They said *Notes* on them. These weren't notes, though, that Tess was writing, but the detailed story of her life – her regrets, her hopes, her ambition, the three wishes she'd love to have granted, and something that oughtn't to be a secret but which, hitherto, she'd kept from Joe. No more secrets, she wrote.

It was almost midnight when she wrote, *I'm sorry to have hurt you.* There was room for little more than the final full stop. Her fingers ached. She had no need to read it through, she knew exactly what was written because it was everything she wanted to say. But the silence of Joe not being there was hard on the ears so she wrote more; her words to fill the emptiness in his house. *I love you*, she wrote. And, after that, there really was nothing she could add.

'The only problem is I don't know where to send it, Wolf.'

And then she thought perhaps that wasn't relevant. It was written, it was said, it was the truth and it would last as long as she did. Whenever it was that Joe came to read it, wherever she might be by then, nothing would have changed. It had been cathartic and exhilarating and revelatory and liberating and draining and painful; she had to haul herself upstairs, collapsing onto the bed without the energy to undress or pull the covers over herself.

She was in a fug of thick, dreamless sleep when she felt something on her cheek. Her eyes sprang open and her consciousness beat back her reverie with a nauseating shove.

'What's –?'

'Shh.'

Joe was sitting beside her in the darkness.

She jerked herself into a semi-seated position but he just said shh again and pushed her shoulders gently so that she lay down.

'What are you –?'

'I've been with the woman I love for the last two hours,' he said. 'I had to wake you to tell you so.'

Even though Tess was still in a woolly-headed blear from being abruptly woken from an exhausted sleep, she told herself, listen up, you need to hear this – this will be key in forcing you to move on. Because of this haze, she didn't consider it the least bit crazy for suddenly wondering whether KL was Kate Ell after all and whether this was the woman of whom Joe now spoke. It seemed ludicrously plausible just then. But then she thought if this was the case then she'd rather be alone and could Joe please go now. She suspected she needed to wake up a little more to be able to cry herself back to sleep. She tried to block out Tamsin saying, well, at

407

least he was honest. And she tried to block out Lisa saying, so sorry for you, pet – but you'll be OK.

Cry. Sleep. Wake up. Run away again.

'It's three in the morning and I've been sitting here, all this time, just watching you.'

The Tamsin and the Lisa in Tess's head were at once awed into silence.

'Watching *me*?' Why would he do that?

'Watching you.'

And then Tess thought, right, I really have to wake up. She thought – could it be? The woman he's been with for two hours – did he really mean –?

'*How* long have you been here?' she asked.

He illuminated his watch. 'Two hours,' he said, 'and a bit. I was at the airport. I was about to get on the plane and then I was just – I don't know – I was *consumed* by this need and this power to make right all the wrong. *All* the wrong, Tess. Because all the wrong has lasted too long and that's not right. They should rename the bloody A66 the Road to Damascus, I tell you. They had to escort me back through passport control and people were staring and I was grinning like an idiot because I was on my way back home to you.'

As he sat and thought about it, Tess noted how he was rocking slightly and smoothing his hands along his thighs. She touched his wrist lightly and he stopped moving and continued to speak.

'I'm not going to let anything – from the past or in the future – jeopardize the blindingly obvious fact that you and I should be together,' he said.

She put her finger up to his lips to say, it's OK, Joe – you don't need to say another thing. But he took her hand and kissed it. Then he laughed. Then it sounded as though he was about to cry.

'I need you, Tess – you make sense of everything, you *are*

everything, to me.' He was stroking her arm, taking her hand between both of his. 'I have to find a way – and I know now that you are the only person on this earth who can bridge over the hostile gorge that's kept my future at bay by my past.'

'Joe –'

But now he put his finger against her lips.

'We can do this together. You have all the raw materials that I need, Tess. I can build it now. You have a love that won't crack under the strain, that will weather any storm, that won't bend to the torsion of my weaknesses and inadequacies. I need these things that your love brings. Will you entrust your love to me, Tess – let me use my love to engineer a future on the firmest foundations that will span the way?'

'Joe.' She pulled him down to her, cupping his face as he came closer. She kissed him very lightly on the lips and rubbed her nose gently against his.

'I'm so tired,' he said and his voice was now hoarse and slow. He lay next to her and there they slept, in their clothes, on top of the covers, side by side, holding hands.

After breakfast, during which Tess thought to herself that anyone looking in on the kitchen might well think this family had been a strong single unit for a long time, she spoke to Em though she looked directly at Joe.

'We're going to go to the pier, Em. Wolfy, Joe, Mummy, Em. We'll buy an ice cream on the way and then we'll find that magic bench.'

She saw Joe's eyebrows give a quick twist of confusion, so she continued. 'We'll find the magic bench again, won't we? Where we all can sit, where things can be said, where secrets have no power because all the bad is washed away by the sea.'

It did strike Tess, when they were within sight of that bench, their ice creams now down to the rim of the cornet, that she could just turn to Joe and say, it doesn't matter what happened, all that matters is ahead of us. She was apprehensive about what he might say, whether he would tell her everything and whether everything might be too much for her to handle. It wouldn't be sweeping it under the carpet, she thought, it would just be letting sleeping dogs lie. And then she thought, enough of the clichés, if Joe wants to speak then let him.

But when they'd been sitting on the bench for long enough to be at the stage of nipping off the point of the cornet to suck the last of the ice cream through, Tess gave Joe a nudge. She had to give him another. She looked at him, he was staring way out beyond Huntcliff. Whatever was on his horizon was very different from the two tankers on Tess's. She put her arm around his shoulders and lay her head lightly and briefly against him, and she waited.

'I didn't have a particularly happy childhood,' Joe began. And that's all he said for a good few minutes.

'In fact, it was pretty bloody miserable.' And that was that, for a long while too.

'But of course, no one would think it – not of the Doctor and the Doctor's Wife.'

Then his sentences came as a series of statements, each one self-contained. They could not flow into a single passage of speech. Their content made that impossible.

'I couldn't say anything to anyone because I knew no one would believe me.

'My mother had a succession of lovers who came to the house when my father was out.

'Eventually, she didn't even bother to send them on their way before he came home.

'Mind you, I caught him with his receptionist once. I was running an errand and I'd gone in to the surgery for Mrs Theberton's ointment. I was nine, I think.

'Everyone hit everyone else in my house. But if they missed each other, I was a convenient bull's-eye.

'The bathroom was cold and dark and dank and I hated it and they'd lock me in it. They'd lock me in it not just when I was naughty. She'd lock me in it when her men came round. He'd lock me in it if he was in a bad mood. I was locked there when they wanted to have their flaming rows without having to lower their voices in case I came into the room.

'But of course he was the Doctor and she was the Doctor's Wife and men coming to the house could just be picking up prescriptions for their wives.

'And it would be preposterous to even think, let alone suggest, that those welts on Joe's backside, or across his back, or along his thigh were from the hand of the Doctor or the Doctor's Wife. He's a lithe, sporty lad that Joe. Must've fallen running across the moors or larking on the beach or swimming 'gainst the tide, or summat.'

Joe glanced at Tess and shrugged as if he'd said little more than that he never had pocket money as a child. She was open-mouthed, her eyes smarting. He smiled sadly at her.

'Thank you for changing the bathroom, pet. It's a lovely room now.'

Joe sat there and felt that some of the badness had indeed drifted out to sea but, by the look on Tess's tear-streaked face, much of it had fallen on her. He wanted to be able to sweep it away from her shoulders as if it was little more than dust. She was sucking her bottom lip and blinking hard against the tears that appeared to be queuing across her eyes.

'I'm OK, Tess,' he told her. 'You've helped me there. You've made that house a home for me for the first time in my life. You've shown me how beautiful a family can be – I mean, there may be only the two of you but to me you and Emmeline are textbook perfect. You with all your love and your lists and your potty systems and routines that suit the both of you. Emmeline with all that sunshine she radiates and the trust she shows because she knows that she's loved, she knows the world is a good place, she knows her mummy'll keep her safe.'

'It must be so hard.'

'I coped. I found a way. I had my sport. My pals. My studies.'

'No, Joe – it must be so hard for you *now*. Your mother, to the world at large, is a sometimes stroppy but usually vague elderly lady.'

Joe looked at his lap then took one of Tess's hands and held it there. He nodded.

'But before the dementia she wasn't the sort of woman, nor he the sort of man, with whom you could sit down and heart-to-heart it out.'

'You and I,' said Tess, 'we're learning to do just that.'

Joe nodded. 'Thank God.'

He paused. 'My father died when I was in my mid-twenties. My mother became bitterer by the month, really. Then five years ago she fell – probably a mild stroke. But that's when her mind started to go. Just small things at first and, as a witness, you'd end up chastising yourself for thinking such things of her.'

'You know she comes back?'

'I know. That's a relatively new thing of hers. The strange thing is that before Swallows, she'd actually been living in a small terrace on Amber Street for a number of years. She said she hated this place but she refused to sell. So I moved back – sold my cottage in Carlton and came back here, for the convenience. I'm a bloke – I can compartmentalize. I can chuck secrets into old boxes like I dumped all that crap into the old boxes you sorted through in the utility room. I employed house-sitters – I swept my secrets and memories into the rooms I never went into.'

'I thought she was a ghost at first.'

412

'I was stupid not to tell you. I was wrong not to tell you.'

'I think I understand why.'

'I could've saved all that hassle yesterday if I'd told you earlier.'

'You'd have a longer night's sleep too.'

They laughed and tucked in close to one another even though it was hot at midday.

'I wonder. If the same thing happened now, would a child be more willing to say something? Would they feel that nowadays their voice might be heard?'

Joe looked sorrowful and his voice was small, vulnerable, young. 'You think no one would believe you. That's why you keep quiet.'

'I believe you, Joe.'

'I said to myself that families aren't worth it. I made myself believe that families bring only discontent. I closed myself off to any kind of meaningful relationship. And then one day, I opened the door and this scruffy girl and her immaculate baby came into the house and started almost immediately to unpick forty-four years of self-sufficiency. You undermined everything I'd trained myself to believe.'

He paused. 'And that's a compliment.'

Tess laughed. She snuggled in close. She could watch the sea all day; watch the sea and sit on the pier next to Joe.

'I liked my time with Emmeline yesterday,' he said.

'I liked your time with Em yesterday too,' said Tess. 'Perhaps today you might like to give her a bath?'

'I do still remember the old bathroom, Tess,' Joe said quietly. 'But because of what you've done, the old bathroom seems to have been not just boarded up but demolished. It isn't at the Resolution any more, that's for sure.'

As they walked home, Tess slipped her arm through Joe's while he pushed the buggy and she pulled Wolf.

'Does she ever – I mean, I don't mean to pry. But when

you visit her – does she ever *talk* as the woman she was, not the one she's become?'

Joe thought about it. 'It's difficult to tell, Tess. Sometimes I rather think she does – but whenever I see her, whatever state she's in, what I do see is a prematurely aged person whose twilight years are cursed with bitterness, with weariness and pain.'

She stole a glance at him. He looked sad and weary. Tess stopped him and looked at him and stood on her tiptoes to kiss him and then she said, smile! And when he did, she peered in very close, very serious, which made him laugh and enabled her to say, I see a lot of love in those eyes, Joe, a lot of love and happiness.

'You see yourself, Tess,' he said.

They lay in bed that night, Tess tracing patterns on Joe's chest.
'Joe?'
'Hmm?'
'Are you tired?'
'Are you horny?'
'No – I mean, yes – I mean, I wanted to ask you something. But it can wait.'
'Wait?'
'If you're horny too.'
'I'd love to be horny – but I'm exhausted.'
'Well, can I ask you something then?'
'What's up?'
'Do you mind – if I still visit Swallows?'
Pause.
'No – not any more. I've heard what you do there – with your tin foil and Vaseline.'
'Clingfilm.'
'I think it's amazing – commendable – what you do. But you could be paid, you know?'

'I know. I know. But I hate money. It scares me. However, I'd like to work at what I'm good at – but I'd just like to do it voluntarily for the time being.'

'Doesn't make much financial sense, you know? Especially with you trying hard to sort yourself out. I'm sure Andy explained all this.'

'I know – but morally it does make sense to me. So do you mind if I continue?'

'I don't mind.'

'And yes, in the meantime, taking Andy's advice, I also need to do paid work. But you see Laura has a friend who works at a care home on Upleatham Street. And they'd have me – on the payroll. What do you think?'

'I think that sounds good and sensible.'

'Joe?'

'Yes?'

'Do you mind if I sort out the other shed? And can I paint it New England Slate Blue?'

'Sure – go ahead.'

'And can I paint your bedroom a warm taupe?'

'Sounds fine to me.'

'And if you're going to be around for the next few days, can I introduce you properly to Lisa?'

'Sure.'

'But you'll have to go off again, mid-week, will you?'

'Yes, I will.'

'But then, you'd be back here a week later – and you could stay home for a little while?'

'That's right.'

'Joe?'

'Yes?'

'Shall I let you go to sleep now?'

Chapter Forty

Joe left, telling Tess that if he just did another week or so abroad, he'd be able to work from home for at least a fortnight before a trip to the US. She'd said, go! go right away – go tonight! But he'd stayed in Saltburn for an extra day before leaving for France and Tess filled his time. He met Lisa properly and helped Tess lug stuff out of the sheds. He fixed the squeaky wheel on the buggy and took her to the Transporter Bridge in daylight. They crossed the river and came back via the Newport Bridge. She called it a thunkingly ugly green hulk of a thing, so he stopped the car and explained how it had worked and he changed her opinion by the time they were on their way again. He told her about Captain Cook and she listened intently. She told him about the Citizens Advice Bureau and he offered to have Emmeline. He took a series of photos of all of them and printed them off. With a sly smile, he put the one Tess took of him grinning for all he was worth, next to the photograph of him in KL.

SOS, he'd written on the back.

'What do you mean by *that*?' Tess had protested. 'It was a lovely day! You thought it was hysterical I'd come across all your old cross-country trophies in that box in the shed. Why the plea for help?'

'Es. Oh. Es,' Joe had said very slowly. 'Saltburn-on-Sea. Mad woman.'

'But it's Saltburn-*by-the*-Sea.'

'Don't argue, Southerner.'

Tess had bided her time until he was in the garden and so was she and the hose was to hand. 'That,' she said, squirting him smartly between the shoulder blades, '*that's* for SOS.'

'That,' he said, grabbing the hose and squirting her back, 'that's for frightening the dog and the child.'

But when Joe and Tess looked at them, the dog and child were regarding the grown-ups with expressions that acted for their limited language to say, 'Happy you may be – but you two are very peculiar and very wet.'

When Joe had packed to leave, Tess had told him about the letter she'd written to him a lifetime ago four days previously. She'd presented him with the scruff of pages but he'd closed his hand around them, around hers.

'But there's nothing you need to prove to me that I don't already feel.'

'But it's a sort of – love letter.'

He'd smiled. 'I've read it already,' he told her gently, 'I know it off by heart. It's written all over your face.'

She'd looked a bit miffed.

'I will take it now, if you want me to,' he told her. 'Or you could keep it here. Keep it for a time when I piss you off and you doubt what you feel for me. Then you can read it to remind yourself that you loved me.'

'OK,' she shrugged, 'but I'll put it in the toby jug on the dresser for now.'

And there it was, Joe observed as he had a last cup of tea before he left. There it was next to KL with SOS propped against it.

*

417

And here he was in France. Working abroad again, where the pattern of his life, the easy tessellation where all the elements slotted into each other whichever way he looked at them, could so easily have been repeated.

He'd gone directly to site. Progress, since he'd last been there, was pleasing. The great pillars were almost complete and the timing was perfect in terms of weather and the generous amount of daylight in June. The timing wasn't so great when he bumped into Nathalie. She came right between him and the hotel he was headed for across the square.

'I didn't know if you were around,' he said a little lamely.

'Of course I am around,' she said. 'Where else would I be?'

He joined her for a drink because he couldn't find a way to refuse. And then they finished the bottle. And shared another. And then he said he mustn't drink any more on an empty stomach after a long day. And she said she'd already made a cassoulet – it only needed heating up. So Joe found himself where he hadn't intended to be again. And if Nathalie had her way – which in his experience, she usually did – then the cassoulet would not be the only thing heating up in her apartment.

And the pattern would be repeated, all the elements of his life slotting into each other again. So easy. The story of his life, thus far. The habit of a lifetime. Why break the mould?

She snaked her arms around his neck, pushed his legs apart a little so that she could enclose his thigh between hers. He put his hand on her waist because he really wanted to ease her away but when her lips found his and her tongue darted along them, for a split second he pulled her against him. Suddenly, he didn't like the taste. He didn't like the feeling – his cock was hard and he hated it.

It was gone eleven and he thought how home was an hour behind. Back at home, it was still only ten o'clock and none of this had happened yet. The present in England was the past in France. He thought how the present in France would be England's future. But whatever he did, whenever he did it and wherever he was, he couldn't turn back the clock. In the here and now, his hands were still on Nathalie's waist. In the there and now, Tess was at home.

It was time.

Joe pushed Nathalie away.

'What's wrong?'

'Look – I need to talk to you, Nathalie.'

'There is a problem?'

'It's not a problem – actually, it's the opposite. It's the solution. Nathalie – I've found someone – someone I want to be with.'

'I know I am not your only one – but that's OK for me too, you know,' Nathalie said archly.

'I know.' He paused. 'In the past, that's why you and I have been so – good. But it's different now.'

'You have fallen in love?' She sounded incredulous.

'Yes,' said Joe, 'I have fallen in love.'

'She doesn't need to know,' Nathalie shrugged. 'There's no way she can find out. What she cannot know cannot harm.'

Joe shrugged back. 'That's not the point any more.'

'OK. So we fuck now and say goodbye. You can go home and kiss and make up later.' She ran her finger slowly up the shaft of his cock, still hard and delineated behind his trousers. 'No one gets hurt.'

He stepped back and pushed his hands deep into the pockets of his trousers. 'The thing is, Nathalie – for me, it's not about having a secret. It's no longer about getting away with it, it's about not fucking around with what I have.'

She looked confused. 'Love is love, sex is sex – you are a guy. Guys can separate this. That's why you like me so much, because I think like a guy too.'

'You're right – it *is* about love. And it *is* about sex. But

419

it's about not wanting to have secrets from the girl I love who has recently become the only girl I want to have sex with. I'm sorry. Look, I ought to go. I should take my stuff from here, too.'

Nathalie blew through her lips and swept her hand about as if Joe's proclamation was on a par with an annoying fly in the room.

'The hotel is shit – you will have only a small room. Stay here. Stay with me. We don't have to fuck if you say you don't want to.'

Joe knew the hotel wasn't so great – he'd stayed there before he'd met Nathalie.

'No, honestly – it is better for me to stay there. It's where I want to be.'

There was a single bed and it was very hard. Everything else about the hotel room was thin. The walls, the mattress, the towels, the overly-perfumed soap wrapped in waxy paper, the camel-coloured veneer of the bedside unit, the chair, the table, the cupboard. But Joe felt comfortable. He'd give Tess a call in a while but for the moment, he was content to lie on the small bed and let the facelessness of the room serve as a blank canvas for his thoughts.

There had been so many revelations recently for him – bare facts that carried with them great emotional profundity. The details of Tess's dire financial predicament made him long to help her. Hearing the truth about Dick caused him some distress; feelings of intense pity, anger too, but also deep pride for how she'd coped and triumphed. Discovering her visits to Swallows, he'd felt extreme consternation – which he realized only later masked pure fear. And then he'd been able to face that fear head on.

It was this last element that had made Joe feel like a superhero. He had run away – once more repelled from home – and then, in the departure lounge, he had stopped running. Standing waiting to board, he felt the terrible comfort in sensing his own impenetrable metal shutters coming down. It was then that he finally tested his own strength. By returning home, he'd stopped those barriers closing. By opening up, he'd been able to break their mechanism. For the first time ever, he'd entrusted the bare facts of his life to someone else and the reward for doing so was to be given love and support that were as generous and gentle as they were indestructible. And it was only tonight, in France, in the last few hours, that the facts and experiences and emotions of Joe's recent past had collided and enmeshed to give him a new protective armature, a new form, one that was invincible enough to withstand temptation – temptation to run away, temptation to close down, or the temptation of Nathalie and any other Nathalies he might know or yet meet.

The ease of secret sex. He'd always assumed it preferable to the rigmarole of conventional relationships. He thought about this now, as he changed position to lie on his side. You could have what you liked, when you pleased. And he acknowledged that it had provided him with a lot of exciting sex over the years. But it wasn't anything like what he'd experienced with Tess. He could have fucked Nathalie tonight – easily. The invitation had been as flattering as ever, and her later consternation and attempt to emasculate him had been titillating. They could easily have had a fast, violent shag with an explosive come. Tess would never know and never be hurt by it. But he'd know – that was the difference now, for Joe – *he'd know*. And the point he wanted to prove was not to Nathalie that he was the best fuck she'd ever have, nor to himself that he could satiate his needs while hurting no one. Instead, it was now an unspoken point he wanted to make to Tess.

He sat up. He had it.

'It's as if a lack of love made me what I was for the first half of my life. But then love came along and stopped me in my tracks at the age of forty-four and will now shape the last half.'

He walked over to the mirror, edged in thin, fractured veneer.

'If I get to ninety,' he laughed.

His mobile woke him. With a start, he saw that it was seven in the morning and the caller was Tess and he was still wearing his clothes from yesterday. He had fallen dead asleep without phoning her the night before.

'I'm sorry I'm sorry,' he laughed before she had the chance to say anything, 'I was completely and utterly whacked yesterday. I didn't even eat. I had a bottle of wine and I fell asleep on this jail-hard single bed wearing yesterday's clothes. I'll buy you a big present, I promise. I'll scrub all the floors and you can flog me. I'll cook for you seven days in a row, lunch and dinner. I'll be your sex slave until Christmas. Sorry, Tess – I know I said I'd call.'

'Joe? You need to come home. It's your mother.'

*   *   *

When the phone had rung at just before six in the morning at the Resolution, Tess had stayed in bed. She thought, why should I stagger out of bed just because now is a convenient time for Joe to call? The phone rang off and though she listened for a message to be left, it appeared there wasn't one. The phone rang again almost immediately. This time she decided to stomp down and say, oi, mate! Tell him he'd better buy her a great big present, or be her sex slave for the next month or cook all the meals and scrub all the floors until Christmas. On picking up the receiver, she said nothing – she

422

was looking forward to hearing Joe splutter and panic over his apology. She was grinning in anticipation.

'Hullo?'

Oh, but it's not Joe at all. It's a woman.

'Hullo – is Tess there? Or Joe?'

'*Laura?* Is that you?'

'Tess – yes, it's me. It's me. Oh, love – it's Mary. Is Joe there? She's had a stroke. A big one. Is Joe there?'

'Oh, my God. Oh, no. Oh, shit. Oh, shit.'

'Is Joe there, love?'

'No – he's not, Laura, he left for France again yesterday.'

'He needs to know. I could phone him – but perhaps you should?'

'Of course. Of course. I will. That's fine. But Laura – how is Mary?'

'She's very very poorly.'

'But is she going to be OK?'

'I don't think so, Tess. No – I don't think she is.'

Tess had kept Laura on the phone long enough only for the essential details. Then she phoned Joe.

Chapter Forty-one

'What a day, Tess, what a day. She's gone – and I keep saying to myself that I'm pleased for her sake that she's gone. They said she wouldn't pull through. I'm pleased for her that she didn't have to live with further decimation of herself. And, selfishly, that I didn't have to experience it or cope with it. They told me she wouldn't have known a thing really – and that's the way to go, isn't it? After all, she always seemed unhappy in this life, Tess, and that's no way to live, is it?

'I'm very tired and totally poleaxed, really – but underneath the rawness of the more immediate, reactive emotions I reckon a sense of relief will be what lasts. My sense of relief both for her and for myself.

'Today was the day I watched my mother die. This time yesterday she was alive – in fact, let me see, just four hours ago she was alive. And now she'd gone. I saw my mother alive – and I saw her dead – all today. This morning I was in a hotel in France, this afternoon I was in a hospital in Middlesbrough and now I'm back home in Saltburn, in the house I grew up in, sitting next to you in the garden of my childhood home. I used to have dens in this garden. I'd spend

424

hours in those dens – they were just glorified spaces amongst the shrubs. But they were my boltholes.

'It all seems a bit unreal. When people ask me from now on, I'll have to say my parents are not alive, they are dead. Does that make me an orphan, Tess? Or am I too old to be an orphan?'

'I don't remember feeling like this when my father died, though. No sense of relief back then. I had my mother to cope with – I remember having to do a lot of tongue-biting as I mopped up all her displaced grief. I don't know if it was guilt or a twisted love that had existed between them but she did take his death badly. Predictably, she took it out on me too. She was very embittered, poor old thing. What a life, hey, to be weighted down by so much that was so negative. She never really got over it. It certainly didn't bring us closer. Nor did her illness – her first stroke. All that brought closer was senility. We've always been – distant. We remained that way until the end. No last words, Tess, none at all.

'It's silly. It's daft. It's stupid – but do you know something? As I was driving to the hospital I was imagining what if, what if I go in there and I take her hand and she stirs from her state and for a moment there *is* recognition? While I drove, I spun it out – and that tiny what-if became the stuff of Hollywood in my head. I saw myself going into the room and everyone would leave and I'd be by her bedside and I'd say, "Mum, Mum, it's me, it's Joe." And suddenly her fingers would twitch and I'd take her hand and she'd close her fingers around mine and she'd murmur, "Joe, Joe, is that you? Is that Joe? Oh, son – oh, son."

'Something like that. Stupid, really, isn't it.

'But it enabled me to drive, to get there in one piece and in time.

'But she wasn't in a room; she was on a ward – a small one – with the curtains drawn right around her bed. I sat

425

and I touched and I spoke – I did say, "Mum, it's Joe" – but there was nothing. The doctor told me when I arrived there was nothing to be done; whenever a nurse came in they'd put a hand on my shoulder with a kindly "not long now" expression. I know that stuff about hearing being the last sense to go but I don't think she was there at all, Tess. And when she died, it wasn't just her and me; there were two nurses too. And there was a bizarre wait – a sort of hiatus between life and death during which I thought, has she? hasn't she? My heart started to race a little at that point. They did lots of checking of pulses and then they gave me a long, sympathetic nod and some more shoulder touching and then they left me alone. I don't actually know precisely when she went.

'And when I was alone in there, I kept wanting to say, "Mum?" out loud – just to check. But I couldn't do that, could I? That would have been crazy. And not fair on the other poorly people around. But I did put my hand over hers and I was pleased it was warm still. I found that surprisingly comforting. I also liked it that her face was actually peaceful too. Like I've never seen it before – not once. Peaceful that it's done, it's over. She looked happy to go.

'Wolf made her happy, though. And do you know something – well, I'm sure you do, I hope you do – Emmeline brought her happiness too. When I went to Swallows last time – Christ, was it really so recently as that – she didn't know you when I asked her but she volunteered information about the baby the beautician brings with her. And her eyes did brighten, Tess, and her smile lasted. And she referred to Emmeline by name.

'But God, Tess, the time she spent with Wolf or with Emmeline – it could only amount to a handful of hours. That's not a lot of respite from seventy-five seemingly miserable years, is it?

426

'I didn't think she'd go. Not this year. Not next. I didn't really think about it or wonder. I was used to my image of her as a steely old battleaxe.

'My father looked dreadful dead.

'My mother looked good – she looked better. As if death had released her and had made her feel better.

'I hope so.

'What a life. A sad, complicated one.

'I've seen, first hand, that where there is no love, there's only loneliness and discontent.

'I don't want that for myself.

'I'm glad that my life is nothing like hers. I hope she'd be glad for me too.'

Tess and Joe are sitting on the backless bench in the garden. Joe is facing one direction, Tess the other. Their bodies are close, side by side, their arms are linked. He's talked and she's listened, her head sometimes resting against his shoulder.

'And you, Joe,' Tess ventures, 'how are *you* doing?'

The light is failing now but they both feel they could sit here all night. They might do just that.

'I think I'm OK, Tess. I think so. When I was a kid I used to fantasize about them dying, then I could go and live by the Golden Gate Bridge. It wasn't so much the bridge that captivated me as the name – I heard the words "golden gate" as symbolic for the way through to a new life. When I was a teenager I used to think darkly, "I won't be sorry when you two are gone." Then when I left home, it was a struggle to remind myself to visit, that they were getting old.

'So here I am and how do I feel? How do I feel on the day my mother died? I don't know. I don't know. I think I'm still pumped with adrenalin. My mother – Mary Saunders née Holt – died today. Aged seventy-five. On the twentieth of June. Born December sixteenth. Died June twentieth. Rest

427

in Peace. Peace on earth is certainly something she didn't have, Tess. Mostly, when I saw her, I was aware of that fact. I found the times when she was away with the fairies easier – even though it was less real and pretty depressing.

'But to answer you straight? I feel sad – I feel a little lost – because I'll be burying my mother next to my father and what I'll mourn for my mother is what I mourned for with my father – for what they never were to me.'

*　　*　　*

On the day of the funeral, Tess went to Swallows as usual in the morning. Joe asked her if she'd mind leaving Emmeline with him.

'I could stay too,' she told him, 'if you'd like the company.'

'You can't do that,' Joe said, 'they're expecting you. They'll want their nails nice – for this afternoon. For my mum.'

'She was a funny one, wasn't she,' Mrs Corper said to no one in particular as Tess buffed her nails. 'But she did love Emmeline,' she said to Tess.

Laura caught up with Tess as she made to leave. 'Joe all right – for this afternoon, like?' she asked. She looked troubled, which was an expression Tess had never seen in Laura. 'Tess – I wish I could say that she left letters and diaries and whatnots, but she didn't.' It was as if Laura felt it was she who'd failed in some way.

'Silly,' Tess said soothingly.

'But she did, once or twice, say something about Joe.'

'Oh?'

Laura shrugged unhappily. 'Once or twice she talked about him. And those times she called him "Joe, dear little Joe". She looked ever so sad, though.'

'What did she say – do you remember?'

'Both times she said something like, "What a life he's made." I'm pretty sure those were her words – or very close. I wish now I'd drawn a little more out – but you know me, always bustling about for smiles and happy stuff.' She paused. 'I feel I've let Joe down, now.'

'Don't be daft, Laura.'

'Do you think he'd like me to tell him? What do you think, Tess – you know him best.'

Tess stood on the steps of Swallows thinking about Joe. Joe currently at home with Emmeline and Wolf. She thought back to all he'd said that night on the bench after Mary's passing. It seemed to Tess that actually, here was a man who'd somehow been able to rise above resentment or cynicism to become positive about the role of love in life. All the unhappiness and loneliness he'd experienced he'd overcome to be accepting of a sorry past and that it needn't sour his own future. So, did she think Joe would want to know that once or twice his estranged mother had referred to him as 'Joe, dear little Joe', that she'd all but acknowledged the life he had made all by himself? That in spite of the impression she gave to the contrary she was actually very proud of him?

'I don't know, Laura.'

They thought about it quietly.

Laura looked at her feet. 'I hope Mary wouldn't mind me saying so, but she had ample opportunity to call him "dear" to his face – and to give the compliment to him herself.'

Tess touched Laura's arm. 'Joe said something really moving on the night Mary died. He said how he'd seen, first hand, that where there is no love, there's only loneliness and discontent. He said how he does not want that for himself.'

Laura nodded thoughtfully.

'If you're asking me, Laura, I would probably say that Joe would not benefit from hearing about what Mary said to you. I think he had worked her out and he worked out how

429

he felt about their relationship. To me, he's a very grounded man because he's figured out for himself that it is best to have something good, something happy, come from something not so good.'

'We put manure down for the roses,' Laura said, looking out at the bushes full of fat creamy roses in the garden. 'See – that's something lovely that comes from plain shit.'

Tess burst out laughing. 'Oh, Laura, I do love you,' she said and she really meant it, Laura could tell.

'See you this afternoon, pet,' Laura said. 'We'll give Mary a good send-off.' She became teary. 'She was an awkward old mare, but I did like her.'

＊　　＊　　＊

'Dead and buried, hey,' Joe says, 'gone but not forgotten.'

The funeral had been straightforward; dignified, not too long and quietly sad. Laura was there, as was the matron of Swallows. Four of the residents came as well as a few elderly people from town.

Joe and Tess are home now. He is surprisingly hungry, even after the sandwiches and the cakes at gone tea-time after the funeral. He's polished off the sausage, mash and beans that Tess has made him and she's passing her plate over for him to finish.

'It was a nice service,' she says.

'Do you think I should have spoken?'

'That's personal, isn't it?' says Tess. 'I wanted to speak at my grandma's funeral but everyone said it was for my mother to do, not me. Only she ended up not saying anything. And I had so much to say. But I liked the vicar today. And he knew your mother well. It's a lovely church too. I love it that they have those two resident sheep to keep the grass down.'

Tess goes to the fridge and finds yoghurt and fresh fruit

and she brings these over for Joe. She cuts a slice from the sponge cake they found on the doorstep when they came home. Lisa had left it, with a sympathy card for Joe that was now with the others, on the Welsh dresser on the shelf below the KL and SOS photos.

'God, what a week,' he says, 'what a week.'

'Can you take some time off work? Will you?'

'I suppose so,' Joe spoons yoghurt thoughtfully. 'Actually, do you know something, Tess, I'm going to. I'll take a week – maybe longer. I'd just really like to have a rest, actually. Do the walks and the picnics and the ice creams and the weekly shop and the bath-times. To be right here – with you and Wolf and Emmeline.'

Chapter Forty-two

Tess had made a picnic lunch. Another one. For the week that Joe had stayed home, the weather had been far too good to squander with meals indoors. Though the garden was at its most beautiful and lush, its place in their lives was restricted to long mornings and evenings. Middays, however, were for going further afield with lunch for four and a picnic blanket rolled into a rucksack which Joe happily hoicked. They didn't venture too far – sticking to the meadows, the woods, the cliff, the pier. There were two reasons for this. Firstly, the aftermath for Joe from Mary's death and funeral was an unexpected tiredness coupled with a need for a gentle routine. Secondly, town at the moment was a fun place to be.

Visitors were swelling Saltburn's ranks every afternoon in addition to each weekend and the local tradespeople used this to their advantage: the shops and stalls presented a plethora of wares, colourful and crammed window displays, and town was awash with vibrant hanging baskets and a flourish of leaflets. There were queues for the cliff lift and the miniature train; there were lines of people of all ages salivating for a milkshake or ice cream. It was frying time from sun up until sun down at the fish and chip kiosk and the unmistakable seaside scents of malt vinegar and candyfloss magnetized passers-by. Swimmers and surfers bobbed in the sea like pink gulls, pony trekkers mooched up and down the beach and school leavers lounged about the sand either fully clothed or else practically naked, all nodding in varying tempos to the joys of their MP3s. The elderly, whether townsfolk or visitors, were granted long hours in the fresh air to people-watch. Elsewhere, in the residential streets came enticing wafts from many a barbeque and homeowners were to be seen manicuring their front gardens or just sitting and enjoying their vistas with a glass of wine or a cup of tea with friends or neighbours. The traffic increased, undoubtedly, but so did the good spirits of the place. The car parks were full; a massed glinting of multi-coloured metal; boots wide open while a fidget of wet dogs and barefooted children were towelled off.

'It's a great time of year to be a local, isn't it,' Joe remarked. They'd had their lunch by the river and had decided to stroll to the front for a *frappé* before returning home. Tess, busy saying hullo to various people, linked arms with Joe to agree. She queued with Wolf and the empty buggy while Joe let Emmeline lead him to where she'd been pointing with great conviction.

'Where are they, Wolf?'

It was surprisingly difficult handling three cups of cold liquid when a medley of scents lured the dog in various directions.

'Oh, look – there they are. Wolf! Heel, you mad dog.'

Em was beaming.

'Hope you don't mind,' said Joe. 'It wasn't expensive – and it was the one she wanted.'

Em was brandishing a bucket-and-spade set, emblazoned with Spider-Man.

'Seems she's fickle in love, your daughter,' Joe said. 'She didn't give the Iggle Piggle bucket and spade more than a passing glance.'

Tess stared at him. 'How do you know about Iggle Piggle?'

'Emmeline introduced me – quite some time ago.'

They sipped their drinks walking along the lower promenade; stopping to watch a juggler do a bad job and a fire-eater do a good job.

'So Emmeline,' Joe said, 'what are you going to do with your bucket and spade?'

Emmeline shook her new present in reply. The items were still encased in lurid green netting.

'Want to build a sandcastle?' Joe asked. 'I'm king of the sandcastle, little rascal.'

Tess knew what was coming. She thought of the letter rolled up in the toby jug in the kitchen.

'Coming to the beach, then, Tess?' Joe asked as if he'd suggested nothing more controversial than a cup of tea at precisely the appropriate time.

'Not today,' Tess replied quickly and she walked on ahead though well aware that Joe and Em and Wolf had all stopped.

'Why not?' he called after her.

She stopped, but did not turn to face them. She concentrated hard on the three huge iron ammonite sculptures mounted on the wall.

'You live beside the sea,' she could hear Joe say. 'Your daughter would love the beach. Why do you hate it so?'

She could see the chimneys of Redcar in the distance, a similar fug filling her mind as billowed out from them.

They had caught up with her, she could sense them just footsteps away.

'Why do you hate it so?' he was asking her kindly but her heart was racing and tears were smarting and if there hadn't been so many people around she might well have turned on her heels and run away.

'What's wrong with the beach, Tess? Why won't you go on it? Look at it – it's beautiful.'

She was paralysed to the spot. But Joe didn't mind, he walked right round in front of her and put his hands on her shoulders.

'Tess? Can't you talk to me – can't you tell me why you hate it?' Wolf and Em had joined him. They were all looking at her intently. And then, it lifted – the pall that had rested heavy over her since she was eight years old disappeared in much the same way that the sun can make a previously enveloping sea fret evaporate within moments. Something far stronger flittered it away into nothing.

I *can* tell them, Tess thought, looking at the three of them. Here is my family and look at them – ready to listen, wanting to help.

Tess glanced at the beach and then she looked from Wolf to Em, finally fixing on Joe. In her peripheral vision, she was aware that people were having to walk right round them, that hand-holding teenagers or arms-linked pensioners had to let go briefly to skirt around them before rejoining.

'I don't hate the beach,' Tess told Joe, 'I'm scared of it.'

Of course his response was, but why? However, Tess felt compelled to make a point strongly before finally, at long last, she could give her reason.

'Do you remember telling me how you didn't tell anyone – about the stuff that went on at home? You said, *I couldn't say anything to anyone because I knew no one would believe me?* Something bad happened – and you couldn't tell anyone about it?'

Joe nodded.

'Well, something bad happened to me, Joe – and I told everyone and no one believed me,' Tess said.

'Jesus, Tess – what happened?'

He couldn't imagine.

And when she told him, he thought to himself, bloody hell, you couldn't make that one up.

'I found a hand, Joe,' she said. 'I found a hand on the beach.'

'You found a *what*?'

'I found a hand on the beach. It was in seaweed. Near the shoreline. It was the last family holiday we had before we fragmented. I had been sent off to look for crabs – I thought my parents were suggesting something nice to do; actually they were packing me off because they weren't talking to each other and I don't think they could handle having all my noisy joys of the seaside in such close proximity. So they said, go and search for crabs, Tess. Take your bucket with you. I joined my sister but she was looking for perfect shells and she didn't want me getting in the way so she told me to go off, go over there, where the seaweed is. That, she said, is where crabs like to be. So I went over there and I dug around a bit in the sand and I shifted the weeds around with my foot. I couldn't find any crabs. It was an overcast day – headachy weather and actually, it wasn't a very nice beach. It was in Norfolk somewhere, I forget the name. There was the odd coke can and bottle and jag of plastic in and amongst the seaweed. And there was a hand. I was looking for crabs, Joe – but I lifted up a clump of seaweed with my toes and I found a hand.'

'What the fuck did you do?' Joe looked appalled.

'I didn't scream. I kept saying to myself, scream, scream – get the grown-ups. But my scream was inward – I was physically incapable of making a sound. I was held captive by that hand, terrified into silence. It looked rubbery and grey but I knew it wasn't grey rubber. It was as if it had physically grabbed me tight and wasn't letting go of me, I

436

couldn't free myself from the grip of the hand I found on the beach.'

'Jesus *Christ*, Tess.'

'And the moment the horror of it released me – the moment my voice came through – was precisely the moment that my father bellowed for me. I ran to them, panting and sobbing. They were all together by the time I got there – my parents, my sister with all her pretty shells. I was pointing to where it was and I was telling them, there's a hand, there's a hand, a dead hand in the seaweed. There are no crabs.'

'What did they do?' Joe's incredulity butted in.

'Nothing. They didn't believe me. Unlike you, I thought – deludedly – that if I told them, of course they'd believe me – they'd help, they'd do something.'

'Why the hell didn't they?'

'Because, Joe, then as now they were wrapped up in themselves. They'd obviously had some flaming row and we all had to frogmarch off the beach in time to their temper. Stop crying, they kept telling me. You can go crabbing another time, they said. But I saw a hand, I sobbed. Oh, for God's sake, they said, that child!'

She paused. Joe saw her glance out to the beach, wide and golden, at Saltburn. He followed her eyes. There was little seaweed with today's tide, though there was some, lying in straggly lines a few yards from the water.

'I don't know, Joe,' she said and she sounded so forlorn. 'Over the years, I've wondered if I imagined it. But of course I know I didn't. I don't know the story behind the hand but I've always hoped that the family of that person didn't need to know about it. I hope I don't hold the key to some dreadful mystery, some unsolved crime or some terrible tragedy. I used to go to bed at night and pray: please let the rest of that person wash up nicely so that at least they are found and the missing hand won't matter to anyone but me.'

437

'Christ, I'm so sorry, Tess – I didn't mean to trivialize your phobia. I just had no idea it was anything as hideous. I would never have come up with *that*.'

She shrugged. 'I know it makes me a rubbish mother to deny my child a romp along the sand – a paddle and a wade.' She paused, then she looked at him. 'But you know something, Joe – in a similar way to you coming round to me visiting Swallows, so I'm happy for you to take my place on the beach with Em. I know you've done so already. I didn't mind that you didn't say. I saw the sand in her nappy that day. It was in her room too. I tried to sweep it up. Most went through the gaps in the floorboards.'

Joe thought about this.

'OK,' he said, 'if you're happy for me to do so, then OK.' They walked back along the promenade until they came to the cobbled ramp down to the beach. Tess ground to a halt. Em had been holding her hand and Joe's. Tess wriggled from the clasp of her daughter's fist.

'Off you go, baby girl,' she said. 'Joe's going to build sandcastles on the beach with you and Wolf will probably demolish them.'

Joe looked at Emmeline a little sadly. 'Say, bye bye, Mummy,' he said. 'Mummy's going home to make you your tea.'

They parted, Tess pushing the empty buggy inland.

'Tess!'

Was that Joe? Did he just call? She wasn't sure – there was such a joyous cacophony coming from the sands already.

'Tess!'

That *was* him.

She turned. He was waving. He was beckoning. She retraced her steps. She came to the railings. She recalled her first morning in Saltburn, when Joe had shown her around town and had taken Wolf for a blast on the beach and she'd stood

438

at these very railings calling him, mortified that she had no money to buy the bread and milk like she said she would. When was that? Last year? The year before? A lifetime ago? It was earlier this year, Tess, when winter was becoming spring. About three or four months ago, that's all.

Wolf was bounding between the latticework of the legs of the pier trestles. Em, it appeared, was eating sand off the spade. Joe was walking over to her; turning every few steps to walk backwards so he could check on Wolf and Emmeline. Tess held onto the railings, looking down at him.

'Tess,' he said, squinting at her. He was slightly breathless. 'Tess.'

He sucked his lip pensively.

'Tess, let *me* hold *your* hand. Look – you don't have to if you don't want to but if you do feel you are able, you don't have to go any further than you feel comfortable.' But she stayed clinging to the railings.

'This is our life, here,' Joe said, 'this is our playground. This is where Emmeline will grow up – healthy and fit, her skin kissed by the sun, the sea breeze in her hair.' Cautiously, Tess took one hand away and Joe gently reached up for it.

'Please join us, *please*.' He didn't pull and she didn't move. 'You can trust me, Tess. It is my mission to keep you happy – and safe. And not just on beaches.'

Gradually, she let go with the other hand which Joe slowly reached up to take.

'That was your "then", Tess – this is our "now".'

He glanced quickly over his shoulder. Dog was fine. Child was fine. 'I just want us to discover and share the many things that can make us happy which previously we'd been conditioned to believe would make us miserable.'

Slowly, she pulled one hand away from him but she didn't back off. While she held his other, she descended the slope as if it was treacherous with black ice though the sun was beating down from a cloudless sky.

'Beaches. Love. Money. Family. Dogs. Kids – neither of us need fear these things a moment longer, Tess.'

She took her first steps onto sand in almost quarter of a century. At first, it felt like she was walking on shattered glass though she was wearing trainers. Joe had not let go of her hand and now his other arm was around her waist, his hip pressed against hers, his lips close to her forehead.

And it occurred to Tess that Joe was the only person she'd ever told about all of this and not only did he believe her, he was actually as appalled as she had been. More, he felt for her, he'd taken on her pain. Best of all, he wanted to show her that she could feel much, much better because he carried the cure.

'You OK?'

It was Tess who asked this question of Joe.

'Very OK,' he said.

*　　*　　*

That night, tucked into Joe for *News at Ten*, Tess looked up at him when the programme ended and, with the volume muted, Joe was flicking through channels.

'I feel like I've climbed some mountain, or run a marathon, or taken all my exams again – I'm exhausted,' she said.

He looked down at her. 'I guess rampant sex is off the menu, then?'

She punched his chest with mock indignation but he caught her fist and said, I know what you mean, I know how it must feel – it was your own personal challenge and boy, did you triumph.

'Next time,' he said, 'next time we may get you taking your shoes *off*. And if I'm very lucky, it won't be long before

440

you're prancing through the surf to me in a minuscule bikini.'
He had a tight hold of her hand. She wouldn't have punched
him anyway – she loved what he just said and she thought,
yes, maybe.

'Tess?'

'Yes?'

'That explains the beach,' he said, 'I now know the reason.
But what about your fear of heights? *I don't do beaches and
I don't do heights* is one of your mantras. What happened
up high? You didn't find a leg on some twenty-first-floor
balcony, did you? A severed foot on top of a mountain?'

Her laughter was a relief for Joe to hear – his blunt approach
had been a calculated risk.

'No,' she said, 'no leg. No foot.' She paused. 'But an ear.'

'A *what?*'

'My ear.' She sat upright and stroked gently where her
cheek met her left ear. 'I burst my ear drum when I was in
my early twenties – I had a really bad middle-ear infection.
Ever since then, I've had distorted balance – vertigo, I suppose.
That's why I don't do heights. I *can't.*' She thought about it.
'Or depths, for that matter, for the same reason. So don't
take me diving when you whisk me off on our luxury tropical
honeymoon.'

Joe thought about it. 'Are you going to marry me then?'

Tess didn't have to think about it. 'It depends,' she said.

'On what?' he said.

'On whether you ask nicely.'

Chapter Forty-three

And so a beautiful summer, whose seeds were sown earlier in the spring, remained in constant bloom for Joe and Tess. For Wolf, the combination of warmth and seawater – now that Tess was prepared to explore the beach – aided an almost complete recovery. He looked odd without his tail – but he'd looked odd with it. He'd always have a slight stilt to his gait, but it wasn't really noticeable on account of the movement from the shreds and tassels and stringy swings of his coat. And anyway, a familiar section of Saltburn society had a certain stiffness or wobble to their limbs too – the elderly and the toddlers. It was the people in between who cared for both ends of the age spectrum in town: just regular folk like Laura and the other care workers, like Lisa and Tess and the other local mums.

Joe continued to travel for work but ensured he was never away for more than ten days at a time. He liked the home-comings – the discordant thrill voiced by Tess, Wolf and Emmeline simultaneously, the physical challenge of them all clambering over him, the way Tess laid claim to his kisses because she could reach whereas Emmeline had to tug at his trouser leg and Wolf could only head butt his waist. He liked how, after a day's excitable chatter and frantic, realigning sex, he and Tess settled into their dynamic.

'It's always like the start of a three-legged race, the first day I'm back,' he told her on one occasion. 'All over the place at first – and then we fall into step with one another. And we could walk that way for miles.'

But they didn't walk for miles. They stayed close to home. They threw an extravagant barbeque in the garden, which provided lunch, tea and supper (or dinner, tea and teas according to everyone apart from Tess) for everyone they knew.

'I didn't know you could be so sociable,' Tess said to Joe while they were clearing up at gone midnight.

'I didn't know you could scrub up so well,' he said to her, holding her fingertips and making her twirl under his arm so he could admire the pale-patterned cotton halterneck dress he'd bought for her on his recent trip to America.

Their hospitality was reciprocated with dinner in Stokesley at Andy's. The deep creases in Tess's finances were now in the very slow process, but steady progress, of being ironed out.

'Why not make like a supermarket?' Andy suggested much to Tess and Joe's initial bewilderment. 'You know, buy one get one free?'

'Buy what?'

'Your services, Tess. I know you say you want to work voluntarily – but until you're in the black you can't afford to raise suspicion. So why not charge for one session and do the other for free?'

'And please *please* consider a little freelance pampering,' Andy's wife said. 'There are plenty of us who'd gladly come to *you* for a facial, or for fingers or toes.'

'You know,' said Joe, 'you could make it even easier by inviting them to bring their own preferred products and giving them a pretend discount for doing so. Then you'd have no outlay costs at all.'

She ate her pudding while mulling over the advice, then she turned to Andy's wife.

'It's funny, isn't it,' Tess said, 'you don't work either, do you? But you did – didn't you say you were something in publishing?'

'Once upon a long long time ago,' she laughed.

'But that's part of my point – it's odd, isn't it, that with the emancipation that feminism brought, women had the choice to work rather than the confines of being just homemakers and child-raisers. But there's a strange backlash – our generation feels obliged to work. We feel guilty if we don't – so we must juggle home and kids so that we can work too. Too often we're made to feel we're wasting ourselves if we don't go back to work whether we need to financially or not. The craft of homemaking and the art of child-raising has been demoted. They're not considered much of a career. I dispute that.'

'I agree,' said Andy. 'I worried about her giving up her job when the kids came along – but then I thought, if she says it's what she wants and if she's as good at making a career at home as she was in her industry then she'll be just as much of a success.'

'I will work,' Tess looked at Andy and Joe, 'because I want to set things straight, settle my debts, close my current account with the past. I'm honest and I want my pride back. But actually, since living here, I've come to realize that I really like being a home bird and I'm really good at it. I never thought how utterly fulfilling I'd find it.' She paused. 'I want to learn by my mother's example – and work my damnedest to do everything completely differently for me and Em.'

'And me,' Joe said to her when they set off for home that night.

'And you what?'

'You said, when you compared yourself to your mother, that you wanted to do everything differently for yourself and Emmeline.' He paused. 'You forgot to add me to the end of the sentence.'

'Actually,' said Tess, 'I ballsed up that sentence completely. What I meant to say was *we*. *We* want to do everything completely differently from the examples we were set.'

'Ah,' said Joe.

'Just a slip of the tongue,' said Tess and she put her hand on his leg and left it there all the way back to Saltburn.

* * *

Summer eased into autumn, visitors still came down Saltburn Bank on sunny days in September but when it was overcast or rainy the locals had their town to themselves. The cliff lift and the miniature railway followed their low-season timetable and some of the kiosks along the parade began slowly to batten down their hatches for the year. People still came to surf and Seb was still there to loan out boards and wetsuits and training. He came across Tess on the beach one day. He noticed Wolf first, stilled his board and sank his body down into the water to rub the sea salt from his eyes and check that Wolf's dog walker was who he thought it was. He'd come from the sea looking half human half seal in his wetsuit, all slinky black. She'd seen him on his board; she was with Joe that day. For a moment, she hoped Seb wouldn't notice her but when he gave her his expansive wave, she waved back. Who's that? Joe asked. Oh, that's Seb from the Surf Shop, Tess told him. Is there anyone in this town you don't know? Joe asked though he remembered now how Seb had come up to the house. But Tess just laughed while Seb walked towards him.

'Now here's a sight I didn't think I'd see,' Seb said as he approached. He turned to Joe. 'How did you manage that, mate? Tess – on the beach?'

'Hard cash,' said Joe.

'Come on, Tess,' Seb said, 'what'll it take to get you up on a board?'

'Do they do wetsuits in pink?'

Joe and Seb looked at her in disbelief until she winked at both of them and changed her answer to, 'Only a bloody miracle.'

As October approached, the shops tempered their window displays; a couple of businesses closed for the season, a couple of others closed down to change hands before the next one. Tess felt that it was the townsfolk who were being provided for and prioritized once more; the tourist industry was in semi-hibernation. The hanging baskets in the Italian Gardens were removed, the decorative stone pillars from which they had swung in such a glorious profusion of colour now stood bare and plain. The beds were turned and bulbs were planted for the spring. The nature centre closed its decorative iron gates and Wol looked like he needed a lick of paint. It was as if all the activities of the summer had taken their toll on his shorts, much as had he been a real ranger and not a wooden cut-out. Tess still referred to him as Wol though Em was now happy to call him Owl.

She was now working five mornings a week – three paid, two voluntary. There were five different playgroups and singing groups that Em could attend. Tess dropped her off and Em was happy to be chaperoned by Lisa who herself was more than happy to take the job because Tess paid her with a treatment of her choice. Consequently, Lisa had the nicest nails in town and her skin was radiant. Tess did four or five private treatments a week, either when Em was having a nap or in the early evening. She'd started to provide a glass of wine for her private clients and sometimes they'd phone and ask if they could bring a friend. A glass of wine and a giggle. They'd sit and sip and gossip while Tess did their fingers or toes. And she thought to herself that the only difference between these ladies and her pensioners was simply a few decades in age. It was lucrative and because it was lucrative, it was enjoyable and Tess thought to herself that life seemed good. For the first time, she found balance between what she wanted to do and what she could do.

She'd had one blazing row with Joe when he'd given her an envelope full of cash, telling her it was for August.

'I don't want you to pay me any more,' she said.

'That was the deal,' he said. 'Nothing's changed apart from the fact that I fell in love with my stroppy house-sitter.'

'Right. Fine. I'll pay you rent, then.'

'Bollocks you will, Tess. If you think about it, you're using less now than before. We're in the same bed, woman – that halves the amount of laundry and it's one less room to heat and sometimes, when I'm lucky, you sneak into the shower with me and that means we've saved on the hot water too.' He'd paused and observed her silently rummaging around for an objection. 'Makes me think I should have slept with my other house-sitters,' he said.

The glint in her eye belied the attempt she was making with her mouth not to smile but still she looked at the money unhappily.

'Look, Tess – how about this? How about I put the monthly wage into a separate bank account with Emmeline as beneficiary? Would you allow me to do that? It would be in my name – in case there's any problem if we were to set one up with your name. But I'll give you the card and the pin number and that way, what you need for Emmeline can come out of that money.'

Tess took a while to digest the concept.

Joe thought, oh God, I didn't mean to make her cry.

He needed to take his calculated risk with bluntness again.

'I mean, poor little fatherless mite,' he said.

This didn't stop Tess crying but it did make her hug him and thank him and tell him that Em was so lucky to have a man like him in her life.

October came.

The month arrived on a Thursday and it brought with it the greatest shock of Tess's life. She'd been at Swallows in the morning, had collected Em from Lisa's and was walking home, jabbering to Em about the afternoon's plans though her daughter was on the cusp of nodding off.

As she approached home, something in her peripheral vision struck her as odd. Something had changed since this morning. Something was different. She couldn't work out at first whether something had been added or taken away. Had the council come and trimmed the verges? Had a neighbouring house had its window frames freshly painted? Was that gate over there always that colour?

No.

No.

Yes.

And then she saw it. The sight paralysed her. She remained stock-still with shock and abject horror. Then, she ran and as she did she shouted, no! no! no! and she wasn't aware that the buggy was careening about with her daughter rudely awoken and now crying.

For Sale

For Sale

There were two estate agents' boards either side of the gate to the Resolution. And both of them were emblazoned with *For Sale*.

*　　*　　*

Tess was beside herself. She didn't know what to do. She paced the entrance hall in the way Wolf did when a bluebottle flew in.

'It must be a mistake!' she cried. But she thought to herself how one errant board might be a mistake, but two of them couldn't be. Phone and check, she chanted to herself, phone and check.

Em and Wolf were banished to the sitting room with rice cakes and the TV. Tess ran out of the house with a biro and scribbled the telephone numbers down onto her arm. She told herself to steady her voice; she told herself to calm down, she told herself not to worry. She told herself no bloody way could this be true. She sat down by the phone then stood up, sat down again and dialled.

'There's a *For Sale* sign outside my house!' she cried. 'What's it doing there? Come and take it down!'

They asked for the address.

'But madam,' they then said, 'your house came on the market today.'

Word for word, the response from the other agents was the same.

Phone Joe.

Why doesn't he answer?

Because he's in bloody America and it's however many hours behind.

She went outside and physically shook the stakes of the boards but they were wired tight against the gateposts.

She looked up at them and felt them glowering down on her like a pair of hostile eyes. All her plans for the afternoon were scrapped. No way was she leaving the house – no *way*. She didn't dare – who knows what would happen next if she did. Removal vans? Changed locks? This couldn't be happening.

'Hullo?'

'The house! The house!' Her voice came through hoarse and manic.

'Tess?'

'What are you *doing*? What are you thinking? The house!'

'Christ – it's the first of October today, isn't it?'

'There are two *For Sale* signs outside, Joe.'

'I know.'

'Tell them to take them down!' She was shouting.

'Take them *down*?'

'The Resolution isn't for sale!' Her voice suggested that the concept was not just ludicrous, but heinous.

'Pet, it is. It is. It was a decision I had to make and I had to make it on my own. I don't want you thinking I've been devious. I know it's a big deal for you – but it's a bigger deal for me and I had to keep it secret until I was absolutely sure, until it was all official. I meant to tell you today before the signs went up – of course I did. But I forgot about my trip and I forgot about the bloody time difference and for that I am truly, truly sorry.'

'Joe, *no*. Please no.'

'Listen. *Listen.* My mother's will. The house is mine now. I love you, Tess, I love how at home you've made me feel in a house that I hated.'

'You've told me I've made it your home.'

'Spiritually, yes. But physically, it's still a place I don't like.'

'Joe, no. Please! *Please*. It's *my* home. I've made it my home.'

450

'My home is with you, Tess.'

'That's just fluffy semantics, Joe.'

'No, it is not.' Now he was indignant. 'I mean it. Will you listen – just for a moment? My needs are actually little different to yours. I found you – or you found me. And, like you, I want our future to close the door on our pasts. I want to lay foundations with you. And I'm looking forward to that being done somewhere new, somewhere ours, somewhere for us to raise our family.'

'But I can *do* it.' Tess was crying now. 'We'll completely reconfigure the layout – we'll get proper *professional* decorators in. An *architect*. We'll pave the driveway and change the gate. Rip out the old kitchen. Have a new front door.'

'Stop it!' he shouted and it silenced her. When he spoke again, it was with a voice she had never heard before.

'It's still That House. It always will be. Though I've loved playing home with you I have to tell you that sometimes I lie awake while you sleep. I cuddle up next to you, I hide behind you, because though the secrets are out, there are still ghosts there that haunt me.'

She'd never heard him say anything like it. His voice was forlorn, stripped. She'd had no idea. And suddenly, she hated to think that she'd slept through such moments.

'I know you love the place,' Joe said, 'because it means something so profound to you. It's as if it's your first home. The walls protected you, enabled you to come out of your shell and it provided a base from which you felt safe enough to confront the big bad world that had chased you up to the Resolution in the first place. You found your feet there, didn't you? You found your métier – not as house-sitter but as talented homemaker. But Tess, you can take all of that with you. It'll be in the first packing box. That's why I have no doubts, that's why actually, I'm really excited. Any place we move to, you can use your very great skill and, with a wave of your magic paintbrush, you'll turn it into our dream home.'

She thought, Joe's right – it was my first home. I grew up here.

But Joe grew up here too. And he had a very different experience to me.

A detached house, built in 1874. Of rosy-hued brick with stone-mullioned windows and a slate roof with decorative lead flashing. Four grand chimneystacks of different designs. The Resolution. The Doctor's House. Who will it be home to next? Tess trailed her fingers along the dado that not so long ago she'd painstakingly sanded, treated and repainted. She sat down halfway up the first flight of stairs. The sound of the grandfather clock gradually instilling a sense of calm. She looked around her, all around her. She looked at the cornice and the coving and the ceiling roses; she looked at the different hues that the velvety evening light elicited from a single paint colour. She looked down to the soft gleam from the flagstone slabs, the sheen off the cherrywood banister. The sturdy wide doors. Brass knobs – they needed a polish. A job for tomorrow.

As she looked all around her, she also found her voice.

'I love you, house, thank you. Thank you for sheltering me while I grew. Thank you for so much happiness and for memories that will last my life.'

Chapter Forty-four

The house sold – of course it did. And to everyone's surprise it sold not only quickly but for quite close to the asking price. There were three viewings that first weekend and it was off the market by the middle of the following week. Initially, both Joe (who was still in America) and Tess worried about her being there when potential buyers came to peruse. He was worried about the pain it might cause her. She was worried that she wouldn't be able to control a scowl; nor resist grumbling about the warped windows, exaggerating the dodgy electrics – 'violently unpredictable' – and calling the hot-water system 'unbearably noisy'. She didn't want people poking around the kitchen cupboards or knocking their knuckles against walls or seesawing on the floorboards to see how uneven and creaky they were. She didn't want to hear their ideas for new uses for the rooms. She didn't want to see them planning where to put all their furniture. She didn't want to hear what changes they planned to make.

However, the three sets of potential buyers who came to see the house fell in love with it on crossing the threshold. And they all loved what Tess had done and they marvelled that they could move right in and they murmured that really, they wouldn't need or want to change much at all. And they all had small children – two of the women had one on the way as well. One set told her that they had a dog and they fussed over Wolf and these were the people Tess hoped would buy it.

Joe agreed the deal on his last day in the United States. He asked the agent to say nothing to Tess. He needed to tell her himself.

There were tears – abundant and plaintive on Tess's part, silent and inward on Joe's.

'How long do we have?' she asked.

'Six weeks. Ish.'

'That'll never give us enough time.'

'We'll rent, then.'

'But it's Em's birthday on November the twenty-first.'

'Well, that gives us a date to work to, doesn't it – a joint housewarming and birthday party.'

'Joe?'

'Yes, Tess.'

'Where are we moving to?'

'Well, I was thinking four bedrooms – a period property, preferably detached with a good-size garden. With a shed or two for me to hoard and for you to blitz on an annual basis.'

'But *where*, Joe, *where* are we moving to?'

'Well, Staithes is glorious and Runswick Bay is exquisite. Or we could go inland a little – say, Stokesley or around Great Ayton? There again, we could go further south – Robin Hoods Bay is called the Clovelly of the North you know. Or, if you fancy something more urban, Pickering perhaps. We could always venture further north to the Durham Dales or move to the moors but Tess, do you not want to stay right here, in or around Saltburn?'

'Thank God for that,' said Tess. 'I was beginning to worry.'

'You *do* want to stay?'

'What a daft question.'

At first, Tess closed off her imagination and narrowed her breadth of vision until it was blinkered. If the places didn't look like the Resolution – if they weren't detached or the brick was too red or not rosy enough, or if there was too much stonework or the windows were too small or large, the roof too steep, or if the garden was too long but not wide enough – then she rejected them with a grave shake of her head at Joe.

'You'll not find another Resolution House,' the agent warned her.

'Oh yes, we will,' she told him. 'We've only been looking a fortnight.'

'You've only a month to find somewhere,' he said, sotto voce to Joe.

With three weeks to go, they took a six-month let on an expansive ground and first-floor apartment on Albion Terrace, not far from the Resolution. At the front, it alternated bay and box windows which looked out to the woods and the playground. To the back was a sizeable square garden though Wolf was really of the age when he wasn't that fussed by acreage. He knew where he was, he was in Saltburn and wherever they lived, he'd be off to the beach or the woods each day, or allowed to sprawl over the pavement with his lead looped around the railings while the family made merry in the playground.

It was when the packers arrived at the Resolution that Joe had to go.

'I can't watch,' he told Tess. 'I'll take Emmeline and Wolf and drop them off at Lisa's, shall I? Leave you to tell them what's for storage and what's coming with?'

455

Tess nodded. She walked over to him and touched his cheek.

'It'll be OK, Joe.'

He looked down and tapped his foot along the line between two of the flagstones in the hallway.

'I know,' he said quietly, 'but I didn't know it would feel so weird.'

'Look, take the child and dog – and thank Lisa again, won't you – then why don't you and I go out somewhere? I don't know – go for a drive? Go to the Transporter Bridge – or have lunch in Yarm or a walk up Roseberry Topping? Do something different – but get away from the house. It feels – I don't know –'

She looked around them as if the right word was in one of the packing crates.

'Undignified. Packers swarming around, bashing furniture against walls and swamping our stuff in newspaper – it's not nice.'

Joe nodded.

'OK,' he said, 'it's a plan.'

They didn't get very far. They had planned to drive to Whitby and have fish and chips there. But after Joe left for Lisa's with Emmeline and Wolf, the agent phoned the house and Tess battled through the maze of boxes to take the call. She knew it was perhaps the last time she'd be able to answer the phone. Resolution House – hullo? Goodbye.

'He said just to have a look – it may not be for us. It's just a little way out of town – off the Loftus road but way before Brotton,' Tess told Joe when he returned.

'Well, we're headed that way anyway,' said Joe.

They turned left off the coastal road and passed two tiny cottages before the single-track lane made a sharp right, straightened out a short way and then came to an abrupt end.

Joe switched off the engine and he and Tess just sat and looked – just as the agent had told them to do.

'That's it, isn't it?' Tess said eventually.

'Yup,' said Joe, 'looks like this is it.'

'I mean – it's *it*.'

'I know you do – and I totally agree.'

Fish and chips and a trip to Whitby were all off the menu. Joe made a call to the agent who called him back and said, sorry, the vendors are out. But then he said that he had keys and if Joe could wait half an hour, he'd come along with the particulars and show them around himself.

Joe and Tess lifted the latch on the gate and stood just inside it. The driveway was gravel and a little like a comma, ending in a generous circle in front of the house. Only it wasn't a house, it was a cottage. It wasn't brick, it was stone. The roof looked new but was in old slate. There were stout chimneystacks at either end. The entrance was a white wooden porch, proudly central, with a pretty fanlight above the front door. There were three windows to either side. Seven windows on the next floor, attic rooms above that. A hedge of hawthorn and hazel edged the perimeter and to one side of the house, an iron gate was cut into it. Tess followed Joe who was already walking towards it. It wasn't locked. They intended to see the back of the house, to peer through windows in advance of the agent arriving. But if the garden wasn't a distraction in its own right (a mature shrubbery rolling down into billowing herbaceous borders demarcating a wide, even lawn in a horseshoe-shaped embrace) then the view rooted them to the spot. Straight out to sea.

'We're about a fifteen-, twenty-minute walk from town,' Joe said eventually.

'The view comes free with the house,' the agent said, suddenly at their side. 'Come on, I'll show you around.'

It would take a little work, but nothing too daunting. Mainly cosmetic – getting rid of the chintz, rubbing down the woodwork, modernizing the bathrooms, changing the use of the reception rooms downstairs, swapping gloss paint for eggshell, replacing PVC windows upstairs with wooden frames.

'Emmeline's room,' said Joe at the precise moment Tess thought the very same.

'You could easily put an ensuite to the master bedroom,' the agent said, taking them through. But both Joe and Tess were not concerned with anything other than staring and staring at the view they could potentially wake up to every morning.

The agent couldn't gauge their reaction.

'Look,' he said, 'I know it's a cottage not a house. I know the building is older than the Resolution, the ceilings are lower and it's not a central location. It doesn't have the grandeur of Resolution House and it doesn't have a garage or the fancy entrance hall. But it's light – don't you think? It's a find, wouldn't you say?'

'But it *is* just like the Resolution,' Tess said.

The agent had long thought she was a little peculiar but who was he to judge, so he just nodded as if he was about to say, yes, you're so right, it's a carbon copy.

'Isn't it?' She turned to Joe.

Joe nodded thoughtfully and his face was lit with a contented smile. 'I think it is, yes.'

'It's home. We live here, don't we, Joe? This is us.'

*   *   *

It was a trip Joe had to make alone. Tess understood this. We'll see you back at the flat, she told him, there'll be something in the oven for you.

Apart from a pile of newspapers the packers hadn't needed

for wrapping, the Resolution was completely stripped of its contents when Joe went back. It was just the building; the walls and floors and ceilings and windows and doors. He walked from room to room with his eyes wide and his ears peeled. All the way up the hill, his pace had slowed with trepidation, as if he feared this final visit would be one last confrontation – flashbacks of his past in each room he went into.

But it wasn't like that.

He went into each and every room.

He took his time.

He didn't shudder once.

He felt neutral.

It was bare.

It was empty.

It was quiet.

It was just a fine old house awaiting its new residents. A family of four with one on the way and a chocolate Labrador.

Joe thought, this house has absorbed the secrets of the Saunders into the dust deep within the bricks.

And yet those secrets had left no negative trail. In fact the house had consumed them to no ill effect whatsover.

Joe thought, its past has no relevance to its future – and the same goes for me.

He thought about the new residents, the new family. The Resolution's future lay in what the new family would bring to the house, what they would make of it.

Laughter will continue to decorate this place, Joe thought. As it has done for most of this year.

Love will be the central heating.

Unity will keep the building standing strong.

And in return, this house will let them know that they are in the safest place in the world.

He locked up and strolled off down the gravel. He didn't look back. He didn't need to.

Epilogue

It turned out that there were to be three separate celebra-
tions: two were for birthdays before Christmas and the other
was the housewarming some time in the new year. Em turned
two on a bright Sunday in late November, the weekend after
the sale was completed on the Resolution. Although the rental
apartment wasn't really home, Tess managed to throw a lovely
party for her little girl. She even invited the children who had
moved into their old house – and they came. You must come
to our housewarming party, the new family at Resolution
House told Tess and Joe as they took their leave with balloons
and party bags and portions of birthday cake wrapped in
napkins.

'Our housewarming won't be until February, probably,'
Tess told them, 'but you must come to ours too.'

Joe's birthday fell on a Sunday too. Tamsin had finally made
it up from London for a long weekend. The pretext, not
that one was needed, was that she could babysit so Tess
could take Joe out for a fancy birthday dinner on one of
the evenings. In the event, Joe ended up babysitting on the
Friday night and Tamsin, Lisa and Tess ended up with a

name for themselves after one too many at the Vista Mar. They had a cold, squally Saturday to recover and when Tess was busy preparing a roast that evening, Joe took Tamsin to one side.

Tamsin listened intently.

'It's a deal, Joe,' she said. 'Anyway, I'm always up for a bit of sightseeing.'

Sunday dawns sunny and crisp, and Tess is surprised that Joe expresses such an interest in the weather. He never lets it impede his day; she's often teased him that he has the largest selection of cagoules possible for one man.

'Shall we take Tamsin to see the new place?' she suggests. She's pleased by how easily Tamsin and Joe have established a rapport.

'Sure. Yes. But this afternoon, perhaps, before she catches her train. This morning I thought we'd take her sightseeing,' Joe says. 'You know – sell the charms of the area to her.'

'Oh, she's pretty sold on it already,' Tess tells Joe. 'Where did you have in mind?'

'Well, how about the Tranny? They might be bungee jumping off it this morning. Dopes on ropes – it's a crazy sight to behold.'

'OK,' says Tess. 'Tamsin likes a little bit of crazy. I'll get people ready.'

*   *   *

'Some crunky old bridge? In Middles-bloody-brough?'

Joe looks startled by Tamsin's response until, very fleetingly, he catches her eye in the rear-view mirror.

'It's my birthday, woman,' he tells Tamsin and Tess smiles that they're already at the affectionate-insult stage.

'On Joe's tenth birthday, they detonated the Halfpenny

Bridge,' Tess tells her. 'He watched it happen. That's what inspired him to build bridges.'

Tamsin doesn't know what or where the Halfpenny Bridge was – but she has no doubt Tess will be telling her all about it given half the chance.

'This afternoon we're going to show you our new home,' says Joe.

'That's more like it,' says Tamsin.

She is, however, bowled over by the Transporter Bridge when they arrive. The vivid cerulean blue appears to etherealize the steel massiveness of the structure.

'Look, Em, look up there!' Tamsin says to her goddaughter who is hitched to her hip. 'Stark-raving mad people about to throw themselves off with only a glorified elastic band around their ankles.'

Em claps her hands accordingly.

As they crane their necks, the bridge seems to move but it's only the clouds passing by. They watch the bungee jumpers for a while, listening out for their faint countdown from on high. Three. Two. One. Bungee!

'How do they get up there?' Tamsin asks.

'Steps – see over there – like fire-escape steps,' Joe points to one of the tower legs on this shore. 'Only steeper.'

'Then they walk along the middle bit? Right at the top? But it looks little more than a narrow grille a mile above the river!'

'Kennedy open mesh grating, to be precise. It's quite safe,' Joe tells her, 'there are handrails to either side. And it's not a mile – it's only 160 feet.'

'I love bridges,' Tess says dreamily. 'Until I met Joe, I never really gave them much thought. But now I totally get them.'

'That's a good thing,' Joe turns to her, 'because I'm taking you all the way up and along this one, right now.'

*

'No, you're bloody not.'

'Yes, I bloody am.'

'You're swearing in front of the children, you two,' says Tamsin.

* * *

'I'm not, Joe, I can't.'

'You can.'

'Don't you remember what I told you?'

'You told me you don't do beaches and you don't do heights. But you've proved to me and to yourself that the first half of that is no longer true.'

'Joe, I really, really don't want to.'

'I'll make it worth your while, pet. I promise you. You can trust me. You know you can. Hold my hand. I will hold your hand every step of the way.'

Tess looks up at the bridge. The walkway is suspended 160 feet over the river Tees. The walkway really is a steel grille. Apparently it is 10 feet wide though from the ground it looks far narrower. Apparently there are railings either side, but you can't really see these from way down here. The clouds are moving quite fast, giving a false but credible sensation of instability. Tess feels queasy with nerves. Her legs feel unsteady and her heart is beating faintly and way too fast. Of course she knows she can trust Joe. She knows he'll look after her and he'll hold her hand physically and emotionally without letting go. She's vaguely aware that, rationally, it's safe – the bridge has stood for almost a hundred years. But she's terrified. She simply and categorically does not want to do this. Just looking up there is making her quake.

However, then something happens to Tess. She's not sure what's caused it or how it came to be. It's an epiphany of sorts, out of the blue. She suddenly thinks to herself, bugger what I think I can or can't do – Joe wants to take me up there and if he knows I can do it, then who am I to argue. I'll do it. I'll do it. I'll do it for him and I'll do it for me. Happy birthday, Joe – happy, happy birthday.

However, Tess can't speak; she can only tremble out her hand towards Joe. He takes it and they set off for the steep steps up. He glances over his shoulder and mouths 'thank you' to Tamsin.

'Mummy and Joe are going all the way up there, Em,' Tamsin says to Em. 'Utterly bonkers, the things that people in love will do.'

The constriction in Tess's chest seems to have a direct effect on her vision, which is simultaneously darting but bleary. She is beyond the power of speech, desperate to focus, to take herself into a zone where she can suspend time and make a nonsense of height and just go up there, walk along it and climb back down again. The steps are very steep, very narrow, with sharp and tricky returns. Their footsteps clang. If she thinks about her footfalls she falters. Joe is talking to her, he's chosen to go behind her so she can dictate the pace and he can keep his hand steady in the small of her back. It takes a long time to climb 210 steps at that speed.

Finally, they reach the top. Tess has never fainted but she thinks that this may be what she's about to do. Breathe. Breathe. Focus. You're safe. Joe takes her hand in his and puts his other arm down her back and around her waist. They've been in this embrace before, they've been in this situation before; those first baby steps he helped her take onto the sand at Saltburn in the summer.

'I'm going to imagine that actually, we're only a foot or so above the ground. I'm not going to look down. I'm just going to look ahead, Joe, to the other side of the bridge.'

He doesn't respond. He just lets her move onto the gangway and set the pace. There are no bungee jumpers; they've all gone now. It doesn't occur to Tess that there's no one else on the bridge at all now. She hasn't twigged that while she was bombarding Tamsin with facts and figures about bridges, Joe had walked off to greet the bridgemaster like the long-lost friend he is.

Joe observes the commitment and determination and total focus etched across her face. He sees how, every now and then, the vertigo wreaks havoc with her balance, which in turn destabilizes her resolve. But he sees how she stops and steadies herself and then moves forward again.

She'd taken baby steps on the beach that first time. But up here, though she shuffles, these are huge strides.

'Just a little further,' she says.

They reach the other side. She has walked 571 feet and it's taken her over ten agonizing minutes.

'Thank God,' she says and her voice breaks. 'Thank God for that.'

Oh God, thinks Joe. Oh God.

'Tess, babe – we have to turn and walk all the way back now. There's only the one flight of steps, you see.'

She's pale. She's quiet. She's motionless. She gives herself a private moment to fight the smart of tears.

'OK,' she says to Joe but she can't nod because it makes her more dizzy. 'Will you hold my hand again?'

'I haven't once let go of it.'

'Oh yes. Silly me.' She sounds hypnotized and in some ways she is, steeling herself for the journey by compressing herself into a zonal state.

Slowly, she sets off again. But not quite so slowly as before. She is able to say to Joe, I can't believe I'm doing this! I can't *believe* this is *me* up here.

You're incredible, he tells her. I'm so proud of you.

They are two-thirds of the way over, back towards the steps. Past the point from where the bungee jumpers leap.

'Tess, can you manage to stop a minute?'

She finds she can just about manage to do so.

'Can you hear me?'

She says, yes, she can.

'I'm going to ask you something,' Joe says, 'and I can tell you for free that I'm currently shaking far harder than you have during this entire expedition. But I want to ask you something, Tess.'

'Go ahead, Joe,' she says. 'I know I'm looking straight ahead – but I am listening to you.'

She's looking ahead, he thinks to himself. And he smiles and feels much calmer.

She's looking ahead – and that's precisely the direction my question points to.

Tamsin thinks, come on come on come on.

But it's not their return she's impatient for. It's been a thrill, watching them journey across and then walk back again. They had seemed to pick up the pace just a little. But now they've come to a complete stop. And, although Joe didn't tell her this was part of his plan, she already had an inkling as to why he wanted to cross this bridge with Tess. Tamsin is suddenly flattered and moved that he'd chosen her visit to make this journey because now she senses that he didn't want her here just so she could look after Em. Come on come on come on.

Tamsin keeps her eyes trained on Joe and Tess and she points them out to Em. Look at Mummy and Joe, she says. Look at them way up there.

They continue to stand stock-still.

Then she hears it.

A voice triumphant. Far stronger than those declaring *bungee!*

Joe is yelling his head off, yelling his heart out on top of the Transporter Bridge.

'Yes!' he's yelling. 'She just said yes!'

We build too many walls and not enough bridges

Isaac Newton (1643–1727)

Acknowledgements

My sincerest hope is that I have done justice to Saltburn-by-the-Sea – one of my favourite places in the world. I am immensely grateful to the people of this lovely town and environs and I've enjoyed many years of happy visits whatever the weather. My thanks, in particular, to Frank Sutton (www.haveyoubeenhere.co.uk) and Rebecca Hilton (www.saltburnbysea.com). I hasten to add that the key characters in *Secrets* are entirely fictitious, as are The Resolution, Swallows and The Everything Shop.

At the Transporter Bridge, I am indebted to Bridgemaster Alan Murray for encouraging me to go up and over, and to Rodger Wakerley for his after-hours support, also to the knowledgeable and friendly staff who add extra colour to that great big sky-blue bridge. Thank you, David Pinder, for letting me hold on tight and for telling me to get a move on when my knees were knocking 160 feet above the River Tees that sunny Sunday in July.

For local knowledge and hospitality, my gratitude goes to my friends and family in the North East, particularly Nigel and Jennifer Garton, David and Victoria Pinder, Lorna Sutcliffe, Jane and Jonny Sutcliffe. And of course to Andy

Sutcliffe for accompanying me over the years and in all seasons to the end of Saltburn pier, as well as up the Cliff Lift, down the Valley Gardens and along the coast in both directions – and for taking me to the Transporter Bridge at all times of the day . . . and night!

At Haringey Library Services, my thanks go to Sandra, Lai-Ming, Hilary, Germaine and to my fellow unofficial writer-in-residence Jonny Zucker.

In terms of general research, I am grateful to David Boughton and Bill Smith, also Darren Thwaites and Paul Delplanque at Gazette Media. In terms of general relaxation, a big thank you to my Parelli pals up the yard (Souki, Sue and Sarah) and to my friends at the John Baird (Keith, Sharon and Sean).

My children Felix and Georgia, my parents, my brother Dan and my network of beautiful friends have all played a vital part in this book's creation.

In memory of Liz Berney 1968–2005

www.saltburnbysea.com   www.haveyoubeenhere.co.uk
www.chocolinis.co.uk   www.realmeals.co.uk
www.camfields.co.uk   www.hawkinsgallery.net
www.middlesbrough.gov.uk   www.transporterbridge.net
www.clevelandbridge.com   www.gazettelive.co.uk
www.ivaadvice.org.uk

Inside:

- Freya's photos
- Freya and Saltburn
- Up close and personal with Freya
- Don't miss Freya's other bestsellers
- www.freyanorth.com

The Halfpenny Bridge 1869, demolished 1974

Photographs Frank Sutton

The Transporter Bridge, 1911

At the Transporter Bridge – on a very chilly Boxing Day 2008

On the walk way 160 feet over the Tees, 2007

The bridge, under construction

Freya and Saltburn

Saltburn-by-the-Sea, Christmas Day, 2008

For me, the greatest perk of my job is not glitzy soirees with fellow writers trying to out-syllable each other (I don't think I've ever been to one of those), it's research. A snippet in a newspaper can fire my interest in a certain subject (sleepwalking for *Pillow Talk*) or a prior passion or hobby of my own can be indulged (pottery classes for *Chloe*, a lot of massage for *Love Rules*, an access-all-areas pass in the Tour de France for *Cat*). My accountant tells me that if I set novels in exotic, far-flung places, 'research trips' are tax deductible. But thus far, no heroine has appeared in my mind's eye insisting on an adventure in the Maldives, or the Seychelles – North Yorkshire is fine, thank you very much.

Which brings me to Tess Adams – the heroine about whom you've just read. I don't plan my novels, I simply start with Chapter One and then let the story unfold organically until I think to myself, 140,000 words later, oh boy, that was the final full-stop. Before I started *Secrets*, I knew Tess lived in London. And I knew she needed to run away. But I also knew that she was not well travelled and she'd have scant knowledge of suitable hiding places. Lucky for Tess, I knew Saltburn-by-the-Sea. Lucky for me, *Secrets* meant I had to return frequently to a place I already loved, all in the name of research.

It was fascinating disciplining myself to see Saltburn through Tess's eyes. When you are familiar with a place (and Andy had introduced me to Saltburn over a decade ago), the tendency is to forget to look up and around, to stop focussing on details, to no longer ponder the scents in the air, to take the feel of a place for granted. Therefore, I couldn't just stroll along the beach yakking to my children, or mooch along the pier with an ice cream, or daydream away while rambling through the Valley Gardens. I had to see Saltburn anew; to smell it, taste it and think about it as Tess might. I made many visits with my camera, my Dictaphone, my notebook, sometimes my sun cream and flip-flops, sometimes my North Face jacket and thermal gloves, and usually with my designated driver and packhorse (thanks Andy).

I'm a southern girl, a city girl, but I'm mad about the specific part of the North East in which my last two novels have been set. This part of North Yorkshire doesn't have the brooding drama of Brontë country, or the picturesque 'ee by gum' of Herriot country. Cleveland is different. It is as gritty and grimy as it is beautiful and unspoilt, it is as thoroughly mundane as it is majestic, it is unarguably grey

Under the pier, Christmas 2008

The Cliff Lift and pier, June 2008

and hard but also colourful and gentle, it is rich and it is also deprived. All of these bind to make it real. I love the way the sci-fi landscape of the vast ICI chemical works – all monstrous towers, pipelines and flares (the inspiration for Ridley Scott's *Blade Runner*) – sprawls at the foot of the beautiful, melancholy, quiet Cleveland Hills. I like the dichotomy of the elegant Regency towns like Stokesley sitting so sedately a stones throw from Middlesbrough. The accent and local vernacular isn't that pretty but the sense of humour is warm and I like it that people call me 'pet'. There are no-go areas, certainly – but these are off-set by so many places where open arms await. In the landscape, in the towns, along the coast – down-to-earthness and drama coexist so seamlessly.

In the Cliff Lift, June 2008

Keiths Sports, Milton Street, July 2007

Personally, I'm as happy slogging through the industrial drabness of Middlesbrough's nether regions in order to come across the sudden bright blue wonder of the Transporter Bridge, as I am happy gulping lungs-full of clean air from the end of Saltburn Pier. To me Saltburn exemplifies the black and white, the yin and yang, the poetry and prose of the entire area. From the pier, look one way and you see the mighty cliff of Huntcliff Nab. Look the other and you see the bellowing factories at Redcar. The Victorian architecture is beautiful and extravagant and, in some cases, quite flamboyant. Though the 'jewel' streets are a stark contrast, somehow they add to the balance of the place. That's why the town works so well – there's room for the fantastically stocked modern deli as well as for the dodgy pub around the corner. The mouth-watering, fancy high-class chocolatiers courts trade alongside the 1970s time-warp dress shop. Saltburn's Victorian heritage is preserved brilliantly – the residents ensure it; quite rightly they are passionately town-proud, house-proud and landscape-proud and that makes them especially friendly and welcoming.

Huntcliff Nab, Christmas Day 2008

Saltburn does not have the chocolate-box beauty of Staithes, or the breathtaking, postcard-perfection of Runswick Bay. It's not as famous as Scarborough or Robin Hoods Bay. It might not be a big place but it's quirkily grand. The beach is unbelievably vast and so are the skies. The pier is plain but it marches out confidently into the grey slab of

Poohsticks Bridge, The Valley Gardens, July 2007

North Sea. I've experienced Saltburn changing over the last few years – but it's growth is clever – the spirit of the place has not been compromised but there's a

On the pier, Christmas 2008

growing energy and the town seems increasingly fresher and more vibrant. It really wouldn't matter at all if you couldn't get a cappuccino in Saltburn, but that you now can is actually quite nice. The town's founding father Henry Pease would approve of modern day Saltburn-by-the-Sea. And if an apartment comes up for sale at what was the Zetland Hotel, the world's first railway hotel, would someone please, please let me know...

Up close and personal with Freya

Q. *How do you write?*

On my gorgeous Apple laptop, from my local library. There are too many distractions at home – not least the fridge, the invisible weeds in the garden and atrocious daytime TV... I love the reverential hush in the library – plus being surrounded by books, of course. I don't plan my novels, I do a few months of research and then I simply sit down, start with Chapter One and trust that the characters will show me what happens and when.

Q. *Do you ever suffer from 'writer's block'? If so, how do you overcome it?*

I haven't yet been stuck for what to write – but I have come up against how to write...You need a surprising amount of physical energy for 5-6 hours at the keyboard, plus a large reserve of emotional energy too because, though fictitious, your characters need you to 'feel' their lives. I've had periods when I've felt so drained or simply tired that I've sat in the library thinking bugger this, shall I just nip off to Brent Cross shopping centre for a couple of hours. But actually, I'm pretty disciplined – you just have to knuckle down and squeeze one word out after another. Strong coffee, Red Bull and Skittles help, it must be said...

Q. *Is there one character in all your novels that you secretly have a soft spot for?*

One? But that would be like having a favourite amongst your children! I do feel an affinity with Thea in *Love Rules* and Petra in *Pillow Talk*. As for my heroes, well I continue to hope that there just might be an attractively stroppy potter called William living on a Cornish cliff with a goat called Barbara. And then there's Django McCabe, who has appeared in four of my novels and who I miss so much I'm considering writing a prequel set in the early 1970s so I have the chance to meet him at his most eccentric!

Q. *What makes you happy?*

The funny things my children say and the funny things my horse does.

Q. *What makes you sad?*

Seeing loneliness in an elderly person's face. I was blessed with close relationships with my grandmas and great aunts. I hate to think of elderly people on their own without company – when they themselves are such good company.

Q. *If you were only allowed to take three things to a desert island, what would you take?*

Oh good God – only three? For starters, I'd hate being on my own on a desert island. So I'd take a solar-powered laptop fully loaded with photos and I'd write stories and invent characters for company. And I'd take a bottle of Jil Sander 'Woman Pure' – which is a perfume I've worn since I was 15. It's not made anymore and I'm down to my last few dabs. I'll look such a state, I may as well be fragrant. Finally, my pillow.

Q. *What's your favourite recipe?*

Donna Hay is a marvellous chef and my favourite dish is one of hers – it's spaghetti with rocket, parmesan, fresh chilli, garlic, capers and lemon juice. I can happily eat my weight of that!

Q. *What's your 'brain food'?*

This is a dreadful thing to admit, because actually I'm a relatively healthy, quite fit, long-term vegetarian. But in my experience nothing beats a can of Coke (proper 'fat coke') and a bag of ready salted Kettle Chips and a Curly Wurly (or a Fab ice lolly in summertime). All readily available from the little shop opposite the library...

Q. *Do you remember your first kiss?*

Of course I do! And I bloody well hope he does too....

Q. *What's your all time favourite book?*

Well, I don't want this to sound poncey, but it really would have to be *Moll Flanders* by Daniel Defoe, because it's such an extraordinarily rich, colourful book – bawdy, humane, original, outrageous and it still romps along at such a pace almost 300 years later.

Q. *What's your most treasured item of clothing?*

My Repetto silver mary-jane high heels which I bought in the Liberty sale and wore to the *Pillow Talk* launch party. And my Horka breeches – which I wear daily for riding, cool in the summer, warm in the winter. Perfect.

Q. *Is there somewhere you've always wanted to visit?*

Alaska. Since watching *Northern Exposure* twenty years ago.

Q. *What's the best piece of advice anyone's ever given you?*

"Everything passes". That's what my Dad says. And it's so true. If you hold on tight to that concept, you won't take the good times for granted and you'll manage to muddle through the bad times too.

Q. *If you weren't a writer, what job would you do?*

Oh blimey. I can't answer that. I love my job. Let me think... Well, at a push I'd quite like to have a very small café in North Yorkshire that's open only for Elevenses, Lunch and Tea. Oh! Well there's an idea for a future novel...!

Q. *What's the last film that made you laugh (or cry)?*

I sobbed at *The Waiting Room*, a lovely understated British movie. And I laughed hysterically at *Tropic Thunder* – I have a pretty puerile sense of humour!

Q. *What's the last book that you couldn't put down?*

A remarkable first novel *What Was Lost*, by Catherine O'Flynn.

pillow talk

Freya North

The sleepwalker.

By day, Petra Flint is a talented jeweller working in a
lively London studio. By night, she sleepwalks. She has
40 carats of the world's rarest gemstone under her
mattress but it's the skeletons in her closet that make
it difficult for her to rest.

The insomniac.

Forsaking a rock-and-roll lifestyle for the moors
of North Yorkshire, Arlo Savidge teaches music at
a remote boys' boarding school. But, like Petra,
ghosts from his past disturb his sleep.

Putting the past to bed.

Petra and Arlo were teenage sweethearts.
Now, years later, in a tiny sweet shop one rainy day,
they stand before each other once more.
Could this be their second chance?

home truths
Freya North

*Our mother ran off with a cowboy from Denver
when we were small.*

Raised by their loving and eccentric uncle Django,
the McCabe sisters assume their early thirties will
be a time of happiness and stability.

However, Cat, the youngest, is home from abroad to
begin a new phase of her life – but it's proving more
difficult than she thought. Fen is determined to be
a better mother to her baby than her own was to her –
though her love life is suffering as a result.
Pip, the eldest, loves looking after her stepson,
her husband, her uncle and her sisters – even if
her own needs are sidelined.

At Django's 75th birthday party, secrets are revealed
that throw the family into chaos. Can heart and home
ever be reconciled for the McCabes? After all, what does
it mean if suddenly your sisters aren't quite your sisters?

love rules

Freya North

Love or lust, passion or promise?

Thea Luckmore loves romance and lives for the magic of true love. She's determined only ever to fall head over heels, or rather, heart over head.

Alice Heggarty, her best friend, has always loved lust – but she's fed up with dashing rogues. Now she's set her sights on good, sensible husband material. And she's found him.

For Thea, a chance encounter on Primrose Hill ignites that elusive spark. Saul Mundy appears to be the perfect fit and Thea's heart is snapped up fast.

However newly-wed Alice finds that she's not as keen as she thought on playing by the rules and she starts to break them left, right and centre. At the same time, a shocking discovery shatters Thea's belief in everlasting love.

When it comes to love, should you listen to your head, your heart, or your best friend?